THE CHILDREN GOD FORGOT

GRAHAM MASTERTON is best known as a writer of horror and thrillers, but his career as an author spans many genres, including historical epics and sex advice books. His first horror novel, *The Manitou*, became a bestseller and was made into a film starring Tony Curtis. In 2019, Graham was given a Lifetime Achievement Award by the Horror Writers Association. He is also the author of the Katie Maguire series of crime thrillers, which have sold more than 1.5 million copies worldwide. Visit www.grahammasterton.co.uk.

BY GRAHAM MASTERTON

Ghost Virus

The House of a Hundred Whispers

The Children God Forgot

THE KATIE MAGUIRE SERIES

White Bones

Broken Angels

Red Light

Taken for Dead

Blood Sisters

Buried

Living Death

Dead Girls Dancing

Dead Men Whistling

Begging to Die

The Last Drop of Blood

THE BEATRICE SCARLET SERIES

Scarlet Widow

The Coven

GRAHAM
MASTERTON

THE CHILDREN GOD FORGOT

HEAD
of
ZEUS

First published in the UK in 2021 by Head of Zeus Ltd

9 7 5 3 1 2 4 6 8

A catalogue record for this book is available from
the British Library.

ISBN (HB): 9781800240209
ISBN (XTPB): 9781800240216
ISBN (E): 9781800240230

Typeset by Siliconchips Services Ltd UK

Printed and bound in Great Britain by
CPI Group (UK) Ltd, Croydon CR0 4YY

Head of Zeus Ltd
First Floor East
5–8 Hardwick Street
London EC1R 4RG

WWW.HEADOFZEUS.COM

THE CHILDREN GOD FORGOT

I

'*Oluwa mi o!* Oh, my God!'

Chiasoka was driving close behind a red 177 bus when she was stabbed by an excruciating pain in her stomach. She felt as if a ten-inch carving knife had been thrust into her, just below her navel, right up to the hilt.

She bent forward over the steering wheel. Her foot slipped off the clutch and her Mini jolted forward, its headlights smashing against the rear of the bus. She narrowly missed hitting a mother and her two young children who were starting to cross the street.

'You dey *crazy?*' the mother shouted at her, flailing at the bonnet of her Mini with her woven shopping bag. '*Ode buruku!* You nearly kill us!'

But Chiasoka was in so much agony that she couldn't hear her. She couldn't see anything or hear anything. After the initial stabbing sensation, she now felt as if her intestines were being churned up by some monstrous blender, tangled and untangled and stretched and pulled. She brought up a thick mouthful of the fried plantain and eggs that she had eaten for lunch, and her bowels let out a small squirt too. Her car was now surrounded by six or seven passers-by, and the bus driver was walking back to see how much damage she had done. But Chiasoka's eyes were tightly closed and her teeth were clenched, and she felt that she was going to be swallowed up by endless darkness, and die.

She was aware of her car door being opened, and a man saying, 'Look at this woman, man. She's well sick. Hold on – I'll call for an ambulance.'

'I have – I have to—' Chiasoka managed to whisper.

'You have to what, love? Listen, don't worry, we've called for an ambulance and look – there's a cop car just turned up.'

'I have to pick up my daughter... from school.'

'Don't you fret about it, darling. I'll tell these coppers. They'll take care of your daughter for you. What school does she go to?'

Chiasoka was gripped by another agonising spasm, so that she jerked forward and banged her forehead against the steering wheel. The man held her shoulders and said, 'Try to keep still, okay? The ambulance won't be too long, I hope.'

'John Donne Primary,' Chiasoka told him. 'Her name is Daraja.'

The pain eased for a while, but she still felt as if her intestines were sliding around. It was a deeply disturbing sensation, as if her seat was sliding around beneath her too. She opened her eyes after a few moments and saw a plump blonde policewoman crouching down beside her, with a concerned look on her face.

'What's your name, dear?' the policewoman asked her.

'Chiasoka. Chiasoka Oduwole. I live in Lugard Road. Last house on the corner by Bidwell Street.'

'Do you have your phone on you? Is there anybody we can contact?'

'My cousin. We live with my cousin. Her name is Abebi. My phone – here – my phone is in my pocket.'

Chiasoka could hear an ambulance siren warbling in the distance. She was just about to tell the policewoman her cousin's surname when she was seized by a pain so overwhelming that she went rigid from head to foot, gripping the steering wheel tightly in both hands and biting her bottom lip until a bead of blood slid down her chin.

She was vaguely conscious of the policewoman leaning across in front of her to unfasten her seat belt, but then she passed out and was plunged into absolute blackness.

*

When she opened her eyes, she found that she was lying on a hospital bed, wearing a flowery hospital gown and white surgical socks. She was in a private room, with a washbasin and two empty armchairs, and out of the window, she could see leafless trees, and a brown-tiled rooftop, and low grey clouds.

She rubbed her stomach. It still felt tender, and swollen, too, although the intense pain that she had felt in her car had subsided. She eased herself onto her left side and sat up, but immediately, she felt swimmy and strange, and the bed felt as if it were rocking up and down like a rowing boat moored to a harbour wall. She lay back down again and took several deep breaths.

She was still trying to steady herself when the door opened and a young gingery-haired nurse came bustling in.

'Ah, you're awake then, sweetheart! How do you feel?'

'I feel very… very weird. Where am I?'

'You're in the Warren BirthWell Centre, at King's College Hospital, in Denmark Hill. They transferred you here from A & E.'

'I don't understand. What is the BirthWell Centre?'

'You've not heard of it? It's for foetal medicine. Prenatal and neonatal. Best in the country, by far.'

'But what am *I* doing here?'

'I think I'd better leave that to Dr Macleod. He'll be along in a minute. He's just having a chat with the sonar technicians. Meanwhile – are you still feeling any pain?'

'Only a little sore, that's all. What about my daughter? I was supposed to be picking her up from school when I was taken sick.'

'As far as I know, the police got in touch with your cousin and your cousin went to collect her. As soon as you've had all your tests, we'll be calling her, and she can come in and see you.'

'Tests? Tests for what? What is wrong with me?'

'You've had a blood test already. I think Dr Macleod wants to give you an ultrasound on the basis of that. But he'll explain it.'

Chiasoka sat up again and swung her legs off the side of the bed. When she tried to stand up though, the floor seemed to surge underneath her like a tidal wave, and she had to snatch the windowsill to stop herself from pitching forward.

'Here, love, you need to lie down again,' said the nurse, taking hold of her arm to steady her. She helped her to climb back onto the bed and pressed her fingertips against her neck to check her pulse. 'It's the painkillers they gave you, that's the trouble... they haven't worn off yet.'

'Do you have my phone? I need to call my cousin and make sure that my daughter is okay.'

'I'll find out who's got it and fetch it for you. Oh, look – here comes Dr Macleod now.'

A tall doctor in a grey three-piece suit appeared. His silvery hair was parted in the middle, and he wore heavy-rimmed tortoiseshell spectacles which looked as if they were just about to drop off the tip of his nose. He was accompanied by two younger doctors, an Asian man with a neatly trimmed beard and a white woman with a very flushed face. The man was smiling but the woman looked anxious.

'Good afternoon, Ms'—Dr Macleod began and then frowned at the clipboard that he was carrying—'Ms Oddy-wolly. I hope I've pronounced that correctly.'

Chiasoka didn't answer. She didn't care how he pronounced her name so long as he told her what was wrong with her and reassured her that it was nothing serious.

'My name is Dr Macleod and I'm a consultant in foetal medicine. This is Dr Bhaduri and this is Dr Symonds. You were brought across here because you were suffering severe abdominal trauma and a blood test showed a high level of hCG.'

5

'What does that mean?' asked Chiasoka.

'HCG stands for human chorionic gonadotropin. It's a hormone that indicates that you're pregnant.'

'*Pregnant?* But I can't be *pregnant*! It's impossible!'

'Well, that's why we need to double-check by giving you an ultrasound scan. Apart from your high level of hCG, there's some fairly boisterous activity going on inside your uterus, and that's what's causing you so much pain. You say that you can't be pregnant, but all of the external indications are that you are. Not only that, but your foetus is highly agitated for some reason.'

Chiasoka could hardly breathe. 'I can't be pregnant. Whatever it is, whatever is making me feel like this, it isn't a baby. I haven't been with anyone. My husband left me and went back to Nigeria. I live with my cousin. I haven't been with anyone.'

'Well, we'll soon see, if you'll agree to a scan. And I do advise you most strongly to agree, because we really need to find out what's going on inside you, Ms Oddy-wolly. And to be perfectly honest with you, I can't imagine what else it could possibly be, apart from a foetus.'

Chiasoka looked at the young woman doctor, and the expression on her face was so concerned that Chiasoka's eyes filled with tears.

'I can't be pregnant,' she wept. 'How can I be?'

'I promise you, you have nothing to worry about. The scan doesn't take long, and it will cause you no discomfort. The technicians will explain to you exactly what they're doing every step of the way.'

'I *was* pregnant, yes. But that was in April.'

'You *were* pregnant?' asked Dr Macleod, taking off his spectacles. 'What happened?'

'I ended it. I had an abortion.'

'You arranged this through your GP?'

Chiasoka nodded. 'She gave me the first pill, and then I went back for the second pills to take at home.'

'One mifepristone tablet, I imagine, followed forty-eight hours later by four tablets of misoprostol?'

'I don't remember what they were called. They made me feel very sick.'

'How many weeks were you?'

'Ten.'

'And the termination was successful? You're sure of that?'

'Yes. I saw it.'

'And you believe that there's no way you could have become pregnant again, after that termination?'

'I was made pregnant by my cousin's husband. I never told my cousin what happened because my daughter and I have nowhere else to live, except for my cousin's house. I never told her husband that I was pregnant either. But I warned him that if he ever try to touch me again, I will take a knife from the kitchen and when he is sleeping I will cut off his *kòfẹ.*'

'Oh, dear. Yes. I believe I understand what you mean. But anyway, whether you're pregnant or not, a scan is essential. In fact – if you're *not* pregnant – I'd say it's urgent.'

Chiasoka closed her eyes for a moment. She couldn't believe that this was happening to her. It was the same unreal feeling she had experienced when she had come home from her day on the till at Peckham Sainsbury's and found that Enilo had packed his bags. He was waiting for her to come back to their flat only so he could tell her that he was leaving her and going back to Lagos. It was bitterly ironic. In Yoruba, the name 'Enilo' means 'the one who went away'.

'What about me and Daraja?' she had asked him.

'You have a job. You can keep the car.'

'But I can't afford the rent. Not on my own.'

'I don't care, Chi. I just don't care. This is not the life I want any more. In this country I feel like a piece of shit. I get no respect from nobody, not like home. I did not tell you, but on Saturday, two policemen stop me in the street and search me for a knife.'

'Didn't you tell them that you are an accountant?'

'Yes. But they said it made no difference. In other words, I am black so I must be a criminal.'

'Don't you love us, Daraja and me?'

Enilo had looked away, as if his eyes were already focused on the future. 'How can I love anybody if I can't love myself?'

The nurse came back into the room, accompanied by a porter who was pushing a wheelchair.

'All ready to go?' she asked cheerfully.

Dr Macleod looked down at Chiasoka and gave her the most sympathetic of looks, almost as if he were her foster father.

'Whatever the outcome, we'll be taking good care of you, Ms Oddy-wolly.'

***

It was five o'clock and growing dark outside by the time Dr Macleod and his two assistants came back with the results of Chiasoka's ultrasound scan.

The nurse had found Chiasoka's phone for her, and she had spoken to Daraja and told her that she was suffering from a tummy ache but would soon be coming back to cousin Abebi's. She had received a message too, from Peckham police, telling her that her damaged Mini had been driven back to Lugard Road and parked at the back of her cousin's block of flats.

She was still light-headed, and she still felt as if something was sliding around inside her stomach. About twenty minutes ago she had been given a cup of milky tea, but as soon as she had swallowed the first mouthful she had promptly brought it back up, and it had splattered onto the floor.

Dr Macleod pulled up a chair and sat down next to her, while his two assistants stood at the end of the bed. She was unsettled by the way they were looking at her now, almost as if she were a living exhibit in a freak show.

'I've had the results of your scan,' said Dr Macleod. 'I have to tell you that you are indeed pregnant.'

'How can that be?' Chiasoka protested. 'How can that possibly be? I had the abortion. I saw it with my own eyes, in the toilet. And I swear to God that I have been with no man since then.'

Dr Macleod held up a green cardboard folder, although he didn't open it, and he kept it out of her reach. 'I'm sorry to say, Ms Oddy-wolly, that the scan clearly shows that you have a living foetus in your uterus. I have to add though, that the foetus is somewhat abnormal. In fact – without beating around the bush – it's *severely* abnormal. Abnormal to the extent that we'll almost certainly have to remove it by C-section.'

Chiasoka stared at him. 'What do you mean, "severely abnormal"?' she whispered. 'What is wrong with it?'

'I have never asked an expectant mother this before, but are you sure you want to see? I can assure you that, given its abnormalities, there is no possibility whatsoever that this foetus could survive, and you may prefer us to proceed with a termination without further delay. Let me put it this way: it is not something that you will be able to *unsee*.'

'How can it be that bad? I do not even know how it could exist at all.'

'Once we've terminated your pregnancy, we can carry out DNA tests, which may enable us to establish who the father is.'

'There is no father.'

'Can I take it then, that we can proceed with a termination?'

'How can you expect me to abort it without even knowing where it came from or what is so wrong with it? I have to see it. I don't care how bad. Wherever it came from, half of it is me.'

'Are you quite sure about this?' asked Dr Macleod.

'Show me,' said Chiasoka.

Dr Macleod turned around to look at his two assistants. Then he opened up the green cardboard folder and took out a 3D ultrasound scan which showed the foetus inside

Chiasoka's womb in three dimensions and in colour.

Chiasoka took it and held it up. Then slowly, she lowered it, her mouth opening wider and wider. She stared at Dr Macleod in utter disbelief, and then she heaved and brought up the rest of her lunch into her lap.

2

Detective Constable Jerry Pardoe had paused by the front desk of Tooting police station to chat to PC Susan Lawrence when his iPhone rang. It was DS Bristow.

'Where are you, Pardoe? Have you taken yourself off home yet?'

'I'm on the verge, sarge.'

'That's all right then. I'm going to need you to do a spot of overtime. There's been a stabbing outside that karate club on Streatham Road, the one over Tesco. There's two squad cars and an ambulance on the way there now. Mallett can go with you.'

'Oh, shit. What is it, fatal?'

'Don't know yet. Two blokes having a barney over some bird, apparently.'

'Hope she was worth it. Okay. You can tell Mallett that I'll meet him out the back, in the car park.'

He turned to PC Lawrence and pulled a face. He had fancied her ever since she had been posted to Tooting, three weeks ago. She had high cheekbones and feline eyes and short-cropped light brown hair, and her white uniform blouse only emphasised her very large breasts.

He had said to his friend Tony at the garage that she had the face of a TV weather girl and the figure of a *Playboy* model. He had been just about to ask her if she fancied a Thai at the Kaosarn restaurant in the High Street when she finished her shift, but now it looked as if he was going to be spending the rest of the evening trying to get some sense out of bloodstained teenagers out of their brains on dizz.

'Oh well, duty calls,' he told her. 'You don't happen to be free tomorrow night, do you?'

'Tomorrow? No. It's my partner's day off. We're going ice-skating.'

'Won't catch me doing that, I'm afraid. Last time I tried I spent most of the time sliding around on my arse.'

'I'm not that good either. But my partner – she's brilliant.'

'Oh. Been together long, have you, you and your... ah, partner?'

'Nearly a year now.'

'Oh. Well, have a good time.'

Jerry went out of the back door of the police station and across the car park to his silver Ford Mondeo. *Just my bleeding luck*, he thought, as he sat behind the wheel. *The tastiest-looking bit of crumpet that's turned up at Tooting nick ever since I've been here and it turns out she's the L bit of LGBTQ.*

DC Bobby Mallett came hurrying out, trying to zip up his windcheater while holding on to a half-eaten cheese-and-tomato roll. He was short and tubby, with prickly black hair and bulging brown eyes and a blob of a nose. Everybody at the station called him 'Edge'og.

He climbed into the passenger seat and twisted around to find his seat belt.

'I hope you're not going to be dropping crumbs all over the shop,' said Jerry, as he started the engine. 'I just spent a tenner having this motor valeted.'

'Bloody kids stabbing each other,' said DC Mallett. 'What's that? About the fourth one this week? They don't get it, do they? All carrying knives and machetes around and threatening each other. They don't seem to understand that when you've snuffed it, that's it. You don't wake up the next morning and say, "Cor, that was horrible, that was, being splashed like that."'

'That kid yesterday afternoon, that one who was stabbed outside Chicks; he snuffed it last night.'

'Yes, I heard. What was he? Only about fifteen?'

'Fifteen last week,' said Jerry. 'And the kid who stabbed him's only seventeen.' He put on his drill rap voice. '"He was trapping round my ends and it was peak. No way man was going to stand for that."'

'What a pillock.'

'It's your Generation Z, 'Edge,' said Jerry, as he turned down Links Road toward Streatham. 'They might be tech savvy, but when it comes to anything else, they don't know their arse from their elbow.'

It took them less than five minutes to reach the crime scene. Two squad cars were already parked outside Tesco's supermarket, with their blue lights flashing, and an ambulance was parked outside the Polski Sklep grocery store. A small crowd had gathered, but they were already being held back by police tape. Jerry pulled up behind the ambulance and he and Mallett climbed out. It was a chilly evening, and their breath smoked so that they looked like old-fashioned coppers in a black-and-white 1950s' crime film.

The victim of the stabbing was lying in the bus shelter outside S. Ayngaran's Asian and Caribbean food shop, which was only five metres away from the entrance to the karate club. He was a young Asian with a pompadour fade hairstyle and a sharply trimmed beard. He was wearing a white Fresh Ego Kid tracksuit which was drenched in blood, so it looked as if he had been knifed in the stomach and the chest at least eight or nine times, maybe more. His eyes were open, and he was staring sightlessly at the boots of the bulky police constable in a high-vis jacket who was standing over him.

'Evening all,' said Jerry. 'What's the SP?'

'Bit of an altercation, apparently,' said the constable, sniffing and tugging out his notebook. 'Victim's name is Attaf Hiraj, twenty-one years old. Suspect's name is Rusul Goraya, twenty-three. He's inside, in the changing room. They're both members of the Kun'iku Karate Club. According to their instructor, there seemed to be bad blood between them this evening. In his own words, they were kicking the living shit out of each other.'

'I see. Did he have any idea what the beef was about?'

The constable shook his head. 'He thought it was over some girl that they'd both been going out with, but he couldn't be sure, because the only thing they were saying to each other was "you're clapped" and "you're a wasteman", apart from a fair amount of effing and blinding.'

'Forensics on their way?'

'Should be here in ten minutes or so.'

'Witnesses?'

'That lot over there. Five of them altogether. They all saw the suspect stabbing the victim. A couple of them tried to stop him while he was doing it, but he threatened to stab them as well. It was only when he started to leave the scene that one of them ran after him and brought him down with a karate kick in the bollocks. Then the rest of them jumped on top of him and took the blade off of him.'

'All right, thanks,' said Jerry. 'We'll have a word with them in a minute. First of all, I think we need to have a bit of a chat with our stabber. 'Edge? You coming?'

Mallett was prodding at his iPhone. 'Oh? What? Sure. Yes. Just telling Margot that I'm going to be late.'

They went in through the door to the karate club and up two steep flights of stairs. Jerry could smell Tiger Balm muscle rub even before they reached the changing room – camphor and menthol – which helped to mask the underlying mustiness of stale sweat.

The changing room was long and narrow, with dank karate kimonos and JD sports bags hanging along both sides. The suspect was sitting at the far end, handcuffed, two uniformed constables standing beside him, their arms folded, looking monumentally bored. When they saw Jerry and Mallett enter the changing room, one of them took hold of the suspect's elbow and pulled him up onto his feet.

'Evening, lads,' said Jerry. He didn't have to introduce

himself. They were both based at Tooting too. 'This is Mack the Knife, is it? What's your name, mate?'

The suspect was only about five feet eight inches, but very muscular, with the thick corded neck and bulging biceps of somebody who visits the gym every day. His hair was braided into cornrows, and he wore a large silver hoop in each ear. Jerry thought that he was spectacularly ugly, as if his face were being pressed flat against a window. He was still wearing his white gi, and it was splattered on the left-hand side with a Jackson Pollock action painting of dried blood. His breath smelled fruity and sweet, which told Jerry that he was probably dosed up with lean, a mixture of cough syrup and codeine. Some of the kids drank three or four bottles a week, or more if they could afford it.

''E deserve it,' he said, defiantly cocking his head up.

'That's your name, is it, mate? "Eedy Zervit"?'

'No, bruv. Man's name is Rusul. I was just sayin', like, Attaf was askin' to be shanked.'

'Rusul what?' asked Jerry, in his flattest job-interview voice. 'How old are you, Rusul? And what's your address?'

'Rusul Goraya. Man's twenty-three. Man lives at 79 Sumner House.'

'On your own or with your parents?'

'Wiv 'is 'rents, bruv. Man ain't got no job now. Man can't afford a gaff of 'is own.'

'What are you, Gujarati?'

'That's right.'

Jerry didn't have to ask Rusul why – as a Pakistani – he was speaking in slang that was mostly Jamaican. All the kids around London spoke like that. There was even a poster pinned up in the squad room at Tooting with a list of young people's slang, and it was constantly being updated. Even if Rusul had been 'making gains' – building up muscle – he was still 'butters' or a 'two', meaning that he was ugly – only two out of ten.

'So you're admitting that you stabbed Attaf?'

'Like I say, 'e deserve it. 'E was guilty of murder, so man was only givin' 'im justice like the court would've done, so it's not that deep. Best believe a court would 'ave only banged 'im up, like.'

'Attaf killed someone?'

''E only murdered 'is kid, didn't 'e?'

'Whose kid?'

Rusul was about to speak, but then his mouth tightened and his chest rose and fell as he took several deep breaths. Jerry could see that his defiance was abruptly collapsing, and his expression was changing to one of inconsolable anguish. He clasped his manacled hands together and shook them and tears burst out of his eyes.

'*My* kid, bruv! *My* kid!'

'Attaf murdered your kid? How? When? Why didn't you tell the police?'

''Cause the pigs would've done nothin', that's why!'

'And why not?'

''Cause they don't pull you in for abortions, that's why! Me and Joya we was goin' together for nearly a year and then this Attaf shows up and takes 'er off me. But Joya finds out after she and me break up that she's expectin' my baby. It 'as to be mine, because she's six weeks gone and she and Attaf 'ave only been together for a mumf.'

'So she arranged for a termination, is that it?'

'Attaf knew this woman doctor in Brockley, and she give Joya the pills. But that's the same as murder, innit? Like, if you fix it for somebody to kill somebody else, even if you didn't do it yourself, like, you're still guilty, innit?'

'And that was your justification for stabbing Attaf? You considered him to be a murderer, and therefore you thought you'd get away with killing him?'

'Perhaps you thought you'd even get a medal,' put in Mallett, 'or a year's free happy meals at McDonald's. I don't know. You melt.'

Jerry looked at the two uniformed constables and shook his head. Then he said, 'Rusul Goraya, I'm arresting you for the murder of Attaf Hiraj. You do not have to say anything. But it may harm your defence if you do not mention when questioned something which you later rely on in court. Anything you do say may be given in evidence.

'Take him down the nick, lads.'

★

Jerry and Mallett talked briefly to all the five witnesses, who included Ken the karate instructor, a former SAS officer who had served in Iraq. They all had the same story to tell. Rusul and Attaf had been pacing around each other all evening like angry pumas, trading insults, and when they had fought together, they had been hitting each other so viciously that Ken had pulled them apart and stopped them before one or both of them suffered a serious injury. Then just after Attaf had walked out of the club's front door, Rusul had come running down the stairs after him with a long kitchen knife, rammed him hard against the side of the bus shelter and started furiously stabbing him in the chest and stomach.

'And this was all over this girl Joya, so far as you know?' asked Jerry.

'That's right,' Ken told him. 'She used to come to the club with Attaf every now and then. Pretty girl, if that's what you go for. Don't know what she saw in Rusul, though. He's built, I'll give you that, but you know – face like a bag of spanners.'

'Don't happen to know where she lives, this Joya? Don't worry if you don't. We should be able to get in touch with her through Attaf's phone.'

'Or by waterboarding Rusul,' put in Mallett.

'I think she lives in Streatham. Not sure where.'

'Her dad runs a halal grocer's shop on Streatham High Road,' said one of the young men who had witnessed Attaf's stabbing.

'Well, that narrows it down to the nearest two dozen,' said Jerry. 'Thanks.'

They took down the names and contact details of all the witnesses, and by now, the forensic technicians had arrived and were waddling around in their blue Tyvek suits, taking flash photographs of Attaf's body and the sticky bloodstains on the surrounding pavement. Jerry and Mallett waited around until they had completed their initial examination and Attaf's body had been lifted onto a stretcher by two paramedics.

Mallett smoked half a cigarette, but then he started coughing so much he had to punch himself repeatedly on the chest, and flicked the rest of it into the gutter.

'You want to try them e-cigarettes,' said Jerry.

'What? And go around smelling like a poof? Leave it out.'

The ambulance drove away. No siren, no lights.

'Fancy a pint before we go back to the nick?' asked Jerry.

Mallett stared at him. 'What are you? Some kind of mind reader?'

3

'We've found out what the problem is,' said Gemma, clonking down her white safety helmet on Martin's desk and tugging down the zip of her white protective suit. 'And I'm afraid you're *not* going to be happy.'

'I didn't become a drainage engineer to be happy, Gem,' said Martin, staring at her helmet with distaste, as if it were going to infect his paperwork. 'I derive my happiness from other pursuits. Squash, mainly. And box sets. Tell me the worst.'

Gemma went over to the large map of London that was pinned on the wall of Martin's office. She pointed to the red line that ran diagonally up through Peckham, from south-east to north-west. 'We have a fatberg blocking the Earl Main Sewer from here, just past Peckham Road... to here.'

'Tell me you're joking. How big is it?'

'Only about half the size of the Whitechapel one, but it's at least a hundred and thirty metres long, and my estimate is that it probably weighs well over a hundred tonnes.'

'Oh, crap.'

'Well, crap, of course, but all the usual rag too. Cooking

fat mostly, but wet wipes and tampons and condoms and cotton buds and even more wet wipes. We even found a litter of newborn puppies that some animal lover must have flushed down the toilet.'

Martin stood up and joined Gemma beside the map. He had waves of dark wiry hair, and he was blandly handsome, like a leading character from a Netflix drama. Today he was wearing a charcoal-grey jacket, with a Paisley handkerchief in his breast pocket, and a matching Paisley tie. He always dressed smartly because he had recently been appointed field manager for Crane's Drains, and he was very conscious of his new authority, especially over engineers who had been working down in the sewers since before he was born.

Next to him, in her white protective suit, Gemma was tiny. She had blonde hair drawn back into a bun and a heart-shaped face, with large brown eyes and slightly pouting lips. When she was younger she had thought of becoming a nurse, but when she was at secondary school, she had taken a tour of London's Victorian sewers and been fascinated by the complex hidden world beneath the capital's streets – all those miles of tunnels and chambers and ladders and secret doors. It reminded her of *The Time Machine*, in which the hideous Morlocks laboured in the darkness underground while the elfin Eloi danced blissfully in the sunlight up above.

'So... have you found what caused it?' Martin asked her.

'Tree roots, by the look of it. They've penetrated the brickwork just here at the junction with Charles Coveney

Road, and of course, the rag started catching on to them. There's lots of snotty noses on the walls there too, from the last time they were patched up. I've checked the records, and it's over three years since that was done.' By 'snotty noses' she meant cement drips, which could catch non-human waste like wet wipes and tampons and start the gradual build-up of solidified cooking fat.

'Right then,' said Martin. 'If you can start drawing up a schematic, Gem, we can plan how we're going to clear this monster out. I'll come up there and take a shufti myself later. But as much CCTV as you can provide us with, please – and samples, of course.'

Gemma said, 'Some of the fat's still softish, but most of it's saponified, and in places, it's as hard as concrete. I don't think digging's going to get us anywhere. It's going to be all high-pressure hoses.'

'Thames Water are going to be pleased, aren't they? Nearly two million it cost for that Whitechapel job.'

'Mr Crane won't be complaining though, will he? Did you hear what he said when he came down the other day, about wet wipes?'

'Can't say that I did.'

'"If it hadn't been for wet wipes, I could never have afforded my holiday house in Marbella." That's what he said.'

She didn't add that Mr Crane would be less than delighted that Martin had allowed a fatberg of this size to build up under his watch. Mr Crane liked to turn a profit, but this blockage was big enough to make headlines in the *Evening Standard*, and he was almost religious about his company's reputation for keeping the capital's sewers flowing freely. The company's logo was a crane sitting on a rooftop with a musical semiquaver wafting out of its beak, and the slogan 'Crane's – Clean As A Whistle'.

★★★

Gemma drove back to Peckham Road in her mint-green Fiat 500. Her three-man crew was still there, gathered around the open manhole on the corner of Southampton Way. They had just brought up the Quickview camera, which they had first used to discover the northern end of the fatberg by Charles Coveney Road where raw sewage and shreds of wet toilet paper had been intermittently bubbling up from underneath the manholes. They had lowered the Haloptic camera down the manhole on a pole, and its bright reflected light had enabled them to see along the sewer for a distance of nearly two hundred metres.

Gemma parked and climbed out of her car, pulling on her thick, red protective gloves. She had already been down the manhole at Charles Coveney Road. Now she needed to go down and take a first-hand look at this end of the blockage, to see how seriously it had solidified.

'So what did his nibs have to say?' asked Jim Feather, who was her most experienced flusher. He was about fifty-five years old, with a grey moustache, a broken nose and no front teeth. About ten years ago, he had been accidentally hit in the face with one of the high-pressure hoses they used to dislodge hardened fat. They pumped out water at 15,000 p.s.i., and if you weren't careful they could blow the skin clear off your fingers, like pulling off a rubber glove.

'He's coming up here later to take a look for himself.'

'What? He didn't believe you?'

'Oh, don't be too hard on him, Jim. He's only trying to show that he's down with the team and that he doesn't mind getting his hands dirty.'

'He wouldn't know a macerating toilet from a monkey's rear end, that one. God knows why they made him field engineer.'

'He's good with the council and his uncle's a director of Thames Water. Didn't you know that? Field engineer, that's only a title. Everybody knows that all the real engineering is done by you, and all the rest of you guys down the pipes.'

'Do you know what you are, Gem?' Jim snorted. 'You're a flipping flirt, that's what.'

Gemma covered her eyes with her grey smoke-tinted goggles, buckled on her helmet and zipped her suit right up to her neck. Newton, her young camera technician, would be coming down into the sewer with her. He would be taking pictures of the fatberg and videos of Gemma as she rooted through the sewage and dislodged chunks of fat to see how hard it had become and what it would take to clear it.

Jim shifted aside the orange plastic barrier so that she could climb down the open manhole. The ripe smell that was rising from the sewer was almost overpowering, and she flapped her hand in front of her face.

'Bit on the niffy side, isn't it?' said Jim. 'Oxygen level's okay though. We've checked the hydrogen sulphide and the methane levels too. Still – no farting when you're down there, Newton. Don't want you pushing the levels over the safety limits.'

Newton gave him the finger, but grinned. Jim never stopped ribbing him about the strong-smelling packed lunches that his mother made for him, which always included àkàrà, fritters made from peeled black beans. 'The amount of beans you eat, Newton, I reckon you could blast away a fatberg on your own.'

Gemma climbed down the rungs in the manhole wall. She sploshed into the tawny, turgidly flowing sewage, which came halfway up her knee-length rubber boots. Then she started to wade her way slowly northward, with the halogen lamp on her helmet illuminating the curved tunnel walls. Newton followed close behind. The dazzling light from his iPEK camera cast dancing shadows on the brickwork, as if they were being accompanied by dark distorted ghosts.

About thirty metres along the sewer, the lumps of fat in the sewage began to thicken, and Gemma found it increasingly difficult to force one leg in front of the other. Ahead of her, a greasy blockage gradually rose up until it left a gap that was less than twenty centimetres below the ceiling. The sewage was trickling through the fatberg, but not rapidly enough to cope with the tidal waves of foul water and faeces and wet wipes that came surging along here every morning and every night when the population of Peckham took baths and showers and went to the toilet and did their washing.

Gemma sniffed. The sewage smelled like sewage always

smelled, but she thought she could detect an unusual lemony aroma to it too.

She stopped and said, 'Can you smell that?'

'I can't smell anything except menthol,' Newton told her. 'I always shove Vicks up my nose before I come down the sewers.'

'All right,' said Gemma. She waded along a few metres further, then she beckoned Newton to stand beside her so that he could film her picking up handfuls of nappies and tampons and saponified cooking fat. Some of the sewage was still reasonably soft and easily separated into lumps, but as she dug deeper, she found layers of fat that had become almost as hard as limestone.

As she was pulling two lumps apart, she came across an onyx bracelet. She couldn't imagine how that had found its way into the sewer, or what the story was behind it. She had found so many objects that appeared to be of sentimental value – rings, brooches, and once, she had come across a locket with a photograph of a small child in it.

She dropped the bracelet into the plastic bag that she always had attached to her wrist. She would clean it once she returned to the office and post it on Twitter, in the hope that somebody would claim it.

On the left-hand side of the sewer, stratified fat rose up at an angle like the white cliffs of Dover. Gemma beckoned Newton again to come closer, and then she took hold of the top of the cliff and started to tug it clear of the sewer wall. It was the consistency of old-fashioned kitchen soap, and it was stuck so hard to the bricks that she had to prise it away in thick crumbly lumps.

'Bloody hell,' she said. 'We're going to need the high-pressure box unit to clear this lot. There are *so* many tree roots in it... look. That's the main cause of it – roots – and this sloppy grouting didn't help.'

The roots had grown down from the plane trees that were planted all the way along the road above. They had wriggled their way in between the bricks so that they were dangling down into the sewer, trapping the tides of waste that flowed through it. Now they were threaded through the solidified fat as thickly as human veins and arteries. They were too fibrous for picks and shovels to cut through them, and so they would have to be blasted away with high-pressure water jets.

Newton scanned the fatberg with his video camera from all angles and took close-ups of Gemma breaking up chunks of fat of different densities, as well as chunks of soiled wet wipes that had stuck together like layers of filo pastry.

'Right,' she said, after ten minutes of digging. 'I think we've got more than enough to show Martin what we're up against. I don't know about you, but I'm absolutely gasping for a breath of fresh air.'

She was rubbing her hands together to wipe the fat off her gloves when she thought she glimpsed a movement in the gap at the top of the fatberg. It didn't alarm her. It was almost certainly a rat. In fact, she was surprised that they hadn't come across a single rat since they had been down here. The sewers were usually teeming with them, especially around fatbergs, which they fed on greedily.

She lifted her head a little, so that the lamp on her

helmet lit up the root-hairy brickwork on the ceiling. The only sound was Newton splashing his way back to the manhole, and the trickling of sewage as it percolated through the crevices in the mountain of fat. She wished she had never learned that poem at school, 'Where Alph, the sacred river, ran / through caverns measureless to man.'

No, she thought. *It was only a bloody rat.* But as she was about to turn away, a face suddenly appeared in the gap, a face as white as milk.

Gemma stood motionless, staring at it. She felt a crawling sensation down her back, as if her protective suit was infested with woodlice, and although she opened her mouth, she couldn't speak.

It looked like the face of a very young child, but a child whose head had been stretched so that its skull was narrow and its features were elongated. It had black glistening near-together eyes that seemed to have no irises, with gaping nostrils and a downturned mouth, as if it were about to start sobbing. It was bald, and its skin gleamed with the same opalescence as the fat all around it.

Gemma had never seen anything as terrifying as this in her life, not even down in the sewers. What made it even more terrifying was that it didn't appear to be aggressive, like rats could be, especially when they were cornered, but neither did it appear to be frightened of her. It was simply staring at her with eerie curiosity, as if it were wondering what she was and what she was doing down here.

At last, she managed to croak out, 'Newton.'

Newton was still splashing towards the manhole, so she had to call out louder. '*Newton!*'

Newton stopped and turned around, but when he did, the white-faced thing immediately slithered out of sight. Her heart beating hard, Gemma waded up closer to the fatberg and cautiously peered into the gap. Further along, the light from her helmet caught something moving – something pale, that glistened, and for a split second, something that waved, like a tentacle. But then she could see only tree roots, and craggy white fat, and shredded ribbons of toilet paper.

'What's up, Gem?' Newton asked her. His expression was what she always called his 'Eddie Murphy' face – half concerned, but half looking as if he were about to burst out with sarcastic laughter. 'You look like you seen a ghost.'

'There's something down there. I mean something *alive*. And before you say "rat", it wasn't a rat.'

'Well, if it isn't a rat, maybe it's an alligator.'

'What the bloody hell are you talking about – alligator?'

'I never heard of any here in London, but it happened in America, didn't it? People bought baby alligators as pets and when they got tired of them they flushed them down the bog. I heard stories that some of them grew up to giant size down in the sewers.'

'It wasn't an alligator, Newton. No way. It was more like... I don't know. It was more like a child.'

'*What?* What's a child doing down a sewer? It couldn't be a child, any road. How would a child get down here in the first place. Not unless *they* were flushed down the bog.'

'I don't know. It looked like a child, that's all. Only its head was all long and thin. It scared the shit out of me.'

'Well, you're in the right place for that.'

Gemma peered down into the gap again, but whatever the white-faced thing was, it had been completely swallowed up by the darkness. She hesitated for a moment, wondering what to do next – whether she ought to organise a shovel party down here, to see if they could dig it out. If they used a high-pressure hose, it was highly likely that they would kill it.

But then she thought, *Don't be ridiculous, it couldn't have been a child. No child could survive if it was deformed like that, and what could it live on, down here in the sewers? You're probably hallucinating from methane and a shortage of oxygen. You've had hallucinations before. You remember that time in Blackheath when you thought you heard women's voices in the tunnels, calling your name, or that time you panicked because you felt that the sewer was going to collapse on top of you. This is probably the same, only different.*

'Come on, let's get out of here,' she told Newton. 'I think I've got a serious case of the heebie-jeebies, that's all.'

4

Dr Macleod had been staring at the scan for almost ten minutes before Dr Symonds said, 'Well? What are we going to do with it?' After a moment's hesitation, she added, 'Sir?'

Dr Macleod took a deep breath and then slowly let it out, in the same way he did when he was about to tell a mother that her baby was stillborn.

'To be absolutely honest with you, Caroline, I don't have the first idea. Will it survive once we've taken it out of her? *Can* it survive? And if it *does* survive – which Heaven help us I pray for its own sake that it doesn't – what kind of a life can it expect?'

Dr Bhaduri had been examining the scan over Dr Macleod's shoulder. 'It's difficult to tell if it's male or female.'

'It's difficult to tell if it's even *human*,' said Dr Macleod. 'Well, of course it must be, because it's been conceived inside this poor woman's womb. It seems to have a brain, and a spinal column, but its body is severely underdeveloped. And all these *limbs*. I think the question of its gender hardly comes into it. It's never going to have to decide whether to wear trousers or a skirt, is it?'

He paused and said, 'Sorry. That was flippant. But I've never come across anything like this in all my twenty-seven years of practice, and I've come across some dreadfully deformed foetuses in my time, I can tell you. Compared to this, conjoined twins were a doddle.'

Duncan, the anaesthetist, pushed his way in through the double swing doors. He was bald and his belly strained against his tight white surgical jacket so that he looked more like a chef. 'She's all prepped for you, doctor.'

Dr Macleod took one last look at the scan, and then stood up. 'Very well. Let's meet this unfortunate little creature face to face, shall we?'

They followed Duncan into the theatre, where Chiasoka was lying on the operating table covered by a light green sheet. One of the centre's more experienced midwives was standing on the opposite side of the table, next to the 4K surgical display screen. A young nurse was counting the instruments that Dr Macleod would be using for the C-section.

As Dr Macleod came in, the midwife lifted the sheet and folded it back to expose Chiasoka's swollen stomach. He said, 'Thank you, Glenda,' and gave her a smile, although it was the queasy smile of a man who is deeply reluctant to do what his professional duty demands of him. He tugged up his surgical mask and was relieved that he could now keep his grim expression to himself.

'Vital signs all within normal parameters,' said Duncan, sitting down beside his monitors. 'Blood pressure 90 over 60, temperature 37, pulse 75. Sixteen breaths per minute.'

On the table next to his instruments, Dr Macleod saw that a large stainless-steel kidney dish was waiting for the foetus, once he had removed it. *Hardly a foetus,* he thought. *But what else can I call it?*

'Let's get this over with, shall we?' he said, and beckoned Drs Bhaduri and Symonds to come and stand on either side of him. Usually he liked to have music playing while he operated, Debussy's *La Mer*, but today he wanted absolute silence, apart from the beeping of the heart monitor. The nurse handed him a No. 10 scalpel and he deftly made the first horizontal incision into Chiasoka's abdomen. Blood ran down on either side, which the nurse quickly swabbed. Next he cut open the thin glistening tissue of her uterus.

Dr Bhaduri inserted retractors into the incision to open it wide and to hold it open so that Dr Macleod could reach inside and lift out the foetus.

'Oh, Jesus,' whispered Dr Symonds, behind her mask.

Normally, when they opened up the womb, they were presented with the top of the baby's head, and then with its face, its eyes squinched tight. All they could see inside Chiasoka was a mess of tubes, like a bowlful of thick cannelloni, although some of the tubes appeared to have rows of small nobbles on them, which could have been rudimentary fingers.

Of course, Dr Macleod had already seen these tubes, or tentacles, or whatever they were, in the ultrasound scan, and he had studied them closely. That didn't diminish his disgust and his horror when they came bulging out of the bloodied incision in Chiasoka's abdomen, because it was obvious by the way in which they slid over each other, winding and unwinding, that they were very much alive.

Dr Symonds turned away, went over to the corner of the operating theatre and retched. Duncan opened and closed his mouth, but he was speechless, and Glenda the midwife and the nurse stood stunned, even though Dr Macleod had shown them the scans and warned all of them beforehand that the foetus was 'catastrophically deformed, with supernumerary limbs, among other defects'.

While the scans were detailed, they were just stills. It was the way that the tubes were writhing and struggling that appalled them most of all.

Dr Bhaduri looked at Dr Macleod, his chestnut-coloured eyes wide over his surgical mask. 'What do we do now, sir?'

'The first thing we do is get it out of her. Then... then I don't know what. Duncan, how are her vitals?'

'Her pulse is a little quicker and her blood pressure's down, but there's nothing to panic about. Except for that bellyful of calamari she's got there. I mean – bugger me.'

While Dr Bhaduri stretched open the incision as wide as possible, Dr Macleod slid his hand into Chiasoka's womb and took hold of the foetus as gently as he could, although it wriggled furiously as soon as he tried to get a grip on it. He could feel that the tentacles were jointed, with thin stick-like bones inside them, like frogs' legs. So – deformed as they were – they *were* limbs.

'Come on,' he breathed, behind his mask. 'Come on out, you little monster.'

He had to tug harder and harder, because the foetus seemed to be resisting every effort to extract it. He would manage to pull it out six or seven centimetres, and then it would immediately slither back into the incision. After this had happened three times, he buried the fingers of his right hand deep between its squirming tentacles so that he could use all his strength to drag it out. It clung on for a few moments, but then Dr Macleod gave it one final wrench, and it slopped out on to the sheet between Chiasoka's thighs, bloody and slippery with amniotic fluid, and still angrily writhing.

It continued to writhe for a few more seconds as Dr Macleod clamped and cut its umbilical cord. He was panting with effort. Over the years he had performed scores of grisly operations, but the feeling of this foetus's tentacles flopping against his hands caused him to bring up a mouthful of acidic bile, which he had to swallow. Dr Symonds was still standing in the corner of the theatre with her back turned, while both Glenda and the nurse had turned away too, and Duncan was staring at the foetus in disbelief.

'Dr Bhaduri,' said Dr Macleod. 'Oxytocin.' This was a hormone injection, which would help Chiasoka to expel the placenta. Dr Bhaduri picked up the hypodermic and lifted the sheet so that he could inject it into Chiasoka's thigh, but he couldn't bring himself to look at the foetus and his hands were trembling uncontrollably.

'I-I...' he began. 'I'm sorry, doctor. I don't believe I can—'

Dr Macleod said, 'It's all right. Let me do it.'

He reached across and gently took the syringe out of Dr Bhaduri's hand. To his relief, the foetus's tentacles had stopped their furious writhing and were slowly untangling themselves. *Dear God*, he thought, *please let this creature be dying*. But as the tentacles unfolded, they gradually revealed a white oval shape in their centre, still glossy with slime and streaked with blood. It was a shape that hadn't shown up clearly in the ultrasound, because the tentacles or limbs or whatever they were had been wrapped all around it, effectively masking it. It had registered only as a mass of tissue, like a tumour, but because it had appeared to be connected to a small deformed spine, Dr Macleod had assumed that it was the foetus's brain.

Now that the tentacles had fallen away though, he could clearly see that it was a distorted human head, with a face. The tentacles were growing out of the back of the head, and from its neck, two bulging balloons of thin skin protruded, semi-transparent and laced with red capillaries. These balloons were rhythmically inflating and deflating, like lungs, and Dr Macleod could only assume that they *were* lungs.

Beneath the lungs, there was a rudimentary body, no bigger than a child's glove, with tiny male genitals and floppy, undeveloped legs.

Dr Macleod had seen some freakish foetuses – foetuses deformed by drugs or alcohol or genetic abnormalities. But the face of this creature chilled him to the core. It was beautiful, like a cherub. He had rarely seen a newborn child look so perfect. Its eyes were closed as if it were peacefully sleeping. Its bow-shaped lips were slightly parted as it breathed. And yet, by any definition, it was a monster. He couldn't believe that it not only existed, but that it was still alive.

'What are we going to do with it?' said Dr Bhaduri. 'It's …it's… I have never seen anything like it. Its *face*.'

Dr Macleod snapped himself back to reality. He lifted the sheet that covered Chiasoka's thigh and injected the oxytocin. He had to think of *her* welfare above everything. The oxytocin would stimulate her to release the placenta, and then he would try to remove it from her uterus by controlled cord traction. That would lessen the risk of infection.

'Her blood pressure's dropping,' said Duncan. 'Heart rate's okay though.'

Glenda the midwife said, 'The *thing*, doctor. The foetus. Look – it's having trouble breathing.'

She was right. The foetus had started to snuffle, twitching its head from side to side, and Dr Macleod could see that its nostrils were blocked with mucus. Its tentacles had started to twitch again too, so that its head was joggled up and down.

If this had been anything like a normal birth, he would have told the nurse to use an aspirator and clear out its nasal passages immediately, but now he hesitated. Despite its angelic face, perhaps it would be kinder to let this poor creature suffocate. In fact, he was already thinking about a massive dose of morphine to finish it off.

It spluttered and choked, and then to Dr Macleod's horror, it opened its eyes. Clear, sapphire-blue eyes stared at him in the same way that all babies stared at him when they were first born. Who are you, and what am I doing here?

Glenda looked across at him, biting her lip. 'I know what you're thinking, sir. I'm thinking the same.'

Dr Symonds had turned around and come slowly back to the operating table. Her face, usually flushed, looked as pale as if she had powdered it in cornflour.

'It's so beautiful,' she whispered. 'How can anything so horrible be so beautiful?'

The foetus continued to snuffle, and Dr Macleod could see by the way its balloon-like lungs were only half inflating that it was having more and more difficulty breathing.

'I don't even understand how it can still be alive,' he said. He wished that it would stop staring at him, as if it were appealing to him to save it. *I can't breathe, doctor. Please, I'm begging you – I can't breathe.*

'I'm not God, but my feeling is that we could do no greater kindness to this unfortunate child than to allow him to pass away, with or without our intervention.'

He was aware that he had called the foetus a child, and that he had also called it 'him', but he had found it impossible to say 'it' when the child was staring at him like that.

'What do we all think?' he said. 'Are we in agreement?'

'Yes,' said Dr Bhaduri; and 'Yes,' said Dr Symonds. Glenda the midwife nodded.

'Nurse, would you fetch me 200 milligrams of morphine, please,' said Dr Macleod. Then with great care, he lifted the tangled foetus off the operating table. It couldn't have weighed more than three or four pounds. Its bony tentacles wriggled a little, and it was whining for breath, and even when he set it down in the stainless-steel kidney dish, it continued to stare at him with those unblinking blue eyes.

'I'm sorry,' he told it, even though he knew that it couldn't understand him.

But then it took a clogged-up breath and started to cry.

5

Jerry said, 'Where'd you get the knife, Rusul?'

'The shank? Man bought it in Asda.'

'It's not a "shank", you twat. It's a Victorinox kitchen knife for cutting up cauliflowers. I doubt if it said anything on the packaging about murdering your mates with it. When did you buy it?'

'Yesterday morning.'

'So you bought it with the specific intention of killing Attaf?'

'Man don't know, blud. Man wanted to teach that paigon a lesson, like, but man didn't think about him actually being *dead*, like.'

'You didn't think that if you stabbed him eleven times with an eight-inch kitchen knife there was more than a remote possibility that he might snuff it?'

'Man was so aggy, man didn't not think about that. That Attaf, he was always irking me, like, but that was always just jokes, you know what I mean? But then he started chirpsing with Joya, and took her off me, even though she was my wifey, you know? And she had my baby inside her, and he only offed it. How would *you* feel, blud, if this pig here offed *your* baby? Would you forgive him?'

Jerry turned and looked at Mallett.

'I think the chances of that happening are what you might call infinitesimal. And here in the nick, Rusul, we usually refer to ourselves as "officers". Otherwise, blud, we get irked. We might even get aggy.'

It was 11:30 in the morning, and they were sitting in the bare, beige-painted interview room. Jerry and Mallett were facing Rusul across the table, and Rusul's duty solicitor was sitting next to him – a thin young man in a blue Marks and Spencer's suit. He had a prominent nose and thinning blond hair, and Jerry reckoned that he would be bald in less than three years.

'Well,' said Jerry, closing the file in front of him. 'I don't think there's a lot more that I need to ask you. You've admitted that you purchased a knife earlier in the day with the deliberate intention of taking your revenge on Attaf. It wasn't as though you picked up some random knife that was lying around the karate club and stabbed him in a spontaneous fit of rage. You purchased the knife to kill him, and you had all day to think it over, so you could have changed your mind, but you didn't.'

He turned to Rusul's solicitor and said, 'Anything you want to add, Mr Teape?'

Mr Teape was wiping his nose with a crumpled-up tissue. 'I'm going to apply for my client to undergo a full psychiatric examination. I am strongly of the opinion that he suffers from an underlying mental disorder, and that this disorder led to his violent over-reaction when he discovered that his former partner had been encouraged to terminate her pregnancy.'

'You didn't know that Joya was pregnant when you and she split up though, did you, Rusul?' asked Jerry.

'That's beside the point,' said Mr Teape. 'Whether he was aware that she was pregnant or not, it was a tragedy, nonetheless. Supposing she had gone full term and given birth to the child, and then years later he had found out that he was a father but had never known?'

'But she had an abortion, and she was well within the twenty-four week limit, and the choice was totally hers. If he was going to be angry at anybody, he should have been angry at her, but it was *her* body, and ultimately, it was *her* decision, and it certainly gave him no justification to murder Attaf.'

'I'm sorry,' said Mr Teape. 'Manslaughter on the grounds of diminished responsibility, that's what we'll be going for.' He picked up his cheap leather briefcase and tucked his notes into it.

Mallett switched off the voice recorder. 'Don't count on it, Mr Teape. Murder on the grounds of being a jealous dim-witted arsehole, that's what *we'll* be going for.'

***

They found Joya in the back of her father's grocery store. It was halfway along Streatham High Road, a wide two-mile stretch of the main A23 into central London, lined on either side with a tatty collection of discount stores and Chinese restaurants and travel agencies and vaping shops.

Sanghavi's Halal Foods was gloomy inside and smelled

pungently of cinnamon and turmeric and allspice and cloves. The shelves were packed with Najma chorizo sticks and Royal gajar halwa dessert and Haloodies chicken fillets, as well as brown rice and parathas and poppadoms.

Mallett took a deep breath and said, 'Blimey. If this doesn't clear me catarrh, nothing will.'

A tubby Pakistani man in a green striped apron was standing behind the counter, prodding furiously at a tablet. He had a shiny bald head and circular spectacles and a heavy black moustache that reminded Jerry of the brushes in front of a road sweeper.

'Looking for a young lady by the name of Joya,' said Jerry, holding up his warrant card.

'Joya? Yes. I am her father. What do you want of her?'

'And your name is?'

'It is over the front of my shop. Sanghavi.'

'Okay, Mr Sanghavi. Any chance of having a word with Joya? Gather she comes in to give you a hand now and again. Is she here in the shop today?'

'Is this about Attaf?'

'We need to speak confidentially to your daughter, Mr Sanghavi. I'm afraid we can't discuss it with you.'

'She was told about Attaf late last night by one of her friends. She is very upset, but she insisted on coming in to help me in the shop today. She said she did not want to let me down.'

'So she's here?'

'I told her so many times that I did not approve of her friends from that karate club. They were all *nimna varga* – low-class. I met that Attaf once though, and he was not as bad as some of the others. Clean and very polite, and called me "*Sāhēba*". But Joya promised me faithfully that she would not see any of them again. Please do not tell her this, but we will be taking her to Pakistan next month in order to marry her to her cousin. That will put an end to all of our worries about who she is mixing with.'

'Oh. Lucky girl,' said Mallett. 'How old's her cousin?'

'Forty-three. But a fine man. He has made a lot of money in mobile phones.'

'So... can we talk to her?' asked Jerry.

'Yes. She is in the stockroom in the back. Just come with me.'

Jerry and Mallett followed Mr Sanghavi down one of the narrow aisles to the back of the shop. The stockroom was piled high with sacks of rice and boxes of Pakistani food and drink, like Khalai Khaas almond and cardamom biscuits and tinned goat curry and cans of cow urine. Sitting on one of the boxes was a young woman of about eighteen or nineteen, wearing a red silk headscarf, a loose pink sweater and jeans. She had been talking on her iPhone, but as soon as her father appeared, she switched it off and pushed it into her pocket.

'Joya, these are police officers. They wish to speak to you about Attaf.'

Joya stood up. 'What about Attaf?' she demanded. Jerry immediately recognised the defiance of somebody who is stricken by grief but is trying hard not to show it. 'Attaf is dead.'

'Well, that's what we want to talk to you about. And in particular, *why* he's dead.'

'How should my daughter know why he is dead?' Mr Sanghavi demanded. He was standing in the doorway with his arms folded. 'Surely, you should be asking that of the fellow who killed him.'

'Mr Sanghavi, we do need to talk to Joya in private.'

'She is my daughter, officer. She lives in my house. She is a member of my family. What is the business of a member of my family is also my business.'

'Not in this case, sir, with all due respect.'

'And why not, may I ask?'

'Because she may want to confide in us information that she's reluctant to share with you. And since this is a murder case, that information could be of critical importance in prosecuting the offender.'

'That is ridiculous. She tells me everything.'

'All right then,' said Mallett. 'Who's her favourite pop singer?'

'How should I know?'

'There you are then. QED. She *doesn't* tell you everything.'

Mr Sanghavi stayed where he was, in the doorway. Jerry took a deep, patient breath then said, 'Look, sir, I'm sorry, but we have to talk to Joya in confidence. If we can't do it here, we'll have to ask her to come down to the station with us.'

'Well... very well. But I am sure she has nothing to tell you that can help you. Why should she? You don't, do you, Joya?'

Joya said nothing but lowered her eyes, her hands clasped together like a meek and dutiful daughter.

47

Mr Sanghavi made a snorting noise then went back into the shop. Jerry closed the storeroom door. He knew that Mr Sanghavi wouldn't be able to hear them even if it were open, but he wanted to give Joya the feeling that their conversation was going to be truly held in private.

'How long were you dating Rusul?' asked Jerry.

'Not quite a year,' said Joya. Her accent was a strange blend of South London and Pakistani. She pronounced 'quite' as 'qvite' but 'year' as 'yurr'. 'I met him at my friend's walima.'

'Walima? That's a wedding party, unless I've got it wrong.'

'No, that is right. And because it was a walima, Rusul was dressed very smart and he was behaving very polite. It was only after I had been dating him for two or three months that I found out how rough he could be. His room was like a pigsty, and even his flatmates used to give him a hard time for being so messy. He never changed his sheets, and all his dirty clothes he just dropped on the floor.'

'So why didn't you dump him?' asked Mallett.

'Oh, come on, 'Edge,' said Jerry. 'Same reason women don't walk out on blokes who give them a regular pasting. They always believe they're the ones who can change them. And then there's l-o-v-e, of course.'

'I did love him, yes,' said Joya. 'He was rough, and not so clean, but he never hit me. Sometimes we had bad arguments, but most of the time, he was funny and he was very generous and... well.'

'He was good in bed?'

Joya blushed and looked away.

'I'll take that as a yes,' said Jerry. 'When did you find out you were expecting his baby?'

'Who told you such a thing?'

'Rusul himself.'

Joya didn't answer for almost a quarter of a minute. Jerry could tell by the way she was breathing and biting her lip that she was close to breaking down.

Eventually, she said, 'Two months ago. August the eleventh.'

'But you didn't tell Rusul? Why not?'

'We were going through a difficult time. Rusul had lost his job at the garage because he was always late for work. And also—'

'Yes? Also, what?'

'I went to see my *bhavishya kahēnāra.*'

'Oh, you did, did you? And what's one of them when they're at home?'

'My fortune teller. She is a friend of my aunt. Her name is Hazeema, and she lives in Mitcham. Somehow she knew that I had come to see her because I was pregnant, even before I told her that I was expecting Rusul's baby.'

Joya paused and sat silent again, her black eyelashes sparkling with tears. Jerry and Mallett stood patiently and waited for her to collect herself.

Eventually, Joya said, 'Hazeema gave me a blessing. Then she laid her hand on my stomach and closed her eyes so that she could tell what the baby's life was going to be like. When she took her hand away, she told me that there was something wrong with the baby. She wasn't sure exactly what it was, but it wasn't growing proper.'

'How did she work that out?' asked Mallett. 'She's got X-ray hands, has she?'

'Everything she has ever told me in my life has always come true,' said Joya. 'She told me when I was only fourteen that I would meet a man who liked to fight and that I would give him a strange baby. She also told me that after that, I would marry an old man with lots of money.'

Jerry looked at Mallett and pulled a face.

'Have to meet this Hazeema,' said Mallett. 'Maybe she can tip me the wink about Friday's lotto numbers.'

'I love Hazeema,' said Joya. 'I love her and I trust her. I can tell her things that I could never tell my mum or my dad.'

'So... after what she told you about the baby... that's why you decided on a termination?' asked Jerry.

'Not straight away. But it put me off Rusul even more. I went to the karate club to meet him one evening and that's when I met Attaf.'

'And that's when you gave Rusul the old heave-ho?'

'Attaf was so sweet and gentle and understanding. His family welcomed me too. I used to go to his house and his mother taught me how to cook cardamom kheer.'

'But it was Attaf who arranged for you to have a termination?'

'Yes. I told him that there was something wrong with the baby and he said that I should. He said that Ibn Hajar Al Asqalani believed that it was the right thing to do, when a baby isn't right.'

'Oh well,' said Mallett. 'So long as old Ibn Hajar Al-What's-His-Name thought it was okay, no worries.'

'He's a great Islamic scholar,' said Joya.

Jerry said, 'As I understand it, you got the pills off a doctor in Brockley that Attaf took you to, and you had the termination at home?'

'At Attaf's parents' house, when they were away for the weekend.'

'And I'm sorry to have to ask you this, and I know that it probably wasn't nearly developed enough for you to tell, but did you see any evidence that the foetus wasn't properly formed?'

Joya shook her head, and shivered at the recollection. 'I felt it, when it slipped out, but I didn't look.'

'Only one more question then. Did Rusul say anything to you about how he felt about Attaf? Did he say he was angry or jealous? Did he threaten to hurt him at all?'

'When he found out about the baby, he came to me and asked me if it was true. He didn't shout or scream when I said that it was, but I could tell that he was very angry. All he said was, "*Jīvana mātē ēīka jīvana*". That means "a life for a life". At the time, I didn't really understand what he meant. Of course I do now.'

'Would you be prepared to repeat that in court, if you were asked to?'

'He killed Attaf. I loved Attaf. If this was Pakistan, he would be hanged.'

'So that's a yes then?'

6

Martin climbed out of his silver-grey Audi and crossed the road, narrowly avoiding being hit by a Deliveroo rider on a moped. The Deliveroo rider shouted something at him that included the words 'fucking *blind* or what?', but he didn't catch the rest.

Jim Feather was waiting for him by the barriers, smoking and talking to Newton. As soon as he saw Martin, he flicked his cigarette into the gutter and blew out a long stream of smoke.

'So, how's it going, Jim?' Martin asked him. 'Hallo, Newton, everything okay? I've had a shufti at your videos. We've got ourselves a fair old blockage here by the look of it. Where's Gemma?'

'She'll be back in a minute. Just gone across the road to get a coffee and a doughnut.'

'Blimey,' said Martin, flapping his hand in front of his face. Even out here on the open pavement he could smell the rancid fumes from the sewer. 'She must have a stronger stomach than me.'

He kept reminding himself that he was the boss here, but he was acutely aware that his white protective suit was brand new and shiny, without a single dirty streak on it, and that his helmet was new too, and not battered and scratched like Jim's. He felt the same as he had on his first day at his secondary school, with a blazer that was two sizes too big for him and a stiff new plastic satchel.

Gemma came across Peckham Road from the Payless store, carrying a cup of coffee and a doughnut, as well as two cans of Coke, which she handed to Jim and Newton.

'Sorry, Martin, I didn't realise you'd be here so soon. Do you want a drink of anything? Doughnut?'

'I think I'll wait until I've checked out this fatberg, thanks. Bit of a dicky tummy, don't know why.'

'Give yourself a couple more years, and you'll get used to it,' Jim told him. 'You think this is bad? You should've gone into the khazi straight after my old man. You'd have needed a bleeding gas mask.'

They waited until Gemma had finished her coffee and eaten her doughnut and Jim had smoked another cigarette. Gemma was trying hard not to appear edgy, but she was still in two minds whether she ought to tell Martin about the white-faced child-thing. If she told him, and it never appeared again, even when they started to blast away the fatberg, he might think that she was cracking up, that the job was too stressful for her. He had already said that he didn't know what a pretty girl like her was doing down in the sewers. If she *didn't* tell him, and the child-thing was injured or killed by their high-pressure hoses, she would feel unbearably guilty. But she had almost completely convinced herself that she had imagined it.

She dropped her empty coffee cup into the nearby

rubbish bin, smacked her hands together and said, 'Right, Martin, we're ready now.'

Martin caught the tension in her voice and gave her a questioning look, but she turned away.

They all buckled up their helmets and pulled on their protective gloves. Jim Feather would be joining them this time, so that he could give Martin an assessment of the most effective way to clear the fatberg and start the sewage flowing freely again. After that, it would be Martin's job to work out how much it was going to cost, especially if they decided to attack it from both ends with two clearance crews. Martin knew that their high-pressure hoses would almost certainly damage some of the brickwork too. It dated back to 1865 when Joseph Bazalgette had supervised the construction of London's first citywide sewer system, and it was always expensive to repair.

Jim lowered himself down into the manhole first, followed by Newton, Gemma and Martin last. The sewage was swirling around at a higher level than it had been that morning, almost up to the top of Gemma's boots, and floating around on the surface there were tampons and what they called 'unpolished turds'.

'This lot should be running through here at full whack,' said Jim. In the fitful lights from their helmets, his face was lit up like a ghost. 'Give it a couple more weeks at this rate and we'll have shite spouting out of the manholes and into the street.'

'Well, let's take a look at our fatberg, shall we?' said Martin. He had been down plenty of sewers, but because of the blockage, the stench in this one was even more noxious than any he had ever smelled before. Not only was it strong, but it had an unusual sharpness to it. As he waded along the tunnel behind Gemma, he sniffed, and sniffed again.

'Is it just me, Gem, or can you smell something *acidic*?' he asked her.

Gemma sniffed too. 'You're right. I noticed it before. More lemony, really. It's like verbena, isn't it?'

'More like Cif lemon toilet cleaner to me,' said Jim.

They waded along in single file until they reached the fatberg. Newton lit up the sheer wall of saponified fat from a variety of different angles so that Martin could see how dense it was, and how thickly laced it was with tree roots. Gemma couldn't stop herself from glancing up at the narrow gap between the ceiling and the fatberg, just in case the white-faced child-thing was watching them.

She showed Martin how much effort it took to prise the fat away from the bricks, and how it was beginning to form craggy stalactites on the ceiling, which would eventually occlude the sewer completely.

'Actually, Gem, it's a damn sight worse than I thought it would be, even after seeing your samples. I think we can only attack it from the north end though. Obviously we could get it flushed out quicker if we could attack it from both ends, but think how much water the crew will be pumping out to clear this lot away. We'll never be able to drain it away fast enough from this end. It won't take five minutes and they'll be drowned.'

'It's effing rock-hard too, some of it,' said Jim. He was

hacking with a broad-bladed chisel at the fat on the wall beside him. 'Even at Whitechapel it wasn't as hard as this.'

He broke off a large yellowish lump, which must have weighed at least four kilos, and it tumbled into the thick beige sewage with a splash.

'Look at this. There's so much rag mixed up in it, as well as roots. And stuff you don't normally see – not just your teabags and your Tampaxes and your rubber johnnies.'

He dug into the fat with his chisel to expose something that looked like a flat black stick. He tugged at it and waggled it from side to side with his fingers, and after a few seconds, he pulled out a tarnished dessert spoon.

'I mean, who throws their cutlery down the crapper? I ask you.'

He started digging again, but this time, he stopped suddenly.

'Whoa,' he said, wading back a step. It was noticeable now that the sewage was rising. It was at least five centimetres deeper than when they had first entered the sewer.

'What's up?' asked Martin.

She didn't really know why, but Gemma's first instinct was to glance up at the gap again. There was no sign yet of the white-faced child-thing, if it existed at all. But then she looked down and saw why Jim had backed off. Half buried in the fat was a severed human hand – a woman's hand by the look of it, greenish-grey because it was partly decomposed. Its nails were painted with chipped orange polish and there was a thin gold wedding ring on its third finger.

'Bloody hell,' said Jim. 'That's enough to make a maggot gag. Wonder where the rest of her is?'

Martin didn't come any closer. He felt nauseous enough as it was. He swallowed, and he was sure that his saliva tasted of lemony sewage.

'I don't believe this,' he said. 'We're well and truly buggered now. We'll have to notify the police before we start flushing, and God alone knows how long *they're* going to hold us up. You remember what they were like in Catford last month, when we found that missing kid's trainer. They'll want to dig out all of this fatberg, inch by inch, in case the rest of her body's buried in it, too.'

Jim thought for a while, frowning at the woman's severed hand as if he were trying to put a value on it. Then he said, 'Not necessarily, guv.'

'What do you mean?'

'I mean if it wasn't for this fatberg, her hand wouldn't be stuck here, would it? It would have floated down to the Thames and out to sea by now, along with any other bits and pieces of her, if there *are* any other bits and pieces of her dotted around.'

'So?'

'So we could just give nature a hand, no pun intended. Dig it out, take it up to Butler's Wharf, drop it in the river and think no more about it. That's where it would have been anyway if half of Peckham hadn't poured their bloody cooking fat and coffee grounds down the sink and wiped their arses with Washlets.'

Martin shook his head. 'No, Jim, sorry, we can't do

that. That would be, what-do-you-call-it, tampering with evidence.'

'All right, guv. You're the boss. I'm only trying to think of a way to save us time and money. And she's brown bread anyway.'

'Yes, but think of the poor woman's family. Supposing she just disappeared and they have no idea what happened to her. They're going to be desperate for closure, aren't they?'

'And what about whoever it was who cut her hand off?' Gemma put in. 'He could still be roaming around, couldn't he, looking for vulnerable women to chop up? You know, like Jack the Ripper.'

'Take a few pictures, will you, Newton?' said Martin. 'We'll run them straight along to the cop shop and see what they have to say. They may want to dig around this end of the fatberg, but that shouldn't necessarily hold us up from making a start on the other end.'

Newton waded forward with his camera, switched on its lamp and began to take bursts of photographs of the severed hand. The light was so bright that even with her tinted goggles, Gemma had to lift her forearm in front of her face to shield her eyes.

Then, with no warning at all, the light went *ping!* and went out. A split second afterward, their helmet lamps went out too, and they were plunged into total, seamless blackness.

'What the hell just happened?' said Martin.

Newton said, 'Hold on – I've got a spare flashlight.'

'Don't anybody move,' Martin told them. 'I don't want you slipping over.'

They waited without speaking for almost half a minute. The only sound was the lapping of the sewage against their boots. But then Newton said, 'The flashlight don't work neither. I don't know what's wrong with it. I've only just put a new battery in it too.'

'Oh, *bollocks*,' said Martin. 'Listen – we're going to have to make our way back to the manhole. But let's take it slowly, shall we? Newton, you go first; Gemma, you put your hand on Newton's shoulder, and Jim, you put your hand on Gemma's shoulder, and I'll bring up the rear.'

Gemma reached out into the blackness with both hands, trying to remember exactly where Newton had been standing. She took three cautious steps forward through the sewage but even with her arms held out straight in front of her, she couldn't find him.

'Newton, say something,' she said.

'I'm here,' he told her. 'I haven't moved.'

'Where's "here"? I'm waving my arms around, but I still can't feel you. Keep talking.'

'I haven't moved since the lights went out. Keep coming. I think I can hear you splashing. That's it, keep coming.'

'I'm sure you weren't that far away from me. Keep talking. Anything.'

The blackness was so total and so overwhelming that she was beginning to panic. She had been terrified of the dark when she was younger. She had always insisted that her parents left the landing light on at night. In her early teens though, she had gradually grown out of her fear, and she no longer believed that witches were hiding in her wardrobe or that her dressing gown was going to drop off the hook on the back of the door and come scuttling under her bed. But this was different. This was underground and the stench was stifling her, and she could feel by the pressure on her boots that the sewage was rising – slowly, but relentlessly, and she knew that at this time of day it wouldn't subside.

Suddenly, she felt Jim's strong hand on her shoulder. He gripped her firmly and gave her a reassuring squeeze.

'Got you, love. Have you found Newton yet?'

Now that Jim was holding on to her, Gemma felt confident enough to take a sloshing step forward, and then another, and at last she felt the slippery back of Newton's protective suit. She grasped his collar and held on to it tight.

Newton said, 'Gah! Strangle me, why don't you?'

'Sorry, sorry, but I thought you'd vanished.'

'Martin? You there?' Jim called out. 'Newton and Gemma and me, we're all ready to go.'

'Hold on,' said Martin, somewhere in the blackness. 'I can feel the wall but I'm kind of disorientated here.'

'Just keep walking forward,' Jim told him. 'We won't move until you catch up with us.'

As they waited for Martin, Gemma saw a flicker of light further down the sewer. It was thin and pale, and it appeared only for the briefest of moments, but she thought it looked like a slender figure twisting itself around and throwing up its arms.

'Did you see that?' she asked Newton.

'What? I can't see sod all.'

'It was kind of a light, but I don't know... it looked like a child, dancing.'

'Phosphorus, probably.'

'No. Phosphorus is green. This was white.'

'You're not seeing things again, are you?'

'I still can't find you!' said Martin. He was beginning to sound anxious. 'Are you sure you haven't started walking off?'

'We're right here, guv,' Jim told him. 'Haven't budged an inch.'

It was then that Gemma saw another flicker of light, closer this time, and this time, it didn't immediately disappear. It looked like the child-thing – pale, with an elongated head and smoke-black near-together eyes, and arms that waved disjointedly, as if they were broken.

Newton must have seen it too, because he said, '*Shit!*' and stumbled backward, so that Gemma lost her grip on his collar. By the dim light that the child-thing gave off, she saw him hit his shoulder against the greasy sewer wall, lose his footing and splash onto his knees with sewage almost up to his waist.

'What's *that*?' he screamed. 'What the fucking hell is *that*?'

Jim said, 'Gas, it's just gas!' but then the child-thing began to move toward them, with its boneless arms waving, and it opened its dragged-down mouth and let out a harsh, high-pitched cry.

'Christ almighty, no it's not!' Jim shouted. 'What is it?' He kept his grip on Gemma's shoulder with his left hand but he raised his chisel defensively in his right.

As the child-thing came closer, its waving arms were reflected in the rippling sewer water. The reflections flickered on the brickwork so that the whole sewer was filled with stroboscopic patterns of light. Then Gemma saw more reflections, further down the tunnel, and more shining figures began to materialise out of the darkness, at least five or six of them. Two of them were slender, like the child-thing, with stick-like limbs, but the others were distorted in different ways. One was hunched, with a low, deeply dented forehead, and it dragged itself toward them, chin-deep through the sewage as if every step was a hideous effort. Behind it came a girl-child, who appeared to be disembowelled. Her looped intestines were hanging down and trailing in the sewage, and the bones of her ribcage were exposed. Above her clavicle though, her neck was white and swan-like, and she had a face of bleached Pre-Raphaelite beauty, with wavy reddish hair that defied gravity and flew up almost to the ceiling.

Gemma was desperate to call out, *Who are you? What do you want?* But she couldn't take enough air into her lungs to utter a word, and all she did was open and close her mouth and let out a tiny froglike croak. She was so frightened by these deformed, radiant figures coming toward her that she couldn't even work out how to move her legs so that she could back away.

Martin said, 'Jim! I can see you now! Hold on!'

Gemma turned her head and saw Martin wading his way up behind Jim, but before he could reach him, the sewer was abruptly plunged into darkness again. Utterly, totally, seamlessly black. Something as tensile and slippery as a snake struck Gemma across the shoulders, and she yelped and tried to duck away from it, but then a claw-like hand groped in the darkness at the back of her helmet, as if it were trying to lever it off her head. She ducked forward again, colliding with Newton, who was climbing back onto his feet.

'What the fuck are you *doing*, Gem?' he shrieked at her, but then Jim shouted, 'Get off me! Jesus, get off me!' and then, 'Newt! Gemma! Guv'nor! Let's get the hell out of here!'

More claws snatched at the crumpled folds of Gemma's polypropylene suit and scraped and squeaked against her helmet, clearly trying to wrench it off her. She struck out against them as hard as she could, over and over, and as she beat them off, the child-thing let out another high, weird cry, half baby and half animal.

Newton grunted and swore and Gemma could feel his arms flailing around, so he was obviously fighting off the tentacles too. He hit her arm, and as soon as he did, and realised it was her, he seized her wrist and shouted, 'Come on!' He pulled her into the darkness, back along the sewer toward the manhole, tugging her so forcefully that she almost fell over.

'Jim!' shouted Gemma, as Newton dragged her along. 'Martin!'

'Right with you, love!' Jim panted. She could hear his boots splashing in the sewage close behind her, and feel it splattering up against the back of her legs.

They jostled and stumbled through the blackness, and it seemed to Gemma to take forever before they saw the autumnal daylight gleaming down through the open manhole, although it couldn't have been more than three or four minutes. They reached the bottom rungs, all of them gasping, and Gemma started to climb up first. Halfway up though, she stopped and said, 'Martin! Where's Martin?'

They looked back into the darkness. It was suddenly quiet, except for the wallowing sound of the sewage that they had run through, and the swishing of traffic from Peckham High Road above their heads.

'He was right behind me, I could swear it,' said Jim. He lifted off his helmet, and shouted out, 'Guv'nor! Are you there, guv? *Guv'nor!*'

Gemma climbed down from the rungs and took off her helmet, too.

'Martin! Can you hear me, Martin? Martin!'

'Maybe he fell over,' said Newton. He was holding on to one of the rungs as if he were desperate to climb out of the sewer and back up into the fresh air.

'Try your lamp again, Newt,' said Jim. 'There's no point in going down there after him unless we've got some light.'

'And those *things*,' said Gemma. 'What do you think they are? One minute they were all lit up and then they went dark. And it was like they were trying to tear us to bits. Look at me, I can't stop shaking.'

'I haven't the first fucking clue *what* they are, love. Not the foggiest, and I've seen some strange-looking animals down the sewers in my time. I saw a rat with one head and two bodies once. And down Chancery Lane I came across a bloke with no legs. I tried to catch up with him, but he went swinging off so fast on his hands I couldn't keep up. For all I know he's still down there somewhere.'

Jim paused, and then he said, 'P'raps that's how that woman lost her hand. P'raps those things ripped her to pieces. Blimey. It doesn't bear thinking about, does it?'

Suddenly, Newton's lamp blinked on again. Two or three seconds later, the lights on their helmets lit up again too. They stood looking at each other, and they all knew what they were thinking.

Jim said, 'I'm going in after him. You coming?'

'What if the lights go out again?' asked Newton.

'Then we'll have to turn around and come back, won't we? But we can't just leave him there, can we?'

'Come on,' said Gemma. 'If the lights go out, we'll have to bring down some portable LEDs and make a daisy chain, but with any luck, we won't need to.'

'But what if those things are still there?'

'Newton!' Gemma almost screamed at him. 'I'm as scared as you are, but Martin's still there, and he could have broken his ankle or God knows what!'

Newton didn't answer, but Jim had already started to make his way back along the sewer, and after a moment's hesitation, Newton followed him, holding his lamp up high so that the brickwork was lit up as far ahead as possible. Gemma waded after him, her mouth dry and her heart beating hard, trying not to imagine what those child-things might have done to Martin. They had tried to pull off her helmet; why had they wanted to do that?

Their lights stayed on, and at last, they reached the wax-white cliffs of the fatberg. There were several deep scratches in the fat, and on the right-hand side, large lumps had dropped into the sewage, and the woman's severed hand had dropped in with them. But there was no sign of Martin.

'Where the hell's he disappeared to?' said Jim. 'There's no side tunnels... and don't tell me he managed to climb up *there*.'

He shone his helmet lamp up to the gap in between the ceiling and the fatberg. Its edges were scored with sharp triangular grooves, which they hadn't been before, but it still seemed unlikely that Martin had climbed up the fatberg and crawled right into it.

'Not unless those things pulled him into it,' said Gemma.

Newton shone his lamp into the gap, but it lit up only the same fibrous tree roots and fatty stalactites that Gemma had seen before. Beyond the range of the light, there was only darkness.

'Guv'nor!' Jim shouted, into the gap. 'Guv'nor, can you hear me? Guv'nor!'

They waited, but there was no response.

'Right,' said Gemma, her voice trembling, 'we need to go right back and call 999. I'll call Michael too, and get him to bring over the GPR.' She meant the ground-penetrating radar equipment they used to trace underground pipes and cables.

Jim said, 'I've got a bad, bad feeling about this, Gem. I really have. It's the spookiest thing I've ever come across, ever.'

'You and me both, Jim. But let's go. It doesn't matter how spooky it is, we don't have any time to lose.'

7

When Professor Karounis returned from his meeting with the hospital's trust managers in central London, Dr Macleod was waiting for him outside his office.

'Stuart? Is something wrong?' asked Professor Karounis as he approached. 'You look as if your cat just died.'

'I'm afraid it's rather worse than that, professor – not that I actually own a cat. I carried out a termination this morning. If I told you that it didn't quite go as planned, it would be the understatement of the century.'

'Is it the mother?'

'No, the mother's recovering well. It's the foetus.'

'You'd better come in,' said Professor Karounis, opening his office door. His secretary was sitting at her desk close by, and since she was only a temporary, he didn't want her to overhear anything confidential. Medical liability lawsuits could cost millions.

He closed the door behind them, took off his dark grey overcoat and hung it up, and then crossed over to his huge mahogany desk. He had been director of the Warren BirthWell Centre for eight years now, and although he had developed a certain arrogance, it was probably deserved.

He had drummed up huge financial support and made sure that the centre led the country in prenatal and neonatal care, with some of the most advanced techniques and medical equipment anywhere.

He was a small, neat man, with a gleaming bald head like a giant horse chestnut, a close-clipped beard and rimless spectacles, and he had never been seen at the centre wearing anything but his grey three-piece suit and red bow tie.

'So... what's the problem?' he said, sitting behind his desk and indicating that Dr Macleod should sit down too. Dr Macleod remained standing.

'The mother's a Nigerian woman, thirty-five years old. She was brought here from A & E suffering from acute abdominal trauma. We scanned her and discovered that she was pregnant, although she couldn't understand how she could be, since she had only recently had an abortion, and according to her, she had had no sexual relations since.

'The ultrasound showed that the foetus was congenitally malformed. And when I say "congenitally malformed", I mean that it was difficult to determine if it was even human. We could see that it was suffering from polymelia, with an unprecedented number of extraneous limbs, a severely underdeveloped body, a small curved spinal column and gastroschisis.

'Here...' he said, handing Professor Karounis the green cardboard file. 'Here are some pictures of it. It has male genitalia, so I suppose to be quite accurate we should call it a boy. But you can see for yourself that it is nothing much more than a head with multiple arms and legs and only rudimentary organs.'

Professor Karounis opened the file and studied the photographs inside. After he had examined them all carefully, he looked up at Dr Macleod, and it was clear that he was shaken.

'I don't know what to say, Stuart. I have been in obstetrics for twenty-six years and never have I seen anything like this. Never.'

'Well, professor, that makes two of us.'

'All these extraneous arms and legs... and the lungs exposed like this! But the *face*, Stuart! I mean – *O Theós ston ouranó!*'

'I know. He's like a cherub, isn't he? But I'm afraid that there's something even more disturbing about him. I removed him by C-section, but he's still alive.'

'*What?*'

'He's still alive, and breathing. He's in an incubator, in a room of his own, of course, in isolation. We wouldn't want any other parents to see him.'

'How can it... *he*... How can he still be alive?'

'I have no idea, professor. I was about to euthanise him with morphine, but he opened his eyes, and he started to cry like a normal baby, and I have to admit that I couldn't bring myself to do it. I thought that if God has allowed such a boy to exist then perhaps He has a reason, and He'll take him when He sees fit. In any event, I doubt if he can survive for very long.'

Professor Karounis stood up and handed back the file of photographs. 'I need to see this for myself. Nobody else knows about it, do they? Apart from the team who assisted you with the C-section? It's very important we keep this confidential. If the media get to hear about it, they'll be all over us before you can say "freak show".'

He led the way out of his office and along the corridor. His secretary looked up and said, 'Professor Karounis—' but he gave her an abstracted wave and said, 'Later, Mandy. Later.'

'How long do you think it can survive?' he asked Dr Macleod, as they waited for a lift to come up to the third floor.

'I don't know. Hours perhaps. Maybe a day, if we feed him.'

'Is it *capable* of being fed? Does it have a stomach?'

'He has a very diminutive digestive system, yes. Whether that can cope with preemie formula or not, I really couldn't say.'

'O *Theós ston ouranó!*' Professor Karounis repeated. 'God in Heaven!'

They went down to the second floor. In a large well-lit room, all of the nine premature babies who had recently been delivered at the centre were being kept warm and nourished in incubators or given kangaroo care by their mothers. Professor Karounis looked in briefly, giving the mothers a quick salute, but then he and Dr Macleod continued walking along to one of the small private rooms at the end of the corridor.

As they reached the door, a young Chinese nurse ran to catch up with them.

'Nurse Chen!' said Dr Macleod. 'I thought you were

supposed to be in there, keeping a constant watch on him.'

'I was, doctor. I am. But the formula ran out. I went to fetch more.' She held up a 200 millilitre bottle of NeoSure to show him.

'You should have called for the pharmacy to bring it to you. You shouldn't have left him unsupervised.'

Nurse Chen blushed and lowered her eyes. 'I also needed toilet, doctor. I'm sorry.'

'There's a toilet in there. You could have used that.'

'Yes, but—'

'Yes, but what?'

Nurse Chen looked up again. 'It *stare* at me. The foetus. It stare at me all time. Never blink.'

Dr Macleod pushed the door open. 'In that case, you should have called for Charge Nurse Rudd to send up somebody to keep an eye on him while you were gone.'

'Yes, doctor. I'm sorry, doctor.'

They went inside. It was a dull day outside, and so the room was gloomy. Dr Macleod had decided to keep the light subdued in case the foetus's eyes were hypersensitive. On the right-hand side of the room stood a Dräger Caleo incubator. It was one of the most sophisticated, with sensors to monitor a premature baby's body temperature, as well as keeping it enclosed in a perfectly balanced microclimate. It was designed with much wider ports than normal incubators so that a mother could have maximum access to her baby for natural bonding, and to allow minor surgical procedures to be carried out while the baby remained inside.

'Here, professor,' said Dr Macleod. 'Tell me what you think.'

As he crossed the room, the grey light from the window was reflected on the incubator's clear plastic cover, so that he couldn't see inside it. When he came closer though, he realised that the incubator was empty. The thick white gauze pad on which the foetus had been resting was still dented, but the foetus itself had gone.

'Stuart,' said Professor Karounis, coming up behind him, 'what is this? There's nothing there.'

'Where is it, Nurse Chen?' said Dr Macleod. 'What's happened to it?'

Nurse Chen hurried over to the incubator and lifted the cover, as if she expected the foetus to suddenly materialise out of thin air.

'How can it be disappear?' she wailed. 'It can't be disappear!'

'Somebody must have removed it,' said Professor Karounis. 'But why in the world would anybody remove it? Do you think it could have been one of your surgical team?'

'Absolutely not. I mean, why would they? Apart from that, none of them would have wanted to go anywhere near him. They found him totally repulsive, if you want to know the truth.'

Professor Karounis took out his phone. 'I'm calling security. Whoever took it may not have had time to leave the centre yet.'

Dr Macleod looked all around the room. The door to the toilet was open but there was nothing in there except a lavatory and a small washbasin.

'This is insane,' he said. 'Whoever took him must have been waiting outside in the corridor for Nurse Chen to leave him unsupervised. But how could they have possibly known that she would? And surely they would have needed something to carry him off in, wouldn't they? A bag or a box. I suppose they could have wrapped him up in a coat or a blanket.'

Professor Karounis put down his phone and said, 'Only two people have left the centre in the past ten minutes. One was delivering a book from Amazon. The other was Nurse Nanda, going off duty, and she was carrying only her handbag. It seems as if our foetus thief must still be somewhere in the building. I have instructed security to search the centre from bottom to top.'

'Have you told them what they're looking for?'

'I simply said that a premature child appears to have been abducted – a child who is badly deformed. I didn't say *how* badly deformed. I don't think they would have believed me.'

'My God, this is like a bad dream,' said Dr Macleod. 'I keep thinking I'm going to snap out of it in a minute, and none of it will have happened.'

Nurse Chen said, 'I'm so sorry, doctor. Please forgive me.'

'Never mind, nurse. You shouldn't have left him alone, but you couldn't possibly have foreseen anything like this. None of us could.'

'But what if he dies?'

'If he dies, quite frankly, I think he'll be doing us all a favour, including himself. He couldn't have gone on living for much longer, not like that.'

Professor Karounis said, 'There's no CCTV along this part of the corridor, but the landing and the stairs are covered, and so are the lifts. David Brennan is going back through the recent footage now. He said that the only way somebody could have left here carrying our foetus without being caught on camera would have been via the fire escape, but if they had done that, the alarm would have gone off in his office as soon as they opened the fire door.'

'I still can't work out why anybody would have wanted to take him,' said Dr Macleod. 'How did they even know he was here?'

'Perhaps the mother mentioned to a friend that she was going to have a termination.'

'Well, that's possible. But the impression I got was that she was too embarrassed to tell anybody about it. Her husband left her months ago and went back to Nigeria, and the only man with whom she's had any kind of relationship is her cousin's husband. He was the one who made her pregnant before she had her abortion, and she says that after that she warned him in no uncertain terms never to touch her again. Even if he did, and even if it *was* him that made her pregnant again, that still doesn't give us any idea why he or anybody else would have taken the foetus.'

'I have to confess that I am the same as you, Stuart. *Berdeménos* – totally baffled.'

*

They returned to Professor Karounis's office.

'We should call in the team who assisted you with the

C-section, one by one,' said Professor Karounis. 'They are the only ones who saw the foetus and apart from Sister Rudd and Nurse Chen, they are the only ones who know that it is still alive. Or *was* still alive, the last time it was seen.'

'Yes, very well. But I can't believe that any of them would have taken him. It makes absolutely no sense at all.'

Professor Karounis's secretary located all of Dr Macleod's surgical team and called them up to his office. Glenda the midwife was first, and she sat with her mouth open in shock and bewilderment when Dr Macleod told her what had happened.

'I thought this day was mad enough already,' she told him. 'That shook me so much, the state of that foetus, I was just on my way to ask Mary Masimba to take over my next delivery for me.'

'I'm afraid I have to ask if you took the foetus yourself,' said Professor Karounis, with his hands steepled in front of his face like a prosecuting barrister. 'Or, if you *didn't*, if you have any idea who might have done.'

'Of course I didn't take it! Heavens above! It frightened the wits out of me! That face, and the way it kept staring at me! I shall be having nightmares about it for the rest of my life!'

'So you can't hazard a guess as to who might have taken it, or why anybody would have wanted to?'

Glenda pursed her lips and shook her head but said nothing. It was clear that she was deeply upset that Professor Karounis had considered even for a moment that she might have been responsible for the foetus's disappearance.

When she had left the office, Dr Macleod leaned over and said quietly, 'If you don't mind my saying so, sir, I think you need to go a little easy on the accusations. We don't want to find ourselves in court, accused of harassment.'

'What are you suggesting? That we forget the whole thing?'

'Not exactly, sir. Well, maybe we should. How many malformed foetuses do we dispose of every year? This one was unusual, yes, because of the severity of its malformation, but we have to face it – there was no possibility at all that it could have survived for any length of time. We have to ask ourselves whether it was a living human being or simply a collection of malformed tissue.'

'Stuart – you said yourself that you hesitated to euthanise it, because of the way it looked at you. But in any case, that's not really the point. The point is that someone breached security and removed a foetus, whether it was alive or dead or somewhere in between. We should call the police. Next time it could be a perfectly healthy newborn, and you can imagine what kind of trouble we would be in then. Our good name would be tattered. That's the right word, isn't it – tattered?'

Dr Macleod wasn't in the mood to correct him. 'Very well,' he said. 'But before we involve the police, let's at least wait until David Brennan has finished searching the building and checked his CCTV footage. For all we know, whoever took the foetus made a perfectly innocent mistake. Perhaps it stopped breathing while Nurse Chen was out of the room, and somebody took it away to resuscitate it.'

'Oh, come on. They took it away to resuscitate it? Something that looked like... I don't know, something that looked like an octopus? Would *you* have taken it away? And how would you have tried to start it breathing again? With mouth-to-mouth? I know it has a face like an angel, but I really don't think so.'

Dr Macleod didn't answer that. He knew how unlikely it was that anybody had taken the foetus to give it artificial respiration, but he was becoming desperate to think of a logical explanation for somebody to remove it. Regardless of its condition, he was still responsible for it.

Dr Bhaduri knocked at the door. When he came in, Dr Macleod could tell by his expression that he had already found out what had happened. Before Professor Karounis could say a word to him, he lifted both of his hands as if he were under arrest and said, 'It wasn't me, sir. I didn't take it. I swear by Gita.'

8

Jerry sat down at his desk, peeled the lid off his marocchino and prodded the 'on' button of his desktop computer. It was raining hard outside, and his hair was wet because he had left his umbrella at Charlene's flat the last time he had gone round to see her. They had argued in the morning and he had stormed out in a huff and he hadn't seen her since. He had texted her six or seven times to say sorry, but she hadn't replied. Bloody Charlene.

He had decided that his love life was doomed. He still had a tattoo of a heart with an arrow through it on his left shoulder, and the name 'Jane', but he couldn't even remember what Jane looked like, except that she was mousy-haired and very skinny, with an overbite. Pretty though.

DS Bristow came into the squad room, red-faced and prickly-moustached and paunchy. He had a small round plaster on his chin where he had cut himself shaving.

'Seems like your reputation has predeceased you, Jerry,' he said, in his clipped military tones. 'I've just had a call from DCI Walters from the Major Investigation Team that covers Peckham.'

'Yes, I know DCI Walters. I was on his team at the Kremlin when that MP got bashed on the head with a cricket bat. Remember that? He was only a DI then. What does he want?'

DS Bristow squinted at the note he had scribbled on the back of an envelope. 'He's got himself a missing person, presumed expired under unusual circumstances.'

'So? What's that got to do with me?'

'The misper's name is Martin Elliot, and he's the field manager in Peckham for Crane's Drains. That's the company that keeps all of the city's sewers flowing. They herd the turds, so to speak. He went down a sewer off Peckham High Road yesterday afternoon with three of his staff, and he hasn't been seen since.'

'What about his staff? All of them okay?'

'Everybody else was unblemished.'

'So what were these unusual circumstances?'

'It seems like their lighting went out *blonk!* for no apparent reason and there was a total blackout. When they did manage to restore their illumination, Martin Elliot was nowhere to be seen. His staff went back down the sewer to look for him, and they tried searching for him with that radar equipment they use for finding underground pipes and whatnot, but after five hours they had to give up. That's when they notified the Peckham nick.'

Jerry looked at the paper bag on his desk with the warm Cornish pasty in it. He was hungry, and he wished DS Bristow would get to the point. 'I don't quite see where I come into this, sarge.'

'You come into it because of what this Martin

Elliot's staff said when they were interviewed about his disappearance. They were questioned individually so there was no collusion between them. All three of them swore that before he disappeared they saw a number of what they could only describe as ghostly figures.'

'Ghostly figures? Oh, come on, sarge. How did they manage to see ghostly figures? I thought you said it was a total blackout. In any case, ghosts are supposed to be transparent, aren't they? Not that I've ever seen one myself.'

'They gave off a light of their own, that's what they said, like they were luminous, or what do you call it, fluorescent. That's how they could see them.'

'They're having a Turkish, aren't they? I'll bet they knocked the poor bugger on the head because he wouldn't give them holiday pay or something like that. They knocked him on the head and flushed him down the sewer, and now they're trying to blame it on some spooks. Talk about the dog ate my homework.'

'Whether it was ghostly figures that did it or not, Jerry, it has all the makings of a possible homicide, so that's why Peckham passed the investigation on to DCI Walters.'

'I still don't see what this has to do with me.'

'The three staff from Crane's Drains were interviewed again late last night by two officers from the MIT. DCI Walters said that their stories may have been bonkers, but they were like *consistently* bonkers. They were asked all kinds of trick questions, but they never tripped up once. It could have been that they were pissed or else they were high on monkey dust or spice or something when they were down that sewer, but if they were, they were all sharing exactly the same hallucination, right down to the last pernickety detail. And that's just not possible, is it?'

Jerry didn't answer, but he had a fair idea of what DS Bristow was going to say next.

'What *you* did, you and DS Patel between you, sorting out that weird business with those clothes that seemed to come to life – that shows you've got an understanding of what we might call the superstitious. You know – stuff that's outside your usual run-of-the-mill police work.'

'Sarge, that was a one-off. I still don't understand all of that, how that happened. Those clothes were all infected with some kind of bug, so far as we could make out. Okay, DS Patel and me, we got it sorted, but that was mostly by accident. We're not ghostbusters.'

'I'm not suggesting you are, Jerry. But you and DS Patel are the only two officers in the Met who have proven experience of successfully dealing with a case that doesn't come within what you might call the normal parameters. MITs investigate homicide cases that call for specialist needs, and if you two aren't specialists then I don't know who is. DCI Walters has asked if you could be seconded to his team in order to look into the disappearance of Martin Elliot, and he's also requested that DS Patel be seconded to join you.'

'Have you told the guv'nor?'

'I've had a word with DI Karim, yes.'

'And is he quite happy about me going up to Peckham?'

'Happy? I'd go so far as to say that he's delighted.'

***

DS Patel was already waiting for him at Peckham police station when he arrived. It was still raining hard, but he had helped himself to an umbrella from lost property. He hadn't seen Jamila for nearly seven months now, even though he kept meaning to take a day off and go up to north London to meet up with her. She was back in Redbridge, working with a specialist team that investigated honour crimes among the Asian community, and somehow neither of them ever seemed to have the time to get together.

There she was, in her black silk headscarf and her dark grey trouser suit. She was still as pretty and demure, with those enormous eyes like a Disney princess, and those slightly pouting lips, but he thought she looked a little older than when he had last seen her, as if the job was wearing her down. He felt the same way himself.

She was perched on a chair in DI Grant's office, nursing a cup of Starbucks coffee. DI Grant was sitting behind his desk in his shirtsleeves, a bulky man with bristling blond hair, protuberant blue eyes and a double chin that bulged over his shirt collar. Standing by the window staring out at Peckham High Street was DCI Walters, the senior investigating officer for the area's MIT. He was thin and stooped, with his receding black hair combed straight back from his forehead, and a large complicated nose like an eagle. He looked almost as if he could swoop down to the street below, pluck a child from its buggy and flap away with it.

There were two other MIT detectives there – a chunky ginger-haired man in a bronze Puffa jacket, and a plain woman in a thick white roll-neck sweater, who reminded Jerry of his old headmistress. Maybe it was the dry, dark-brown bob and the heavy eyebrows, as well as the large mole just above her lip.

'Sorry I'm late,' said Jerry. 'Traffic was even crapper than usual.'

'That's all right,' said DI Grant. 'Gave us plenty of time to talk about Brexit. DCI Walters – this is DC Pardoe.'

DCI Walters turned around and looked Jerry up and down. 'I must say you're not what I expected.' His voice was whispery and dry, and there was a faint hint of a Scottish accent.

Jerry was about to say, 'So what *did* you expect? Father Karras?' but he decided against it. In his experience, detective chief inspectors were almost always lacking in any sense of humour, especially if they were Scottish.

'Of course you know DS Patel. And this is DC O'Brien and DC Pettigrew, both from the MIT. It was these two officers who interviewed the three staff members from Crane's Drains who were down in the sewer with Martin Elliot when he disappeared.'

Jerry sat down next to Jamila. She looked across at him and smiled and said, 'How are you, Jerry?'

'Bearing up. Still trying to lose weight. If only we didn't have a Gregg's just around the corner.'

'And the job?'

'We've had a surge in knife crime round Tooting in the past six months. I think the kids are bored of *Fortnite* and think it's more fun to go around shanking each other.'

'Oh. It's acid attacks in Redbridge. Mostly against

girls who want to marry a lower-caste boy. Or married women who are suspected of being unfaithful.'

'That's right. Nothing like a faceful of the old sulphuric if her indoors starts to misbehave herself, eh?'

'DC Pardoe?' DCI Walters interrupted.

'Oh yes, sorry.' He turned to DCs O'Brien and Pettigrew. 'Sorry, you two. Just having a quick catch-up.'

Jamila said to them, 'I understand that you interviewed each of those three witnesses separately. But each one of them insisted that they had seen "ghostly figures".'

'That is correct,' said DC O'Brien. With his ginger hair and a name like 'O'Brien', Jerry had been expecting him to speak with an Irish accent, but he sounded like one of those East Enders who emphasises the ending of every word with a snap of the tongue, such as 'correct-*ah*!'

'What were they doing down in the sewer in the first place?'

'They was inspecting a fatberg – a blockage in the main sewer between Peckham Road and Charles Coveney Road. That's a shade under a hundred and fifty metres. Same constituents as the fatberg under Whitechapel – cooking oil gone solid, wet wipes, that kind of thing.'

'They were digging into the fat to see how solid it was when they exposed a woman's severed hand,' put in DC Pettigrew. She not only looked like Jerry's former headmistress but spoke like her too, as if she were saying 'Now then, class, these are the principal crops that are harvested in Namibia'.

'That was when all of their lights unexpectedly went out, including their helmet lamps. At first there was total darkness, but they claim that after only a few seconds they were approached by several illuminated figures. They all counted five figures, or possibly six, and each of their descriptions tallied exactly. The female staff member, Gemma Bright, even drew me some pictures of them.'

DC Pettigrew unzipped her leather document wallet and took out three sheets of paper in a clear plastic envelope, which she handed to Jamila.

Gemma had sketched the child-thing, with its smudged black eyes and its arms flailing, as well as the hunched-up figure like Quasimodo and the beautiful girl with her intestines trailing in the sewage.

Jamila passed the drawings one by one to Jerry, and he examined them closely. 'Bloody hell. She's got some imagination, this woman. She should get herself a job drawing horror comics. Better than spending her life down the sewers.'

'The trouble is, mate—' DC O'Brien began.

'Jerry,' said Jerry.

'Okay, Jerry. The trouble is, Jerry, the other two witnesses gave us descriptions of those same figures that were identical in almost every respect. As you very well know, you don't often find that eyewitness accounts tally in every detail, especially after a traumatic incident like this one, but these three did. Five or six illuminated figures – a skinny one with waving arms, a hunchback, one with all her guts hanging out. And what was more, these figures attacked them.'

'*Attacked* them? What, like had a go at them? You're joking.'

'No, they attacked them, and all of them said that the ghostly figures were hitting them and trying to pull off their helmets. Martin Elliot was still with them when that happened. The last words they heard him say were something about him being confused about where he was, and then he just said "hold on". After that everything went dark again, and the three of them made their way back to the manhole, in the belief that Martin Elliot was following them. When they reached the inspection chamber and realised that he wasn't, they went back along the sewer to look for him, but there was no sign of him nowhere.'

DCI Walters came away from the window. He looked as if he hadn't laughed since he was at primary school. 'They brought in specialists from Crane's Drains with ground-penetrating radar equipment. We've called in the same specialists ourselves in the past, once or twice, when we've suspected there might be a body or some weapons buried or suchlike. They also sent out teams of experienced flushers – that's what they call them, the engineers who keep the sewage flowing. They've searched all the surrounding sewers for him, but no luck so far. We've also notified the Marine Unit at Wapping in case his body's already reached the river.'

Jamila put down her coffee. 'I am truly sorry, sir, but I am not at all certain how DC Pardoe and I can be of any assistance to you in this case. I specialise in domestic crimes among ethnic minorities, and DC Pardoe's main area of expertise is in dealing with suburban street gangs.'

'Yes, DS Patel, but there are *ghostly figures* involved – or what are alleged to be ghostly figures. Nobody else in the Met apart from you two has any experience in investigating what you might call the occult. Granted, it may all turn out to be some kind of elaborate hoax or a shared hallucination brought on by drugs or inhaled gases. But the witness statements are so convincing that we need somebody with your take on the supernatural to look into Martin Elliot's disappearance and tell us if it really could have been caused by some other-worldly phenomenon.

'I make no bones about the fact that I myself am extremely sceptical. But you know what unrelenting scrutiny we're under these days from social media. We can't leave any avenue unexplored or any stone unturned.'

'Well...' Jamila shrugged. 'If that is what you want us to do. I must tell you though, that I have never personally encountered anything that you might call a ghost. Of course we will need to speak to the witnesses ourselves. Where can we find them?'

DC Pettigrew took out her iPhone. 'I'll call Ms Bright and find out for you. So far as I know, they're staying on site at Peckham Road. Their boss may have disappeared, but they still have the fatberg to deal with.'

'Gordon Bennett,' said Jerry. 'I hope that doesn't mean we have to go down the sewers too. I didn't bring my clothes peg with me.'

9

Jenny had meant to get up early so that she could go to Aldi and do some shopping, and then meet her friend Carol for lunch at Persepolis Café. But this was her first weekday off in two months, and last night, she and Mick had gone to The Rye pub, and she had drunk about three fruity bangers too many. She couldn't even remember walking home to their flat. Maybe Mick had carried her.

She had a throbbing headache, and her tongue felt as rough and dry as glasspaper. She knew they had run out of baked beans and coffee and milk, and they had nearly run out of toilet paper, but the bed was warm and comfortably rumpled, and it was gloomy outside, and she could hear that it was raining. She could always meet Carol for lunch and go shopping afterward. Or maybe she could go shopping early tomorrow morning before she had to go to work.

She turned over in bed and looked at the framed photograph of her and Mick sitting on their hotel balcony in Gran Canaria. She was lifting her glass of sangria and smiling, but Mick was frowning. That photograph had been taken about half an hour after he had asked her to marry him, and she had said *no* – well, more like not yet. She was only twenty-three, and even though she loved Mick, she didn't want to settle down yet. She wanted to party and have fun, and she also wanted to build her career as an actress. She had already been given a small part in *EastEnders* as a waitress. It had been a speaking part too. Her line had been, 'Ready to order yet, love?'

She closed her eyes and dozed off again. She dreamed that she was walking around Peckham trying to find her friend Tina's house, but the streets in this Dream Peckham were all different from the streets she knew, and wet, and deserted, and she was lost. Although it was daytime, all the houses had their curtains closed, so she felt that even if she rang their doorbells to ask for directions, nobody would answer. It was still raining, and she was barefoot and wearing nothing but her white nightshirt, which was soaking.

She saw a newsagent's shop on the corner, with its windows lit. When she reached it, she found that a CLOSED sign was hanging in the door, although she was sure she could see a hunched-up shadow moving around inside.

She was about to knock at the window when she was woken up by her cat, Persephone, mewling in the corridor outside her bedroom. She opened her eyes and stared at the side of the chest of drawers next to her bed. Persephone mewled again, and then hissed, and Jenny was sure she could hear her clawing at the carpet. Perhaps she had cornered a mouse, although they hadn't had any mice in the flat since last year, after the landlord had arranged for most of the small overgrown garden at the back of the house to be bricked over.

She sat up in bed. The bedroom door was half open so that she could see the opposite wall of the corridor, with a framed reproduction of a print by M. C. Escher of people climbing up endless flights of stairs, but she couldn't see Persephone, and she couldn't see a mouse.

'Perse?' Jenny called out. 'What's the matter, sweetie?' But Persephone had stopped mewling and hissing, and all Jenny could hear was the rain pattering against the window.

'Perse?' she called, one more time, and then she flopped back onto the pillow and dragged the duvet right up to her chin. Another twenty minutes' dozing wouldn't make any difference. In fact, she might even ring Carol and tell her that she didn't feel well and couldn't make it for lunch.

She closed her eyes again, but as she did so, she felt the duvet being lifted at the end of the bed, and then a brief, cold draught. She heard a scratching sound too.

'*Perse!*' she complained, kicking her feet from side to side. Persephone had done this before, when it was chilly – crept under the duvet and tried to snuggle up next to her. She knew that Persephone was only being affectionate and wanted to keep warm, but she purred like a football rattle and her breath smelled of tuna.

Something touched her bare left calf, but it wasn't furry like Persephone. It was sticky and cold and it was crawling up between her legs like a giant spider. Jenny instantly threw back the duvet and rolled herself sideways, standing up beside the bed in shock and horror.

There was a creature in the bed with her. It was still

mostly hidden under the duvet, but she could see two moist eyes looking up at her, and what could have been a finger sticking out, except that it had a bunch of small nobbles on the end of it.

Whatever it was, the creature didn't move for nearly twenty seconds, but then it gradually inched its way back under the duvet until it was completely covered over.

Jenny's brain was a jumble, and she couldn't think what to do. She knew that one of Mick's golf clubs was leaning in the umbrella stand beside the flat's front door. Perhaps if she tiptoed out of the bedroom and went to fetch it, she could beat this creature to death. But what was it, and where had it come from? And why had it crept into her bed?

She edged her way out of the bedroom, without taking her eyes off the small hump under her duvet. She found Persephone in the corridor, cowering among the untidy heap of shoes and wellington boots. Persephone's gingery fur was standing on end, and her little sharp teeth were bared. She hissed as Jenny approached, as if she were trying to warn her that the creature under her duvet was something dangerous and that she was right to be frightened of it.

'It's all right, Perse,' Jenny whispered. 'Mummy will deal with it.' Then she thought, *Why am I whispering?*

She picked up Mick's sand iron and made her way back to the bedroom, feeling as if she could hardly breathe. The hump was still in the same place, not moving. She didn't know if she ought to start hitting it, or if she should leave it where it was and phone Mick. She knew that he wouldn't be able to come home straight away, because he had gone to Sheffield for a meeting with his suppliers, but at least he could advise her what to do. If only she knew what the creature was, that would help. If it was some kind of stray animal, perhaps she ought to call the RSPCA. Or Rentokil, if it was a rat.

She approached the end of the bed. She hesitated for a moment, then she turned the golf club around and poked at the hump with the end of its handle. The creature retreated a few inches further across the bed, but then it stopped still again.

Oh my God, this is scaring me to death. I'll have to call Mick. But the first thing he's going to ask me is – what the hell is it, Jen? And I'm going to feel like a fool because I'm too frightened to look and find out.

She took hold of one corner of the duvet in her left hand, gripping the sand iron tightly in her right. She counted to three, then she whipped the duvet sideways off the bed and dropped it onto the floor. When she saw the creature that had been hiding underneath, she took two stumbling steps backward and gasped. She didn't have enough breath in her lungs to scream.

It was about the size of a small child's hand and shaped like a crab. It had a small bulbous head supported by four limbs that resembled fingers – although each limb had those bud-like protrusions on the end. They reminded Jenny of the stunted arms of children deformed by thalidomide.

What stunned her the most was that the head had a *face*. It was a baby's face, with its eyes closed, and its pale lips puckered, and only two small wet holes where its nose should have been. It was breathing quickly and stickily, as if it were panicking.

Jenny dropped the sand iron onto the carpet and stood staring at this creature, shaking with shock. She couldn't believe that it was real, and that she wasn't still sleeping, and having a nightmare. How could such a thing like this exist, and how had it managed to crawl into their flat and into her bed?

Still shaking, her teeth chattering, she circled cautiously around the end of the bed to pick up her phone from the top of the chest of drawers. She had nearly reached it when the creature opened its eyes, and she froze. It stared at her, unblinking, then it opened its lips and let out a sound like nothing she had ever heard. It was a thin, plaintive whistle that ended in a cry, almost as if it were appealing to her to help it.

Its finger-limbs started to move, and it crawled across the bed toward her. It was then that Jenny completely lost it. She snatched up her phone and stumbled out of the bedroom, across the corridor and into the living room, slamming the door shut behind her. She jumped onto the couch, lifting her feet clear of the floor in case the creature somehow managed to follow her, and jabbed frantically at her phone.

Please answer please answer please answer! Oh God Mick please answer!

'Jen? What is it? I'm right in the middle of a meeting. Can I call you back in half an hour?'

'Mick, there's a horrible thing in the flat! I don't know what it is, and I don't know what to do.'

'What do you mean, a horrible thing?'

'It's like a giant spider except that it isn't a spider. It's got a face. It crawled right into the bed with me. It's still in the bedroom now. Well, I hope it is.'

'Hold on, Jen. A giant spider with a face? Sorry, guys, it's my girlfriend. She's throwing a bit of a wobbly for some reason.'

'It's got a face like a baby, and it crawled right into bed with me. Right under the duvet.'

'Jen, are you still pissed? You sound like it.'

'I'm not pissed, Mick! I'm scared shitless! This thing frightened Perse and then it came into the bedroom. What am I going to do?'

'Listen, Jen, try to calm down. Honestly, try to calm down. Whatever this thing is, maybe Bill downstairs can get rid of it for you. Go down and ask him. If he can't, phone up the letting agents.'

'I've shut myself in the lounge, Mick. I don't want to go out there.'

'Try to keep calm, Jen. I'd come down myself if I could, but it's going to take me three hours at least. Take a look outside the lounge and, if this thing's still in the bedroom, run down and knock on Bill's door. He'll help you. He was in Afghanistan, Jen. I bet he's seen spiders a damn sight scarier than this one.'

'I'm too scared, Mick. It's horrible. You'd feel the same if you could see it.'

'Just open the door a crack and take a look. Think about it, Jen. It might look scary, but I'll bet it's a lot more scared of *you* than you are of *it*.'

'All right. I'll look, but if I can't see it, I'm not going out there.'

'Fair enough. Call me back when you've decided what you're going to do.'

'Can't you stay on the phone?'

'I'm right in the middle of a meeting, Jen, and everybody's staring at me and drumming their fingers.'

'All right. Sorry.'

'You don't have to be sorry, sweetheart. Just go down and fetch Bill.'

Jenny put down her phone. She knew that Mick was right, and that the creature was probably much more frightened than she was. With its four finger-like limbs it looked like a giant spider, but it had the face of a vulnerable baby, and its cry had been desperate rather than aggressive.

She climbed off the couch and went over to the door. She listened for a while, with her ear pressed against it. Nothing. Only the rain, and the intermittent clonking of the central heating. But she was just about to turn the handle when she heard a scuffling sound, and then a scream from Persephone. A harsh, high-pitched scream, more like a child than a cat.

She flung open the door. Persephone was struggling among the shoes and wellingtons in the corridor. She was lying on her back and the creature was on top of her, furiously tearing at her stomach with its finger-like limbs. It looked as if claws were sticking out of the bud-like nobbles and bits of ginger fur and red flesh were flying everywhere, sticking to the boots and shoes and the wallpaper too.

Jenny rushed up and screamed at the creature, '*Get off*

her! Get off her!' But the creature carried on ripping at Persephone's stomach, staring up at Jenny with no emotion in its eyes at all, its moist nostrils flared and its lips tightly pursed. With a sharp crackle it split open Persephone's ribs and Jenny could see her cat's dark red heart, still beating.

She tried to seize the creature's limbs, but they were slippery and strong, and they wriggled so much that she couldn't get a grip on them. Its claws scratched her fingers, too, and the scratches stung. She managed to force her hand underneath its head, into the bloody, furry mess that it had made of Persephone, and she pulled it upward as hard as she could, but the creature jerked and jumped and scrabbled so ferociously at her wrist that she had to let it go. As she staggered back, the creature let out another high-pitched whistle, but this time it sounded more triumphant than appealing.

Whimpering with pain and distress, with both of her hands covered in scratches, Jenny limped back to the bedroom and picked up the sand iron. Now she was going to do what she should have done before, and smash the creature into a pulp. She could worry if it was human or animal or giant spider once she had killed it.

She went back out into the corridor with the sand iron held high. Persephone was lying on top of the shoes and wellingtons, her head still intact but her stomach ripped wide open and her legs splayed apart, like a tiny tiger-skin rug. The creature, however, was no longer on top of her, and there was no sign of it.

Jenny cautiously made her way along the corridor to the front door, still holding up the sand iron, ready to strike. *Where are you, you demon? Where are you hiding yourself?*

The bathroom was off to the right, and its door was slightly ajar. Jenny poked the door open wider with the sand iron and then quickly reached inside to snatch down the light pull. The bathroom was small and windowless, so if the creature had crawled in here, there was no way for it to escape. Before she went in, Jenny bent down so that she could see under the washbasin. Nothing. The creature wasn't hiding there.

She stepped inside, immediately swinging the door back, but the creature wasn't hiding itself behind the door either. The bathroom was too small for a bathtub, although there was a shower with pale-green polyester curtains, with a seahorse design on them. Jenny hesitated, but then she took hold of the left-hand curtain, counted to three, and yanked it aside, holding the sand iron ready to beat the creature to death.

The shower tray was empty, except for Mick's sodden orange sponge.

Jenny immediately left the bathroom and hurried back along the corridor, trying not to look at Persephone's mutilated body. She was so frightened that she felt she was going to be sick. If the creature wasn't in the bathroom, where was it? She hadn't seen it run back into the bedroom when she had gone to pick up the sand iron, but she supposed it might have scuttled past her into the living room or into the kitchenette. There was a small airing cupboard too, halfway along the corridor, although that was tightly closed.

She went into the living room first. There was no sign of the creature in there – not behind the curtains, or under the couch, or hiding in the small corner beside the bookcase. She even looked up at the ceiling, in case the creature was able to scurry up walls, like a spider.

Next she looked in the kitchen. She opened the larder, and all the cupboards, and looked in the oven and the dishwasher. She didn't see how it could possibly have climbed into any of the kitchen units, but she wanted to make sure for her own peace of mind.

She ended up by searching the bedroom. She knelt down, peered under the bed and slid out every drawer in the chest of drawers. Nothing. However it had managed to escape from the flat, the creature had disappeared. If it hadn't been for poor Persephone's remains lying on top of the shoes and boots, Jenny could almost have persuaded herself that she had imagined it.

She looked into every room one more time, just to make absolutely sure. There was no point in going downstairs and asking Bill to help her now. He would probably think she was going doolally. He might even think she had killed Persephone herself and was making up a story about a spider-like creature with a child's face so that she wouldn't be blamed for it.

She was even reluctant about calling Mick again now, but before she could decide what to do, her phone rang. She went into the living room and picked it up.

'Jen? How's it going? Have you got rid of that thing yet?'

'It's gone, Mick.'

'Blimey, Jen, you sound terrible. Did Bill come up and help you?'

'He didn't have to. It's gone, Mick. It's disappeared. I don't know how.'

'Listen, I've finished all my meetings and I'm catching the first train back.'

Jenny was about to tell him about Persephone, but tears started to stream down her cheeks, and her throat tightened so much that she couldn't speak.

'Jen? Are you still there, Jen?'

She managed to croak out a *yes*, but that was all.

'I'm on my way home now, Jen. Just hold on. You were supposed to be having lunch with Carol, weren't you? Why don't you call Carol to come over?'

Jenny managed another *yes*, but then she had to put down her phone. She sat on the couch, numb with shock, while the rain continued to trickle down the window and Mick's tiny voice kept repeating, 'Jen? Are you still there, Jen?'

IO

It had stopped raining by the time Jamila and Jerry turned into Southampton Way and parked behind the large white Crane's Drains van. They unbuckled their seat belts, but before they climbed out of their car, Jamila turned to Jerry and said, 'You know, Jerry, I have very grave doubts about this.'

'Me too, sarge, to be honest. I mean, weird isn't the word. But what's bugging *you* about it?'

'It was DCI Walters. He said he was sceptical, but it seemed to me that he was too quick to assume that Martin Elliot's disappearance had something to do with the supernatural.'

'I reckon he wanted to wash his hands of it, do you know what I mean? It's all too screwy for the MIT, so he passed it across to us. Didn't want to spoil his success record.'

'You're probably right. But I find these ghostly figures really hard to believe in, don't you?'

'Well, yeah. I suppose they could have been some kind of hallucination, couldn't they? There's methane down the sewers, isn't there? And carbon monoxide, and if you breathe in too much of those you can start seeing things. And God knows what other solvents might have been dumped down the drains. But to be fair to Walters, how can three people all have the same identical hallucination?'

'It's very rare, but it has happened. In psychology they call it "*folie à deux*", or a madness shared by two people. In this case it would be "*folie à trois*". There's even "*folie à plusieurs*".'

'Sorry, sarge. I've forgotten all my Frog.'

'It means madness shared by many. My friend from the Crime Branch in Delhi told me about a case that he had to deal with in Burari, in the summer of 2018. Eleven members of the same family hanged themselves from the ceiling of their house, all together. Apparently they had talked a lot about *śūnyata*, but otherwise they were a normal family and they were not into the occult or anything like that. A psychiatrist decided they were suffering from shared psychosis, or what they sometimes call induced delusional disorder.'

'What's *śūnyata* when it's at home?'

'It means emptiness, or voidness. It's a meditative state of empty awareness.'

'Like when you look down into your glass and realise you've finished your beer?'

'No, Jerry. It's a belief that all things are empty of intrinsic existence.'

'Sorry, sarge, you've lost me. But it doesn't sound like something that's worth hanging yourself for.'

'I simply feel that the MIT should have brought in a

forensic psychologist first, to interview the witnesses, before they called on you and me as ghostbusters.'

'Why didn't you say that to Walters?'

'Because I didn't want to question his judgement – not in front of his own detectives. And also because I think that you and I are quite capable of making an intelligent assessment of the witnesses' credibility. If they do need to be seen by a forensic psychologist then I think we will know, once we have talked to them.'

'I get the feeling you're even more sceptical about this than Walters.'

'Jerry – I was brought up among people who believe absolutely in the existence of ghosts and demons. My uncle used to sacrifice goats to ward off evil spirits, so I know what's real and what isn't. Those clothes that came to life – that wasn't supernatural, that was an actual virus. I do accept that people see ghosts, but there is always an explanation. As you say, methane and carbon monoxide can give you hallucinations. How many times have you heard people with faulty boilers say that they have seen intruders in their house?'

'Only once. But then the fellow who reported it was pissed as arseholes too.'

They climbed out of the car and walked along to the orange plastic barriers on the corner. Three engineers were standing around talking and smoking, and as they approached, Gemma was climbing up out of the manhole, and Jim was holding out his hand to help her. Newton came after her, lifting up his camera so that it wouldn't knock against the manhole's metal frame.

Jamila lifted her hand in greeting.

'Ms Bright? Detective Sergeant Patel. And this is Detective Constable Pardoe.'

Gemma came over to the barrier and dragged it aside so that Jamila and Jerry could join her beside the open manhole.

'Oh yes,' she said. 'Those other detectives told me you'd be coming to talk to us.'

'Did they tell you why?'

Gemma took off her helmet and shook her hair. 'Not really. Only that you were specialists.'

'Did they tell you specialists in what?'

'No. Not exactly. They just said that you'd dealt with this kind of thing before.'

'You could say that, yes. But what you told those detectives... what all three of you told those detectives—'

'About those things, you mean?' said Gemma. 'We can hardly believe it ourselves. Honestly, it was like being in a horror film, except that it was real. But those things did attack us, and I think they would have hurt us if we hadn't managed to get away.'

'Hurt us?' put in Jim. 'They would have bloody torn us to bits, if we'd let them, and had us for lunch. We would have been three shit sandwiches, and don't think I'm joking.'

'I'm sorry,' said Gemma. 'This is Jim Feather. He's our senior flusher. And this is Newton Akamba. He's our lighting and camera engineer.'

'You've got yourselves a fatberg down there, as we understand it,' said Jerry.

'That's right. The sewer's almost totally blocked, all the way from here to Charles Coveney Road. That's about an eighth of a mile. We went down there so that Martin could take a look at it and decide how we were going to clear it.'

'You found a severed hand apparently.'

'That's right. A woman's hand, stuck in the fat. It was just after we'd found it that all our lights went out and those things appeared.'

'Luminescent, they were,' said Jim, wiping his nose with the back of his hand. 'Bit like a watch dial, you know what I mean? Glowing in the dark.'

'And you all saw them?'

'That's right,' said Gemma. 'They weren't hallucinations, because the methane and hydrogen sulphide levels were well within the safety limits, and there was no evidence of any unusual gases. Sometimes we can detect arsine from the semi-conductor industry, but that smells like garlic, or fishy, so you can always tell. Then there's ethylene oxide, which they use in antifreeze and for sterilising food. That can give you headaches and hallucinations, but again, there was no trace of that.'

'A crime scene team will be coming down later to examine the location where Martin Elliot was last seen,' said Jamila. 'Meanwhile, we'd like to take a look for ourselves, if you can show us.'

'We've protective suits and boots and helmets in the van,' Jim told her. He looked her up and down, and then he said, 'Not sure we've got one small enough for you, love, but you don't mind baggy, do you?'

'This isn't a fashion parade, Mr Feather. Any size will do.'

★

It was growing dark by the time Jerry and Jamila had struggled into their white protective suits and boots, buckled on their helmets and were ready to climb down into the sewer. Newton had set up a portable LED light tower on the corner so that the area around the manhole was lit up like a film set.

'I feel like I'm on a mission to the Moon,' said Jerry, tugging on his thick black nitrile gloves.

Gemma said, 'We'll be walking single file, and quite slowly, because we don't want too much splashing. You'll find it slippery underfoot in places, so watch your step. If the smell's too much for you, or you start feeling faint, please shout out immediately. The sewage is knee-deep this time of day, especially with this blockage, and we don't want you falling over and going under. If you do though, shut your eyes tight, keep your mouth closed, and hold your breath.'

'In the Met, that's what we call redundant information,' said Jerry.

Gemma gave him a ghost of a smile. 'Perhaps. But two of our flushers have drowned in the sewers in the past eighteen months, and if you did happen to go under, and we fished you out, we don't really want to be giving you mouth-to-mouth.'

Jerry thought, *I like this girl. She gives as good as she gets.*

Newton climbed into the manhole first, so he could switch on the daisy chain of LED lights that he had strung along the walls of the tunnel. Jim went down after him, followed by Jerry, Gemma and Jamila.

Jerry carefully lowered his boots into the slowly moving tide of pale brown sewage. He sniffed, and then he said, 'To be honest with you, it doesn't smell as bad as I thought it would. It's no worse than the bogs at the Tooting nick after Sergeant Khaled's been in there, getting rid of last night's vindaloo.'

'Now you're being racist,' said Jamila.

'You think so? You want to tell him that. I reckon he's taking his revenge for the Raj.'

Jamila took several deep breaths. 'I can smell something lemony.'

'Yes, we could too,' said Gemma. 'We're still not sure what it is. One guess is that it could be dipentene, which is a paint thinner and a by-product of waste tyres. But we haven't had the time to carry out an analysis yet, as you can imagine.'

'Maybe it's lemons,' Jerry suggested. 'There's plenty of pubs around here serving their drinks with ice and a slice.'

Gemma went first, with the rest of them wading slowly behind her. 'We've searched the whole length of the fatberg with ground-penetrating radar,' she said, over her shoulder. Her voice echoed from the curving brickwork so that it sounded as if there were two of her speaking in chorus. 'We've also sent flushers all the way north along the sewer from Charles Coveney Road as far as the Thames outflow.'

'But no sign of Martin Elliot?' said Jamila.

'No. Only the usual rag.'

'What about that severed woman's hand you saw? Did you find that?'

'No. We couldn't find that either.'

'You're sure it was a woman's hand and not a glove, or something like that?'

'It was a real hand all right,' Jim put in. 'It was going green, because it was rotting, and you could see a bit of the wrist bone sticking up.'

'But the GPR didn't pick it up?'

'No, but then it does have its limitations, especially with high conductivity soil like clay. The hand could still be there, buried in the fat. If it is, we'll find it soon enough, when we get the high-pressure hoses on it.'

They arrived at the glistening wall of fat and sewage clutter. Jerry said, 'Jesus!' and shook his head in disbelief. He had seen pictures of fatbergs on the TV news, but the reality of dripping solidified grease, stratified with layers of toilet paper and wet wipes, prickly with cotton buds, was more repulsive than he could have imagined. He glanced across at Gemma, who was frowning at her hand-held four-gas monitor, checking for methane and hydrogen sulphide, and wondered why on earth a pretty girl like her had chosen a career in drainage. Jamila caught him looking, and she gave a quick one-shouldered shrug, as if she'd read his mind. He had begun to suspect that Jamila was telepathic, or if not, the shrewdest woman he had ever met. He knew one thing for certain: she could always tell when somebody was lying to her. She said that she could see their eyes turn glossy black, like black olives.

Gemma said, 'Right here – this is where Martin was standing the last time we saw him. Look – you can still see his fingermarks where he grabbed at the fat to try and keep his balance. I was standing here, next to him... Jim was here... and Newton was almost exactly where he's standing now.'

'So take us through it,' said Jamila. 'The light went out, and then what?'

Newton said, 'I was carrying a Haloptic camera, which has a very powerful lamp attached, twenty times brighter than your standard lamp, and that suddenly switched itself off. I say "switched itself off" because the lamp and the camera were not damaged in any way and afterward they worked fine, no problem at all.'

'Next second, all of our helmet lamps went out too,' said Jim. 'It was pitch-dark, and that's when those ghosty things came at us.'

'But you could see them, even though it was totally dark?'

'That's right. They sort of *glowed*. Almost like they was radioactive.'

'And they attacked you?'

'They were all over us,' said Gemma. 'One of them was snatching at my helmet as if it was trying to pull it off. I truly honestly felt that they were trying to kill us.'

As she said that, the LED lights that Newton had strung along the sewer wall started to flicker. They flickered rapidly at first, like strobe lights, so that when the five of them turned around to look at them their movements appeared to be jerky, like characters in a silent movie.

'What's happening, Newton?' asked Gemma. 'Don't tell me there's a loose connection.'

'No, it can't be. Maybe that bloody generator's on the blink again.'

The lights stopped flickering, but then they went out completely, so that they were left with only their helmet lamps. After a few seconds though, the lights came on again, but now they began to shine much brighter than they had before, brighter and brighter – so bright that the interior of the sewer was almost completely bleached of colour.

'*Newton* – what the hell?' said Jim, holding up his arm to shield his eyes.

'I don't know! I don't know what's going on!' Newton protested. 'These lights never did nothing like this before!'

Then, abruptly, the lights all turned green. Not just the LED lights along the wall, but their helmet lamps too.

Gemma checked her gas monitor again. 'I don't know what's causing this. There's no gas warning. But I think we need to get out of here, fast.'

They started to slosh their way back along the sewer. Gemma went first, with Jamila and Jerry close behind her, followed by Newton and Jim. The lights stayed green and almost unbearably bright, so that everything was green – the brick walls, the sewage, their faces, their hands, their white protective suits.

They were not even halfway back to the inspection chamber when they heard a low moaning sound. It was coming from behind them, and it grew louder and louder. At the same time, a foul draught started to blow along the sewer. It gained strength with every splashing step they took, until it was shrieking in discordant chorus with the moaning sound. The sewage lashed against the backs of their legs, and Jerry felt it spray against his neck and splatter against his helmet. It was like being caught in a storm, except that it was underground, and everything was blindingly green, and the rain was human waste.

Gemma shouted something, but the moaning and the shrieking were so loud now that Jerry couldn't hear what she said. The moaning sounded like a woman in terrible agony, and the shrieking reminded him of a traffic accident he had once attended, when a school bus had caught fire and all the children had been trapped inside.

He wanted to walk faster and escape from this claustrophobic hellhole as soon as he possibly could, but the sewer was slippery underfoot, and he had nearly lost his footing twice already and had to reach out for the wall to stop himself from falling over.

They were less than fifty metres from the inspection chamber when he was struck on the right shoulder by some small hard object. Then he was hit again, on the back of his helmet, and this object clanked, as if it were metallic. Three or four more flew past him, and one of them hit Jamila. They dropped into the sewage before he could see what they were, but they had felt like nails.

Jamila, right in front of him, slipped and stumbled forward. She fell on to her hands and knees in the sewage, which was almost thigh-deep now and rippling in the draught like an incoming tide. She almost went under, but

Jerry bent forward and put his arms around her waist and lifted her up. She was so light it was like picking up a small girl. She staggered and nearly slipped again, but then she regained her balance. She turned around and looked up at him and even in the bright green light he could see how relieved she was.

Gemma looked back to see what had happened, and Jerry raised his hand to reassure her that they were fine. Before Jamila continued to follow though, she held up an object in her glove so that Jerry could see it. It was a large old-fashioned key, with a bow shaped like a star, and he guessed that she had picked it up from the sewage when she fell.

'Let's get out of here first!' he shouted at her, although the shrieking was so piercing now he doubted that she could hear him.

The children in the bus had shrieked like that, and he had never really got over it.

At last they waded into the inspection chamber below the open manhole. As soon as they did, the moaning and the shrieking died away. The draught subsided, although the sewage was still gurgling around their boots and slapping against the sides of the chamber. Jerry looked back along the sewer and saw that the green lights were gradually fading and changing back to white.

He looked at Jim, and he didn't think he had ever seen a man with such a grim expression on his face.

'What was that all about?' Jerry asked him. 'It's all stopped now. That makes me think that somebody must have known we were in there, do you know what I mean?

I reckon that was all for our benefit. Somebody wanted to scare us out of there.'

'Well, they bloody well succeeded, didn't they?' said Jim.

'I stink,' said Jamila, holding up both arms and looking down at her sewage-streaked suit. 'I have to get out of here and wash myself.'

Jerry said, 'Technically though, what did we just witness down there? Do you have any idea what could have made an effing awful noise like that, and turned the lights green, and started that wind blowing?'

'I cannot understand how the lights changed colour,' put in Newton. 'They are standard LED lights. They cannot turn green without a filter. It's not possible.'

'Well, you say it's not possible, but it obviously is. And what about the noise? And the wind?'

'I know what you're asking me, detective,' said Jim. 'But the answer is no, I can't explain how that was done. I can't even understand how anybody apart from Crane's Drains operatives knew that we were down there.'

'Okay,' said Jerry. 'Maybe the forensic technicians can come up with some kind of answer, when they go down to take a look.'

'Well, bloody good luck to them,' Jim told him. 'Right now, all I need is a stiff double Scotch.'

Gemma stood to one side so that Jamila could climb out of the inspection chamber first. Two of the sewage engineers helped her out of the manhole and Jerry heard one of them say, 'Went for a swim, did you, love? You'd be better off down the leisure centre. Not quite so smelly.'

Jerry climbed up after her.

'Didn't you hear anything?' he asked the engineers, stamping his foot to shake off a piece of toilet paper that was wrapped around the toe of his boot.

'Hear anything? Like what?'

'Like somebody howling. *Aaaaaaahhh!* And like the wind whistling. *Phweeeeeee!*'

The two engineers looked at each other in bewilderment. 'No, mate. Didn't hear nothing like that.'

'Nothing at all? How about the lights? Didn't you see the lights going green?'

'What lights?'

'The LED lights, the ones you've strung out along the sewer.'

They both shook their heads. 'No. But then we wasn't really looking, to tell you the truth. We was over there, having a quick snout.'

Gemma climbed out of the manhole and pulled off her gloves. 'You can come back to our offices if you like, detectives. We have showers there that you can use.'

'Thank you,' said Jamila. 'And when we've cleaned up, we need to talk about this. You're the experts on sewers; you must be able to come up with some explanation. I'm going to tell the forensic team to delay their inspection until we have some understanding of what just happened down there. Maybe the fatberg is giving off some type of unusual gas that you don't know about. I don't want anybody else going missing, or worse.'

They walked over to the Crane's Drains van and Jim slid open the side door for them. Jamila sat down, and Jerry bent over to pull off her boots for her.

'Still convinced that it's nothing supernatural?' he asked her, keeping his voice down so that Gemma couldn't hear him.

'There's something down there, Jerry, I'll grant you.'

'You don't really think it's some kind of gas?'

'No, I don't. There may be gases that can turn lights green, and there may be gases that can cause dramatic changes in air pressure, and that was why that wind started blowing. And that moaning sound, maybe that was gas blowing through holes in the fatberg – you know, like organ pipes.'

'But you don't believe that, sarge, do you? Not for a moment.'

'No,' said Jamila, and she held up the key that she had picked out of the sewage. 'Whatever extraordinary properties gases may have, they can't throw keys at people.'

11

Dr Macleod was locking his office door when Professor Karounis appeared at the end of the corridor. 'Stuart! You're not going yet, are you?'

'Well, yes. I don't have any more patients booked in for today, and I thought I might pick Beverly up from the library.'

'Have you told her that you would?'

'No. It's a surprise. I was thinking of taking her for supper at the Peckham Bazaar.'

'Perhaps you can treat her another evening. I've called the police, and they're sending an officer over to talk to us. He should be here in ten minutes or so.'

'You called the police? I thought we were going to give David Brennan a chance to look into it first.'

'He has. He has combed the building high and low, and he has talked to everybody who was here at the time the foetus disappeared, but he hasn't found anything to suggest who could have taken it. But *somebody* must have done, and that is why I called the police. We have a reputation to uphold here, Stuart, at the Warren. Our security must be of the highest order. Who is going to trust us if babies can be taken, even if they are stillborn or have only a limited time to live?'

'I completely understand your concern, professor,' said Dr Macleod, as they walked along the corridor toward the lifts. 'But if we don't announce that this foetus went missing, who's to know?'

'The birth mother knows. She may well be asking, where is it, and what was it like? She didn't realise she was pregnant, did she? She may ask us for a DNA test to establish who the father was, and what can we say to her then? Oh, sorry, madam, but your foetus has mysteriously vanished, and we don't know how.'

'We can simply tell her that it couldn't survive and that it's been disposed of.'

'Yes, but that would not be completely true, would it? And I know that you trust your surgical team, but it would only take one of them to let slip what had happened to the wrong person, and the story would be out.'

They reached Professor Karounis's office. Once they were inside, Professor Karounis indicated with a wave of his hand that Dr Macleod should sit down.

'You are deeply worried that this might botch your copybook, aren't you, Stuart?'

'*Blot*,' Dr Macleod corrected him under his breath, but he didn't think that Professor Karounis heard him.

'When you delivered it, the foetus was living and breathing, and its continuing welfare was your responsibility, after all, no matter how deformed it was, or how distressed, until it passed away. I agree with you that there was no chance of its survival, but that is not the point.'

At that moment, Professor Karounis's secretary knocked at the door and poked her head around.

'You've two visitors, professor. They're police officers.'

'Good, thank you, Mandy. Please show them in.'

Two uniformed constables came into the office, one stocky man in his mid-thirties with a crew cut and cheeks that looked as if they had been sandblasted, and a plump young woman with pale green eyes and the smallest nose that Dr Macleod had ever seen on an adult.

'I thank you for coming so promptly,' said Professor Karounis. 'I know that the police are very hard-pressed these days, what with all the stabbings and the lads on mopeds snatching people's mobile phones. I am Professor Karounis, the director of this clinic, and this is our chief surgeon, Dr Macleod.'

'You reported a suspected abduction, sir,' said the young woman constable flatly.

'I did, yes, indeed. The circumstances are that a woman patient was referred to us complaining of acute pain. A scan showed us that she was pregnant, but the foetus that she was carrying was cataclysmically malformed. Dr Macleod immediately performed a C-section to remove the foetus, but contrary to his expectations, it survived the operation. We were keeping it in isolation in an incubator, under supervision, but it was momentarily left unattended, and in that very short period of time when the nurse was out of the room, it disappeared.'

'You have your own security staff here, don't you, sir? And CCTV?'

'Yes, we do. But they could find no evidence of how the foetus might have been taken. The closed-circuit television covers all the entrances and exits, as well as the landings and the stairs and the lifts, but they recorded nobody acting suspiciously and no comings or goings that could not be accounted for.'

The male constable turned to Dr Macleod and said, 'The foetus was "cataclysmically malformed"? What exactly does that mean, sir, if you don't mind me asking.'

'I think Professor Karounis meant "catastrophically". It's not easy to describe it to you, so perhaps I can show you a picture.'

Dr Macleod took out his phone and prodded at it until he found a photo of the foetus in the picture library. He handed it over to the constable, and said, 'There. That's it. I took that about five minutes after I removed it from the patient's uterus.'

Both constables stared at it for nearly ten seconds. Then they looked back up at Dr Macleod, and both of them had stunned expressions on their faces.

'Is this real?' asked the male constable. 'I mean, this isn't some kind of a wind-up, is it?'

'He's real all right. Do you honestly think that we would make up a creature that looked like that, for a joke?'

'You say "he"?'

'If you look closely, you'll see that he has male genitalia. Diminutive, but unmistakable.'

'Blimey.'

'Don't think that I wasn't as shocked as you are,' Dr Macleod told them. 'Probably much more so, because there he was, living and breathing in the palm of my hand. I've never seen anything like him, ever, not in all my years as a surgeon, and believe me, I've seen some desperately deformed foetuses in my time. Two or three of them would have given you nightmares.'

'And you think that somebody might have taken it?'

'It could hardly have left the clinic on its own, could it?' said Professor Karounis, with a sharp hint of impatience.

'No, of course not. But can you think of any reason why anybody might have *wanted* to take it?'

'There could be any number of motives,' said Dr Macleod. 'He might have been taken by a dealer in human organs. A human head can fetch up to five hundred pounds when sold for dissection. Hospitals and universities pay very respectable money for livers and kidneys and other organs. So you can imagine what a dealer might be able to ask for a very unusual specimen like this.'

'But what would a dealer in human organs be doing, wandering around this clinic?' asked the female constable. 'You don't sell stillborn babies for dissection, do you? Or do you?'

Dr Macleod was about to speak when Professor Karounis raised his hand and said, 'Please! That question is not at all relevant to this disappearance, madam. Dr Macleod was only making a conjecture. As he said, the foetus could have been taken for any one of a number of motives, and not necessarily for dissection.'

The male constable handed back Dr Macleod's phone.

'I'm afraid this is rather out of our league, sir, to be perfectly honest with you. Missing children, yes. Stolen property, yes. Like you say, there must be a reason why this foetus was abducted, but considering its deformity, I think Constable Lake and me need to hand this over to officers who specialise in this kind of thing.'

'What do you mean, "this kind of thing"?' said Professor Karounis. "Don't tell me there are more foetuses like this.'

'No, sir. I meant cases that are out of the ordinary. Not like your everyday common-or-garden stabbings or robberies or drug-dealing or internet scams. I'm talking about cases that defy rational explanation, and I certainly think that this disappearance has all the characteristics of one of those.'

'So what action are you going to take?'

'I'm going to return to the station, sir, and inform the DCI in charge of the Major Investigation Team of the circumstances under which this foetus disappeared. Of course I'll show him a picture of the foetus, if you can send it to me, please, along with any details such as its size, weight and general physical condition. Do you think it could still be alive?'

'I simply don't know,' said Dr Macleod. 'I couldn't even guess. I was staggered that he was still alive after I delivered him. As you saw, his lungs and other organs are external and his heart is no bigger than my fingernail. It depends very much on how he's been treated by whoever took him.'

'Okay then, sir. We'll get back to you just as soon as the DCI has assessed the case and decided how to go forward from here. Is it possible to have a word with your security people before we leave?'

'David Brennan, of course. My secretary will take you downstairs to his office.'

When the constables had left, Dr Macleod stood staring at the door as if he expected them to come back in again.

'Why do I think that this is going to have a very bad ending?'

'I don't know, Stuart,' said Professor Karounis. He sat down behind his desk, picked up a folder, frowned at it, and then dropped it. 'My feeling is that it will have no ending at all, and that we will never find out why that foetus was malformed the way it was, or what happened to it. My feeling is that we will never know the answer to these questions before we are six feet below the ground.'

'Oh, not me,' said Dr Macleod. 'I'm going to be cremated. I never fancied being eaten by grave-worms.'

Professor Karounis gave an odd, off-key bark, like a surprised dog. 'You're not intending to donate yourself to science? You surprise me. You've just said that your body parts can make very good money.'

*

As soon as he had left Professor Karounis's office, Dr Macleod called his wife, Beverly. She had already left Peckham Library and was on her way home to Dulwich, and in any case she said that she was exhausted and didn't feel like going out to eat.

'Oh well,' he told her. 'Maybe another day.' After talking to the police, he didn't have much of an appetite himself.

He looked in on Mrs Adams to see how she was recovering from the C-section he had given her that afternoon. She was drowsy but smiling, and her husband was there too, and gave him a grateful handshake that almost broke his fingers.

He was halfway across the car park when his phone rang. It had started drizzling again, so he climbed into his Mercedes and closed the door before he answered it. It was Dr Bhaduri, and he sounded breathy and over-excited.

'Dr Macleod? Are you on your way home yet?'

'I'm about to. What is it?'

'It's Susan Nicholls. That young woman who suffered a placental abruption.'

'Yes, I know who you mean.'

Dr Macleod had treated Susan Nicholls yesterday after she had lost her baby at nineteen weeks, which was unusually late for a miscarriage. It was sad, but the operation had gone smoothly and there had been no complications. He had given her a D & C, and she was due to be discharged early tomorrow morning.

'About two hours ago she started complaining of acute abdominal pain,' said Dr Bhaduri. 'It became so severe, ten out of ten, that she couldn't even speak, and so I put her on an opioid drip. She was vomiting too, which made me wonder if it was mesenteric ischemia, and so I sent her for an urgent scan.'

'Why didn't you tell me this before?'

'You were in surgery, sir. And I thought I would wait until I saw the results of the scan.'

'All right, Dr Bhaduri. Calm down. Have you been given those results?'

Dr Macleod could hear Dr Bhaduri take a deep, quivering breath. He sounded as he were just about to start crying.

'She's pregnant. That is to say, she has a foetus in her uterus.'

'Dr Bhaduri, she can't be pregnant. It's less than forty-eight hours since she miscarried. Are you sure her ultrasound hasn't got mixed up with another patient's? It has happened.'

'But it looks like the same foetus, sir. The foetus you removed from Chiasoka Oduwole. The foetus that has gone missing.'

'That's impossible. They've given you Mrs Oduwole's ultrasound scan by mistake. They must have.'

'No, sir. I have double-checked it. I took it back down to the technicians, and they confirmed absolutely that this is the scan of Susan Nicholls.'

Dr Macleod felt chilled all over, and even in his thick Crombie overcoat, he shivered.

'I'm coming back in,' he said. 'Where is Susan Nicholls now?'

'Two-oh-three. I took her out of the ward because I didn't want to upset the other mothers.'

Dr Macleod climbed back out of his car and walked quickly through the fine rain back to the centre. The receptionist looked at him quizzically as he strode, grim-faced, to the lifts. As he went up to the second floor, he stared at himself in the mirror in the back of the lift and thought, *This can't be happening. This can't be true. This is like something out of a horror film.*

Dr Bhaduri was waiting for him in the corridor. Dr Symonds was with him, and Sister Rudd. Without a word, Dr Bhaduri handed Dr Macleod the cardboard folder containing the ultrasound scan and nodded toward the open door of room 203.

Dr Macleod went inside. Susan Nicholls was lying on her bed with her eyes closed, attached to an intravenous opioid drip. She was twenty-three years old, quite pretty in a punky way, with her spiky dark brown hair bleached blonde at the tips, a stud in the side of her nose and a tattoo of a mermaid on her left forearm. A nurse was sitting close beside her, but she stood up when Dr Macleod came in.

'She's sleeping now,' said Sister Rudd. 'She went through more than an hour of absolute agony, and it's worn her out.'

'Vitals?' asked Dr Macleod.

'Her blood pressure's slightly elevated, 140 over 90, but apart from that, normal.'

Dr Macleod opened the folder and looked at the ultrasound scan. He couldn't help shivering again. It showed the foetus that was curled up inside Susan Nicholls's womb, and it looked exactly like the malformed foetus that he had removed from Chiasoka Oduwole. Its spidery limbs were wrapped around its head so that its angelic face was obscured, but he was in no doubt that if it wasn't the same creature, it was that creature's identical twin. It had the same external lungs, although they weren't inflating and deflating as they had when the foetus was breathing air, and it had the same diminutive genitalia.

Dr Bhaduri pointed to the way in which the foetus was pressed against the wall of the womb.

'You see? It can only have been lodged there for a very few hours, and yet it has already put out microvilli to attach itself to the lining of the uterus. It is my guess that within a very short space of time it will be taking nutrition and oxygen from Ms Nicholls, like a normal foetus.'

'Is she aware that she has this foetus inside her?'

'Not yet,' said Dr Symonds. 'We thought it important to discuss it with you before we told her. She's only just lost a baby halfway through her pregnancy – a baby that she'd already felt moving – as if that wasn't enough for her to contend with.'

'She'll have to know,' said Dr Macleod. 'A C-section is going to be the only way to get it out of her, and we can't do that without her permission. Not unless her life is at risk, and at the moment it isn't, no matter how bizarre this thing is.'

'I can't understand how it got into her,' said Dr Bhaduri. 'I mean – did it *crawl* all the way from Room 207 into the ward? And then what? It's like some terrible kind of parasite.'

Dr Macleod turned to Sister Rudd. 'We have to remove this, and as soon as possible. Let her sleep until we've organised an anaesthetist and prepped the theatre. When she's awake I'll come back and explain how this thing has somehow invaded her body and what we'll have to do to extract it.'

'And when we *have* extracted it?' asked Dr Symonds. 'What are we going to do with it then?'

'What I should have done before. Euthanise it.'

'It's not "him" anymore?'

Dr Macleod didn't answer that. He handed the ultrasound scan back to Dr Bhaduri, then he walked off to tell Professor Karounis that the foetus had reappeared, and that instead of calling for the police, he probably should have called for an exorcist.

12

Back at Crane's Drains' red-brick building on Copeland Road, Jerry and Jamila were shown to the washrooms so that they could both take a long hot shower. Even after soaping himself twice though, Jerry was sure that he still smelled faintly of sewage.

Jim Feather was waiting for them when they came out, their hair still wet. Jerry sniffed his fingers to reassure himself that he didn't really smell, and Jim said, 'You're all right, mate. That's phantosmia. All of us flushers get it from time to time.'

'Phan-*toze*-mia? What's that then?'

'It's when you're worried that you stink of something and your brain conjures up the smell that you're worried about, even though it's only imaginary. You'll probably smell it again, on and off, maybe for three or four days. But you only smell of Lynx, believe me.'

'Bloody hell. That's bad enough.'

Jim led them to Martin Elliot's office, whistling between his teeth as he walked. Gemma had already contacted John Crane, the company's founder and owner, so that she could tell him about the lights turning green and the howling draught, and update him on their continuing search for Martin, whether he was alive or dead.

As Jerry and Jamila came in, she was still talking to him on Skype on the fifty-five-inch television in the corner of the office. He had a broad northern face, with deep lines in his cheeks and a deeply cleft chin. His hair was grey and combed straight back, like a 1950s' cricketer, and he had a distinctive Yorkshire accent.

'Whatever happens down drains, pet, there's always a logical explanation,' he was saying. 'Sometimes you can see things that look like ghosts flitting around and hear shouting and singing. Once in Beckton the sewage itself caught fire, spontaneous combustion. I saw that for myself. But like I say, there's always a logical explanation. That sewage catching fire, we tracked that down to a fly-by-night haulage firm in Barking. They'd poured thousands of litres of illegal red diesel down the sewers so they wouldn't be caught with it. Somebody probably dropped a lighted fag end into the drain and *blammy*, up it all went.'

'I understand what you're saying, sir,' said Newton. 'But I can't think of any logical way in which those LED lights could have turned green.'

'Not now you can't, lad,' said John Crane. 'But I can assure you that it didn't happen by magic. Any more than that draught that blew you all out of there.'

Jamila sat down at the conference table next to Gemma and introduced herself. 'I am Detective Sergeant Jamila Patel, Mr Crane. I am one of a team that is investigating Martin Elliot's disappearance. This is my partner, Detective Constable Pardoe.'

'How d'ye do, officer. If there's owt I can do to help, you only have to ask.'

'Mr Crane, we saw those green lights for ourselves, and we felt that draught, but there was one thing more. As we were retreating along the sewer, we were showered with keys.'

John Crane's brow furrowed. 'Keys? You mean like door keys?'

'That's right, sir, metal door keys. And they struck us with some considerable force, as if they were being thrown at us to hurt us, or at least to make sure that we left the sewer as quickly as possible.'

'Well, keys, that's right queer, I'll admit. But there must have been some scientific reason for it. I don't know... maybe there was a sudden upsurge of magnetic energy. It's always full of surprises, that bobar, and none of them pleasant. You can never tell what's going to come floating along in it next.'

Jim said, 'I can put together a technical team first thing tomorrow morning, Mr Crane. I'll call in Dale Roberts from safety and Lenny Machin from the lab, and maybe Ken Williams too. Ken really knows his onions when it comes to ventilation. We can carry out a thorough gas analysis and double-check the electrics, as well as take sewage samples all the way from the inspection chamber to the fatberg.'

'That's good,' Jamila put in, 'because as soon as you've done that, we can send in our own forensic experts. Provided, of course, you can assure us that it's safe for us to do so.'

'I'll admit it's a thousand-to-one phenomenon, what you experienced,' John Crane told her. 'But if there's one thing I've learned about sewage over the years, it's never predictable. You can never tell what some misguided barmpot is going to flush down his bog or how that's going to react with what some other misguided barmpots might have flushed down *their* bogs – especially in confined spaces like sewers. But don't you worry, detective, we'll get this sorted in double-quick order. We're Crane's Drains... and when it comes to sewers, we're the bee's knees.'

***

Jamila and Jerry went back to the station to report to DCI Walters. They caught him just as he was leaving the station to go home, and even when they told him about the green light and the draught and the flying keys, he stood beside his desk with his coat on, jiggling his car keys, and they could tell that he wasn't really listening to them.

'What can I say?' he told them, looking at his watch. 'I think that more than justifies my calling you two in to investigate, considering your experience with strange stuff like that.'

Jamila said, 'Mr Crane is quite convinced that there's a logical explanation for what happened.'

'It still sounds pretty weird to me. Somebody was throwing *keys* at you? And you couldn't see who it was? I mean, you have to admit that's *weird*, even if it isn't supernatural.'

'Crane's technicians are going down there tomorrow morning, and if they give us the all-clear we'll be able to send in our own forensic experts. Between them, I think they should be able to give us some answers.'

'Right. Good. I look forward to hearing what they come up with. Meanwhile, I have to love you and leave you, I'm afraid. We're having the wife's mum and dad for dinner tonight.'

'Everyone to his own taste,' said Jerry. 'I was thinking of going for a ruby myself.'

Once DCI Walters had hurried off, Jamila looked at Jerry and said, 'He really doesn't want to get involved in this, does he? I'm sure he thinks that Martin Elliot is never going to be found, and he doesn't want the MIT to be blamed for it.'

'Let's just play it by ear, shall we? Meanwhile, I'm starving. I noticed this little curry house when I was on my way here. Do you want to join me, or have you had it up to here with Indian food?'

Jamila nodded. Jerry could tell that she was upset by DCI Walters' indifference. Personally, he couldn't give a monkey's. He'd been sceptical of senior officers ever since he had worked at New Scotland Yard and found out how many of them were taking backhanders from fraudsters and drug dealers. They hadn't sacked him, because that would have risked him whistle-blowing and creating a public fuss, but that was why they sent him out to the suburbs, where he could cause less trouble.

They drove down to Holly Grove, a narrow residential street with a yellow-fronted Indian restaurant on the corner, and parked right outside.

'Ganapati,' said Jamila, looking up at the name over

the restaurant's front door. 'That is another name for Ganesh, the god with the elephant's head.'

'I used to know somebody in the Kremlin with an elephant's head,' said Jerry. 'But his name was Gordon.'

Inside, the restaurant was plain, with bare wooden tables and utilitarian chairs, but it was warmly lit with lamps made from coloured glass jugs hanging from the ceiling, and there was a fragrant aroma of spices that made Jerry's brain forget all about the smell of sewage. When he took off his jacket and sat down though, he could see himself in the mirror on the wall, and he thought that he was looking scruffy and washed-out.

He watched Jamila study the menu. 'What do you think, sarge?' he asked her. 'Do you really believe we could have been given this job so we could be – you know – like scapegoats?'

'I'm not sure. Perhaps. You told me, didn't you, that Chief Inspector Kelley has been trying to pull the rug out from under you ever since you left the Yard. And I know for sure that I have made many enemies in the Pakistani community in Redbridge. All *men*, of course, who don't like being criticised for the way they treat their women.'

She paused, playing with the turquoise ring on her left little finger. 'After we wrapped up that case against Jokubas Liepa and his ghost virus, you and me, they could hardly dismiss us straight away, could they, after all the press coverage we were given?'

'But?'

'I'm not sure. I'm just suspicious of the way they brought us into this investigation so quickly, as if they had been waiting for some weird case to come up so that they could put us both on to it. If we can't make any headway with it, they might well accuse us of incompetence. Either that, or they'll say that we've been playing on our reputation as ghost hunters to get ourselves assigned to a job that's going to win us even more personal publicity – even if *they* were the ones who assigned us to it.'

'Well, you may be right. But supposing there *is* some kind of a spooky influence at work here? What happened to us down in that sewer – you have to admit that it was totally mad. Especially those keys flying around like a swarm of bloody locusts.'

Jamila unfastened her maroon leather purse and took out the large old-fashioned key that she had picked up in the sewer. She held it out to Jerry, but at first he hesitated to take it.

'Don't worry,' she said. 'Before I took a shower, I washed it in very hot water. It's clean.'

Jerry took it and peered at it closely. It was about fourteen centimetres long, with an elaborate bow, a long shank, and star-shaped key wards cut into the bit. It was iron and pitted with corrosion, so it was obviously old, but exactly how old he couldn't guess.

'We need to ask a locksmith to take a shufti at this,' he said, passing it back to Jamila. 'I know the manager at Kevin's Keys, in the Broadway. If he can tell us what kind of a lock it was used for, maybe we'll have a better idea of why it was being thrown at us.'

'Yes, perhaps. And we'll ask that Gemma Bright if her team can find us any more keys when they go down into the sewer tomorrow. But it's an antique, isn't it? So I think we'll need more than your local key cutter. We'll need somebody who's an expert on historical locks and keys.'

A smiling waiter came over and asked them if they had decided what they wanted to eat. Jamila chose a vegetarian thali, and Jerry asked for the odyian lamb, with fenugreek, tomatoes and green chillies. He also ordered a pint of Fourpure pale ale, brewed in Bermondsey, while Jamila was content with tap water. He knew he shouldn't drink on duty, but he persuaded himself that when they had left the Crane's building they had technically knocked off for the day.

'That Crane bloke, maybe he's right, and there *is* a logical explanation,' he said, snapping a poppadom in half and cramming it into his mouth. 'I mean, he's been in the sewage business for donkey's, hasn't he? And like he said, you never know what some plonker has decided to flush down the khazi.'

'For now, I am keeping an open mind,' said Jamila. 'My teacher always said to me that some monkeys became men, while the monkeys who didn't are still jumping around in the trees making faces at them.'

'Really? My teacher told me to stop flicking ink pellets.'

They were still waiting for their main courses when Jamila's phone rang.

'DS Patel. Yes. Yes, I'm still here in Peckham. I'm having a quick supper before I go back to Redbridge.'

She listened, and as she listened, her eyes widened and she looked across the table at Jerry as if she were being told that there was a bomb in the restaurant and they had only minutes to get out.

Eventually she said 'yes', and 'yes' again, and took a ball pen out of her coat pocket. She scribbled something on one of the paper napkins, and then said, 'Right away. Of course. We'll see you there.'

'What's happened now?' Jerry asked her. 'Don't tell me somebody else has disappeared down the drain.'

'Martin Elliot has just been found. A gang of Tideway construction workers came across him lying in a sewer about half a mile north of Greenwich Pumping Station.'

'Brown bread, I'm assuming?'

'No. He's still alive. But he's seriously injured. He's lost both of his legs and he's been blinded. They've rushed him to King's.'

'He's lost both of his legs and he's been blinded and he's down a sewer and he's still alive? Bloody hell. My Uncle Harry fell over outside the pub and cracked his skull on the pavement and he was playing a harp in Heaven by the following morning.'

'Come on,' said Jamila, standing up and lifting her coat off the back of her chair. 'We need to get to see him as soon as we can.'

Jerry stood up too, just as the waiter was bringing their curries on a tray.

'Sorry, mate. We have to be going.' He took three ten-pound notes out of his wallet and tucked them into the waiter's shirt pocket. 'Keep the change. Don't spend it all on scratch cards.'

With that, he and Jamila hurried out of the restaurant

and back to Jerry's car. It was freezing cold outside now, and the windscreen was already beginning to ice up. Before they could drive off, they had to sit for three or four minutes with the engine running until it had gradually cleared.

'Did you see that nosh there?' said Jerry. 'It looked incredible. And did you smell it? I mean, if nostrils could have orgasms! Why couldn't they have found this Martin Elliot geezer half an hour later?'

'It's part of the job, Jerry, you know that. You wouldn't like to be sitting in some council office from nine to five, would you?'

'My brain wouldn't, no, but my stomach wouldn't mind, believe me.'

★

It took them only ten minutes to drive to King's College Hospital on Denmark Hill. When they arrived, the receptionist showed them through to a chilly waiting room, where two young constables from Lewisham police station were sitting next to an aquarium full of listless goldfish, looking bored. One constable was short and thickset, while the other was tall and thin and mournful-looking. Jerry thought they looked like an unsuccessful comedy act.

Jamila introduced Jerry and herself, and then she asked the constables for an up-to-date briefing.

The short stocky constable spoke first. Every now and then he jerked his head sideways as if he were being annoyed by a fly. 'We was notified by Thames Water shortly after 7:15 that the victim had been located in a new sewer pipe what they've been drilling as part of the Tideway construction.'

'Did you go down into the sewer yourselves?'

'We did, yes. It's not yet operational, so we was able to follow the ambulance crew. The victim was lying on a shelf at the side of an inspection chamber. He was missing his legs, and it looked like his eyes had been put out too. To be honest with you, we couldn't believe he was still alive and talking.'

'When you say he was missing his legs, were they still there?'

'No, they wasn't, and that was the funny part about it,' put in the tall, thin constable, in a sad tone. 'Well, not funny, but you know what I mean. We walked all the way down the sewer until we reached the tunnel face but there was no sign of them.'

They were still talking to the constables when a doctor appeared. He was Bengali, not much taller than Jamila, with rimless spectacles and a hooked nose, like a parrot's beak.

'I am sorry to have kept you waiting, officers. I am Dr Sanjay Gupta, a consultant in emergency medicine. It has been touch-and-go with Mr Elliot. We have had to resuscitate him twice, although he now seems to be stable.'

'Is he conscious?' asked Jamila.

'At this moment, no. He is under sedation because he was suffering very great pain. His injuries are extremely severe, and we have had to clean them and dress them, and he is now on intravenous antibiotics. However, he was conscious when he was admitted.'

Jerry said, 'Really? Did he say anything?'

'Nothing coherent. He was shouting very loud, like he was angry at somebody. He kept saying that it wasn't his fault, whatever he meant by that. "It wasn't my fault; it wasn't me who got rid of them!" Very loud.'

'But he didn't say what it was that he didn't get rid of? Or who?'

'No, although he repeated that again and again. With those injuries, I doubt if he was talking sense. Or shouting sense, rather. But I will take you up to the intensive care unit, and you will be able to see his trauma for yourselves.'

He led them along to the lifts. As they were going up to the second floor, Jamila said, 'What do you think his chances are?'

'It's very difficult at this moment to say. To be frank with you, I am staggered that he is still alive at all. But his injuries are most unusual, as you will see.'

Before he took them into the ward, a nurse came up and gave them light-green aprons to tie on, as well as surgical caps and masks.

'I feel like a very hygienic bank robber,' said Jerry, in a muffled voice.

Martin Elliot was lying on a tilted-up bed in a bay screened on either side by diamond-patterned curtains. He was linked up to an intravenous drip, and also to a blood bag. A nurse was standing beside his bed, watching his vital signs monitor and taking notes. In the next bay, a young woman was whimpering like a lost puppy and calling out, '*Mama…! Mama…!*'

'Nurse, if you could…' said Dr Gupta, indicating that

she should fold down the sheet that was covering Martin up to his chest. Once she had done that, he beckoned Jamila and Jerry to come closer.

White crêpe bandages were wrapped around Martin's torso and he was wearing an adult diaper. His legs had both been severed at the upper thigh, so all that remained were two short stumps, both of which had thick gauze pads stuck over them with surgical tape. Both of his eyes were covered with gauze pads too.

'The only reason we have applied dressings is to prevent infection,' said Dr Gupta. 'When he was found, he was not bleeding, despite his rectus femoris and his femoral artery having been cut clean through. This was because somehow his stumps had already been cauterised, as if by a red-hot iron.'

He took a pair of surgical gloves from the dispenser beside the bed and snapped them on, wiggling his fingers as if he were preparing for a puppet show. Then he carefully peeled away the dressing from Martin's right stump so that Jamila and Jerry could see how his thigh muscle had been seared. His flesh was blackened and crusted, like a steak that had been charred on a barbecue. His thigh bone had been cleanly sawn off and then scorched by the heat of the cauterisation to a light tan colour, with a scab of burned bone marrow in the centre of it.

Dr Gupta carefully replaced the dressing. 'Both legs are the same. If you ask me what was used to amputate them, I would have to guess at a circular saw. When he was first admitted, I thought he might have fallen in front of a train, but as soon as I examined him, I changed my mind. A train or any other vehicle will cause severe crushing and will certainly not cut through muscle and bone as precisely as this. Now and then we have to deal with patients who have had limbs amputated by trains, and sometimes they have also suffered serious burns because they have touched the third electrified rail. But this cauterisation could not have been accidental. The heat has been applied too uniformly and too comprehensively and too deeply. Whoever did this did not want his victim to die.'

Jamila turned to Jerry. 'They cut off his legs and blinded him, but they didn't want him to die? So why did they do this to him? Was it out of revenge, do you think – some sort of ritual? Or perhaps could it have been some sort of reprisal? Under sharia law, in Pakistan, if you have blinded somebody a court can sentence *you* to be blinded, as a punishment.'

'The trauma to his torso is quite puzzling too,' said Dr Gupta. 'I don't want to remove his dressings to show you, but I have pictures here that will enable you to see quite clearly what has been done to him.'

He led them across to a shelf on the opposite side of the ward and opened up a laptop. He had taken twenty or thirty pictures of Martin's chest and stomach, some of them highly magnified. Martin's skin had been lacerated with deep V-shaped scratches, about thirty or forty of them in a herringbone pattern, all the way down from his neck to his pubic hair.

'They're in fives,' said Jerry, leaning forward to peer at the screen more closely. 'These were done either with a five-pronged fork, or somebody with very long fingernails.'

'We took DNA samples from several of the scratches,' said Dr Gupta. 'We will be able to pass these over to your forensic technicians. I think your second suggestion is the most likely, that they were inflicted by somebody with long fingernails. You can see *here* and *here* that the spacing between the scratches is inconsistent, so that would rule out the possibility of a fork or some other instrument.'

He swiped across to pictures of Martin's face, with both eye sockets ravaged. Both were cavernous and empty, and one of them still had a shred of optic nerve dangling out of it.

'Jesus,' said Jerry. 'How do you think that was done?'

'By hand, I'd say. Forcibly. And by a hand with long sharp fingernails, like the other wounds.'

'I'll contact forensics and get them over here to examine him as soon as possible,' said Jamila. 'Have you ever seen any injuries similar to these before?'

Dr Gupta shook his head. 'This is unlike anything I have ever encountered, even when I was training at the Apollo Hospital in Kolkata. I treated men whose noses and ears had been cut off for failing to pay their debts, and women who had been beaten or branded or blinded for adultery, but nothing like this. Never. In my opinion, whoever did this was a maniac.'

Jerry and Jamila stayed for twenty minutes longer, but there was no significant variation in Martin's vital signs and Dr Gupta said he was likely to remain unconscious for hours to come. Jamila asked him to contact her immediately if there was any dramatic change in his progress – either for better or for worse – and then she and Jerry left.

Outside, a freezing fog was enveloping the car park so that the street lights all around looked like dandelion clocks.

'How are you getting back to Redbridge?' Jerry asked Jamila.

'Don't worry. I'll call for an Uber.'

'I'll catch you tomorrow then. What sort of time?'

'Make it eight. The traffic's always terrible at that time of day.'

Jerry saw that she was shivering. He could tell that she was not only cold but shocked, as he was. It didn't matter how many mangled bodies he had come across in his career, the sight of serious injuries still chilled him and made him realise how vulnerable human beings are to being cut, or crushed, or burned, or disembowelled, or torn to pieces.

Instinctively, he wanted to put his arms around Jamila and hold her tight and reassure her that everything was going to be all right. Not only did he feel protective toward her, but he was beginning to admit to himself that he was very fond of her too, and that he could almost be in love with her. But of course, she was a DS and he was a DC, and they were working on a case together, and paragraph 2.3 of the Metropolitan Police Code of Ethics ruled that officers should 'not engage in sexual conduct or other inappropriate behaviour when on duty'.

Besides that, he had no idea if she felt the same way about him.

'Go and wait for your Uber inside, where it's warm,' he told her. Then, 'See you tomorrow, all right?' He was almost tempted to add 'love'.

13

Jenny was sitting on the couch with her feet tucked under her watching *Home Alone* when she heard the key turning in the door and Mick call out, 'Jen?'

'In here.'

He appeared in the doorway, still wearing his camel-coloured overcoat.

'Don't come rushing out to welcome me home, will you?' he said.

She looked around the floor. 'I'm worried that it's still crawling around somewhere.'

He looked around, too, but then he said, 'I can't see anything, babe,' and came into the room and kissed her. Immediately, she burst into tears.

'Oh, come on,' said Mick, sitting down beside her and putting his arms around her. 'I'll search the whole flat myself. You said it looked like a giant spider? I can't *believe* it killed Persephone.'

'It crawled around like a spider, but it wasn't a spider,' Jenny wept. 'Like I told you on the phone, it had a face. A child's face. It was so creepy I can't tell you. I went out into the corridor and there it was, tearing Perse into little bits.'

'Are you sure it didn't have a pattern on it that just *looked* like a face? You know, like one of those moths. What do they call them? Death's heads.'

'No, Mick, I swear to you. It was an actual face, with eyes and a mouth, and all the time it was tearing Perse into little bits it was staring at me. It scratched me too. Look at my hands! I went to get your golf club to hit it, but when I came back it was gone.'

'What have you done with her? I mean Perse.'

'She's in a plastic shopping bag in the kitchen. I thought about taking her into the backyard garden and burying her, but I was scared that thing might still be crawling around outside somewhere. In any case, I thought you ought to see what it did to her.'

Mick gave her a squeeze and kissed her again. 'I wish I could've been here, Jen. I really do. But listen, I'll make absolutely 110 per cent sure that it's not hiding in the flat somewhere, and maybe in the morning I ought to call the police and tell them about it. It could have been somebody's pet spider that's got loose, like a tarantula or something. I mean, Christ almighty, if it killed Perse, what if it attacked a baby?'

'It wasn't a spider, Mick! It was like a human hand with a child's face on it! It crawled around like a spider, but it was nothing *like* a spider!'

'*Mom? Dad?*' said Macaulay Culkin. Mick picked up the remote and switched the sound off.

'If it was as big as that, how did it manage to disappear?'

'I don't know, Mick,' said Jenny, wiping her eyes on the

sleeve of her dressing gown. 'But you only have to go and look at Perse to see that I didn't imagine it.'

'Okay, sweetheart, I believe you. Of course I believe you. Let me take a look around.'

Mick took off his overcoat and went back into the corridor to hang it up.

'She's in that Asda bag, on the chair!' Jenny called out.

There was a lengthy silence while Mick went into the kitchen. When he returned to the living room he stared at Jenny with his eyes wide and his mouth open in disbelief. His brown hair was always brushed upward, but with the stunned expression on his face, it looked as if it were standing on end out of shock.

'Shit, Jen. When you said it was tearing her into little bits... I mean, I imagined just bits of fur and stuff. I didn't think – shit, that's all her *insides* and everything!'

Jenny nodded and started crying again. Mick sat down and gave her another hug, and then he said, 'Right. I'll search the whole flat now. If it's still here, that thing, it's going to get flattened. Fucking pulverised. I mean that.'

Jenny stayed on the couch, biting her thumbnail, while Mick went across to the bedroom. He looked under the bed and opened every cupboard and every drawer. He brought in a chair from the kitchen so he could climb up onto it and make sure the thing wasn't hiding itself on top of the wardrobe.

After the bedroom, he searched the bathroom, the airing cupboard and the kitchen. Eventually he came back into the living room and searched that too, kneeling down to peer under the couch and even lifting up the couch cushions. There were two drawers under the bookshelves, and he pulled them right out so he could look into the back of them.

'You're right, babe,' he said at last. 'Whatever it was, it's gone.'

'But what I can't understand is how it could have got in here in the first place. The front door was closed, and the only window that was open was in the bedroom, and that was just the little top window. I would have seen it or heard it if it had climbed in through there.'

'Maybe it got in yesterday, and it was biding its time, sort of thing. Maybe it got in when I opened the front door this morning to go to Sheffield. Maybe it's been here for days, waiting for the right time to come out – you know, when you were alone.'

'Oh, don't. You're scaring me even more now.'

'Well, look, babe, it's definitely gone, so let's try and relax. I'll take poor little Perse to the police station tomorrow morning before I go to work and tell them what's happened. Right now, I'm absolutely knackered, and I could do with a beer and something to eat, then let's go to bed and get a good night's kip.'

Jenny swung her legs off the couch and pushed her feet into her fluffy slippers.

'What about Perse?'

'I'll take her down and shut her in the cupboard under the stairs. Even if that thing's still roaming around the house, it won't be able to get to her in there.'

'There's some of that smoked ham left. I'll make you a sandwich.'

'How about you?'

'I'm still sick to my stomach, Mick. I don't think I'm going to be able to eat anything for weeks. I don't even know if I'm going to be able to sleep. I keep seeing that face. It was like a little baby's face. But the look in its eyes... like it was saying, "I'm scaring you half to death, aren't I, and I'm tearing your cat into pieces, and there's nothing you can do about it."'

Mick took the Asda bag with Persephone's remains down to the cupboard under the stairs. When he came back, Jenny was in the kitchen spreading butter on bread for his sandwich. He stood in the doorway watching her. If she had turned around and seen his face, perhaps she would have guessed that he was wondering, *A spider, with a baby's face? What if she's suffering from some kind of mental problem, and she was hallucinating? What if she ripped Persephone open like that, but scratched her own hands to try and prove that she didn't?*

***

It was past one o'clock when they eventually went to bed. Jenny insisted that they keep the corridor light on and the bedroom door slightly ajar. She didn't want to be lying there in total darkness, and if that thing came creeping around again, she wanted to be able to hear it. She didn't think she was going to be able to sleep.

Mick gave her a cuddle. 'Come on, babe. It was a horrible experience, but it's all over now.'

'You do believe me, don't you? You saw what it did to poor Perse.'

'Of course I believe you. But try and get some sleep. You'll feel better about it in the morning.'

He turned over with his back to her, and after only three or four minutes, she could hear him breathing deeply and then softly snoring. She lay staring at the red numbers on the digital clock as they silently flicked from 1:07 to 2:00 and then on to 2:36. She wondered if she would ever be able to sleep again, but when the clock showed 3:09, she began to breathe more deeply herself.

She dreamed that she was in a strange house, uncarpeted, with no furniture and only naked light bulbs hanging from the ceiling in every room. It was chilly, this house, and dusty, as if it hadn't been occupied for months, if not years. She was walking along the hallway toward the stairs, but when she put her hand on the newel post to start climbing up, she heard Persephone mewling.

Perse? Where are you, Perse?

She went from room to room, but there was no sign of Persephone in any of them. She went back into the hallway, and now she could hear Persephone mewling from upstairs. She started to climb up, but the stairs were like an escalator, and with every step she took, each tread sank down to floor level, one after the other, so that she could never climb any higher.

She stood still, trying to work out how she could make her way upstairs to rescue Persephone. As she was standing there, she felt a cold draught, and she looked around to see if the front door of the house had been opened. The draught subsided, but after a few seconds, she was conscious of a wetness between her thighs and a sensation like fingers touching her, and parting the lips of her vulva.

Then suddenly, she felt something slippery wriggling into her vagina, and she woke up.

'Mick!' she said, slapping at the duvet. 'Not now, Mick, I'm too tired, and I'm not in the mood!'

Almost at once though, she realised that Mick still had his back to her, and that he was still asleep. She screamed and threw back the duvet, scrabbling with both hands to pull up her nightgown. She opened her legs wide and made a grab for the creature that had almost completely squirmed its way up inside her. Between her labia she could feel fingers, or protrusions that felt like fingers, and she tried to pinch them between her own fingers and pull them out, but they were so slimy she couldn't get enough of a grip, and the creature was forcing its way further up into her by expanding and contracting itself like the muscles of an oarsman rowing upstream.

Mick jolted awake. 'What? What is it?'

He lunged across and switched on the bedside lamp, but he knocked it off the nightstand onto the carpet. Jenny was screaming and screaming and bouncing up and down on the bed, trying to wrench the creature out of herself.

'*Get it out! Mick! Get it out! Oh God, Mick, get it out!*'

Mick knelt up beside her, and she pulled her labia apart as wide as she could so that he could see the nobbled tips of the finger-limbs as they gradually started to disappear from sight. He tried to get a grip on them, but they were too strong and too wriggly and too slick with juice.

Jenny had stopped screaming now, and Mick said nothing.

He ripped the pillowcase off his pillow and thrust his left hand into it, so that it acted like a large white cotton glove. Pushing his hand up between Jenny's outstretched labia, he managed to clasp the tip of one of the creature's limbs and hold on to it tight. Then with his right hand pressed flat against Jenny's hip to give him leverage, he slowly tugged the creature out of her, centimetre by centimetre. It tried to cling on, squirming and twisting, but at last, with a slow sucking sound, it came out. As soon as it dropped onto the sheet, its claws came out, and when Mick picked it up, it scratched at the pillowcase, tearing it. Mick flung it hard against the opposite wall so that it tumbled onto the carpet close to the bedside lamp.

Jenny moaned and pulled down her nightgown, squeezing her thighs tightly together and rolling over onto her side.

Mick swung himself off the bed. The creature was lying face down, its finger-like limbs quivering like a spider's legs after being sprayed with insecticide, but that was its only resemblance to a spider.

'Fuck me,' said Mick. He was panting, but more from shock than exertion. 'It's only fucking real. Are you all right, babe? Has it hurt you?'

Jenny was almost incoherent. 'No,' she sobbed. 'Only when you pulled it out.'

Mick's left hand was still wrapped in his pillowcase. He bent down and cautiously flipped the creature over. By the floor-level light from the toppled lamp, he could see what Jenny had seen when the creature had attacked and killed Persephone – its babylike face, with its staring blue eyes;

its nostril holes, which opened and closed as it breathed, and its pouting lips.

It looked up at him and let out a thin, whispery squeak.

'What are we going to do with it?' said Jenny. 'It's alive, isn't it? Do you think we should kill it?'

The creature gradually started to crawl sideways across the carpet, toward the door.

'Babe,' said Mick, 'are you okay to go into the kitchen and get me one of those big Tupperware boxes?'

Jenny sat up. 'What are you going to do?'

'I'm going to call the police. What else can I do? I don't even know what it is. If it's a sort of a human, I don't want to kill it. If it's an animal... I don't know – maybe the RSPCA will know what it is. But it assaulted you, babe. It fucking assaulted you, and it's dangerous.'

Jenny eased herself off the bed and hobbled into the kitchen, keeping her eyes on the creature all the time, in case it suddenly came scuttling after her. She came back with the largest size of plastic storage box, handing it to Mick before she climbed back up onto the bed and clutched a pillow protectively in front of her. Mick peeled the lid off the storage box, held it above the creature for a few seconds, and then suddenly slammed it down onto the carpet, trapping the creature inside. The creature tried to jump to one side, obviously realising what he was going to do, but he was too quick for it. He slid the lid underneath it, and then turned the storage box over and sealed it.

The creature struggled and rattled furiously against the sides of the box, and Mick had to hold the lid on tight, with both hands. He carried it into the kitchen, where he took a roll of duct tape out of a bottom drawer and wound it twice around the box to secure the lid. After that, he found a metal skewer and stabbed six air holes into the lid, taking care not to stab the creature itself.

He left it in the kitchen and went back to the bedroom to pull on a pair of jeans and a sweater.

'Let's have a look at you,' he said. 'Do you want me to call a doctor or anything?'

Jenny lifted her nightgown. She had three red bruises on the inside of her right thigh, but she wasn't bleeding, and otherwise she didn't appear to be hurt.

'You searched the whole flat,' she wept, covering herself back up. 'How did it get in again?'

'Don't ask me,' said Mick, picking up his phone. 'Maybe the police can work it out.'

He prodded out 999. Before the operator answered though, he covered the receiver with his hand and said to Jenny, 'What the hell am I going to say to them?'

14

Back in Tooting, after he had returned to his chilly first-floor flat on Prentis Road, Jerry took another long shower, so hot that it made his face flush red. He felt hungry, but he couldn't think what to eat this late at night. Maybe he should have asked the waiter at Ganapati to pack up their curries to take away with them. A couple of minutes wouldn't have made any difference. But he kept picturing Martin Elliot with his hollow eye sockets and the deep lacerations in his chest and his bandaged stumps for legs, and he didn't know if he would have been able to chew and swallow a cold lamb curry at two in the morning after seeing that.

He went to bed, but he had to force himself to close his eyes, and even when he did, he couldn't sleep. After about an hour he climbed out of bed and went into the living room to watch TV. He started to watch a Netflix crime drama called *Nightstalker*, but he was too tired and too hungry to follow the plot, and the detective was so incompetent that he felt like shouting at him, *You don't touch the door handles, you prick, not without nitrile gloves.*

At 4:10 a.m. he switched off the television, went for

a pee, and then crawled back into his messed-up bed. Usually he slept as if he were dead and never had dreams – not that he could remember in the morning, anyway. But this investigation with Jamila was so surreal that he couldn't stop himself from churning it over in his mind, over and over, and he was sure he could still smell sewage on his hands. Those luminous figures of deformed and disembowelled children – had they been real, or a mass hallucination, as Jamila had suggested they might have been – a *folie à plusieurs*? How had those LED lights along the sewer suddenly started to shine green? Where had it come from, that draught that had howled along the tunnel after them like a banshee? And who had thrown that hailstorm of keys?

He was still awake at 5:27 a.m. when his phone rang. He reached across, dropped it on the floor, and had to lean over the side of the bed to pick it up.

'Is that Jerry?'

'Yes. Who is this?'

'It's Declan.'

'Declan?'

'Declan O'Brien, from the MIT. I heard that you and DS Patel went over to King's yesterday evening to see our misper.'

'That's right, we did. And he's in a right bleeding state, I can tell you. Both his legs were sawn off, both his eyes were pulled out, and he's covered all over with scratches. The doctor has no idea how he survived it, except that the stumps of his legs were cauterised with something red-hot to stop him bleeding to death.'

He rubbed his eyes and blinked. 'What's the bird lime? I haven't checked with the hospital yet this morning, but nobody's called to say that he's snuffed it.'

'Jesus,' said Declan. 'It really sounds like somebody was out to teach him a lesson, doesn't it? Why didn't they just cut his throat and have done with it?'

'Don't ask me, mate,' Jerry told him. He looked across at his bedside clock. 'Bloody hell, it's only half five. Are you calling for anything special, or did you just want to get an update on that?'

'I tried calling DS Patel, Jerry, but she didn't pick up, so DCI Walters told me to call you instead. The thing is, we don't want to overload you, you know what I mean, but it looks like we've got another weird job on our hands, and, well – we'd very much appreciate your expertise.'

'Expertise? Do me a favour. I can guess what Walters actually said. "This job's so bloody screwy we'd better call in those two ghostbusters. I can't make head nor tail of it."'

'Pretty much, yes. I was just being euphemistic.'

'Euphemistic? Don't worry. You can get pills for that these days. So what is it, this weird job? There's only the two of us, remember, DS Patel and me, and I haven't even had any bleeding supper yet, from last night, let alone any breakfast.'

'We had a call early yesterday evening from the Warren BirthWell Centre. That's right next to King's, on the same campus, like.'

'Yes, I know it. A barmaid friend of mine had triplets there. Go on.'

'A Nigerian woman was admitted the day before yesterday because she was suffering acute abdominal pain. She claimed she had an abortion in April, but a scan showed that she was still pregnant. However, the scan also showed that the foetus was severely malformed, and so a surgeon gave her an emergency Caesarean.'

'You're reading this, aren't you? How was it "severely malformed"?'

'I can send you a picture of it. According to the surgeon, it had a proper face, but a whole lot of legs on the back of its head like an octopus, and all of its internal organs – like its heart and its lungs and its stomach – were outside its body. What they couldn't believe though, was that it was still alive. They put it in an incubator, and it kept on breathing and its heart kept on beating.'

'I agree with you, mate, that *is* weird. But those doctors at the BirthWell – they must have to deal with horrible deformities all the time. You know – like conjoined twins and kids with two heads and babies with only half a brain. Those are medical problems. Why would they call for the bizzies?'

'It disappeared, that's why. The foetus. Apparently it was left unsupervised for only a couple of minutes and it vanished, and they couldn't find it anywhere. Walworth sent round a couple of uniforms, but they couldn't work out what had happened to it, either.'

'Somebody half-inched it?'

'Maybe. But it's turned up again. And this is what's *really* weird, and why DCI Walters wanted you and DS Patel to get involved. They've found it inside the uterus of another patient – another woman, who'd had a miscarriage and was supposed to be ready to go home. They're planning on giving *her* a Caesarean too, but they've had to postpone it until later this morning because she's been suffering from heart palpitations.'

'Just a minute. Am I hearing this right? This severely malformed foetus was taken out of one woman and put in an incubator, and then it disappeared, but now it's showed up inside another woman altogether?'

'I know. It sounds cracked, doesn't it? But these were definitely not crank calls, or practical jokes. The first one came from the BirthWell Centre's director, Professor Karounis. He was the one who reported that the foetus had gone missing. The second call came from the surgeon who performed the Caesarean on the Nigerian woman. He said they'd given this other woman an ultrasound scan, and he was in no doubt whatsoever that it's the same foetus.'

'I don't know what to say, mate. I really don't. Look, let me try and get in touch with DS Patel and see what she has to say. Then I'll get right back to you, okay?'

'I think DCI Walters wants this dealt with pronto, Jerry, mostly because he doesn't want it leaking out to the media until we've really got a handle on it. The last thing we want is a crowd of TV and newspaper reporters following us around pestering us to tell them what this job is all about, when we don't have the first notion ourselves. I mean, Jesus, we don't even understand why teenage kids are going around stabbing each other, do we? Let alone why kids who aren't even born yet are starting to assault innocent women. In any case, I'll send you the picture of the foetus right now, and you can see for yourself.'

Declan ended the call, but a few seconds later there was a ping, and the picture of the foetus appeared on the screen of Jerry's phone. He stared at it for almost twenty seconds, unable to grasp what he was looking at. Yet that sweet angelic face was staring at him from out of that tangle of limbs as if it could read his mind and was appealing to him to be loving and understanding.

*

Jerry rang Jamila. At first she didn't answer, so he went into the kitchen and switched on the kettle to make himself a mug of coffee. It was still dark outside, and he could see himself reflected in the kitchen window like a ghost in blue-striped pyjamas.

As he poured the boiling water onto his instant coffee, he rang Jamila again. This time she answered almost immediately.

'Jerry? What is it? Do you know what time it is? I've hardly slept a wink.'

'Sorry, sarge, but that O'Brien from the MIT just called me.'

He told her about the 'severely malformed' foetus and how it had disappeared from the incubator but had now been found in Susan Nicholls and had even started to attach itself to the lining of her womb. He also said that DCI Walters had forcefully suggested that he and Jamila should be assigned to investigate how this possibly could have happened.

Jamila was silent for almost ten seconds.

'Sarge? You still there?'

'What you are saying to me, about this foetus. Is it really real? It's not some sort of a hoax?'

'O'Brien's sent me a picture of it. I'll forward it to you. You won't believe it. I find it hard to believe myself, to tell you the truth, but I asked O'Brien if it was a wind-up, and he swore that it wasn't. Besides, I can't really see the CEO of the country's top neonatal clinic playing off-colour practical jokes, can you?'

'Perhaps they've made a serious surgical error and this is their way of covering it up. You know what surgeons are like, always amputating the wrong foot or transplanting somebody's lungs the wrong way round. My uncle in Pakistan had cancer in his right testicle and they removed the left one.'

'They made a balls-up of that then, didn't they?'

'*Jerry.*'

'Yes, sorry. But the doctors at the BirthWell, they're not going to do an abortion in reverse, are they, even if they did make a pig's dinner of the first one? Besides, two uniforms from Walworth responded to the first call, and they seem to believe that it's all straight up.'

'Jerry, we're already up to our necks. We have to work out who mutilated Martin Elliot, and how, and why, and what really happened down in that sewer. Who does Walters think we are? Superheroes? As if I don't have enough on my plate. When I got back to my flat last night, I had seven threatening tweets saying I would be raped and killed if I carried on arresting Asian men for grooming white schoolgirls.'

'Yes – no, you're right, sarge. But if Elliot regains consciousness, we'll be going back to King's sometime today to talk to him, won't we? So we might as well nip over to the BirthWell while we're there. You know, just to check out the s.p. Take a look at the picture, and I think you'll say yes.'

Jamila was silent again. Then she said, 'This has really aroused your interest, hasn't it, Jerry? This foetus?'

'All right, I can't say that it hasn't. I mean, it's like something out of *Quatermass*.'

'What is "Quatermass"? I have no idea what you're talking about.'

'It's an old science-fiction scrics that used to be on British telly.'

'This is not fiction, Jerry. This is fact. And our priority at the moment is to find out whoever took Martin Elliot down in that sewer and then blinded him and cut off his legs. I will be calling that Gemma Bright later to see what progress their engineers have made. I want to send our forensic team down there as soon as possible.'

'You're the boss.'

'Yes, I am, and the boss is telling you to have a substantial breakfast so that you are ready for a long day's work. I'll get back to you as soon as I've heard from King's.'

'Okay, sarge. Roger and out. But take a look at the picture. I'm not sure you'll want any breakfast when you have.'

Next, Jerry rang DC O'Brien back to tell him that he and Jamila would try to visit the Warren BirthWell Centre sometime during the day, but to keep them posted if there were any urgent developments.

It was still only 5:40, too early for the other calls he wanted to make. First he wanted to ring 'Edge'og Mallett to find out if a date had been fixed yet for Rusul Goraya to appear in court. Then he needed to get in touch with his ex-wife, Nancy, to fix a time for him to pick up their daughter, Alice, on Saturday. He and Alice were going to eat popcorn and watch her favourite Japanese animated film together, *Mary And The Witch's Flower*, even though they had already seen it five times.

Alice even knew the words by heart. '*Tonight, I really am a witch!*'

15

With his mouth full of *bakarkhani* flatbread, Hamid Sanghavi turned around and said to his wife, 'Where is Joya? If she doesn't hurry up and come down for her breakfast, she's going to be late.'

Farita turned over the spicy omelette that she was frying. 'Let me finish cooking your eggs, and I will go up and see why she's taking so long.'

'I won't be able to wait for her. I have to open the shop at 6:30 sharp for the papers to be delivered. If she doesn't hurry, she will have to catch the bus.'

'She told me last night that she wasn't feeling too well. Maybe she's coming down with a cold.'

'Well, she can always take some Lemsip, can't she? I am going to need her today. I have a whole heap of deliveries coming in from Amar's, and Ibrahim won't be able to come in to help me until this afternoon.'

Farita turned off the gas and came over to slide the omelette on to Hamid's plate.

'You work her too hard, you know, poor girl.'

'Well, it keeps her out of trouble. Keeps her away from those good-for-nothing boys like Rusul and Attaf. And once she's married to Faisal, I won't have her to help me anymore, will I? So I might as well make the most of her while she's still living at home.'

'Attaf is dead, Hamid. Don't speak ill of him.'

'He wasn't all bad, I'll give you that. But that was the price he paid for going out with Joya. He should have had the sense to realise that a respectable marriage was going to be arranged for her by her parents.'

Farita said nothing. She knew about Joya's pregnancy, and her abortion, but she had never said a word about it to her husband. She had not been a virgin herself when she and Hamid were married, but she had kept that a secret from her own father and mother, and from him. On their wedding night she had cut her finger and wiped blood on the sheet of their hotel bed, so that Hamid believed that he had been the first man to penetrate her.

She left Hamid eating his breakfast and went upstairs. When she reached the landing, she heard Joya softly groaning. She went quickly across and opened her daughter's bedroom door, to find Joya kneeling on the floor in her nightgown, rocking backward and forward and clutching her stomach.

'Joya? What's wrong?' she said, but then Joya sat up, and Farita saw that the front of her nightgown was soaked in blood, and that her hands were bloody, and that the pale-green carpet all around her was spattered with blood, too. A six-inch kitchen knife lay on the floor next to the chest of drawers.

'Mama,' Joya whispered, holding out her hand. 'Mama, I can't get it out of me.'

Farita dropped down on to her knees beside her and lifted up Joya's sodden nightgown. Her stomach was sliced open from side to side and her intestines were bulging out, some of them cut open, too. Blood was still pouring out of her, and her thighs were slippery with it.

Farita screamed, 'Hamid! Hamid! Call for an ambulance! Hamid! Call for an ambulance now!'

There was a long pause, then Hamid called back from the bottom of the stairs. 'Ambulance? What are you talking about? What's wrong? I'm trying to have my breakfast.'

'Joya is hurt! She's badly hurt! Call for an ambulance now or she could die!'

Hamid came stamping up the stairs and across the landing. He took one look at Joya and Farita kneeling beside her, both of them smothered in blood, and his mouth opened and closed in shock.

'*Hamid!*'

'What has happened? Who has done this to her?'

'Nobody! She did it herself! Now call an ambulance, or you will lose your daughter forever!'

Hamid hesitated for a moment, still bewildered, but then he turned around and blundered back down the stairs. Joya moaned and then coughed, and dribbled a long string of bloody phlegm. Farita took hold of her shoulders and gently turned her over so that she was lying on her side. Then she straightened her legs and laid her on her back. Her stomach was gaping so Farita unwound her beige headscarf, hurriedly folded it into a pad, and pushed it into the wound to try and stop the bleeding.

'It's all right, Joya, your father is calling for an ambulance. Stay quiet and calm. I love you, my darling, please don't die. Why did you do this to yourself?'

Joya didn't answer. She had lost consciousness now, although she was shivering as if she were feeling desperately cold. Farita's scarf was rapidly being soaked dark red, and Farita knew enough about first aid that if Joya lost more than two litres of blood, she might be past saving.

'Hamid?'

'I've called for an ambulance. I still have them on the line. They say ten minutes.'

Hamid came back upstairs, holding his phone to his ear. 'They say to put pressure on the wound, not to worry about cleaning it. Also to raise her legs. How is she?'

'She's lost so much blood. Oh, please, tell them to hurry.'

Farita pressed harder on Joya's stomach, but when she did, she felt something squirming inside her. It reminded Farita of the time when she was nineteen weeks' pregnant, and Joya had first quickened. She pressed deeper with her fingertips, and she could definitely feel a lump – a lump that was rolling from side to side, as if it were trying to escape from the pressure she was putting on it.

'She has something inside her,' she told Hamid. 'I can feel it. Something alive.'

Hamid knelt down beside her, still holding his phone to his ear. He laid his other hand on Joya's forehead.

'What do you mean, alive?'

'Alive like a baby.'

'No, no, it can't be. She has never been with a boy, not in that way anyway. What you can feel, that must be just her muscles twitching. She's in shock. She's so cold, and so sweaty.'

The emergency operator spoke to him, and he said, 'Yes... yes. I will look out for them.' He leaned over and kissed Joya on the cheek, then he stood up and said to Farita, 'They are telling me five minutes, maybe sooner. I will go downstairs and open the door for them.'

'Hamid, something is inside her, I swear to you. I can feel it.'

'Maybe it's a tumour. I read about that, a girl who thought she was pregnant, but she gave birth instead to this massive tumour.'

Farita was about to answer him when Joya jolted, as if someone had violently shaken her, opened her eyes and let out an agonised scream. Farita screamed too, so that both of them were screaming in chorus. Out of the gaping wound in Joya's stomach, a small bloodstained hand had appeared, like a baby's hand, only with sharp curved claws. It had torn apart the muscular wall of Joya's womb, and now it was tearing at Farita's scarf, trying to rip it aside. Farita snatched at it, and even though it clawed at her fingers, she started to pull it out of Joya's body.

Hamid came back into the room and dropped down beside her. Without hesitation, he pushed up his sleeve and plunged his right hand into Joya's bloody wound. He grunted and struggled for a few seconds, but then he managed to drag the creature completely out from the ragged tear in her womb and slap it down onto the carpet.

Joya by now had lost consciousness again and was lying motionless, her face drained white and her lips blue, although her chest was rising and falling, indicating that she was still breathing.

'What *is* that?' said Farita, in a haunted voice. 'How could that have been inside her?'

Hamid could only shake his head. The creature that he had pulled out of Joya was about the size and shape of a baby squirrel, but it had no tail, and instead of four legs like a squirrel, it had two stunted arms, with tiny five-fingered hands, with curved claws. It had two stunted legs too, and on each side of its body, connecting the arms and the legs from wrists to ankles, there was a web of semi-transparent skin.

It lay on the carpet, smeared in blood and amniotic fluid, not moving. It looked as if it could be dead.

'Get it out of here,' said Farita. 'Please. Get it out of here and throw it away. Where is that ambulance?'

Hamid stood up. 'I think we should let the ambulance people take it. The doctors will want to know what happened to her, and how can we explain it, otherwise, except by showing it to them?'

Almost as soon as he had spoken, the front doorbell rang, and he hurried downstairs to open the door for the paramedics. Farita kept up the pressure on Joya's wound, pressing it even harder now that the creature had torn her flesh open wider still, but by now her scarf was totally sodden with blood.

'Oh, Joya,' she said, as softly as a prayer. 'Please don't leave me. You are so young, my darling.'

As if it had heard her, the creature opened one pale-blue eye and then the other, and stared at her. She stared back at it, too unnerved even to shout to Hamid. But then two paramedics bustled into the room, one of them carrying a large jump bag and the other a defibrillator, and the creature slowly closed its eyes again.

16

Jerry hadn't had time to read about last night's football in the back of the *Daily Mail* before Dr Gupta came into the waiting room and said, 'Good morning to you, officers. You will be pleased to know that Mr Elliot is now conscious.'

Jamila stood up and Jerry folded his newspaper. 'How is his general condition?' asked Jamila.

'Considering the physical trauma that he has suffered, as well as the psychological trauma of discovering that he is now blind, he is bearing up far better than I would have expected. He is still in some delayed shock, of course, and I doubt if he has yet fully grasped the enormity of what has happened to him.'

Dr Gupta took off his glasses and frowned at them short-sightedly. 'As I said yesterday though, it still appears to me that whoever injured him went to some lengths to ensure that he survived. I find it very strange. It is almost as if they were *operating* on him, rather than deliberately mutilating him, no matter how crudely. But why they should have amputated his legs and taken out his eyes, and yet taken every precaution not to kill him, I have no idea.'

'He's talking?' asked Jerry.

'Yes, he is. A little deliriously, I have to say, but I think it may be cathartic for him to go back in his mind and relive what was done to him. And of course it may be useful for you in your investigation, although that is not my prime consideration, as I am sure you appreciate.'

'Yes, of course, doc, but we don't want it done to nobody else,' said Jerry. 'I mean, you wouldn't want your whole hospital crowded out with blind legless blokes, would you? Bloody hell – that would be nearly as bad as the Queen's Arms on a Saturday night.'

Dr Gupta gave him a tight little smile that showed he didn't understand the joke but still appreciated that Jerry was having a dig at the priority he always gave to his patients. 'Come with me,' he said. 'We have now installed him in a private room. It is quieter, and also, the sight of his condition was causing some distress to the visitors of other patients.'

'Has he had any visitors himself?'

'We have received several phone calls enquiring about him from his relatives and his workplace, but we will not be permitting visits until we are confident of his continuing survival – or unless it becomes apparent that he does not have very much longer to live.'

'So it's still a bit touch-and-go?'

'Come and see for yourself.'

He took them up in the lift and along the second-floor corridor. Before he opened the door to Martin Elliot's room, he lifted his hand and said, 'He is calm at the moment. But I will have to ask you, if he becomes distressed, to leave the room immediately. His mental state is very important to his recovery.'

'Gotcha,' said Jerry.

Inside, Martin Elliot was lying propped up on his bed. He was still on a drip, but no longer being given a blood transfusion, and the stumps of his legs were protected by a metal cradle with a loose-woven blanket draped over it. A pretty young Filipino nurse was sitting at a small table in the corner, making notes in Martin's folder.

Dr Gupta went up to him and touched his shoulder. 'Martin... I have brought the two police officers I told you about. They are standing next to me now. If you feel able, and if you are willing, they would like to have a few words with you.'

'Yes, yes, of course,' said Martin, in a slurred voice.

Jamila stepped close to the bed and laid her hand on his arm. 'Mr Elliot... may I call you Martin? My name is Detective Sergeant Jamila Patel, and I have with me Detective Constable Jerry Pardoe. We are both extremely sorry to see the terrible injuries that you have suffered.'

'Just as well that *I* can't see them,' Martin told her. 'Never will, either.'

'Do you feel up to answering some questions? We have already talked to your colleagues Gemma Bright and Jim Feather and Newton Akamba. They've given us quite a good description of what happened in the sewer tunnel before your disappearance. What we really need to know is what happened after that.'

'Did they tell you that it all went dark?'

'Yes, they did. But then they said that some figures appeared. Luminous figures.'

'They were like children – and, yes, they were shining, although God knows how. I say children, but only because they were the same size as children. But they had all kinds of things wrong with them. Hunchbacked, one of them, and another had all her insides hanging out. It was unreal. It was... *ugh*, I can't describe it.'

'Yes, Martin, your colleagues described them in some detail. They even drew pictures of them for us. They said they attacked you – tried to pull off your helmets.'

Martin lifted one arm and flapped it as if he were still trying to beat the creatures off. 'They were so *strong*. All right, they weren't any bigger than children, but they grabbed hold of my sleeves and they pulled at my belt, and I couldn't get away from them. I heard the others shouting at me – Gemma and Jim – and I kicked and I struggled to get myself free, but I couldn't.'

Jerry had come around the other side of Martin's bed and pulled a chair across, so that he could sit close to him. 'What happened then, mate?' he asked him. 'Can you remember, or is it all still a bit of a blur?'

Martin turned his face toward him, even though his eyes were thickly bandaged with white gauze.

'I heard Gemma calling me again, but she sounded like she was further away. Then it all went dark again. I mean like *pitch*-dark. Totally black. Even the glow from the children died out, but they were still there, pulling me. I can't tell you how many there were, because I couldn't see them, but it felt as if there were dozens, all tugging at my suit and my belt and my boots and my hair. I'd lost my helmet by then – I don't know what happened to that.'

Martin was talking in a soft, hoarse monotone, strangely unemotional, as if he were reading a report on sewage flow to a meeting of Crane's board members. It seemed to Jerry that he was almost exploding to get to the point of what he was saying, yet was too technically minded to leave out any details, or to describe what happened out of sequence.

'They must have pulled me through the fatberg, because I could feel myself sliding against the grease and the rag. To begin with, my shoulder was scraping against the brickwork on the roof of the sewer. I began to get the feeling though, that there must be a whole network of different tunnels running through the fat, because sometimes I was sliding downward at quite a steep angle and other times they were dragging me upward. Some of those tunnels were okay to start with, reasonably wide, but after a while, we came to a long stretch of tunnel that was really tight and claustrophobic, and the children were struggling to pull me through it feet first. I could hardly breathe, and of course, the air stank, and I was sure that I was going to get jammed down there in the middle of that fatberg and suffocate.'

'How long did this go on for, Martin? Have you any idea?'

'I couldn't tell you for sure. It seemed to last for hours. It was totally dark, like I say, and I lost all sense of direction. I knew that the fatberg runs approximately south to north, but more than once, I felt that they were pulling me off sharply to the right or the left, and at times there was no fat at all, and they were pulling me through liquid sewage right up to my chin, so that I nearly swallowed it.'

Martin tried to sit up straighter, but when he did, he gritted his teeth in silent agony for a few seconds before letting himself drop back on to the pillows.

'Are you all right?' Jamila asked him. 'Shall I call the nurse for you?'

Martin shook his head. 'It's all right. I just forget sometimes that I haven't got legs any more.'

Jerry and Jamila stayed silent for a while to let Martin recover. There was no sound except for the endless beeping of his vital-signs monitor and the squeaking of trolley wheels in the corridor outside. The rain pattered soft and cold against the window, as if long-dead spirits were trying to get in, or at least trying to remind the living that they too, had once been alive.

Jerry held out a glass of water and guided Martin's hand toward it. Once Martin had taken a drink and cleared his throat, he said, 'At last they stopped dragging me along, and I was able to sit up, even though I was up to my arse in sewage. It was still dark at first, although I could hear the children all around me, splashing and talking to each other.'

'Could you hear what they were saying?'

'No, not really. They were whispering very quietly, like kids do when they don't want adults to overhear them. I did pick up a couple of snatches, but they were speaking in a very strange accent.'

'Any idea what kind of an accent? Can you describe it?'

'I don't know. I'm trying to hear it again in my head. If

anything, I'd say it was American, or West Country. Lots of rolling of "r"s. You know, almost like the way that pirates were supposed to speak.'

'Okay,' said Jamila. 'And then what?'

Martin paused and licked his lips. 'Then...' he said. '*Then...*'

They waited. Jerry looked across the bed at Jamila, because it was obvious that Martin was finding it hard to explain to them what he had encountered next. His hands jumped two or three times on the blanket as if he had been given a mild electric shock, and his head jerked too.

Standing by the window, Dr Gupta said quietly, 'I'm sorry, officers... I think it may be necessary for you to bring this questioning to a conclusion.'

Jerry stood up and pushed back his chair. At that moment though, Martin started to pant – faster and faster, as if he couldn't get enough oxygen.

'There's a *light*... it's off to the left... it's in that sewer that comes in from the left. It's dancing... jumping around... and it's green. It's like somebody's walking this way along the sewer, and they're carrying a green lamp. And I can *see* now... I can see that I'm sitting in this sewer chamber where two sewers join. It looks... it looks like the sewer chamber under New Cross Road... I'm sure of it...'

Jerry pulled back his chair and sat down. Martin groped frantically across the blanket until he found Jerry's hand, and he clenched it tight. He was still panting, and now and then, he gave a convulsive shudder. Jerry realised that behind the gauze bandages that covered his empty eye sockets, he was visualising whatever it was that he had encountered down in that sewer chamber, just as clearly as when it had first appeared in front of him. His fingers were icy cold, but perspiration was trickling down the sides of his cheeks.

'It's coming out... it's coming out of the sewer... and there's green light shining all around it... this bright green light, so that everything's green. The walls are green, the sewage is green. My hands are green. Everything's green.'

'What is it, Martin?' asked Jamila gently. 'What can you see?'

'Officers, please—' Dr Gupta repeated, stepping forward, but Jamila held out her arm to keep him back.

'It's... it's a *woman*, I think,' said Martin, so quietly that Jerry almost had to lip-read to follow what he was saying. 'A tall, tall woman. I can't see her face because she's wearing a hood... a hood and a cloak that's so long it's dragging through the sewage. She's coming up closer, but I still can't see her face...'

Martin's head dropped forward, and for almost half a minute, he said nothing, although he continued to breathe in quick, erratic snatches through his nose.

'I think that is all he has to tell you for now,' said Dr Gupta. 'Perhaps when he is stronger he will be able to tell you more. So, really, if you don't mind...'

Jerry tried to stand up again, but Martin wouldn't let go of his hand. Jerry tried two or three times to tug himself free, but before he could manage it, Martin abruptly lifted up his head again and whispered, '*She has a saw.*'

'Go on, Martin,' Jamila coaxed him. 'What kind of a saw?'

'It's like... it's like a tenon saw... but the end of it... the end is more pointed. She's taken it out from underneath her cloak, and she's holding it up like this.'

With that, he suddenly let go of Jerry's hand and lifted his right arm like a starter at a racetrack.

'She's coming nearer, and she's speaking to me... but I can't understand what she's saying. It doesn't make any sense. I'm freezing cold and the sewage is freezing cold and I feel numb all over and I can't move... why can't I *move*?'

Now, with his arm still raised, he turned his head slowly from side to side. 'They're coming up behind her... the children... the things that look like children... there's so many of them... they're crawling through the sewage, some of them... and some of them hopping like big toads... oh, my God!'

Martin began to shake violently, clonking the back of his head against the bed frame. The whole bed rattled and shook, and he waved his arms around so wildly that he ripped out the cannula for his intravenous drip. Jamila and Jerry backed away while Dr Gupta and the nurse bustled forward to restrain him. The nurse pinned his wrists down to the mattress, while Dr Gupta quickly opened the medicine cabinet beside the bed and took out a hypodermic syringe. He filled it from a small clear glass bottle and gave Martin an injection.

'Fosphenytoin,' Dr Gupta explained. 'This will relax his muscles.'

Martin shook three or four times more, but then he stopped shaking, his head tilted sideways, and he started to snore.

Dr Gupta looked across at Jerry and Jamila and pulled a face, as if to say, *Sorry, but this is the condition he's in. He's lucky to be alive at all, let alone alive and telling you what was done to him.*

'Perhaps we can come back later,' said Jamila. 'There's a lot more we need to ask him.'

'Well, perhaps. But I would prefer it if you were to wait until tomorrow. I want to see how he manages to get through the night – even though, for him, from now on, it will *always* be night.'

★

As they went down in the lift, Jerry said, 'Well, sarge? What did you think?'

'I really don't know, Jerry. I really don't know what to think.'

'Let's put it this way: if those three others hadn't sworn that they saw luminous children too, I would have put him down as delirious. Or a full-blown nutter.'

'Well, me too, I have to admit. But look what's been done to him, and the doctor definitely believes that it was done deliberately. You have to ask yourself why – why would anybody want to amputate a man's legs and put out both of his eyes? As a punishment? As a warning?'

'Could be. Or maybe it was a freak who gets a sexual kick out of mutilating people. When you see some of the things those S & M-ists get up to. A couple of months ago we had this schoolteacher in Streatham – Billings, his name was. He paid his dominatrix to cut off one of his fingers so that he could—'

'Jerry, I don't want to know. I don't think that what was done to Martin Elliot was anything to do with sadomasochism. Perhaps he was hallucinating. He said himself that for a long time he was being pulled through a very confined tunnel and that the air was polluted. The chances are that it contained a high percentage of methane. Then again, perhaps he was making it all up about the woman in the hood, with her saw, although I can't think of any logical reason why he should lie to us. He lost his legs somehow, even if this woman didn't do it. As you know, I can usually tell if somebody is lying. I can see their eyes turning black. But Martin Elliot no longer has eyes, so I couldn't say for sure.'

They left the lift and walked across the reception area. An old white-haired man in a shabby brown tweed coat watched them as they passed, as if he recognised them, which Jerry found strangely disturbing. He turned around when they reached the front doors, and the old man gave him a gap-toothed grin.

Jamila hadn't noticed him. As she buttoned up her coat, she said, 'What he was saying about that green light though – that rings true, doesn't it? That sounds almost the same as the green lights that we saw, and he couldn't have known about that, could he?'

'That's right. And he also said that once this spooky woman appeared and the sewer was lit up, he knew where he was... or at least, he thought he knew where he was. An inspection chamber under New Cross Road, where two sewers join together. That Gemma must know where he was talking about. We can send forensics down there to check it out.'

'I was thinking exactly that,' said Jamila. 'The doctor said that the stumps of his legs were cauterised, probably with some kind of red-hot iron. There might well be evidence of what was actually used to do it, or how it was heated. Scorch marks on the brickwork perhaps, or the remains of some combustible material, or ash. And there could well be some DNA from Martin Elliot's legs – blood, or bone fragments. Who knows? Perhaps even the severed legs themselves.'

'I don't know. Maybe. But I have the feeling that his legs were cut off because this woman wanted them. His eyes too.'

'Really? What for?'

'Don't ask me. It's a feeling, that's all. Maybe she's putting a monster together, like Doctor Frankenstein.'

He held open the door so that Jamila could step out into the rain. She turned up the collar of her raincoat and said, 'You know, Jerry, sometimes I can't believe the things that people do to each other in this world. Sometimes I want to quit this job and stay home by the fire and read a good book with my cat sitting on my lap and purring.'

'I didn't know you had a cat.'

'I don't.'

Jerry checked his watch. 'Listen, we've got plenty of time. Let's go across to the Warren BirthWell Centre, shall we? And check out this weird foetus that Walters is so worried about.'

'I don't really want to be taking on another case, Jerry. As if we don't have enough to do.'

'You saw the picture.'

'Yes, of course. But I found it very hard to believe that it was real. Even if it is, I don't see why it should be a matter for you and me. There are many deformed children born in Pakistan, for various reasons, but their doctors don't call the police.'

'Fair enough. But it wouldn't hurt just to take a butcher's, would it?'

'You are such a voyeur.'

'I thought that was part of our job. That, and sticking our noses in where they're not wanted.'

17

Susan Nicholls was awake now, although she was still under the influence of the midazolam that Dr Macleod had prescribed for her to relieve her pain. Her eyes were misty, and she was speaking in a dreamy murmur, as if she were floating out to sea. However, her heart rate and her respiration were almost back to normal, and Dr Macleod wanted to operate on her as soon as possible, before the foetus implanted itself even more tenaciously into the lining of her womb.

The anaesthetic room was quiet and dimly lit. When Dr Macleod and Dr Bhaduri came in, a red-haired nurse was standing beside Susan's trolley, holding her hand and talking to her.

Dr Macleod went up to her and smiled. 'Hallo, Susan. How are you feeling?'

'Like I'm dreaming. I still can't believe that I'm pregnant again.'

'As I said before, you are and you aren't. This is not a normal pregnancy. It's more like some invasive tissue that has to be removed.'

'It's not cancer, is it? You'd tell me if it was cancer.'

'No, I promise you it's not cancer. But we do need to remove it from your uterus immediately to relieve the pain you've been suffering and so that it doesn't threaten your general health.'

'It's not a baby, is it? I mean, it's not like a twin of the one I miscarried, that got left behind?'

Dr Macleod smiled again and shook his head. Before she was sedated, he had tried to explain to her why she had to have a C-section. He had told her that it was urgent, but he hadn't gone so far as to tell her that she was carrying inside her a foetus that possessed the face of an angel but the writhing limbs of a sea creature.

The door from the operating theatre swung open, and Duncan the anaesthetist came in, wiping his mouth on a paper napkin. Dr Macleod had never seen him look so serious, but then he knew in advance what they were going to be removing from Susan Nicholls's womb. It had been traumatic enough seeing it the first time, when it was lifted out of Chiasoka Oduwole.

'Ready for a little nap?' Duncan asked Susan, rubbing his hands together and trying to sound cheerful.

'I *will* be all right, won't I, doctor?' Susan asked Dr Macleod, lifting her head from the pillow. 'I'll be able to have other babies after this, won't I?'

'Of course, Susan. Absolutely no reason why not. Don't worry. You'll be fine. I'll see you later, when you come to.'

Dr Macleod and Dr Bhaduri left the anaesthetic room. They were walking along to the scrubs room to prepare themselves for surgery when Dr Macleod's iPhone pinged. He had been sent a text from the front desk, telling him that two detectives had arrived in reception and wanted to talk to him.

I'm going into theatre, he texted back. *Tell them to come back in an hour.*

'The police,' he told Dr Bhaduri.

'I thought you didn't want to call the police.'

'I didn't, but Professor Karounis has been fretting about a possible malpractice suit or even a prosecution for sexual assault and infanticide.'

'Professor Karounis is a good director but... I don't know – he can be so cautious sometimes. I wonder if he has an incident in his past that haunts him.'

'Nothing that I know of. The Warren Trust think very highly of him. But from my experience, you can get yourself into deeper trouble if you're too worried about legalities. Personally, I think we should have euthanised that foetus as soon as we took it out of Ms Oduwole. We could have told her it was stillborn. It was my fault entirely. It was the way it looked at me – that sweet, sweet face. It reminded me so much of my own daughter, when she was a baby. And the way it started to cry. I had a nightmare about it last night. I dreamed that I woke up, and instead of my wife, Beverly, lying on the pillow next to me, it was that foetus.'

They walked into the scrubs room and hung up their jackets. Dr Bhaduri obviously didn't know what to say, because Dr Macleod had never spoken to him so intimately before.

'After today though, no more nightmares,' said Dr Macleod, as he washed his hands and his forearms, staring at himself in the mirror over the washbasin and sticking out his lower lip as if he were challenging himself to a fight.

*

Dr Symonds and two nurses were already waiting for them when they entered the theatre, as well as the centre's most experienced midwife, Janet Horrocks. Susan Nicholls was unconscious on the operating table, lit up by the 130,000 lx surgical lamps as if she were lying on an altar.

From his seat on the opposite side of the table, Duncan gave Dr Macleod the thumbs up. Dr Macleod saw that the largest size of stainless-steel kidney dish had been placed next to the instruments, ready as before for the foetus to be dropped into it. *And what if it looks up at me appealingly, in the same way that it did last time? What if it starts to sob? I don't even know if it's human, but it has a human face, the face of a beautiful child. How am I going, coldbloodedly, to kill it?*

'Right,' he said. 'Let's do it.'

One of the nurses lifted the pale-blue sheet that was covering Susan Nicholls's stomach. Her stomach looked swollen, but that was to be expected after she had lost her baby as late as nineteen weeks. The other nurse handed Dr Macleod a scalpel, and he poised it over her skin to make the first incision.

He had only just started to cut, and the first thin runnel of blood was starting to slide down Susan Nicholls's side, when the surgical lamps started to flicker. He hesitated and looked across at Duncan, and then at Dr Bhaduri.

'We're not about to have a power cut, are we?'

'Could be a loose connection,' said Duncan. 'It's only the lamps though. The monitors aren't affected.'

Dr Macleod hesitated. The lamps flickered faster and faster, and gradually they began to shine a lurid green, instead of white. He stepped back from the operating table, both hands raised as if he were being arrested.

'What in the name of God is going on, Duncan?'

'I have no idea, doctor. The monitors are still working fine. I'll call maintenance. I never saw anything like this in my life.'

The whole theatre was lit with shuddering green light so that everything appeared to be jumping – the monitors, the operating table, even Dr Bhaduri and Dr Symonds and Janet Horrocks and the nurses. One of the nurses reached across and twisted off the light control, but the lamps continued to flicker just as brightly. She twisted it again and again, but it had no effect on the lamps at all.

'I'm sorry, doctor,' she said. 'It just doesn't work.'

'Right,' said Dr Macleod. 'I think we'd better call a halt to this operation and get the patient out of here asap. Duncan? Have you got through to maintenance?'

Duncan held up his phone and said, 'I'm getting nothing but a buzzing noise. I think the lamps are interfering with the signal.'

'Nurse Harris... can you go and find somebody from maintenance, quick as you like,' said Dr Macleod. 'Janet... Nurse Yeom, let's get the patient disconnected and into the recovery room.'

Nurse Harris went over to the theatre's double doors,

but when she pushed them, they stayed firmly shut. She pushed them again, but they still wouldn't budge, so Dr Bhaduri went over and rammed them with his shoulder. He rammed them a second time, so hard that he rubbed his shoulder in pain, and then he kicked them, three times, but they refused to open.

'It's like they're locked. But look at the bolts – they're not locked at all.'

Dr Macleod was about to go around the operating table to help him when he became aware of a dark shadowy swirl in the corner of the theatre. He stopped and frowned at it through the flickering green light. At first it looked like nothing but smoke, but gradually it began to take on the shape of a figure. He reached over and touched Dr Symonds's arm to get her attention, and pointed to it.

Within a few seconds, the swirl had formed itself into what looked like a tall, hooded woman in a long cloak, although her outline was blurred, and through her cloak, Dr Macleod could still faintly see the white metal cabinet in the corner behind her.

The woman raised her smoky left arm and appeared to point at Susan Nicholls, still lying anaesthetised on the operating table, although Duncan had now removed her oxygen mask. Susan Nicholls stirred. Her hands twitched, and she gave a violent shiver from head to foot. Then, as if somebody invisible had taken hold of her shoulders and lifted her, she sat up.

Janet Horrocks made a move toward her, obviously worried that she might try to climb off the operating table and hurt herself, but Dr Macleod held her back.

'Wait... I don't know what's happening here, Janet, but wait.'

Duncan slowly rose from his stool, staring at the ghostly figure in the corner. 'Doctor—'

'*Wait*, Duncan.'

Dr Macleod felt that the whole world as he knew it was falling to pieces. He was usually so calm and sane and systematic: he had to be, for the sake of his patients. But what was happening now in this operating theatre – this flashing green light, these doors that wouldn't open, the way in which Susan Nicholls had risen from the table – it was all madness. As mad as it was though, his logical mind told him that there had to be some reason behind it, and that they should hold back and see if that reason became clear.

Susan Nicholls opened her eyes. She turned to Dr Macleod and her lip was curled in contempt.

'You will not touch me,' she told him, in a throaty voice. 'You will not cut me open.'

Dr Macleod took a step back toward her. 'Susan?'

'Stay away from me. Lay down your knife.'

'Who's that talking, Susan? That's not you, is it?'

'You will not cut me open. If you try to cut me open and take out my nestling, you will live to regret it for the remainder of your days.'

'I'm going to ask you again, Susan. Who's telling you to say that?' He pointed to the shadowy hooded figure in the corner. 'Is it her?'

Susan Nicholls didn't answer. After a few moments she sank back on to the operating table – again, as if some invisible helper were gently lowering her down.

As soon as she lay back and closed her eyes, there was an ear-splitting crackle, and all the surgical lamps shattered, showering the operating table in hundreds of shards of glass. For a few seconds, the theatre was plunged into absolute darkness. Nurse Harris screamed.

The emergency lights blinked on. When they did, the theatre looked so utterly normal that it was almost a shock. The shadowy hooded figure had vanished from the corner, and Susan Nicholls was lying with her eyes still closed, breathing quietly and steadily. The only evidence of what had happened was all the glittering splinters of glass that were scattered over the sheets.

Dr Macleod and everybody else in the theatre looked at each other, stunned, not knowing what to say.

At last, Dr Symonds whispered, 'Oh, my God. I mean – *oh – my – God*. What was that? I can't stop myself shaking.'

'I don't know what it was. Some kind of hallucination?'

'How could it be a hallucination if we all saw it?'

'Perhaps it was a ghost,' said Dr Bhaduri. 'The spirit of some person who has died but who has not been able to leave this Earth. My grandmother used to tell me about such phantoms.'

'Whatever it was, this poor young woman still has that thing inside her,' said Dr Symonds. 'What did she call it? A "nestling". But we can't leave it there, can we? Who knows what it might do to her, when it grows?'

Dr Macleod pressed his hand over his mouth. He didn't know what to think. Dr Symonds was right; they couldn't leave that creature to develop inside Susan Nicholls's womb – not only for her sake, but for the creature's sake too. He had aborted foetuses far less malformed than this thing, and the strange beauty of its face was no justification for allowing such a creature to live.

But he couldn't help thinking about the threat that he had been given – by Susan Nicholls herself, or by some kind of ventriloquism from that hooded apparition? *If you try to cut me open and take out my nestling, you will live to regret it for the remainder of your days.*

18

Jerry and Jamila had been sitting in the waiting room for over an hour when Jamila's phone warbled. It was Gemma Bright, and she was ringing to tell them that Crane's engineers had completed their examination of the sewer between Peckham High Road and the southern end of the fatberg.

As far as the engineers could make out, the sewer was safe for the Met's forensic team to go down and carry out whatever tests they thought were necessary. The LED lighting had remained steady and white. The methane and hydrogen sulphide levels were both well within the specified safety limits. There had been no strange draughts or inexplicable noises, and there was no obvious structural damage to the brickwork that might cause a collapse.

The engineers had been categorically instructed not to dig into the fatberg or to remove any unusual items that they might come across during their examination, so they hadn't tried to find the woman's severed hand, and they hadn't picked up any of the keys that were still lying under the surface of the sewage. They had shone high-powered lights into the space between the fatberg and the ceiling of the sewer, but they had seen nothing unusual, only dripping bricks and torn grey shreds of toilet paper.

Jamila called the forensics laboratory in Lambeth Road to tell them that they could send a team down into the sewer as soon as they liked.

'Probably tomorrow morning now,' she told Jerry.

'Rather them than me, sarge. I don't want to go down another sewer as long as I live. The pen-and-ink's enough to kill you, let alone having half of Timpson's chucked at you.' He checked his watch. 'What are we going to do? Hang on a bit longer or call it a day?'

'I thought you were dead set on finding out more about this peculiar foctus.'

'Well, yes, but I'm absolutely Hank Marvin. My stomach thinks my throat's been cut.'

'Didn't I tell you to have a good breakfast?'

'If I hadn't run out of bacon, I would have had bacon, and eggs, if I'd hadn't run out of eggs. All I had was a couple of Marmite biscuits, and they'd gone soft.'

'Well, let's give it ten more minutes. I have to say that I'm quite curious to know more about this foetus myself.'

Jerry was just reaching over for a copy of *Country Life* magazine when Professor Karounis entered the waiting room. He was wearing his usual grey three-piece suit and red bow tie, and he smelled strongly of Christian Dior aftershave, so Jerry guessed that he must be off to some function somewhere.

'You are the detectives? Allow me to introduce myself. I am Barak Karounis, the director of the Warren BirthWell Centre.'

'How do you do, sir. I'm Detective Sergeant Patel and this is Detective Constable Pardoe. We were notified that you called the police about a rather unusual medical situation, and that two officers came down from Walworth to talk to you about it.'

'That is correct. They told us they would have to refer the matter to more specialist officers, and I presume that is who you are. If you would like to come up to my office, I will tell you more. But I have to say to you right away that in the past half hour the situation has become more than simply unusual. To be frank with you, it has become critical.'

Professor Karounis led them up to his office. Dr Macleod was there, sitting in front of the professor's desk. His hair was still sticking up from when he had pulled off his surgical cap, and he looked pale and distracted, as if he had just been sick.

'Please, take a seat,' said Professor Karounis. 'This is Dr Macleod, our senior OB surgeon. I will perhaps leave it to him to explain what has occurred.'

Dr Macleod nodded to Jamila and Jerry and then leaned forward, his fingers laced together. He didn't look at either of them when he spoke, only down at the carpet and around the room. Jerry recognised his posture and the way he was talking as a clear indication that he was in shock. He was like a witness to a fatal road accident, almost disbelieving what he had seen.

'I gather you know about the malformed foetus and how it appears to have lodged itself inside the womb of another female patient?'

'Yes, we do,' said Jamila. 'And we have seen the pictures of it too. I don't really know what to say about it. It's extraordinary.'

'It's far beyond extraordinary, detective. We were attempting to abort the foetus because of the acute physical and psychological risk it was presenting to our patient, Ms Susan Nicholls. She had already suffered a late-stage miscarriage.'

He paused and licked his lips as if his mouth had dried up.

'You say "attempting",' Jerry prompted him. 'That leads me to think that something's gone pear-shaped.'

'If you mean that I didn't succeed in completing the procedure, then you're absolutely right. It's very difficult for me to describe what happened, because I have never experienced anything like it in my life. If there hadn't been six other witnesses – my two assistant obstetricians, my anaesthetist, my midwife and two nurses – I seriously would have believed that I was suffering from some kind of psychological breakdown.'

'So, doctor, please – tell us about it,' Jamila coaxed him.

'I had just started my first incision when the lamps over the operating table started to flicker, faster and faster. At first I thought it was a short-circuit, but then the lamps turned green. I have no idea at all how they could have done that.'

'They turned *green*?' Jerry asked him. He looked across at Jamila, and Jamila looked back at him with what he privately called her 'oh, shit' expression, even though she never swore.

'Yes, bright lime green. And they kept on flickering. And it was then that a woman appeared in the corner of the operating theatre. Perhaps *materialised* is a more accurate word. She looked at first as if she was made out of nothing but smoke. Even when she had taken shape, I could still see through her.'

'What did she look like? Facially, I'm talking about. Would you be able to give us a description for an EvoFIT?'

'No. I couldn't see her face. She was wearing a high pointed hood and what looked like a cloak – although, as I say, she was partially transparent.'

'If you couldn't see her face, and she was so insubstantial, how do you know it was a woman?' asked Jamila.

'It was her shape and her general bearing, I suppose. She was quite tall for a woman, but she had sloping shoulders, and when she extended one arm her gesture was very feminine. I suppose it could have been a man, but for some reason I was in no doubt at all that she was female.'

'And everybody else in that operating theatre saw her too?'

'Yes. And they all agreed with me that she was a woman.'

'Tell me, doctor,' said Jamila, 'how do you think she materialised, as you put it? Do you think she might have been a trick of the light? If the lights were flickering, and they had turned green, do you think she might have been an optical illusion?'

Dr Macleod was still looking down at the carpet, but he shook his head emphatically and said, 'No. She wasn't solid, but she was there. I suppose she might conceivably have been a hologram, but a hologram would have needed a projector, wouldn't it? The smoke could have acted as a screen for a hologram, but where did the smoke come from, even if it *was* smoke? Whatever she was made of, it twisted and turned, but it didn't disperse, not in the way that smoke would have done.'

'And you told me that your patient sat up and spoke, did you not, Dr Macleod?' put in Professor Karounis. 'You told me that she warned you not to continue with your incision and not to attempt to remove the foetus.'

'Yes,' said Dr Macleod. 'She said that if I aborted it, I would regret it for the rest of my life. She called it her "nestling" – almost as if she considered herself to be its surrogate mother.'

'So it's still inside her?' asked Jerry. 'But what's going to happen to her if you leave it there and allow it to grow?'

'We can't leave it there. There's absolutely no question of that. It's a monstrosity already, as you've seen for yourselves. God alone knows what it would turn into if we let it develop to full term.'

'But her threats don't worry you?'

'I don't see what she could do to me... or what that hooded woman could do to me either. I had the feeling that it was *her* talking – the hooded woman – using Susan Nicholls like a ventriloquist's dummy. But even if she's real and not an hallucination, what could she be made of? She must be formed out of some kind of ectoplasm, like those spirits that Victorian mediums used to conjure up. How could ectoplasm hurt me?'

He raised his eyes and said, 'No. As soon as we've prepped theatre number two, and I'm satisfied that Susan

Nicholls can withstand a second general anaesthetic, I intend to operate.'

'And what will you do with the foetus, once you've taken it out of her?' asked Jamila. 'The last time you let it live, and look how *that* turned out.'

'Exactly, and this is one of the reasons I wanted the police to be aware of the situation,' said Professor Karounis. 'In the eyes of the law, is this foetus a viable human being or not? We have no way of knowing the exact date when it was conceived by Mrs Oduwole. She had a termination in April, so it could not have been a residual twin that survived that termination. In any case, such an event has occurred only about once worldwide in several million births. She claimed that she'd had no sexual relations after that termination, but if she was not being truthful, it is arguable that this foetus could be older than twenty-four weeks, and that, of course, is the legal limit for an abortion.'

'We'll be consulting the Met's lawyers, of course,' said Jamila. 'But judging by that picture you showed us, I think it is highly unlikely that there would be any repercussions if it failed to survive.'

Professor Karounis turned to Doctor Macleod. 'There, Stuart – you have the green light to go ahead.'

Jamila said, 'Ah, talking of green lights, Dr Macleod – I would advise you to watch your back for a while after you have performed this termination.'

'I don't follow you, detective. You don't mean those threats that Susan Nicholls made against me could be serious? As I've said, I don't see how.'

'Let me simply say that we are investigating some recent

incidents that bear similarities to what took place in your operating theatre. The appearance of the hooded woman, and the lights turning green. I can't tell you for certain yet if there's any connection. Perhaps there is no connection at all. But I would suggest that you keep your eyes open for anything unusual.'

'Such as what?'

'Well, for instance, a woman in a hood who appears out of nowhere,' said Jerry. 'If that had been me, the very least I would have done was fill my under-grundies.'

***

As they drove back to Peckham, Jamila said, softly but emphatically, 'He was telling the truth, that doctor. And so was Martin Elliot.'

'Yeah, I thought so too,' said Jerry. 'But I'll tell you something for nothing – I'd feel a damn sight more cheerful if the two of them had been making it all up.'

'You are not the only one, Jerry. When they showed us that picture of the foetus, it immediately set me to wondering if it could be connected in any way with those deformed children who attacked Martin Elliot and Gemma Bright and their co-workers down in the sewer. After what we have heard today though, it certainly seems possible, don't you think?'

'I don't know. The more we find out about this, the nuttier it gets.'

'When *we* went down into the sewer, we didn't see any of those children, neither did we see any hooded woman. But we heard that awful moaning, didn't we? And we felt that draught blowing, and those keys were thrown at us, and of course we saw the lights turn green. I find it very hard to believe that it was nothing more than a coincidence.'

'Well, right. Martin Elliot saw a hooded woman lit up all green, and so did Dr Macleod. I suppose the only difference is that she didn't take out a saw and cut off Dr Macleod's legs then pull out his eyeballs, so he should thank his God for that.'

They passed the Crooked Well pub and stopped at the red light at the junction of Peckham Road. For a long moment neither of them spoke. Then Jamila said, 'It was that *one* word that really caught my attention. You know how that can happen? You're interviewing a suspect and they inadvertently say one word that unlocks the whole case, even if you don't realise it, not straight away.'

'Sure. I know what you mean. So what was the word?'

'"Nestling". It suggested to me that this foetus was being taken care of, like a mother bird takes care of her fledglings. It wasn't simply struggling to survive on its own – like, for example, a beetle will scurry away for dear life if you try to step on it.'

'And you think maybe this smoky ghost woman is the one who's looking after it?'

'Dr Macleod felt very strongly, didn't he, that it wasn't his patient who was threatening him if he carried on with his Caesarean, but *her*. Remember that his patient was under a general anaesthetic, and yet somehow, she managed to sit upright and speak.'

'I don't know,' said Jerry, as the traffic lights changed to green and he turned right into Peckham Road. 'It's not just bonkers, it's double bonkers. Treble bonkers. Bonkers to the nth power.'

As they turned, Jamila touched his shoulder and said, 'Look – over there, on the corner.'

Jerry said, 'Hang on,' because the van in front of him had come to an abrupt stop. A curly black mongrel had run across the road in front of it and was now sprinting away along the wet pavement as if all the demons in Hell were after it.

'Blimey, I should have had a bet on that dog.'

'But look,' Jamila insisted. 'There, in that doorway.'

Jerry looked across the road and saw that five children were clustered in the doorway of Elite Shoes. Two of them were quite tall and looked as if they were ten or eleven years old. The other three were much smaller. But all of them appeared to be afflicted in some way. One of the smallest had an abnormally oversized head, as if she were suffering from macrocephaly, and the tallest had one shoulder much higher than the other, sticking up at a sharp angle.

What struck Jerry more than anything else, though, was that they all appeared to be wearing nothing but soiled white nightgowns, and they were barefoot, even though it was drizzling with rain and the temperature couldn't have been higher than eight or nine degrees.

'Pull over,' said Jamila, although Jerry had already switched on the car's flashers and was steering over to the kerb. He parked, and they climbed out and crossed over the road, with Jamila lifting her hand to hold up the traffic.

By the time they had reached the opposite side of the

road though, the five children had fled from the entrance
to the shoe shop and around the corner into Grove Lane.
Jerry and Jamila went after them, but when they turned
the corner, there was no sign of the children anywhere. The
street was wet and glistening under the street lights, but
apart from two cars that were waiting at the traffic lights
and an elderly woman pushing a shopping trolley, it was
deserted. There was no sign of the children anywhere, even
though there was nowhere that they could have hidden
themselves – no shop doorways or front gardens or side
alleyways.

Jerry stopped, and Jamila came up to join him, panting.

'Where have they gone?' she asked him. 'They can't
have vanished into thin air. It's not possible.'

They walked on a little further, but then they stopped
again.

'It's no use,' said Jerry. 'Wherever they've gone, we're
not going to find them.'

'But why did they run away? They looked wet and
cold and miserable. They didn't even have any shoes. You
would have thought they wanted to be helped.'

'I think they knew who we were, and that's why they
ran away.'

'What do you mean? We're not wearing uniforms.'

'Well, what were they doing there, in that doorway?
They were looking across at us, weren't they? It's
almost like they were waiting there to watch us go by. You
know, like keeping an eye on us to see where we went.'

'That's ridiculous.'

'I know it is, but did you see the state of them? They

were all deformed, just like the kids that dragged Martin Elliot off. One of them looked exactly like one of the drawings that Gemma Bright did of them – that kid with the bloody great bonce.'

They crossed back over the road and climbed into their car.

'So what do we do now?' asked Jerry.

'I don't know. We could send out some officers to look for them, but I think that would be fruitless, and a waste of time and money.'

Jerry started the engine, but before he could drive off, Jamila said, 'Did you ever see that film *The Third Man*?'

'I've heard of it, but I've never seen it. Orson Welles, wasn't it?'

'That's the one. He plays Harry Lime, who's a drug dealer in Vienna just after the Second World War. He's followed, but when he's followed, he always manages to disappear. *Poof*, and he is gone! But the way he disappears is down into the sewers, and that's where they eventually catch him.'

'I've got a horrible feeling about this,' Jerry told her. 'A horrible, horrible feeling that we'll be going back down those stinky sewers again and again until we find out what the hell is going on. My sister always told me I was going to end up in the shit one day. I never knew how right she was.'

19

Only five minutes after she had arrived at the station the next morning, Jamila was called by Dr Macleod's secretary, Glynis.

'The doctor asked me to tell you that he's postponed a second attempt to operate on Susan Nicholls. She's still suffering from hypertension after yesterday's anaesthesia. If she's well enough, he may try again later today.'

'All right. But please let me know if he does. I would like to be there, or at least close at hand, if I can.'

Jamila sat down and prised the lid off her Starbucks cappuccino. She had slept for only two hours last night because she hadn't been able to stop thinking about the deformed children that she and Jerry had seen running around the corner on their way back from the BirthWell Centre, and about Dr Macleod's description of the smoky hooded woman who had appeared in the operating theatre.

What unsettled her about the hooded woman was that it reminded her of a story that her grandmother in Peshawar used to tell her about witches called Churels. These were the spirits of women who had died during pregnancy or childbirth, who rose up from their graves to haunt those who had caused their death and the death of their baby.

They were shape-shifters, the Churels. Sometimes they appeared as animals or as pretty young girls in white dresses, but at other times they looked like hideous hags with their faces masked by coarse black hair. Sometimes too, they materialised as nothing more than spirals of black smoke.

All the same, she told herself, *they were stories*. She was open-minded about strange events that seemed to defy any rational explanation, but she was a highly trained police detective too, and first and foremost, she believed in evidence, no matter how irrational, or how strange.

Jerry came into the office, looking almost as tired as she felt, holding a half-eaten chicken-and-mushroom slice in one hand and a copy of the *Express* in the other. He hung up his raincoat behind the door, then he slumped down opposite her and said, 'Bloody hell. Nightmares, or what? I dreamt I was in a fish and chip shop, and when I opened up my chips that foetus-thing was lying there looking up at me. It jumped out the wrapper and ran off across the floor.'

Jamila shook her head sympathetically. 'Myself, I could hardly sleep at all.'

'Hardly surprising. I mean, I can't get my head round any of this. Like, what's the motive? Even the weirdest offences have a motive. Look at that gay bloke who killed his husband because he kept putting the wooden spoons in the dishwasher.'

'This is not necessarily about motive, Jerry, but it's critical that we try to understand what is really going on here. It will not help us simply to dismiss all these events as "supernatural". Not before we have exhausted every other possibility. The more I think about them, the more convinced I am that what we saw in the sewer and this foetus and those children we saw in the street, they're all somehow connected, as we talked about yesterday. And it seems to me that the sewers are central to what is going on.'

'So what's your thinking?'

'Of course we'll have to wait for the forensic reports, but the explanation could be that there has been some unusual chemical spillage that has released a toxic gas – you know, like the Bhopal disaster in India in 1984. That was caused by pesticide leaking into the air, but perhaps *this* gas is like an airborne version of thalidomide, and it can cause severe malformation of unborn children. After Bhopal there were countless stillbirths and children with muscular and exoskeletal growth problems, as well as brain damage. But perhaps this gas can also cause mass hallucinations. Hence this hooded woman that Martin Elliot and Dr Macleod both believe that they saw.'

'That's possible, I suppose. But how can a hallucination drag you nearly a mile through a sewer and then saw your legs off and pull out your eyes?'

'It can't, of course. But it could have been a real person doing it, and Martin Elliot was hallucinating that it was some kind of spectre.'

'Well, all right. Down the sewers is one thing. But how did this gas get into the operating theatre at the BirthWell, so that Dr Macleod hallucinated?'

'I have no idea, Jerry. I am only theorising. But I was brought up on stories of demons and evil spirits, and I know that for the most part they are only an excuse for the cruelty and the negligence and the misdemeanours of men. It wasn't ghosts who killed sixteen thousand innocent people at Bhopal, it was the careless release of a cloud of methyl isocyanate.'

'But the keys? What about the keys?'

Jamila's Skype rang, and she leaned across to her laptop to answer it. DC O'Brien appeared on her screen, sitting at his desk in his shirtsleeves. DCI Walters was standing in the background, talking on his phone and repeatedly waving a ball pen as if he were conducting a church choir.

'DS Patel? Oh, good morning. DC Pardoe told me yesterday that things at the BirthWell didn't quite go according to plan.'

'No, you're right. They didn't. Did he tell you why?'

'Not in any detail, no. Just that the surgeon might have to put the operation on hold.'

Jamila looked across at Jerry, who now had his mouth full. She was quietly relieved that he had refrained from telling DC O'Brien that Susan Nicholls's abortion had been interrupted by the appearance of what had looked like a ghost. After Jamila and Jerry's first case together, when they had confronted virus-infected clothing that had seemed to take on a life of its own, some officers in their Basic Command Unit still regarded the two of them as slightly cuckoo. That was why these investigations had been assigned to them, she was sure of it. Nobody else wanted to have it on their service record that they had spent weeks chasing foetuses with eight legs and hooded figures made of smoke.

'So how can I help you?' Jamila asked DC O'Brien.

'You're going to love this. We've just had reports of two more. One from Streatham nick and the other from Camberwell.'

'Two more what?'

'Two more of them foetuses. Not exactly the same as that one that they're operating on at the BirthWell, but sort of similar.'

'Are you serious? Where did they come from?'

'One of the foetuses came from a young Pakistani woman. Apparently, she tried to give herself a C-section to get it out. She's still alive but she's in intensive care at King's and her condition's critical. The other foetus is hard to believe, to be honest with you. A young white woman claims that it killed her cat and then tried to crawl inside her. Lucky for her, her boyfriend came home and pulled it out of her.'

'It killed her *cat*?' said Jerry. 'You're having a giraffe, aren't you?'

'That's what she said, apparently.'

'How is she?' asked Jamila.

'Shocked, naturally, and she's been given a check-up, but no serious injury.'

'So where are they, these foetuses?'

DC O'Brien held up a photograph of the squirrel-like foetus that had been cut out of Joya and then a picture of the blue-eyed foetus that Michael had managed to extricate from Jenny.

'*Ya Khuadaya*,' Jamila breathed. 'They are not still alive, are they? Where are they now?'

'We had both of them sent over to the forensic lab at St George's. And – yes – the last we heard they were still living and breathing. We've called in a forensic pathologist to take a look at them. Dr Pocztomski. He's the leading pathologist in the south-east group, and he doesn't only examine dead bodies but victims with serious injuries too. And foetuses. Unfortunately, he's not available today, but he'll be there tomorrow about one o'clock, and here's his number if you want to make contact.'

When Jamila had switched off her Skype, Jerry said, 'Gordon Bennett. Two more. It looks like you might be right, and this *is* some sort of toxic gas escape.'

'If it is, we need to know as soon as possible what type of gas we are talking about. We might even have to call for people all around Peckham to be evacuated, especially expectant mothers. Let me get in touch with Lambeth and see what progress they're making with the forensics.'

It took Jamila nearly ten minutes to find somebody at the forensics laboratory at Lambeth Road who could give her an update on the team who had been assigned to examine the sewer along Southampton Way. A lab assistant with a thick Welsh accent told her that there were eight of them, and they had just called in to say they would have completed their preliminary investigation in about an hour or so.

'Right,' said Jamila. 'Let's go and meet up with them. And then this afternoon we can go over to St George's and see this Dr Posthumous, or whatever his name is, and see what he thinks about these foetuses.'

'Oh well,' said Jerry, finishing his chicken-and-mushroom slice and slapping his hands together. 'I suppose it beats chasing after kids who keep shanking each other.'

20

They had intended to walk along Peckham High Street to Southampton Way, because it would have taken them less than ten minutes, but the skies had turned as black as charcoal and lightning was dancing over the rooftops. As they stepped out onto the front porch of the police station, they were deafened by a bellow of thunder directly overhead, and rain started to hammer down so hard that the gutters in the street were immediately flooded and water started to spout from the police station roof.

'The gods are angry about something or other,' said Jerry, as they went out of the back door to the car park and climbed into his Mondeo. 'Chelsea thrashed the Gunners 4–1 last night, that's probably it.'

He turned into Peckham High Street, but almost immediately, he had to slow down behind a bus. Standing at the bus stop, he could have sworn, he saw the same shabby old man in the brown tweed coat who he had seen in the vestibule of King's College Hospital when they had visited Martin Elliot. The man was staring at him, and just before Jerry was able to move off, he gave him the same gap-toothed grin as well as a sly wink, as if he knew him.

'I think I'm losing it, sarge.'

'What do you mean?'

'I just saw the same old geezer I saw at King's yesterday, standing by that bus stop.'

'Coincidence, Jerry. Or else he's a lookalike. You have to admit that one old man can easily be mistaken for another. All the elders in my village look like clones.'

'No, this was him all right.'

'Jerry, there is no law against him visiting the hospital one day and catching a bus in the high street the next.'

'I know. But right at the moment when *I* happen to be passing? World of weird.'

The rain continued to drum down so hard that Jerry had to keep the windscreen wipers whacking away at top speed all the way to Peckham Road. When they arrived, they saw that the forensic team had erected a large blue vinyl tent over the manhole, and that three of them were standing around outside it in their white Tyvek suits. Four white Forensic Services vans were parked on the pavement in a line, and he parked in front of them.

They hurried back to the tent, and one of the team lifted the flap for them so that they could go inside. The noise of the rain clattering on the vinyl was so loud they had to raise their voices. Jerry already knew two of the crime scene investigators, Phil Mullins and Margaret Broadbent, and so he introduced Jamila. Gemma Bright was there too, along with Jim Feather. Gemma looked pale and cold and washed out, and when Jerry asked her, 'All right?' she gave him nothing more than a half-hearted shrug.

'No word of a lie, this is the strangest bloody crime

scene I've ever had to examine, like – *ever*,' said Margaret Broadbent. She came from Durham originally, so she spoke in a broad northern accent. 'I've been down collapsed mines before but never down a blocked-up sewer. I'm going to take a week-long bath in Chanel No.5 after this, and I'll still be worried what I smell like.'

'So how is your examination progressing?' asked Jamila. 'We were told that you were almost finished.'

'We've dug up a whole mess of stuff we need to take back to the lab so that we can scrutinise it in more detail. There's the keys, of course. We've found well over sixty of them under the surface of the sewage, scattered over a distance of about seventy-five metres. Sixty, can you believe it? They're all pretty similar to that one key you fetched out yourself, although every one of them is slightly different. Some of them have stars on and some have crescent moons and others have faces. Yes, I said "faces", although they had plenty of *that* on them too.

'The keys we'll be sending off to Cullen's – they're an antique lock and key specialist in Kensington. With any luck, they should be able to tell us where the keys came from and how old they are and what they were supposed to open.'

'Have you found a woman's amputated hand? It had orange nail varnish and what looked like a gold wedding ring.'

Margaret Broadbent shook her head. 'We've dug up several items of jewellery, as well as kids' toys and sex aids and the remains of more bloody pets than you could shake a stick at. Why people don't take their unwanted kittens to a shelter instead of flushing them down t'toilet, I'll never work out.'

'There seem to be passages or tunnels running through the fatberg. Do you know how these were dug out? Or were they caused by the natural flow of sewage?'

'Some are obviously natural, because the sewage usually finds a way to keep flowing, but some of them look as if they may have been clawed out by hand. In places, you can see that the saponified fat appears to have deep fingermarks in it, and even some broken fingernails. But I wouldn't like to say for sure until we've studied all the photographs we've taken. Some of the surfaces that we've examined we're also going to print out in 3D.'

Gemma said, 'Tomorrow we're going to start clearing out the fatberg with high-pressure hoses, weather permitting, but two or three of the forensic team are going to be staying with us in case anything else turns up. You know, apart from keys, and kittens.'

Phil Mullins checked his watch. 'We've got five of our team still down there, giving the sewer a last going-over. They should be out in a couple of minutes.'

'Newton's down there too – our lighting and camera man,' said Gemma.

'Bloody hell,' said Jerry. 'After all the fun and games we had down there the last time? I've got to admire his nerve.'

Phil Mullins bent over the open manhole and shouted out, 'Terry? How's it going?'

He waited, with his head cocked to one side, listening, but there was no reply – only the trickling sound of sewage.

'I thought he was almost back,' he said, and unhooked

his radio. 'Terry? Where are you now, mate? I thought you said you were just about finished.'

The only answer was a loud crackling noise, and he held up his handset so that everybody else in the tent could hear it, even over the rain.

'Some kind of interference,' said Jim Feather. 'We get that sometimes, in a thunderstorm.'

'Yes, but he should be almost back by now. The last we heard he was pretty much winding up.'

He slapped his radio hard into the palm of his hand then tried calling the forensic team again. 'Terry? Janice? Hallo? Can you hear me?'

The loud crackling continued, but then they heard another sound, and this was coming from the manhole. It started as a thin, edgy whistling, like the wind on a stormy night, although it rapidly descended in pitch to a low, ghostly moan – the same moan they had heard the last time they had ventured into the sewer. The flickering white LED lights that had been reflected from the sewage directly below the open manhole began to shine an acidic green.

'Oh my God, it's happening again!' said Gemma. 'You need to get your team out of there right now! I mean it!'

Phil Mullins knelt down over the manhole and shouted out, 'Terry! Can you hear me? Get the hell out of there pronto! *Terry!*'

There was still no answer. The moaning was growing louder, and the green lights were flickering even brighter so that the whole of the inside of the tent was lit up in epileptic green, which made them all look as if they were jiggling and jumping. Phil Mullins turned to Margaret Broadbent and said, 'I'm going down there. Maybe the methane level's spiked, and they've all been knocked unconscious.'

Jim Feather said, 'Here – I'll fetch you a breathing pack. And I'll come down with you.'

'I'll get help from the fire station,' said Gemma. 'If they're unconscious, all six of them, you won't be able to carry them all out on your own.'

The Peckham fire station was no further than the opposite side of the road, and she lifted the tent flap to go over and alert them. As she stepped outside though, they heard a rushing noise and chilly foetid air started to blow into the tent, as if an underground train were hurtling toward them along the sewer. A huge fountain of sewage exploded out of the manhole, knocking both Gemma and Phil Mullins off their feet and sending Jamila and Jerry and Margaret Broadbent staggering backward. It blasted the tent over sideways with a clatter of aluminium poles, and it spouted across the street, thousands of gallons of stinking brown water. It was more than water though. Out of the fountain, lumps of faeces spattered onto the ground all around them, and then larger lumps, which rolled across the pavement and into the gutters.

'What's happening?' Gemma screamed at Jim Feather.

Jim Feather had one hand lifted to shield himself from the random lumps that kept dropping out of the sewage. All he could do was shake his head.

'The tide!' he shouted back. 'It could be the tide! Maybe it's a freak tide, and they've closed the Thames Barrier, and it's all backing up!'

'How can we stop it?'

'We can't! Not if it's the tide!'

Another lump dropped with a splash at Jim Feather's feet, and when he looked down at it, he saw that it was a torso. It was headless, although it still had a pipe-like neck, and its lungs and its chocolate-coloured liver were still hanging out of it.

Jerry was standing next to him and he saw it too, and when he looked all around him, he realised that all the larger lumps that were falling out of the fountain were pieces of human bodies. Heads, hands, arms, legs and feet. Half a ribcage. A woman's pelvis, wound around with shreds of torn white Tyvek. They were so slathered in shiny dark-brown sewage that it had taken him a few moments to understand what they were.

'Oh my God oh my God oh my *God*!' screamed Gemma. Newton's video camera came tumbling onto the ground right beside her, with its light still lit, followed almost immediately by Newton's left arm, ripped off at the shoulder, but with his bloody grey T-shirt still wound tightly around it.

Traffic along the Peckham Road had come to a standstill, and on the far side of the road, a small crowd of onlookers had already gathered, staring at the fountain without comprehending at first what it was. It was only when sewage started to flood the opposite gutter that they smelled it and began to run away – a few of them at first, and then more and more, shouting in horror.

Jamila and Jerry backed over to the other side of Southampton Way, both of them calling on their phones for reinforcements. The folding doors of the fire station opposite were rolled back, and a fire engine began to nose its way out with its blue lights flashing. It reached the kerb, but the road in front of it was blocked by a stationary skip lorry and, as far as Jerry could see, traffic had already backed up as far westward as Camberwell Green so the skip lorry couldn't move either.

Another torso came spinning out of the fountain and bounced across the road. As it rolled toward them, Jerry could see that its flesh looked as if it had been sliced rather than ripped apart, and its spinal column was cleanly cut through.

'Jesus *Christ*! They've all been chopped into pieces,' said Jerry, as he lowered his phone.

'*All* of them, yes, by the look of it,' said Jamila, and her voice was strained with shock. 'I count... two, three, four... pieces from maybe five bodies anyway.'

'But what the hell can *do* that, sarge? Don't tell me one spooky woman with a saw could have done that, not on her own.'

Gradually, the sewage began to subside. It sank lower and lower until it was only just brimming above the level of the manhole. It gurgled occasionally, as pockets of gas burst out, and Jerry could see that there were still some lumps floating in it. Six firefighters went hurrying across the road on foot, but there was little that they could do except stand next to Gemma and Jim Feather beside the manhole and watch the sewage bubble. There would have been no point in trying to pump it out, because it would have had nowhere to drain away.

Jerry could hear sirens coming from the direction of Lewisham and Walworth, the nearest police stations that were still open. Jamila had called the MIT team back at the Peckham station. DCI Walters had left for a meeting at New Scotland Yard, but DCs O'Brien and Pettigrew were still on duty, and they were already on their way. The most urgent need was to clear the blocked-up traffic and cordon off the area all around.

A police squad car came driving along the pavement toward them, its siren whooping and its lights flashing. Jerry and Jamila stepped back out of its way, but as Jamila turned around she caught sight of a small group of figures about two hundred metres up the street, close to the corner with Charles Coveney Road. She frowned at them, and then covered her eyes with her hand to mask the glare from the street lights, because for some reason she couldn't get them into focus.

'*Jerry*,' she said, tugging at his sleeve.

Jerry turned around too. There were seven or eight figures, all of them blurry, and all of them appeared to be wearing white – long shirts or nightgowns. It was still raining hard, and it was difficult to tell exactly how far away they were, and because of that it was equally difficult to tell how tall they were – whether they were children or adults. They were all clustered together, and they were swaying as if they were trying to keep their footing in a blustery wind.

'Oh, shit. It's more of them,' said Jerry. 'It's more of them spooky kids.'

He hesitated at first, but then he started to walk toward

them, quickening his pace as he went. Jamila said, '*Jerry!*' and she hesitated, but then she followed after him. 'Jerry, be careful!'

As they approached the figures, they could see that Jerry was right and they were children. Some of them were taller, as if they were about eight or nine years old, but the rest couldn't have been more than three or four. Their faces were as white as clowns, with smudges of black for eyes, and they all appeared to be distorted in some way. One child at the back had an elongated head and a jaw that sagged down, so that his tongue hung out between his jumbled teeth. Another had only a gaping triangular hole where her nose should have been. One of the smaller children at the front had a face like a Christ-child from a medieval painting, but underneath its soaking white nightgown, its hips were disproportionately wide, and its ankles and feet were the size of an adult's.

On the opposite side of the road, a young couple with a baby buggy were standing under their umbrellas, transfixed. Their wet black Labrador was cowering down behind them, clearly terrified.

Jerry had no idea what he was going to do when he reached the children. His hair was plastered flat on top of his head and rain was running down inside his collar, and he was so pumped up with adrenaline that he could hardly believe any of this was real. But he was still a hundred metres away from them when they clustered closer together and started to shrink away.

'*Stop!*' he shouted. 'Stay right where you are! Stop! We need to talk to you! *Stop!*'

At that moment, as if it were pouring out of the cracks between the paving stones, a dark twirl of smoke rose up into the rain. It grew thicker and thicker, and started to circle around the children, as if it were protecting them.

Jerry ran the last few metres then stopped dead. The smoke had taken on the shape of a hooded figure, taller than him, and its arms were spread wide as if it were warning him not to come any closer.

Jamila caught up with Jerry, and she stopped too.

'It's just as that doctor described it,' she said.

'This is no hallucination, sarge. This is no toxic gas.'

'I don't know. Maybe it is. In Bhopal, the cloud affected people's perception for miles and miles all around.'

Seconds passed. None of them moved, and none of them spoke. The hooded figure stood in front of the children, its arms still spread, with the sparkling rain seeming to fall right through it. The children huddled behind it, still swaying, clutching each other tightly. The late afternoon echoed from all directions with the sound of police and ambulance sirens.

'I'm asking you to stop right where you are,' Jerry called out, lifting up both hands to show that he meant the children no harm. 'We're police officers, and we need to know who you are and what you're doing here.'

'It's raining, and you have no raincoats,' said Jamila. 'And look at you – you all have bare feet. We can't allow you to wander the streets like this.'

The hooded figure pointed at Jamila and Jerry, and they heard a woman's voice. But the voice wasn't coming from the figure itself – it was coming from the young woman with the baby buggy on the opposite pavement. It didn't sound like a young woman's voice though. It sounded old and ravaged, with a high screech to it.

'Turn away! Do you hear me? Turn away and leave us be! These are my nestlings and nobody may touch them!'

Jamila turned to the young woman in astonishment, but the young woman herself was looking shocked, pressing her hand to her chest as if she couldn't believe that she had just spoken. Her partner was staring at her too.

'Debbie?' he said, shaking her shoulder. 'Debbie, what the fuck?'

'*Turn away!*' the young woman repeated, and this time she screamed it, hurling her umbrella into the road. '*Turn away and leave us be! Touch my nestlings and you will suffer as your friends have suffered!*'

'Debbie!' yelled the young woman's partner. 'For fuck's sake, Debbie!' Their baby woke up and started to cry, and their Labrador let out a howl and then started to whine and whimper, creeping low down onto the pavement.

Jerry said, 'Right! That's enough of this crap!'

He strode toward the hooded figure, almost sure that he could walk right through it, in the same way that the rain was falling through it. But before he could reach it, it let out an ear-piercing whistle. It whirled around like a dust devil, its sleeves sweeping left and then right, and it struck him criss-cross blows on the chest that sent him stumbling backward, with all the breath knocked out of him. Its arms may have looked as if they were nothing but smoke, but he felt he had been dealt two vicious lashes by a braided leather whip. He lost his balance and sat down heavily on the kerb, clutching his breastbone and bending forward in agony.

'Jerry?' Jamila turned toward the High Street to see if there were any uniformed officers in sight who she could call for back-up, but it was a chaos of blue flashing lights and firefighters and paramedics and body parts strewn across the pavement. It looked like some medieval vision of Hell.

She turned back to face the hooded figure. She wasn't armed today, not even with a Taser, and she wasn't even sure that a bullet could have brought it down. The children in white were already starting to run away, some of them hobbling, some of them half loping and half leaping, their hips twisting unevenly. The hooded figure paused for a moment and then followed them, opening out its cloak wider and wider like a pair of huge dark wings.

Jamila started to run after them, but they were rushing away so hurriedly through the rain that she didn't know if she could catch up with them, and even if she did, she didn't know how she could possibly detain them. They reached the corner of Charles Coveney Road, where the hooded figure looked back to see if Jamila was still chasing them. Jamila was sure she could see white eyes glittering like diamonds deep within the shadow of its hood. She stopped and stayed where she was, while the children ran around the corner and disappeared out of her sight. Once they had gone, the hooded figure shuddered and then blew away, as if it were smoke blown from a chimney in a breeze.

Jamila walked back to Jerry, who was still sitting on the kerb, coughing and trying to get his breath back.

'Are you okay, Jerry? No bones broken?'

Jerry shook his head, still gasping for breath. 'Winded, that's all. But bloody hell. I thought that thing was nothing but smoke.'

Jamila patted his shoulder and then crossed over to the young couple with the pushchair. The young woman was crouching down, trying to soothe their sobbing baby. The young man was stroking the dog.

'What the *fuck* was that all about?' the young man asked her. 'Those kids – I mean, *mate*! They looked like fucking *ghosts*, man. And how did Debbie shout like that?'

'I am not at all sure,' Jamila told him. 'But those children you saw, they may not have been what they appeared to be. And what caused your young lady here to shout out like that, I am afraid I have no idea at all. But I would be grateful if you could give me a contact number in case I need you both as witnesses to what happened here. I would also suggest that you go to A & E at St Thomas's or visit your GP as soon as you can, for a check-up. It is possible that what we saw and heard here was caused by the effect of a toxic gas.'

'What, like noz, you mean?' He meant nitrous oxide, or laughing gas.

'Possibly. It is far too early to say.'

The young man told Jamila his phone number, then he nodded toward the high street. 'What's going on down there then? Somebody got themselves cheffed up or something?'

'I can't tell you at the moment, but if you were thinking of going in that direction you will have to find another way home.'

The young man turned to his partner, who had lifted their baby out of his pushchair and was cuddling him to calm him down.

'This is a fucking nightmare, this is.'

'Yes,' said Jamila. 'I think that is exactly what you could call it.'

21

Dr Macleod had given up smoking over twenty years ago, but as he prepared himself for a second attempt to remove the malformed foetus from Susan Nicholls's womb, he would have given almost anything for a cigarette.

Once he had tied on his surgical mask, he stared at himself in the mirror over the washbasin, trying to see if his eyes were betraying any sign of his anxiety, but he was surprised how dispassionate they looked. He held out both hands, to make sure they weren't trembling, but they were rock steady.

'Right, Stuart,' he told himself, out loud, his voice muffled behind his mask. 'Ghosts or no ghosts, this thing is coming out of her. Full stop.'

He had been trying his best to persuade himself that what had appeared yesterday – that smoky apparition – was only an illusion, caused by stress. A *shared* illusion, yes, which was mind-shrinkingly rare, but an illusion nonetheless.

Yesterday afternoon, the centre's maintenance crew had checked the theatre's fuse box and all the electrical circuits but found nothing that could have caused the lights to malfunction. They had also dismantled the air-conditioning unit, but they had been unable to explain how any smoke could possibly have leaked into the operating theatre.

Dr Macleod used his elbows to push open the double doors that led from the scrubs into the theatre. Susan Nicholls was already anaesthetised, lying on the operating table as she had before, like a brightly lit human sacrifice on a catafalque. Dr Bhaduri and Dr Symonds were waiting for him on either side of her, and Janet Horrocks, the midwife, was sitting in the right-hand corner of the theatre, along with another junior midwife, Kisi Adomako.

Duncan, the anaesthetist, gave him a thumbs up and said, 'Heart rate, blood pressure, everything's normal.'

'Any movement from the foetus?'

'Its vital signs are the same as before, so it is still alive,' said Dr Bhaduri. 'The latest scan shows that it is already firmly attached with microvilli to the wall of the uterus, but there is no movement, no. Perhaps it is waiting for us. Perhaps it sleeps.'

Dr Macleod looked across at him but said nothing. He could clearly imagine that angelic face with its eyes closed and its tentacle-like limbs tangled all around it, and the thought of that gave him a crawling sensation down his spine. In a matter of minutes he would have to cut it out and confront it, and this time he would euthanise it, instantly. Nurse Harris had already prepared a hypodermic with a three-milligram dose of fentanyl, which was easily enough to kill an adult, let alone an unformed foetus.

'Okay, everybody,' he told them, 'let's go for it.'

Dr Symonds folded back the sheet that had been

covering Susan Nicholls's stomach. Dr Macleod stepped up to the operating table and held out his hand for the scalpel to make his first incision. He hesitated and looked up, in case there was any indication that the surgical lamps were starting to flicker or change colour, but they remained steady, without even the faintest tinge of green.

Once the thick gauze dressing had been peeled off, he snipped apart the sutures with which Dr Bhaduri had temporarily closed the incision that he had started to make yesterday. Blood slid out again, which Nurse Harris quickly dabbed up. Then he slit open Susan Nicholls's uterus, and a glistening flood of yellowish amniotic fluid poured out, streaked with pink.

He was fully prepared for the foetus to twitch or writhe or shrink away from him. But as soon as the walls of the uterus parted, it boiled into furious life, its limbs thrashing and waving, and its muscles contracting again and again in one powerful spasm after another. For a split second, behind its tentacles, he saw its blue eyes staring up at him through a thin film of mucus, and its look was one of utter hostility.

Susan Nicholls started to jerk up and down on the operating table, thumping on it loudly, and Dr Macleod said, 'Hold her down! For God's sake, keep her still!'

Nurse Harris and Nurse Yeom gripped her knees and her ankles, while Dr Symonds and Dr Bhaduri pinned her shoulders flat. That didn't stop her from repeatedly banging her head, and tossing it wildly from side to side.

Dr Macleod took a deep breath before he plunged his left hand into the wetness of her womb. He buried his fingers into the wriggling bony mass of the foetus's limbs to keep it as immobile as he could. Its slippery, bony tentacles fought furiously against him, but with one deft scalpel stroke after another, he started to slice it free.

Once his last stroke had detached it from the lining of her womb, he paused, his chest rising and falling while he summoned up all of his strength, and then he slowly dragged it out. It came away with an obscene sucking sound, and he held it up in his fist, still squirming.

'*Nurse!*' he snapped, beckoning Nurse Yeom to pass him the stainless-steel kidney dish. Susan Nicholls had stopped jerking now and was lying flat, although she was quaking as if she were suffering from hypothermia. Dr Symonds and Dr Bhaduri were already swabbing her gaping uterus and preparing to stitch it up. Janet Horrocks and her junior had come forward now and were waiting to see if Dr Macleod needed any assistance with the foetus. As inhuman as it looked, it was their duty to make sure that this wriggling mass didn't suffer before it was euthanised.

Nurse Yeom set down the kidney dish on the side of the operating table. Dr Macleod held the foetus over it, prising its limbs away from his surgical glove one by one. Nurse Harris stood close by his shoulder, holding up the hypodermic with the lethal dose of fentanyl.

'Come on, come on, you obstinate little freak,' Dr Macleod whispered at it, with his teeth clenched together. It was hard to believe how strong it was, and how tightly it was clinging on to his fingers.

He had nearly pulled the last tentacle free when the foetus suddenly untangled itself. It slithered out of his grasp and around his wrist, and before he had a chance to snatch at any of its limbs, it burrowed its way underneath his elasticated cuff and up inside his sleeve. In a matter of seconds it had disappeared from sight, and he could feel its nails tearing at his forearm as it pulled itself higher and higher, up toward his elbow.

'Jesus *Christ*!' he shouted, wildly swinging his left arm and smacking at the bump underneath his sleeve. But the foetus carried on climbing, around his elbow and up toward his shoulder. The pain was excruciating, as if he were being clawed over and over again by a vicious cat, and he could feel blood and amniotic slime running down inside his sleeve.

Dr Bhaduri hurried around the operating table and managed to get a grip on the foetus as it bulged up under the shoulder of Dr Macleod's blue polypropylene gown, even though it was wriggling so ferociously. He pulled at it again and again, but at least a dozen of its nails were hooked under Dr Macleod's skin, and it refused to let go.

'Christ almighty, stop!' Dr Macleod shouted at him. 'You're tearing my arm off!'

Dr Bhaduri backed away, his hands lifted helplessly. Dr Macleod reached across to the instrument tray, scrabbling to pick up a scalpel and dropping at least half a dozen of them onto the floor. Raising his shoulder as high as he could, he stabbed at the foetus six or seven times. It reacted to each stab with a spastic contraction, but still it clung on to him, and when he started to slash open the fabric of his surgical gown to get at it, it clawed its way over his shoulder and started to climb down his back.

Now he was staggering around and around, first of all trying to stab at his own back then holding out the scalpel to Dr Bhaduri and shouting, 'Kill it, Kumar! For God's sake, kill it!'

Nurse Harris held up her hypodermic. 'Dr Bhaduri – here, jab it with this!'

But Dr Bhaduri shook his head and said, 'No, no – too risky. If I miss it and jab Dr Macleod, it will kill him in seconds!'

'Just kill it, Kumar! Get it off me!'

Dr Macleod dropped to his knees in front of them, bowing his head like a religious penitent. They could see the bump of the foetus underneath the back of his gown, crawling slowly down his left shoulder blade. Dr Bhaduri danced around him, trying to find the best position to stab the foetus without stabbing Dr Macleod too, but when he lifted up the scalpel like a dagger, Dr Macleod screamed and frantically waved both hands.

'*No! No! Don't do it! Jesus, what's it doing to me? Aaagh! No! Aaagh!*'

Spots of blood appeared on his gown, only four or five of them at first, but then it was flooded with a wide red stain. He fell sideways onto the floor, his legs kicking and his arms thrashing, jerking up and down on the tiles in the same way that Susan Nicholls had jerked up and down on the operating table. He screamed and kept on screaming, not only jerking but rolling from side to side.

Duncan came scrambling around from the other side of the operating table and knelt down beside him. 'Kumar – help me get this gown off him!'

Between them, Duncan and Dr Bhaduri managed to wrestle Dr Macleod onto his stomach, so that Dr Bhaduri could cut the ties that fastened his gown at his waist and the back of his neck. Dr Macleod was in so much pain that he was fighting against them, but they managed to wrench the bloodstained gown inch by inch off his shoulders then lever his arms out of his sleeves. Underneath he was wearing a white T-shirt, now soaked in blood, and pale-blue boxer shorts. The bump of the foetus had shifted now from his shoulder blade to the lower left side of his back, and it seemed to be creeping toward his spine.

While Dr Macleod continued to scream and batter the floor with his fists, Dr Bhaduri cut open his T-shirt to expose his back. It was then that they saw why he was in so much agony. The foetus had used its nails to tear a ragged diagonal hole over his left shoulder blade, and now it was tunnelling its way under the outer layer of his skin, separating it inch by inch from the flesh below. As it crawled across his back, it was flaying him alive, from the inside. Already the skin on the left side of his back was hanging loose and floppy and wrinkled, and through its semi-transparent layers, Duncan and Dr Bhaduri could see the writhing outline of the foetus as it crawled over his backbone. They could *hear* it too, because the epidermis made a crackling sound as the foetus gradually ripped it away from the subcutaneous tissue underneath.

Dr Bhaduri used the scalpel to stab the foetus again, and each time he stabbed it, its limbs bunched up, but it continued its progress across Dr Macleod's back.

'Morphine, that should do it,' said Duncan. 'A damn great shot of morphine. Here – hold him down for me, nurse.'

Nurse Harris knelt on Dr Macleod's left elbow and gripped his wrist to keep him pinned to the floor. Duncan pulled himself up onto his feet and went back around to his station. His hands shaking, he filled a syringe with morphine sulfate solution and then came back, dropping down beside her. By now the foetus was forcing itself under the skin of Dr Macleod's right hip and his screaming had become thin and repetitive, like a child crying.

Duncan located one of the foetus's squirming limbs through Dr Macleod's skin, pinching it hard between finger and thumb to keep the foetus as still as possible while he injected it. But before he could stick the needle into it, all the lights went out, with a loud click, and the operating theatre was plunged into total blackness.

Duncan jabbed blindly at the foetus, but he heard the needle snap, and the foetus twisted its limb free from him. There was nothing that he could do but help Nurse Harris and Dr Bhaduri keep Dr Macleod pressed flat to the floor.

'Open the doors!' he shouted, and he heard Janet Horrocks and Kisi Adomako blundering around in the darkness, colliding with the trolley full of instruments.

After a few moments, Janet Horrocks cried out, 'I can't!'

'What?' said Duncan.

'They're stuck! Just like they were before ! I can't open them!'

'Try the scrubs doors!'

'I am trying that!' said Nurse Yeom. 'I can't open them either!'

Duncan took out his phone and jabbed at it, but it was dead.

'Who's got a phone? We need light!'

'I don't have mine with me,' said Janet Horrocks. 'I never bring it into the OR.'

'I have,' said Dr Symonds. 'Hold on a second. No... no, it's not working.'

Dr Macleod had stopped kicking and rolling from side to side, and his screaming was now reduced to a scratchy, high-pitched whining. He lay still, with only an occasional twitch, and after Duncan was satisfied that he was going to stay that way, he stood up, reaching out for the side of the operating table to guide himself. He stepped over Dr Macleod's legs and shuffled his way toward the doors, his arms held out in front of him. The darkness was overwhelming, without even a glimmer of light from the corridor outside. He bumped into Janet Horrocks then reached out for the doors. He pushed against them, hard, but they remained immovable.

'This is insane,' he said. He took two steps back from the doors and threw his whole body weight at them, jarring his shoulder. The doors stayed shut.

He threw himself at them a second time, and he heard a cracking sound, but they still wouldn't open. He gave them a frustrated kick, and then another, and another.

'Hey!' he shouted. 'Anybody! We're trapped in here! Theatre number two! Can anybody hear us? The doors are stuck and we can't get out!'

'How is this even *possible*?' said Janet Horrocks, and Duncan could tell by her voice that she was beginning to panic.

Out of the darkness behind him, Dr Bhaduri said, 'The foetus… I can't feel it anymore. It was crawling down the back of his thigh, but now I don't know where it has gone to.'

'Anybody!' Duncan shouted out again. 'We're trapped in here! All the lights have gone out and the doors are stuck and we can't get out!'

He kicked at the doors again and again, but they stayed firmly shut. Then he remembered the fire extinguisher hanging in a bracket next to the scrubs doors. Reaching out for the wall to guide himself, he groped his way blindly toward it. Once he had found it, he unfastened it and lifted it out, and started to carry it back to the main doors. All the time, Janet Horrocks and Kisi Adomako kept on screaming out shrilly for help, as if they were on the top floor of a blazing building.

'Help us! Help us! We're trapped in here! Help us!'

'Janet, Kisi – where are you?' said Duncan. 'Stay well back… I'm going to try and bash the doors open with the fire extinguisher.'

He braced himself in front of the doors and then swung the fire extinguisher like a battering ram. It hit the doors with a loud bang, and they shook, and he heard that cracking sound again. With any luck, he could knock the screws out of the hinges and the doors would fall flat.

He swung the fire extinguisher again, but as it struck the doors, they both burst open inward, knocking him backward onto the floor. The fire extinguisher fell on top of him and hit him on the side of his head, just above his left eye, stunning him.

Even though the doors had been flung wide open, the operating theatre was still in complete darkness. Something had entered though, something they could all feel and hear even if they couldn't see it. A whistling draught began to blow, softly at first, but it rapidly grew stronger and louder. Then they heard a low-pitched moaning and that grew louder too, until the glass vials and syringes on the instrument trolley started to rattle and clink, and they could hardly hear themselves think.

The moaning grew higher and higher in pitch, until it sounded like singing.

Dr Bhaduri shouted out, 'What is it? Duncan – what's happening?'

'There's somebody in here!' Janet Horrocks cried out. 'Oh my God, there's somebody in here!'

Duncan rolled the fire extinguisher off his chest so that it clanked onto the floor. He propped himself up on one elbow and strained to see into the darkness. The draught was blowing so strongly now that it ruffled his hair and made his eyes water. He was still half stunned, but he could feel a huge physical presence in the theatre, something that was swirling around and around, invisible in the darkness but powerful, like a thunderstorm at night.

He could *smell* something, too. An acrid smell, like woodsmoke, and a citric tang – an acid overtone of lemons.

'*Duncan!*' Nurse Harris suddenly shrilled out. 'Duncan,

help! It's Dr Macleod! He's... Duncan, I can't hold on to him!'

'The same!' shouted Dr Bhaduri. 'Somebody's pulling him away from me!'

Duncan tried to climb to his feet, but before he could stand up properly, Dr Macleod came sliding along the floor, bumping into him so that he fell backward again. As far as Duncan could tell in the darkness, Dr Macleod was still lying flat on his stomach. He reached out to seize his arm or his gown or whatever he could, but he was gone.

A few seconds passed. The moaning died away, and the whistling draught subsided. The lights in the operating theatre flickered and buzzed then lit up again, with a sharp *ping*.

The seven of them stared at each other in disbelief. Nurse Harris and Dr Bhaduri were still on their knees, but Dr Macleod had disappeared. Several parallel lines of blood were smeared across the beige epoxy flooring – a trail that led out of the wide-open doors. Duncan went out into the corridor and saw that the trail continued for about fifteen or twenty metres then abruptly came to an end, as if Dr Macleod had been picked up.

As he stood there, he heard Dr Symonds's phone playing a marimba ringtone.

'Call security, *now*,' he said. 'Maybe he hasn't been taken out of the building yet. And we need to call the police.'

'I'll do that,' Nurse Harris told him, standing up. She went across to the scrubs doors, cautiously pushed at them, and they opened.

Dr Symonds turned to Susan Nicholls, who was lying anaesthetised on the operating table with her incision still gaping open.

'Kumar – we have to finish closing her,' she said flatly. All of them were so shocked by what had just happened that they could hardly speak.

Dr Bhaduri said, 'That smoke... I can still smell that smoke.'

He bent over to pick up the scattered scalpels and forceps. As he did so, Susan Nicholls's eyelids fluttered, then she opened her eyes. Dr Symonds went over to the operating table and said, 'How do you feel, Susan? We've had a problem, and we may have to give you another anaesthetic, but only a local.'

Susan Nicholls frowned at her. Then she whispered, 'Where's my baby?'

22

The sky was beginning to turn a pale mauve colour when Jamila said, 'I don't think there's anything else we can do here, Jerry. Let's go home and get some rest. I'll meet you at about two o'clock this afternoon.'

'We've still got those two foetuses at St George's to check up on, haven't we? And I wonder if Dr Macleod managed to hoick that octopussy foetus out of that Nicholls girl.'

'One thing at a time, Jerry, and the first thing I need is sleep.'

'No, yes. You're right, sarge. I'm cream-crackered myself.'

It had stopped raining soon after midnight, although the streets were still wet. All through the early hours, forensic technicians in white Tyvek suits had been silently criss-crossing the street like a tribe of lost snowmen. They had photographed and tagged all the body parts that had been blown out of the sewer, where they had fallen, and then collected them up in body bags. They would be taken to the morgue for identification and, as far as possible, for piecing back together.

After that, the pavements had been painstakingly

searched by more than twenty officers on their hands and knees, working under portable LED lamps and headlights from the fire engines. It had taken about an hour for the sewage in the manhole to sink back down to its usual level, still gurgling and bubbling as it disappeared, but once it had dropped right down, the fire brigade had been able to hose down the street and then sluice buckets of disinfectant all the way across it. The early-morning air smelled strongly of diesel fumes and ammonia.

Behind the police barriers, Jerry could see the media gathered, with vans from the BBC and ITN and Sky News parked along the pavement. Helicopters from the TV stations had flown over several times too, and there was still one hovering over Camberwell Green, so that they had to shout to make themselves heard.

DCI Walters came up to them, along with DC Pettigrew. She had called him as soon as she and DC O'Brien had seen the way the bodies were cut up and realised that this could be a major crime scene, rather than some random industrial accident.

In his grey trilby hat and his droopy grey raincoat, DCI Walters looked as much like a bird of prey as ever. All the same, Jerry had noticed him talking intently and seriously to all of the forensic team involved in searching the street, and also to the paramedics who were carefully stowing the smaller body parts into polythene evidence bags. It was obvious that he was meticulous and thorough and that he wasn't the kind of DCI who left all the minor details of any investigation to his underlings.

'I was hoping I'd find you still here, DS Patel,' he

said, with that hint of a Scottish accent. 'I've just been addressing myself to the media. I didn't give them much, but then we don't really *know* much, do we? You two are the supernatural experts. Any ideas?'

'What did you actually say to them, sir, if you don't mind me asking?'

'I said that we have no clear idea yet what caused the sewage to erupt like that. It could have been a spontaneous explosion of methane and hydrogen sulphide, combined possibly with another flammable gas. It could even have been an unexploded German bomb from the Second World War. After all, Thames Water have dug up at least seven of them since they started these new excavations for the Tideway tunnel – hardly a surprise when you consider how many tens of thousands of bombs the Luftwaffe dropped on this area of London during the war.

'Of course, they asked me why I was here from the MIT. I told them I was checking to see if this could have been a terrorist attack – Real IRA or Al-Quaeda or Extinction Rebellion or some other bunch of loonies.'

Jerry said, 'It wasn't a gas explosion though, was it, sir, or a Second World War bomb?'

'*I* know that and *you* know that. You only had to take one look at those poor buggers' bodies to see that they hadn't been blown apart. They were chopped up like joints of meat in a butcher's shop, weren't they, all six of them? Dissected. And that sewage spouting out like that... no bomb in the world could have caused that. So whatever you said about the supernatural, DS Patel – not believing in ghosts and whatnot – I can't think of any explanation that *isn't* supernatural. Can you? If you can, I'm dying to know what it is.'

Jamila looked at her watch. It was 6:07 a.m. 'DC Pardoe and I are leaving now, sir. We're too tired to think sensibly at the moment. We'll see you back at the station early this afternoon. We need to analyse what actually happened here, and most of all, *why* it happened, and if it could have been in any way supernatural, although I'm always very reluctant to use that word, as you know.'

'Suspend your disbelief for a moment and assume that it *was* supernatural. What kind of supernatural, would you guess? Some sort of poltergeist, perhaps, that can throw stuff around?'

'Many different cultures have stories about vengeful spirits, sir, and some of those accounts are quite convincing. More than half of all Muslims believe in witchcraft and various evil jinns, including most of my own family. So from their point of view, this could have been caused by a vengeful spirit.'

DCI Walters took off his hat and frowned at it as if he hadn't realised he was wearing it. He flicked drops of water off the crown and then carefully replaced it. 'A vengeful spirit?'

'Yes, sir. I mean – what do we have here? Six innocent people have been killed, and at first sight it looks as if they have been deliberately dismembered. If it was a supernatural event and not an accident, then there will have been a spiritual motive for it. If we can find out what that motive was, that will be our best chance of discovering what committed it.'

'A vengeful spirit,' DCI Walters repeated, still staring at her. Jerry couldn't work out from his tone of voice if he was being sarcastic, or if he saw this as a possible first step in solving the most inexplicable mass murder with which he had ever been faced.

★

They were climbing back into their car when Gemma hurried up to them.

'Sorry…' she said. 'Before you go, I just wanted to say that I might be able to give you some more help.'

'Believe me, Gemma – any and all help gratefully received,' said Jamila.

'I've been thinking, that's all. We've scanned all the known sewers for three hundred hectares around the Peckham Rye area with GPR, but so far we haven't come across anything that could explain what's been happening here.'

'What exactly were you looking for?'

'I don't know. Anything. Fractured gas pipes, any unusual kind of toxic spillage. To begin with, I wondered if some factory was discharging some prohibited chemical down the sewer, and it got mixed up with other effluents so that it created some sort of hallucinogenic gas. I thought that may have been what made us see those spooky children and turned all the lights green.'

'Well, yes, we thought of that too,' said Jerry. 'But there's no gas that cuts people up into pieces or chucks keys at you or screams and howls or blows thousands of gallons of sewage out into the street like that.'

'Of course not. The sewage... Jim Feather thought it might have been the tide backing up, but it couldn't have been – not with that fatberg 90 per cent blocking it up between here and the Thames. It's simply not possible.'

'So do you have *any* explanation?'

'I don't know. I just don't know. Maybe there's a whole lot of mad people living down there in the sewer who are chopping up anybody who comes near them. But after all that scanning, we haven't found any trace of them.'

'Which leads you to think – what?'

'I'm not at all sure yet. I'm absolutely shattered, so I need to go home. But there was something we were told when I was training for this job, and I want to find my notes about it.'

'Well, we're packing it in for now too,' said Jerry. 'We're having a meeting with the Major Investigation Team about two this afternoon, so why don't you come and join us if you've got any new ideas? It's at the old Peckham police station. You know where that is, don't you? Right on the corner of Meeting House Lane.'

'Okay. If I can dig that stuff out, I'll bring it along. I'll probably come along anyway, if that's all right. You might think it sounds strange, but the sewers are like my whole world. What's been happening, all this weird and horrible stuff, it's like my world's been invaded and taken over. I'm scared to death to go down there now.'

★

Once Gemma had walked off, Jerry said to Jamila, 'Have you called yourself a taxi?'

'Yes. He should be here in a minute.'

'How do you feel?'

'Numb. How about you?'

Jerry looked at her, and it was one of those moments when he wished they weren't serving police officers, so that he could give her a comforting hug.

'I'm okay, sarge,' he said wearily. 'I'll see you later. I'll be interested to hear what that Gemma has in mind. Clever girl, that – like my Alice. Not that I want Alice to grow up to be a sewage engineer. She might expect me to visit her at work.'

He waited until Jamila's minicab had arrived, and then he climbed into his own car and started the engine. He was about to pull away when his phone rang.

'DC Pardoe? This is Inspector Bullock, Camberwell nick. I understand you're currently investigating an incident at the Warren BirthWell Centre at Denmark Hill.'

'That's right. One of the doctors reported an intrusion into the operating theatre, right in the middle of surgery. DS Patel and me, we were supposed to go up there yesterday afternoon, but to coin a phrase, we got bogged down by this bloody sewage thing in Peckham High Street. I'm only just leaving there now.'

'That doctor – that would be Dr Stuart Macleod?'

'That's right. He's their top surgeon, so far as I know.'

'*Was*, you mean. His body was found about an hour ago under the bushes in Max Roach Park.'

'You're joking.'

'No, straight up. Some bloke was taking his dog for an early-morning walk before he went to work, and the dog sniffed him out. I'm not sure of all the details, and at the moment the witness reports are all very confused. What seems to have happened is that there was a power cut in the operating theatre while Dr Macleod was carrying out a Caesarean section.'

'When was that? Yesterday afternoon?'

'That's right, about 4:30, 4:40. But right in the middle of the blackout, Dr Macleod disappeared.'

'I'm not sure I get what you mean. Walked out, or what?'

'Two of the witnesses say he was dragged out by person or persons unknown. And of course, unidentified because all the lights were out.'

'*Dragged* out?'

'There was blood on the floor of the operating theatre, which we have yet to establish was his. He'd only just completed a Caesarean, after all. But here's the really odd thing – the foetus that he'd removed from the patient had disappeared too. No sign of it. And there's still no sign of it, even though Dr Macleod's body has been found.'

'Why didn't anybody get in touch with myself or DS Patel as soon as this happened?'

'Sorry, Pardoe, but nobody mentioned your involvement until this morning. In any case, if you've been tied up with that incident in Peckham High Street…'

'Incident? It's a major disaster. Five forensic officers dead, and one photographer.'

'Yes. I've seen the reports coming in, and it's the leading story on the news. Tragic. Just tragic.'

'So, anyway, guv. Tell me about Dr Macleod.'

'The power cut only lasted a few minutes apparently,

and as soon as it was over, one of the other doctors made a 999 call. We had officers up at the BirthWell in less than fifteen minutes. But as I say – there was no sign of Dr Macleod when they got there, whether he left voluntarily or not.'

'No CCTV footage?'

'None. The CCTV cameras were blacked out for the same period of time. Total power outage.'

'Where's his body now? St Thomas's?'

'No, St George's. He'll have to be given a full post-mortem, so I doubt if that'll be started until tomorrow now, or even the day after, and who knows how long it's going to take.'

'No obvious cause of death then?'

'Well, this is the thing. He was naked, when he was found. In fact, he was a bit more than naked. He was skinned.'

'*Skinned?*'

'Every inch of him. From his face right down to the soles of his feet.'

'What the hell can do something like that?'

'I've been told that's your speciality, Pardoe. You and DS Patel. Things that can do things like that.'

'Oh, come on, guv. Just because we sorted out that madness in Tooting, that doesn't mean we're experts in every weird crime that comes up.'

'Well, perhaps not. But nobody else has got a clue how he could have been kidnapped out of his own operating theatre and then skinned. We were hoping you could give us some input.'

'Not right now. I'm on my way back to my gaff for a couple of hours of much needed kip. I'll need to talk to DS Patel too. She's got more of a handle on this kind of thing than I have. Not only that, it's probably worth waiting until we get the results of the autopsy. Maybe we'll have some idea then of how Dr Macleod was actually skinned. Bloody hell. Gives me the shudders just thinking about it.'

'Fair enough. But put your mind to it, won't you, and get back to me later today?'

'Yes, guv. I wouldn't be surprised if I have nightmares about it.'

23

Dr Pocztomski was over an hour late because somebody had thrown themselves in front of his train at Clapham Junction. When he entered the laboratory at St George's Hospital, he found his assistant pathology technician and two pathology students already waiting for him.

On the bench in front of them stood two portable incubators made of green-and-white plastic. In one was the foetus with the stunted arms and legs that had been cut out of Joya Sanghavi. In the other was the crablike foetus that had tried to penetrate Jenny Gibbons.

Dr Pocztomski had already been sent 3D pictures of both foetuses, as well as read-outs of their latest vital signs, so he knew what to expect. Despite that, he felt his heart beating hard and slow when he saw them lying there in their incubators, still alive, still breathing. Everything he knew about foetal malformation told him that they should never have survived even their first five minutes once they had been expelled from the womb.

'Have you ever seen anything like these two before, doctor?' asked his assistant, Firash.

Dr Pocztomski slowly shook his head. 'Not living, no.

Never. And *two* of them? I would have said the odds against that were millions to one.'

He was tall and stringy, Dr Pocztomski, with fine straw-coloured hair that had receded halfway back from his forehead, a sharply pointed nose and circular spectacles. Firash was a tubby Malay, with a smooth round face and short black hair that stood straight up, as if he had stuck his fingers into an electric socket.

The students were both female – a slim brunette with pouty lips and a ponytail, and a large gingery young woman who reminded Dr Pocztomski of his half-sister, who still lived in Poland. Firash introduced them. 'This is Melanie – Mel – and this is Sinead.'

Dr Pocztomski carefully lifted the clear plastic lid of the incubator in which Joya's foetus was lying. It quivered, as if it were having a bad dream, but its eyes remained closed, and it carried on breathing, although each breath was snatched and shallow.

'Did the AFP give you any background information about these foetuses?' He was referring to the Assistant Forensic Practitioner from the Met's laboratories at Lambeth.

'Only that they were both the result of home terminations. Foetus A appears to be the result of the mother's deliberate attempt to perform a C-section on herself. Foetus B was manually aborted by the woman's partner. Apart from that, all they told me was that you were coming to examine them, and to keep them in their incubators until you arrived.'

Dr Pocztomski peered closely into both incubators and

then shook his head. 'I find it almost unbelievable that either foetus has survived. Yes, Foetus A was removed from the mother's uterus by a crude Caesarean, but Foetus B... its mother claims that it was actively roaming around her flat before forcibly attempting to enter her birth canal. I say "mother", but if her story is true, which I think is highly unlikely, she was obviously nothing more than a very temporary host from which Foetus B was forcibly extricated.'

'They did tell me that the young woman who tried to perform a C-section on herself was taken to the emergency room at King's,' put in Firash. 'The latest news is that her condition is serious but not life-threatening.'

'Well, that's one relief,' said Dr Pocztomski. 'All we have to do now is find out how she became impregnated with a foetus like this. What about the other young woman?'

'Ms Gibbons? She suffered bruising and shock but was otherwise unharmed.'

'It's an extraordinary case. Extraordinary. We need to know where *her* foetus came from... and why it was attempting to force its way inside her. And of course how both of these foetuses have managed to survive for so long after abortion, considering their extreme malformation.'

'I've taken blood and tissue and DNA samples, as you asked,' said Firash. 'I've flagged them with the lab as top priority, but we may not get the results until tomorrow or the day after. But here are the ultrasounds.'

Dr Pocztomski took the folder of scans, laid them on the bench and took them out one by one, holding them up and frowning at them intently.

'I would guess that Foetus A is in about the twelfth week of gestation, while Foetus B has reached about the thirteenth or fourteenth week. Both foetuses have brains, and hearts, and lungs, and livers, even though they're so catastrophically malformed. They have genitalia too. Foetus A is female while Foetus B is male.'

'Both their size and their weight are what you would expect from normal foetuses at those stages,' said Firash. 'Foetus A is sixty-one millimetres in length and weighs eleven grams. Foetus B is 61 millimetres in length and weighs 13 grams.'

Dr Pocztomski was about to answer him when the bench shuddered, and the raised plastic lid above Joya's foetus dropped shut.

'I hope that wasn't an earthquake,' said Dr Pocztomski, peering at Firash and the two students over the top of his spectacles. 'You don't get earthquakes here in Tooting, do you?'

Firash didn't have the chance to say anything before the bench shuddered again, and then the whole floor felt as if it were sliding sideways underneath their feet. A row of glass jars fell off the shelf at the back of the laboratory, with three or four of them smashing into the sink. Test tubes rattled in their wooden racks and an anglepoise lamp tilted over sideways like a skeletal bird and clattered onto the floor.

'It *is* an earthquake!' said Dr Pocztomski.

The floor shook again, much more violently, and he had to reach out and grab the handle of the store cupboard next to him to keep his balance. Sinead staggered back against Mel, and the two of them collided with the left-hand wall.

The shaking gradually subsided. As the rattling died away though, the lights began to dim, like flickering candles. There was a row of small windows between the top of the shelving and the ceiling, but these slowly darkened, as if night were falling outside, three hours early, until they were totally black.

'Firash, what the hell is going on?' asked Dr Pocztomski, still holding on to the handle in case the floor started shaking again. 'Is this a power cut, or what?'

'I'll go and find out, doctor.'

Firash made his way around the bench to the door, but when he tried to open it, he found that it was stuck fast. He jiggled the handle and tugged at it hard, but it still refused to open.

'Phone reception,' Dr Pocztomski told him. 'They can send maintenance.'

Firash took out his phone and prodded at it, but then he pulled a face. 'It's dead, doctor. It's fully charged, but look.' He held it up so that Dr Pocztomski could see the black screen.

Dr Pocztomski took out his own phone, but that too was dead. He went over to the wall phone in the corner and picked that up, but when he put the receiver to his ear, all he could hear was a faint swishing crackle, like somebody wading slowly through autumn leaves.

'No, useless. Try the door again.'

Firash wrenched the door handle again and again, and at

the fifth wrench he tore all the screws out, and the handle dropped onto the floor.

'Well, now we are well and truly trapped,' said Dr Pocztomski.

Both of the students had brought out their phones, only to find that they were dead too.

'What are we going to do?' asked Mel. She was close to tears. 'What if nobody comes to get us out?'

'Of course they will,' Dr Pocztomski reassured her. 'Even if we have to wait for the cleaners to come around.'

'But what's happening? Why has it gone so dark?'

The fluorescent lights in the ceiling blinked and dimmed, and then brightened; but then they dimmed down again.

'Maybe I should try to kick down the door,' Firash suggested.

But Dr Pocztomski didn't answer. He was sure he had seen something stirring in the corner by the sink. Although it was already gloomy in the laboratory, a darker swirl appeared to be forming. He reached across and tugged Firash's sleeve and said, 'Look, Firash... *there* – what is that?'

The darkness clotted together, thicker and thicker, growing taller and wider at the same time, until Dr Pocztomski realised that it was taking on the shape of a human figure. It was dense enough for him to be able to see it, and yet he could also see the shining taps right through it, as well as the faint glitter of broken glass on the draining board.

'Oh my God, what is it? Oh my God!' The two students had seen it too, and they were backing away, clinging to each other. Sinead was making a thin keening sound in the back of her throat, and both of them were clearly terrified.

The flickering light took on a sickly green hue and began to grow brighter again, and steadier. Dr Pocztomski could see that the figure appeared to be wearing a cloak, with wide-spreading sleeves, and that it had a tall, pointed hood, like a member of some religious order, or a witch.

Was it *real*? he asked himself. Or was it some kind of optical illusion? He was hard-headed and relentlessly analytical – both by training and by nature. He was even prepared to believe that this might be a tasteless practical joke that some of the hospital's students were playing on them, using some computer-generated image.

He was about to challenge the figure, but before he could think what to shout out, a high, grating voice echoed around the laboratory – a woman's voice, harsh with rage. To his bewilderment, it wasn't coming from the figure itself, but from Mel. She was almost doubled up, with both her fists clenched. Sinead was staring at her in shock.

'*You will not touch my nestlings! You will not harm them, or I swear that you will suffer as you have never suffered before!*'

'Who are you?' Dr Pocztomski retorted. He was trying to sound authoritative, but he was aware that his voice sounded off-key.

'*You will not rob them of their future life! God and their mothers turned their backs on them and cast them out, but I never will! They are my nestlings now!*'

'I asked you who you are! Or *what* you are!'

'*You want to see what life you might have taken away from them, my nestlings? Then behold!*'

The hooded figure's sleeves swooped and furled, as if it were signalling with two large black flags. Dr Pocztomski caught a smell in the draught that it stirred up: the bitter reek of woodsmoke. Over the two incubators the air started to quiver, so that the hooded figure quivered too.

Out of this trembling air, two small images took shape, one hovering over each incubator, although the foetuses were still lying inside them, their breathing quick and shallow as before. They were clearly visible, these figures, but translucent, like two holograms. Dr Pocztomski was eerily reminded of the hologram of Princess Leia in *Star Wars*.

The image over Joya's foetus had a grossly swollen head, but underneath the crease of its bulging forehead, it had clear cerulean eyes and a face that was almost cherubic, with rounded cheeks and pouting lips. Its shoulders sloped down sharply from its neck, and its arms were little more than stumps, with tiny nodules for fingers. Its belly was swollen, with a protuberant navel that looked like a complicated knot of twisted twine. Its legs were as stunted as its arms, with tiny underdeveloped toes. Two webs of transparent skin stretched from underneath its arms to the sides of its feet, giving it the appearance of a flying squirrel.

Over Jenny's foetus, the image had a far smaller head, with a forehead that sloped sharply back, as if it had almost no room inside its skull for a brain. Its eyes were bloodshot and protuberant and looked as if they were about to pop out of their sockets. It had no nose, only gaping triangular holes that exposed its sinuses, and its mouth was dragged downward like a miserable child. Its body resembled a plastic bag half filled with water, and its arms and legs were nothing more than rows of buds, although both its fingers and its toes had sharp hooked claws on them.

'*This is how my nestlings will grow,*' said the woman's voice, and Dr Pocztomski thought that it sounded more indulgent now, and far less angry. '*You may not love them, and God may not love them, but I love them, because they are alive. Ugliness may be a curse, but it is not a sin. The moment these nestlings were conceived, their lives began, and I will nourish and protect them, for all of their misfortune. It is not their fault that they will never be beautiful in your eyes, or the eyes of God. They will always be beautiful to me.*'

The two images wavered and then slowly faded. The hooded figure remained, its outline slightly blurred, so that Dr Pocztomski became even more convinced that it was formed out of nothing but smoke. It looked like smoke; it smelled like smoke. But how could smoke penetrate this laboratory, and take on a human shape, and create holographic images, and speak through one of his students?

He took a deep breath, and then he said, 'So, what are you telling me? That I mustn't touch these two foetuses? What am I supposed to do with them? They've been aborted. There's no way in the world that they can possibly survive.'

Mel was on the point of collapse. Her head was lolling down and her knees were giving way, and Sinead was having to hold her up to prevent her from falling face down onto the floor. Sinead looked over desperately at Dr Pocztomski, but he felt paralysed, as if every joint in his body had locked up.

'*I will take care of my nestlings, as I have been taking care of them before,*' Mel croaked. '*They are my children. Not yours. Not God's. Mine.*'

There was a moment when Dr Pocztomski felt as if the whole of reality was being twisted out of shape. The laboratory felt as if it were rotating all around him, and he could even see Firash being stretched out impossibly thin. He heard Mel screaming, but this was a piercing scream of pain, not coarse and angry like the hooded figure. He tried to turn around, but as he did so the laboratory was abruptly plunged into total blackness.

'*Fiiirrrr-assshhh!*' he called out, and his voice was dragged out like the soundtrack of a slow-motion film. '*Fiiirrrr-assshhh wheeere arrrrrre youuuu?*'

He was groping his way across the laboratory when there was a deafening bang, and he was hit by the door flying off its hinges. He was knocked sideways against the bench, snapping his glasses in half, and the door clattered down on top of him, one of its broken hinges snagging his cheek.

He heaved the door to one side, and at the same time the lights blinked on. Not green, but normal. Feeling bruised and half stunned, he climbed to his feet, looking around for his glasses. It was then, blurrily, that he saw Firash sitting slumped in the corner by the sink, as if he were drunk. And then he heard Sinead behind the bench, gasping and sobbing.

'Sinead?' he said.

He could see that the transparent lids of both incubators had been ripped off, and that both foetuses had gone. But then he heard Sinead sobbing again, and after that, he paid the incubators no more attention. As he came around to the other side of the bench, he found Sinead crouched down beside Mel, and Mel lying on her back on the floor. Mel's white lab coat was soaked dark, glistening red with blood, and her face was grey with shock.

She was holding up both of her arms, or what was left of them. They had both been torn off at the elbows, exposing the bone. Sinead was trying to wind the tatters of Mel's sleeve around her upper left arm as a tourniquet, but her hands were slippery with blood and she was in shock too, and finding it hard to make her fingers do what she wanted.

Dr Pocztomski took out his phone and saw that it was working. He jabbed out 999, and then he unbuckled his belt and pulled it out from the loops around his trousers with a sharp snap.

'Firash!' he shouted, as he knelt down beside Mel.

'Yes, yes, doctor. I hear you.'

'Firash, go to A & E now. I mean *now*! Mel has been critically injured.'

'What? How?'

'Don't ask, Firash, just go!'

'Yes, doctor. I'm going. I'm on my way.'

The operator answered, 'Emergency. Which service?' and Dr Pocztomski briskly told her what had happened and gave her his location. One way or another, he wanted to make sure that help reached them as quickly as possible. After that, he looped his belt around Mel's upper right arm and pulled it as tight as he could. Sinead had managed to bind Mel's torn sleeve around her left arm and tie that tightly, too. Neither tourniquet was perfect, but they would stem the bleeding until the paramedics arrived.

'Mel, stay with us, darling,' said Sinead. Mel's eyelids were fluttering and she didn't respond. 'Mel, don't leave us. Help's on the way.'

Dr Pocztomski pressed his fingertips against Mel's neck to feel her pulse. It was weak, which was consistent with her losing blood, but her heart was still steadily beating.

Sinead said, 'I don't... I don't understand what's happened.'

Dr Pocztomski was looking around now, trying to see if Mel's severed forearms had been dropped anywhere near, but there was no sign of them, only a spray of blood like a bouquet of roses up the side of the bench, and more squiggly blood spatters on the wall beside the door. Had that hooded figure done this to her? But how? How does a figure made of nothing but smoke wrench off a young woman's forearms and carry them away? And had it taken away those two deformed foetuses too?

'I don't understand what's happened any more than you,' he told Sinead. 'I keep thinking that I'm going to wake up in a moment, and that I'm still at home in bed. But I'm not. I know I'm not. Oh Mother of God, I know I'm not.'

24

On his way to Peckham police station, Jerry stopped off for a double quarter-pounder at the McDonald's on Rye Lane. He hadn't had the time to go shopping for over a week now, and all he had left in his fridge at home was a tub of out-of-date cheese coleslaw and a jar of pickled onions.

Some strategy meetings could go on for hours, and the last thing he wanted was his stomach gurgling because he was hungry.

He carried his burger to the corner by the window and asked two young women if they minded him sharing their table.

'So long as you let us pinch some of your fries,' said one of them.

'You can try, love. I don't fancy your chances.'

While he ate, he scrolled through his iPhone to see if there was any more news about the forensic officers who had been killed in the sewer, but there was none. He had managed to get in touch with Jamila while she was on her way home and tell her about Dr Macleod. However, he had received no more messages from Inspector Bullock about how Dr Macleod had been abducted from the

Warren BirthWell Centre, and it was unlikely that the post mortem on his skinned body would be completed for at least another day or two. Until then, the police would give out no releases to the media.

Jerry had taken only two bites of his burger when he heard a tap on the glass. He looked up and saw the old white-haired man in the shabby brown tweed coat standing on the pavement outside, grinning at him with gappy teeth.

He slowly lowered his burger. The old man continued to grin at him, and nod, and give him the thumbs up, as if they were long-term friends who had happened to bump into each other purely by chance. The two young women looked at the old man and then at Jerry, and they obviously sensed that something strange was going on.

Jerry picked up his phone and took a quick burst of pictures of the old man. Then he said to the girls, 'Keep an eye on my burger, could you, ladies? I need to have a chat with that old geezer outside.'

'Not your dad, is he?'

'I blinking well hope not. The last time I saw my dad he was getting buried in Blackshaw Road cemetery.'

'Oh, sorry.'

Jerry pushed his way out of the restaurant's front doors. Once he was outside though, the old man was nowhere to be seen. The only people on the pavement were a woman pushing a baby buggy and two schoolboys scuffling along and taking turns at punching each other on the arm.

He walked quickly to the corner of Elm Grove. The street was empty as far as he could see. He paused for a moment, in case the old man was crossing the road and was temporarily hidden behind a parked van, but he didn't appear. Then he walked back to the other side of Mcdonald's, to Holly Grove. A man in a hoodie was sitting on a camping stool, selling fake Louis Vuitton suitcases and Prada backpacks, but apart from a woman walking a standard poodle in the middle distance, Jerry could see nobody else.

He went back into the restaurant and sat down. One of the girls said sorry again, but he flapped his hand to show her that it didn't matter. He had never got on well with his father anyway.

He checked the photographs on his phone. He had taken five pictures of the street outside, but the old man appeared in none of them.

He had been about to take another bite out of his burger, but he slowly put it back down on his plate. The old man had been standing right in front of him, he was sure of it. How was it possible that he wasn't in any of the pictures?

He looked across at the girls and said, 'You saw him, didn't you?'

'What? That old man?'

'Yes. You didn't see where he went, did you?'

Both girls shook their heads. 'We wasn't really looking.'

'But you *did* see him?'

'Yes. That's why I thought he might be your dad.'

Jerry checked his phone again, but there was no question about it. There was the street, there was the woman pushing her baby buggy, although the two schoolboys hadn't reached McDonald's yet. But there was no old man.

Suddenly he didn't have an appetite anymore. He stood up and lifted his jacket off the back of the chair.

'Are you going?' asked one of the girls. 'Don't you want your fries?'

'No, love. Take the lot. I've decided to go on a diet.'

★★★

Jamila was waiting for him when he arrived at the station.

'You haven't heard any more from Camberwell?' she asked him.

'Unh-hunh. No. Not a sausage.'

'I called Inspector Bullock myself after you'd told me about Dr Macleod. He sounds extremely confused about the way in which the doctor was abducted from the operating theatre. I think when we've finished here we should go to the BirthWell Centre and talk to any witnesses ourselves.'

'I'm not surprised he's confused. I mean, Jesus, this gets more and more insane by the minute. And listen – you won't believe who I've just seen.'

He was about to tell Jamila about the old man in the brown tweed coat when the station's front door opened and Gemma Bright came in wearing a businesslike grey suit and carrying a briefcase and a long cardboard tube under one arm.

'Sorry I'm a bit late. Traffic.'

'Not to worry,' said Jamila. 'Why don't we go upstairs?'

They took the lift up to the first floor and crossed over to a high-ceilinged room that was bare except for a large desk and a random collection of office chairs. It was stuffy and it smelled of old wood panelling. Out of the cardboard tube Gemma drew several old maps and spread them out on the desk.

'I wanted to show you this one first of all. This is a recent map, and it shows that the sewers haven't changed all that much since Joseph Bazalgette first planned them back in 1865.'

'I don't think I need a map to tell me how old they are,' said Jerry. 'The smell sort of gives it away.'

Gemma gave him an unamused smile. 'Here – this is the Battle Bridge sewer, which serves the Peckham area, and this is the Southwark and Bermondsey storm drain, which takes away excess water when the sewer's overflow. They've survived so long because Bazalgette made them twice the size that was needed at the time, and he insisted on using Portland cement. It sets extremely hard and it's waterproof.'

Jerry leaned over the map and examined it with a frown. Then he turned back to Gemma.

'You said you had some ideas about what could have caused that bloody great fountain of sewage. Not to forget those poor buggers all getting chopped up like that. And then there's all the other weird things we saw down in the sewer. All the lights turning green, and that howling noise. And those keys flying at us.'

'Yes, I do have one or two ideas,' said Gemma. 'I've been thinking it over and over, and I don't believe you can put any of them down to natural phenomena. I'm convinced that some person or persons must be doing this deliberately.'

'But for what earthly reason?' asked Jamila.

'What *un*earthly reason, more like,' Jerry put in.

'I have no idea,' said Gemma. 'And I can't even begin to imagine *how* they're doing it. Our chief flusher suggested that all that sewage spouting out might have been caused by an abnormally high tide and the Thames Barrier being closed.'

'But you don't think so?'

'No. That volume of sewage could never have got past that fatberg. It's far too constricted. And how did all those forensic officers and my photographer get cut to pieces? Even a high-pressure hose couldn't have done that. And what about those mutilated children, and those lights turning green, like you say, and those keys? What about poor Martin being blinded and having his legs amputated? It all seems like some terrible horror story, doesn't it? But it's real. You've witnessed it; I've witnessed it. It must be real. And since it's real, *somebody* must be doing it.'

'But you've searched all the sewers with your ground-penetrating radar, haven't you? And you haven't found anybody hiding in them.'

'That's how I came up with these ideas. And I definitely think they're worth exploring.'

Jamila looked up at the clock. 'It's 2:30... time to meet up with DCI Walters and the rest of the MIT team. Listen, Gemma – why don't you tell us your ideas once we've all gathered together? That will save you from having to explain them twice.'

Gemma rolled up her maps, and the three of them went upstairs to the large chilly office that DCI Walters had been allocated for this investigation. DCI Walters was already there, sitting at the head of a shiny walnut table with his hands steepled as if he were waiting impatiently for the answer to a prayer, and so were DCs O'Brien and Pettigrew. Another man sat on DCI Walters' left-hand side. He looked professorial, this man, with unkempt white hair and half-glasses and a worn-out corduroy jacket in faded beige with leather patches on the elbows. His blue bow tie was tilted askew at a forty-five-degree angle.

'Ah, Mulder and Scully,' said DCI Walters.

'Detective Sergeant Patel and Detective Constable Pardoe,' Jamila corrected him coldly.

'Just my little joke, DS Patel. Don't take it to heart. In fact, you should take it as a compliment.'

'Thank you, sir. But I think the compliments can wait until we can bring this investigation to a close. That's *if* we can. In the meantime, this is Ms Gemma Bright, the engineer from Crane's Drains who's been in charge of the sewer where all of these tragic incidents have been taking place. She says she has some ideas that could possibly help us.'

Gemma said, 'Yes. I believe that I might have.'

'Excellent, good. We appreciate your input, Ms Bright,' DCI Walters told her, without looking at her, although he sounded to Jerry as if he were thinking, *What can a woman possibly know about sewers – especially a young attractive woman like this?*

'Please, take a seat,' he told them. 'This is Alan Pattinson, from Cullen's, the antique lock and key specialists. Probably the most knowledgeable man in the country when it comes to antique locks and keys. He's even written a book about them, haven't you, Mr Pattinson?'

'Two books, actually, detective chief inspector. One about antique locks and one about antique keys. But I don't like to blow my own trumpet about it.'

They all sat down, and Jamila poured herself a glass of water from one of the plastic bottles in the middle of the table. Jerry was already beginning to regret leaving his cappuccino behind at McDonald's.

'Tell DS Patel and DC Pardoe what you've been telling us, Mr Pattinson,' said DCI Walters. 'I think you've shed some quite interesting light on this whole wretched business.'

On the table in front of Alan Pattinson lay a green canvas tool roll. He unfastened it and rolled it out. In each of the sixteen pockets that normally would have contained spanners or screwdrivers there was one of the keys that had been retrieved from the sewer.

'This is the first time I've ever come across one of these keys in the flesh, so to speak, let alone so many of them, and of course, these are only a selection. I've seen pictures of them, in antique books, and they're mentioned in several treatises on locksmithery. But the reason you come across them so rarely is because of what they were used for.'

'Unlocking locks, I should imagine,' said Jerry. 'Why does that make them so rare?'

'Aha!' said Alan Pattinson, raising one finger. 'They were used for *locking* locks, but not for *un*locking them. Once they had locked a lock, they were left *in situ*. They were known as quarantine keys. The designs you can see on the bows all have an occult significance... each one of them different. Sigils, we call them.'

He took out a key and held it up. It had an X on its bow with a crescent moon on either side, and the letters M-U-R-M-U-R around the rim.

'This sigil is for Murmur, who was one of the seventy-two demons listed in the *Lesser Key of Solomon*, which was a book about witchcraft. It was compiled in the mid-seventeenth century, but it was mostly based on material that was hundreds of years older. Murmur was a Great Duke and Earl of Hell, and he commanded thirty-nine legions of lesser demons.

'If you were a sorcerer and you could conjure up Murmur, he would enable you to raise the dead and make them answer any question you might want to put to them. Supposing somebody had died without telling you where they'd hidden all their money... well, this was a way of bringing them back to life so they would *have* to tell you.'

He laid the key down and held up another. This key had a bullet-shaped design on its bow, with an inverted cross and two scissors shapes.

'This sigil is for Malphas, who was a Great Prince of Hell and Satan's second-in-command. He had *fifty* legions of demons under his command. If you summoned Malphas, he could give you the power to make all of your enemy's buildings collapse and also to empty his brain of any thoughts he might have of attacking you... or indeed any thoughts at all. The only trouble with Malphas, though, was that he was never to be trusted, and he was liable to steal all the thoughts from *your* brain too.'

'Do *all* these keys have the signs of demons on them?' asked Jamila.

Alan Pattinson held up three more keys, one at a time. 'Every one of them, and you sent me sixty-four altogether, so I can only presume there are some that you haven't yet recovered. This one has Beleth's sigil on it. This one is for Asmodeus. This one is for Marchosias. And so on.

'As I say, they're all demons listed in the *Lesser Key of Solomon*, but the list was originally compiled in 1577 by a Dutch doctor and occultist called Johann Weyer. He didn't personally believe in witchcraft, and he called his list *Pseudomonarchia Daemonum* – which means *The False Monarchy of Demons*. But there were plenty of witches and conjurors and practitioners of black magic who believed that the demons on his list were real, and that with the right incantations they could call on these demons to work whatever mischief they had in mind.'

Jerry said, 'You almost sound as if you believe that yourself, Alan, if you don't mind me saying so.'

Alan Pattinson let out a laugh that sounded like a horse snickering. 'Let's put it this way, detective. In my business, you always have to keep an open mind. You'd be amazed at some of the uses that have been made of locks and keys over the centuries – some of them extremely *risqué*. I could regale you for hours about it.'

'Well, yes, I'm sure you could. But let's stick to these keys, shall we? Why were they called quarantine keys?'

'They were called quarantine keys because they were specifically made for exorcists to keep the dead bodies of witches and sorcerers sealed in their coffins for the rest of eternity. The coffins would be fitted with seventy-two iron rings all around the lids and each ring would have a padlock. Each padlock would be locked with a key bearing the sigil of one of the seventy-two demons, and the keys would be left in the locks when the coffins were buried.

'The exorcists believed that if the keys remained in the locks, nobody would be able to turn them or take them out. That's because each key had been exorcised with a prayer that paralysed the power of the demon's sigil. In other words, they jammed them, as effectively as if they'd filled them with superglue. Or *spiritual* superglue, anyway.'

'But somebody took these keys out, didn't they? They not only took them out, they bloody well slung them at us.'

'Aha – but this is where it gets interesting. According to the *Lesser Key of Solomon*, a select few have the ability to turn the keys and open up the padlocks. Ordained priests can do it. So can people whose hearts have stopped beating but who have been brought back to life. And the children of the witch or sorcerer inside the coffin, natural or adopted – they can do it, too.'

'So the coffins *can* be opened,' said Jerry. 'But then what?'

'Whoever is lying in them can be revived. Or so the book says. And it doesn't matter how long they've been dead.'

'So what does this all mean?' Jamila asked him. 'Are you trying to tell us the fact that these keys were thrown at us down in the sewer – that's an indication that some witch has been released from her coffin and resurrected?'

Alan Pattinson shrugged and looked almost coy. 'That's if you believe that kind of thing.'

'Jesus came back from the dead, didn't he?' said Jerry. 'A lot of people believe that. Why should a witch be any different? What do *you* think, guv?'

DCI Walters pulled a face to indicate that he had no firm opinion on the matter. 'Something extremely strange is going on – we have to admit that. No matter how it's been done, we now have five forensic officers and one employee of Crane's Drains fatally injured, and of course we have another one of their employees blinded and mutilated. Everything that's happened appears superficially to have a supernatural element – which is why I asked for you and DS Patel to be brought in. But as Mr Pattinson has pointed out, the chap who first made a list of all these demons didn't believe in them himself, so there's a good chance that these keys and everything else that's been happening – the lighting effects, etcetera, etcetera – they've all been the work of somebody who's using them to fool us into believing that something supernatural is going on, even though it's all trickery. You know – like a stage magician saws a woman in half.'

'Or in this case, saws the legs off one poor bloke and cuts up six other people into bite-sized pieces,' said Jerry. He was making the point that DCI Walters's analogy had been less than sensitive.

Gemma raised her hand to be heard. 'I agree with DCI Walters. I was attacked by those strange-looking children myself, and they certainly didn't *feel* like ghosts. They were real, even though they looked so deformed. They felt as if they had claws, and they tried to pull off my safety helmet, and no ghosts could do that, could they? I still think the whole thing could have been rigged, and that they might have been wearing costumes. I mean, how could any child survive with all its insides hanging out? Especially down in the sewers.'

'I have to ask the same question again and again though,' said Jamila. 'And that question is – why would anybody go to such extreme lengths to do such bizarre things? What is their purpose? You talk about a stage magician, DCI Walters, and I would be willing to accept that the lighting and the costumes and the sound effects – yes, they could all have been artificially set up. They could have been a hoax. But how do you make a gale-force wind blow down a sewer? How do you throw dozens of keys through the air, like a blizzard? How do you dismember six people and have their bodies blasted out of a manhole in thousands of litres of raw sewage? And most of all, *why*?'

DCI Walters nodded. 'All good questions, Detective Sergeant Patel. All very good questions indeed, questions that I've been asking myself too. But that's why I've been farming out this investigation to the specialists like Mr Pattinson here, and like you and Detective Constable Pardoe. Because, quite frankly, I'm damned if I know the answer.'

25

Gemma unrolled one of the maps that she had brought with her. It was a scan of an 1847 map that was yellow with age, and which had been folded and refolded so many times that it had been stuck together with Sellotape.

'From my point of view, our first priority is to track down the person who's doing all these things. Until we can find them, I don't think we can possibly understand *what* their motive is. Perhaps they don't even have a motive. It must be the same with some of the murders you have to investigate.'

'That's true,' said Jamila. 'I had a case only last month in which a young woman in Redbridge had been stabbed to death. There seemed to be no motive at all, but when the forensic pathologist examined her wounds, he found that they had been inflicted by a Mahasabha knife.'

'What's that then?' Jerry asked her.

'It's a very distinctive kind of sheath knife given only to Hindus when they are young to protect themselves. The young woman had only one close Hindu friend, and when we questioned him, he admitted that he had murdered her.

His motive was that she had killed a spider that was sitting in the middle of its web.'

'Oh well. She deserved it then. You can't expect to kill spiders willy-nilly and get away with it. Blimey.'

'You don't understand. Her friend was a devout Hindu and to Hindus the spider is the spinner of illusions and represents *maya*, the supernatural force behind the creation of the world. That was his motive. He feared that if he left her unpunished, he himself would be considered to be an accomplice, and when he died he would be reincarnated as a beetle or a rat.'

'When does he come up for trial? I can't wait to see what excuse his defence lawyer is going to come up with.'

Gemma laid the map flat on the table. Even though it was faded, Jerry could see that it depicted Peckham Rye and all the surrounding area as it had been in the mid-nineteenth century.

'This map was used by Mr J. Clarke, who ran a night-soil business – in other words, he employed men to go around at night and empty people's cesspits. They called them "nightmen". A "holeman" would go down into the cesspit with a wooden tub and shovel up the human waste, a "ropeman" would haul it up and two "tubmen" would carry it between a pole to their cart. They would take it back to Mr Clarke's yard, and he would mix it up with manure and rotting vegetables and sell it to local farmers to spread on their fields..'

'Waste not, want not,' put in DC O'Brien.

'You're right,' said Gemma. 'A hogshead of human excrement could dress a whole acre of farmland. Here

– you can see that Mr Clarke has marked all his clients' houses with a cross, along with the date when their cesspit was last emptied. Some cesspits didn't need emptying for years, but if they were allowed to fill up too much they could flood into your garden or up through your floor and into your house. Samuel Pepys had some trouble with that when his neighbour's cesspit burst into his cellar, and he wrote that he went down to fetch a bottle of brandy and found himself ankle-deep in turds. His words, not mine.'

Jerry glanced across at DCI Walters. He could tell that Gemma was impressing him now, and that he was listening to her attentively. DC Pettigrew had her hand clamped over her mouth and her nose wrinkled as if she could actually smell those nineteenth-century cesspits.

'We traced nothing unusual when we searched the sewers with GPR,' Gemma continued, 'but I went back over all the readings we'd taken, and I discovered that there are several locations where disused cesspits are connected to the sewers, either deliberately or because they've broken through where the brickwork has collapsed. I've marked those cesspits with a sticker – here, and here, and here – five of them altogether.'

'And you believe that your ghosts, or your deformed children, or whatever they are – you think they could be hiding in one or other of these disused cesspits?' asked DCI Walters.

'It's a possibility. Where else could they be?'

'We have seen them out twice on the streets, as you know,' said Jamila. 'Or what *appeared* to be them, anyway.

On both occasions though, they turned a corner and disappeared, and we could only assume that they had opened a manhole and gone back down into the sewers. There was absolutely nowhere else for them to go.'

Gemma said, 'Yes. And if they had gone back down into the sewers, they could have easily made their way along to one of the breaches in the brickwork and concealed themselves in a cesspit, which we wouldn't have thought of scanning with radar. The nearest breach from Peckham High Street is on the corner of Talfourd Place. A lot of the streets around there were bombed flat during the war, but there are still one or two large houses standing there from the 1830s, before the sewers were dug.'

'So what's your suggestion?' asked DCI Walters.

'To begin with, I suggest that we scan each of these five cesspits with GPR, and if any of the scans show anything unusual, that we investigate it further. I can get that done early tomorrow morning.'

'But if they come up with nothing at all?'

'I don't know, detective inspector,' Gemma told him. 'It might sound strange to you, but like I've told DS Patel and DC Pardoe, the sewers are my whole world. They're my life, and I want my life back, that's all.'

★★★

As they drove along Peckham High Street, Jerry told Jamila that he had seen the old man in the brown tweed coat again, outside McDonald's.

'Jerry – I'm sure it's just a coincidence.'

'Either that, or he's stalking me.'

'But why would he? And how would he know where to find you each time?'

They were turning into Denmark Hill when Jerry's phone warbled. He took it out and passed it over to Jamila.

'Jerry? It's 'Edge'og.'

'Who? DC Pardoe is driving at the moment.'

'Oh, sorry. Is that DS Patel? This is DC Mallett, from Tooting.'

'Yes, this is DS Patel. Can I help you?'

'There's been a major incident at St George's, involving those two foetuses that were being examined by Dr Wossname, the forensic pathologist.'

'What kind of an incident?'

'An intruder broke into the path lab and took away the foetuses before the doctor had a chance to look at them. Worse than that, they seriously injured a student who was there to watch him. Ripped off both of her forearms, right up to the elbows.'

'Oh my God. When did this happen?'

'Less than two hours ago. I've talked to Dr Wossname and his assistant and another student who was there. They all say that the intruder was wearing a black hooded cloak, but that they looked more like smoke than a solid person.'

'Like *smoke*? That is exactly how Dr Macleod described the intruder who prevented him from carrying out a Caesarean section at the Warren BirthWell Centre. Like smoke.'

'That's right. Sounds like they were smoking something themselves, doesn't it? But they all agreed that's what it looked like.'

Jerry glanced across at her, and she lifted her hand to indicate that she would tell him all the details in a moment.

'The student… will she survive?'

'Yes, apparently. Dr Wossname stopped her arms from bleeding, but she'll probably have to be fitted with prosthetics. Even if they could have sewn her arms back on, there was no sign of them. It seems like this smoky intruder took them away, along with the foetuses. Stone cold unbelievable, isn't it?'

'All right, thank you, DC Mallett. We are on our way to interview the staff at the BirthWell Centre. After we have done that, we will come over to Tooting.'

Jamila handed Jerry's phone back.

'Don't tell me,' he said. 'That spooky hooded smoke thing's done it again.'

'It took away the two foetuses that the pathologist was supposed to be examining at St George's and tore off a student's arms. I tell you, Jerry, this has all got completely out of control.'

'Bloody hell. Let's hope that Gemma's right, and that we can find this thing hiding in one of those cesspits. Even if we *can* though, what do we do with it once we've found it? How are we going to nick something that's made out of smoke?'

'I wish I could ask the pir who used to live in the village next to mine. He was a holy man who was supposed to possess the power to dismiss evil spirits.'

They carried on driving up Denmark Hill until they reached the wide intersection with Daneville Road. Jerry stopped for the traffic lights, drumming his fingers on the steering wheel while he waited for half a dozen pedestrians to cross.

He had shifted into first gear, ready to move off, when one more pedestrian hurried out in front of them. Jerry couldn't believe what he was seeing. It was the old man in the brown tweed coat, his thinning white hair flapping up in the wind. He turned to look at Jerry and Jamila, giving them a triumphant grin, and then he licked his lips.

'That's *him*! And this is no bloody coincidence!' Jerry exclaimed. He revved the engine and turned sharp left into Daneville Road, pulling up close to the kerb. When he tugged his door handle though, he found that the door wouldn't open. He jabbed repeatedly at the unlock button on his key fob, but the door remained shut.

'What's the matter?' Jamila asked him.

'The effing door's jammed! Can you open yours?'

Jamila pulled at her door handle, but her door wouldn't open either.

'I don't effing believe this!' Jerry twisted around in his seat. The old man in the brown tweed coat hadn't crossed the road after all, and now he was standing on the corner by the traffic lights, less than ten metres behind them, still grinning.

Jamila turned around too. 'Why is he smiling like that? Do you think he is stopping us from getting out?'

'How can he? He's nowhere near us! It's this clapped-out bloody car!'

Jerry yanked at his door handle again and again. When the door refused to budge, he pressed the button to put down his window. He was hoping to reach out and open the door from the outside, but the window stayed shut. Jamila tried to open her window, but that wouldn't go down either.

Jerry turned round again. The old man was still standing by the traffic lights, although he was no longer smiling, and he was using both of his index fingers to describe circles and criss-cross patterns in the air. At the same time, he seemed to be performing some kind of shuffle, shifting from one foot to the other.

'What the hell is he up to? Looks like a bloody rain dance.'

'I don't know,' said Jamila. 'But I have a feeling that we ought to drive away from here – now. I can't imagine that he's responsible for locking us in, but let's go anyway and find a garage so that somebody can let us out. I have always suffered from claustrophobia.'

Jerry turned the key in the ignition, but instead of the engine starting, there was a shattering explosion. The bonnet flew up, and the windscreen was smashed into a glittering mosaic, and the whole car bounced up and down on its suspension as if the road had been rippled by an earthquake.

Jamila screamed and Jerry hit his door with his shoulder, but it stayed stubbornly shut. There was a loud groaning sound like metal being twisted and then a sharp crack, and almost immediately, Jerry could smell petrol. The smell grew stronger and stronger, until there was a soft shuddering *whoomph*. The back of the car was swallowed up in garish orange fire, which leaped up higher and higher, as if it were trying to devour them. It took only a few seconds before the rear window split open and the flames started to lick inside.

'*Glovebox!*' Jerry shouted. 'There's a hammer in there!'

Jamila opened up the glovebox and rummaged around until she found the red emergency hammer. Jerry grabbed it from her and hit it hard against his window, although he had to hit it three times before he smashed it. He used his elbow to clear the remaining shards of glass away from the frame, and then he knelt on his seat and climbed out head first. He fell on his right shoulder onto the road and rolled over. A small crowd of onlookers were already standing on the opposite pavement, and a bus driver came over and helped him to his feet.

Jamila had already managed to wriggle herself halfway out of the broken window. Jerry gripped her under her arms and pulled her out completely. The two of them backed away from the blazing car, and as they did so, it was totally engulfed in flames. They were immediately surrounded by sympathetic bystanders asking them if they had been hurt.

'We are all right, thank you,' said Jamila, although Jerry could tell how shaken she was. 'We are absolutely fine.'

'I've called the fire brigade,' the bus driver told them. 'I took the fire extinguisher out of the bus, but it was empty. I'm going to be giving somebody a hard time, man, I can tell you that for nothing.'

Jerry put his arm around Jamila and gave her a reassuring squeeze. She was trembling, but he knew from experience how strong she was. After they had watched their car burning for a few moments, she suddenly looked around and said, 'Where is he? That old man? Is he still there?'

Jerry turned toward the junction. The old man was still standing beside the traffic lights, and when he saw that Jerry had spotted him, he raised one hand and smiled.

Jerry took his arm away from Jamila and said, 'Right – I'm going to have him!'

He started to cross the road, but he had only gone three or four paces before the old man swept one arm sideways like a karate chop, and the burning car erupted in a huge ball of fire. An overwhelming wave of heat stopped Jerry before he could go any further, and he had to lift his hand to shield his face.

The car erupted again, and again, and two more balls of fire rolled up into the air. This time though, the fire was green, the same lurid green as the light they had encountered down in the sewers. The car continued to crackle with bright green flames, fiercer and fiercer, even though it had already been reduced to little more than a blackened shell.

Thick smoke began to drift across the road junction, until it was almost impossible to see the shops on the opposite side. The old man stepped backward and disappeared into the smoke, and when Jerry reached the corner, he had gone. He walked back across the road to join Jamila. A police squad car was approaching from the direction of Wren Road with its blue lights flashing, and he could hear the *hee-haw* siren of a fire engine only a few streets away.

'Better late than never, I suppose,' said Jerry.

'I've called DCI Walters,' Jamila said. 'He's going to contact Lambeth Road and have them send a forensic team over with a pick-up truck. A car will be coming in a minute to collect us too.'

'Are you okay?'

Jamila looked up at him, and for once he couldn't read what she was thinking.

'You've scratched your cheek,' he told her. 'No, your other cheek.'

She dabbed at it with her fingertips. 'I'll live.'

If she had been his lover, he would have pulled out a tissue and wiped the blood from her cheek for her, and then kissed her. But she was Detective Sergeant Patel, his superior officer, and that would have been totally out of order.

The fire engine turned the corner and stopped, its engine roaring, although the green fire had almost completely died down now, apart from a few small guttering flames. The smoke was thinning out too, although it was wafting in their direction and drifting between them.

Jerry sniffed. The smoke smelled like burning wood, but it had a tang to it too.

He sniffed again and said to Jamila, 'Can you smell that?'

She breathed in, closed her eyes, and then said, 'Yes, I can. Lemons.'

'This all has to be connected, doesn't it? There was that same lemony smell down in the sewers. And the way that old geezer in the brown coat keeps showing up. It's all linked up. It has to be. Just don't ask me how.'

He looked across at the skeleton of his car. Two firefighters were circling around it, spraying it with foam.

'Don't ask me what I'm going to tell my insurance company either. "Some geriatric waggled his fingers at me, and my car blew up."'

26

Louise was woken up by a deeply disturbing dream.

She dreamed that she was lost in a forest of tall dark trees and that it was raining, hard. In between the trees the forest floor was overgrown with ferns, and they nodded in sequence as the raindrops pattered down on them. She had the feeling that creatures of some kind were scuttling around, hidden beneath the ferns, rats or giant cockroaches. She could hear them, but she couldn't see them.

She knew there was a reason why she had entered the forest, but she couldn't remember what it was. All she wanted to do now was find her way out.

She forced her way through some bramble bushes, scratching her arms and her legs. On the other side of the brambles she came across a limpid pool, its surface dimpled by the raindrops. As she approached the edge of the pool, she heard crying from the opposite side. A child crying. In fact, as she listened, she realised it was *two* children crying, in melancholy harmony.

It was then that she remembered why she was here. She was looking for her children. She had gone into their bedroom this morning to wake them up, but their cots were both empty, with rumpled sheets, and she had known instinctively that they had gone to the forest.

She started to make her way around the pool. Progress was difficult, because it was boggy in places, and her slippered feet sank into the mud. She was only halfway round when she saw two pale figures emerge from the overgrown reeds. They were both dressed in white nightgowns, although the hems had trailed in the dirt. Their cheeks were streaked with tears and their mouths were turned down in misery, but even though they looked so sad, they were strangely beautiful, like angels in a medieval painting.

'What are you doing here?' Louise called out, although her voice sounded oddly muffled, as if she were shouting into a pillow. 'You need to come home!'

The two children began to struggle their way toward her through the reeds and the nettles, but as they came closer Louise saw that one of them appeared to have thin jointed arms and legs like a spider, while the other was waving hands that were curved into claws.

She felt icy cold. She knew that these were her children, and that she was supposed to take care of them, but they were both monstrosities. As they came nearer and nearer, she suddenly lost her nerve. She turned around and battled her way back through the bramble bushes, flailing at them wildly with both arms, even though they were lacerating her.

She heard the two children scream in fear and bewilderment, '*Mummy! Mummy! Where are you going?*' but she kept on stumbling through the forest until she burst out into the open, into the rain, and woke up.

★

She opened her eyes, and the first thing she did was lift up her arms, to see if they were scratched. Around her wrist was the fine silver bracelet her grandmother had given her, but except for some almost invisible scars from her schooldays, her skin was unmarked. She sniffed. There was an unfamiliar smell in the room, like smoke, but she supposed that the rest home's gardener must have lit a bonfire.

She sat up. The orange hessian curtains were drawn, but it was daylight outside. Last night she had worked the early-morning shift at The Whittington Rest Home, starting at midnight and finishing at eight, and after breakfast, she had gone straight to bed.

She was a large young woman, over 12 stone, and 5 foot 9. Last month, she had celebrated her thirty-fourth birthday and her fifth anniversary of nursing at the Whittington. The old people in the home adored her, because she was endlessly patient with them, even those residents who were suffering from dementia or Alzheimer's, or who were doubly incontinent. Despite her warmth though, she had only ever had one boyfriend – a shy ginger-haired accountant called Alan, who had eventually left her for another young man, called Grzegorz.

She stood up and went into her bathroom. Her stomach felt full and uncomfortable, as if she had eaten far too much, but she sat on the toilet for almost five minutes and all she could manage was a few squirts of urine. Eventually she gave up, washed her hands and brushed her choppy brunette bob in the mirror.

Her mother had always complimented her for having beautiful green eyes, but she had long ago given up believing that beautiful green eyes were enough to attract a man – not if you had a double chin and enormous breasts and a belly that flopped over the top of your tights. She had dieted, endlessly. This morning's breakfast had been nothing more than two slices of Ryvita with low-fat cream cheese and a cup of lemon tea. But dieting made no difference. It only prevented her from growing even fatter.

She sat back down on her bed and picked up her watch. It was 3:17 in the afternoon, so at least she had managed to have five and a half hours' sleep. She had nearly run out of toothpaste and shower gel so she decided she might as well get dressed and go out to the chemist. She just wished that her insides didn't feel so bloated. She lay back on her pillows, frowning and cradling her stomach.

'*Marta, rambling rose of the wild wood...*' a thin voice sang outside her door. She knew who that was: Leonard Bassett, only six months shy of his hundredth birthday. He had once been given top billing at the Camberwell Palace Theatre, but the theatre had been demolished thirty years ago and Leonard couldn't even remember his own name.

She wondered why he was wandering unaccompanied around the care home, and she was starting to get up when she was gripped by an agonising spasm in her stomach. She dropped back onto her bed, gasping with pain, clutching her stomach with one hand and the candlewick bedspread with the other. Something was *moving* inside her, something that was stretching and poking and scratching at her, and when she pulled up her nightdress, she could see that her stomach was bulging and undulating as if she were pregnant and a baby was kicking inside her.

She tried again to sit up, but she was wracked by another spasm, so painful that she hissed and doubled up. She had never known anything in the whole of her life to hurt so much as this. She rolled from side to side, digging her fingers deep into her stomach to try and stop the churning sensation, and when she did that she could actually feel a hard shape rising up and turning over inside her womb. It felt like a crab shell. Almost immediately after, she felt a second shape rise up, and the two shapes seemed to become locked and tangled up together, scratching the lining of her womb as fiercely as the brambles in her dream.

She stretched her mouth wide open, but her senses were blotted out with pain, and if she was screaming, she couldn't hear it. After a few moments though, her door was cautiously opened and Leonard appeared, almost skeletally thin, with long white hair, wrapped in a white towelling dressing gown. He came up to her bedside and leaned over her, his straggly eyebrows knitted in concern, and she could see his lips moving.

Louise reached out toward him, trying to make him understand that she was in too much pain to speak, but silently begging him to go and fetch help, as quickly as he could. If he didn't, she was sure that it would only be minutes before the pain totally overwhelmed her, and she died.

***

'Ah, you're awake,' said a man's voice.

Louise blinked. She looked around her and gradually

realised that she was lying in a dimly lit hospital room, and that it was dark outside, except for street lights. Two doctors were standing beside her bed, one male and one female, one on either side, smiling at her. At the end of the bed, a nurse in a green uniform was writing on a clipboard.

'Where am I?' she asked. Her mouth was so dry that she found it difficult to speak, and her breath smelled like wood varnish.

'You're in KCH,' said the doctor. 'That's King's College Hospital. You're in a room in Beverley Ward, where we treat patients who have birthing problems. My name is Doctor Sanjay Gupta. I am a consultant in emergency medicine. This is Doctor Clarissa Edwards, who is a consultant obstetrician. In fact, she's our head of obstetrics.'

Louise's head was throbbing, and she felt both bruised and nauseous, as if she had been punched very hard in the stomach, not just once, but again and again, so that she had been sick. Her hips were sore too.

'*Birthing* problems?' she said huskily. 'What do you mean, birthing problems? I'm not pregnant.'

'I hope it doesn't come as too much of a shock to you, Louise,' said Dr Edwards. 'But you *are* pregnant, yes.'

'I can't be pregnant. I haven't been with anybody. I haven't even got a boyfriend.'

'You're sure you haven't had any kind of sexual relations with anybody – not necessarily intercourse? Is it possible that somebody could have taken advantage of you while you were asleep, or after you'd had a little too much to drink?'

'I don't drink. And, no, I don't see how anybody could

have had sex with me while I was asleep. Nobody's allowed into the care home without a pass, and all our male patients – well, they're long past that kind of thing.'

'However it happened, Louise, there's no question that you are pregnant. We gave you a sonograph scan as soon as you were brought in here. As a matter of fact, I hate to spring this on you, but you're carrying not only one foetus, but two.'

'*Twins?* That isn't possible. It simply isn't possible.' Louise pressed her hand against her stomach and winced because it was still very tender. 'How long have I been here? What time is it?'

'A quarter past eleven. You were brought in just after three.'

'But before today I haven't been feeling any pain or any movement inside me – none at all. And it was my period last week. How can I be pregnant if I had my period last week?'

Dr Edwards looked across at Dr Gupta, and her expression was serious now. 'You have two living foetuses in your womb, Louise. But the problem is a little more complicated than that. There's no point in my beating about the bush. I have to tell you that the sonograph showed both of them to be suffering from severe malformation.'

'What does that mean? What's wrong with them?'

'It looks as if they're well into the second trimester – perhaps eighteen weeks or more. But although they're unusually active, they simply haven't formed properly. They have brains and hearts and all the other internal organs, but their bodies and their limbs are extremely misshapen. Every foetus develops clawlike muscles in their hands in the early stages of their growth – muscles that disappear before they reach full term. But it looks as if these two foetuses have sprouted all manner of extraneous muscles and limbs, and show no sign of losing them.'

'You're telling me that I've had them inside me for *eighteen weeks*? I can't have!'

'I understand how confused you are, Louise,' said Dr Gupta. 'But the results of the ultrasound are irrefutable. I am going to suggest that we also give you a CVS test. This is when we take a sample of cells from your placenta so that we can examine them for genetic or chromosomal disorders. In normal circumstances, there is a small percentage risk of miscarriage when we do this, but in your case...'

'Go on, tell me. What's so different about my case?'

'I'll have to be frank with you. In your case it seems highly unlikely that you will lose either of these two foetuses because of the unusual way in which they have connected themselves to you. They are attached not only to the lining of your womb, but somehow, they have managed to intertwine their nervous systems with yours by burying nerve rootlets into your spinal cord, and combined their circulatory systems with your inferior mesenteric artery. We have never seen anything like it.'

Louise could feel the foetuses shifting inside her, and her womb went into a painful spasm, which made her clench her teeth and grunt. She looked up at Dr Edwards in desperation.

'When you say I won't lose them... you *can* get rid of them, can't you?'

'Before we can consider termination, Louise, I'm afraid we'll have to carry out far more detailed scans. As Dr Gupta says, both foetuses have connected themselves to you in such a comprehensive and complex way that we can't simply give you a dose of mifepristone or cut them out surgically. If we tried to do that, the risk to your own life would be unacceptably high.'

'In other words, abortion would not only kill *them*, but you too,' said Dr Gupta. 'At least, that is how it looks at the moment. But we will try to find a way to do it.'

Louise started to cry. Her eyes welled up with tears, and she sobbed uncontrollably until she could scarcely breathe. Her womb went into another spasm, even more painful than the last, and she could feel a chilly fizzing sensation up her spine.

Dr Edwards tugged a tissue out of the box beside the bed and wiped her eyes for her. Then she held her hand and said, 'Louise... we're going to be doing everything we can to find out how we can terminate these two. In the meantime, we'll be giving you regular analgesics to suppress the pain. I have to be totally honest with you though. It does appear at the moment that you might have to carry them to full term and let them be born naturally.'

'But they're *not* natural! They're freaks! I saw them in a dream!'

'Excuse me? You saw them in a dream?'

Louise nodded frantically. 'I know it's them. I just know.

One of them was like a spider and the other one had claws like a lobster. But they both had beautiful faces.'

Dr Edwards looked across at Dr Gupta. She said nothing, but Dr Gupta picked up a folder from the side table and took out two 3D colour sonograph prints. He held them up so that Louise could see them, and there they were, clinging to each other, the same children that she had seen in her dream. In these pictures they were much smaller, and naked, and their eyes were closed, but she could clearly see the angelic face of the spidery foetus. Its arms and legs were folded protectively around the foetus with the claw-like hands.

'Oh dear God,' whispered Louise. 'Oh dear God I can't believe this. What are they going to look like when they're born? And what are you going to do with them, once they are? Are you going to kill them?'

27

It was well after five o'clock before Jamila and Jerry arrived at the BirthWell Centre, and it had started to rain.

After Jerry's car had burned out, DC O'Brien had come to Daneville Road to pick them up and take them back to Peckham police station. They had both taken a shower and recovered from their escape by sitting in the staff room with mugs of hot tea and watching half an hour of afternoon television.

DCI Walters had suggested that if they weren't up to it, they could postpone their interviews at the BirthWell Centre until the following day. Jamila had thanked him for his consideration but insisted that they talk to everybody who had seen Dr Macleod's abduction as soon as possible. She knew from experience how witnesses could unconsciously censor and reinterpret their memory of a crime scene, especially if it had been gory and traumatic. She had known witnesses to swear that they had seen people who hadn't even been there and invent car number plates that didn't exist.

The sleeve of Jamila's coat had been ripped open when Jerry had pulled her out of the shattered car window, and so she had borrowed a dark brown anorak from DC Pettigrew, which was two sizes too large for her.

'I hate to say this, sarge,' Jerry told her. 'But that jacket makes you look like an orphan.'

Jamila had studied herself in the mirror. 'My parents have both passed away, so I suppose, technically speaking, I *am* an orphan.'

Professor Karounis was on his way out to a bankers' dinner, so he gave them the use of his office. One by one, they questioned everybody who had been in the operating theatre when Dr Macleod had been skinned by Susan Nicholls's foetus and then dragged away. They weren't able to talk to Susan Nicholls herself because she was still in intensive care, heavily sedated, and Nurse Yeom had called in sick.

Both Dr Bhaduri and Dr Symonds looked tired and distressed. Dr Bhaduri couldn't stop coughing, although his cough was caused only by stress. Their accounts of the Caesarean section were almost identical, as well as their description of the way in which the foetus had clawed its way up Dr Macleod's sleeve and ripped its way underneath his skin.

Nurse Harris told them how she had pinned Dr Macleod to the floor, while Janet Horrocks recalled her panic when she found that she couldn't open any of the doors. Duncan explained his futile attempts to smash the doors apart with the fire extinguisher.

They all described the darkness and the moaning and then the singing sound, and how they had felt that some enormous invisible force had burst open the doors and dragged Dr Macleod out of the operating theatre.

It was only Kisi Adomako who said that she had actually heard distinct words being sung.

She was the last witness that Jerry and Jamila were questioning. She sat with her hands clasped together and her head bowed, and only occasionally looked up at them with her huge, soulful eyes.

'You heard actual words?' asked Jamila gently. 'The others heard singing... but none of them said they heard words.'

'The singing went up very high – so high you could hardly hear it. You know, like a dog whistle. But I felt that whoever was singing was very close to me. I'm sure I could feel their breath against my face.'

'So what words did you hear?'

'"Rise up, you shadows, and fly down, you crows."'

'That's all?' asked Jerry.

Kisi Adomako nodded. 'But she sang it over and over, at least three times. Like this: "Rise *up* you shadows! And fly *down*, you crows!"'

'You say "she"?' asked Jamila.

'I'm sure it was a woman. She was singing so high. And the way she was singing was not like she was pleading with the shadows and the crows to come and help her. It was like she was *telling* them to, or else there would be hell to pay. Men don't sing like that.'

'All right, Kisi. Thank you. I'm not exactly sure how, but that could be really helpful.'

Kisi said, 'I can still hear her. I can still hear that singing, in my ears. I have never been so frightened in my life.'

When they had finished all of their interviews, Jerry and Jamila sat back and looked at each other. The rain pattered against the office window, and it sounded almost as if it had something important to tell them.

'Do you *really* think she heard those words?' asked Jerry.

'Why would she make it up?'

'I don't know. Maybe she simply misheard. You know what it's like when you mishear a pop song. For years I thought "we built this city on rock'n'roll" was "we built this city on sausage rolls".'

'She heard *some* words though, and if she heard words, then we're dealing with a person, and a female person – even if that person *is* some kind of supernatural force, or a spirit, or a ghost.'

'What are the chances that it was the same spooky thing that took away those foetuses at St George's and tore that poor girl's arms off? That same thing we saw in the street with all those kids?'

'Extremely high, I should think. And since we've finished here, we'd better get over to St George's now.'

***

When they arrived at St George's Hospital, forty minutes later, Dr Pocztomski took them immediately into the laboratory where he had been intending to examine the two distorted foetuses. Two forensic technicians were still there, in their crinkly Tyvek suits, taking samples from the pools and splatters of blood on the floor. They had propped the broken door up against the wall and were photographing it with ultraviolet light.

'Give us a couple of minutes and we'll be finished,' one of them told Jamila, tugging down his face mask to reveal a neat little moustache, like Hercule Poirot. 'I can tell you what's really odd though, even before we've carried out any analysis back at Lambeth Road.'

'Tell us something that *isn't* odd,' said Jerry.

'No – you see the floor there, next to the sink? That's where the victim had her arms ripped off. And you see all the footprints, in the blood? Every one of those footprints matches the shoes of one of the pathology team – the doctor here, and his assistant, and the two students who were here to watch. But that's all. The perpetrator, him or herself – they didn't leave a single footprint.'

Jamila pointed to the two portable incubators, with their plastic lids still open. 'There's no fingerprints or DNA on those?'

'Yes, of course, and we'll be matching them with all the hospital staff who might have handled them. But neither of them appear to have any trace of blood on them, which we would have expected if the perpetrator had opened them up after severing the victim's arms.'

After they had looked around the laboratory, Dr Pocztomski led them upstairs to a small quiet waiting room, with an overstuffed sofa and two ill-matched armchairs. On the wall hung a faded reproduction of Ophelia floating in the stream, and on the coffee table lay dog-eared copies of *Country Life* and *OK!* magazines.

'I am not superstitious,' Dr Pocztomski told them. 'My grandmother believed in ghosts and swore that she could have conversations with the dead, but I think she was simply senile. But let me tell you – what I saw in that laboratory today... I can only say that it must have been a ghost of some sort.'

'Can you describe it?' Jamila asked him.

'I've already told the officers who first came here, after we had called the police. It was like smoke, black smoke. It appeared out of nowhere, nowhere at all, but it quickly took on a shape like a priest or a witch with a pointed hood. And it talked to us – well, *shouted* at us, rather, but it had no voice of its own. It used Mel's voice – the unfortunate girl who lost her arms. It used her like a ventriloquist.'

Dr Pocztomski told them as much as he could remember of what the hooded figure had said. '*God and their mothers turned their backs on them, and cast them out, but I never will! They are* my *nestlings now!*'

Jerry said, 'When the figure appeared, did you like *smell* anything?'

'Yes, I did. It not only looked like smoke, but it smelled like smoke. Like a bonfire.'

'Anything else?'

'I don't know. Perhaps a hint of something sour.'

Jamila and Jerry exchanged glances but said nothing, and didn't ask Dr Pocztomski if the sourness reminded him of lemons.

'Those two foetuses you were going to examine... do you have any idea what might have caused them to become so deformed?'

'Many foetuses are malformed – more than you would think. If the malformation is extreme, the foetus more often than not is spontaneously expelled from the uterus. Otherwise, when the obstetricians see that it will be born with disabilities that would make its life intolerable, they will recommend termination.'

'But these two foetuses... they were still living and breathing, weren't they, in spite of being aborted?'

'Yes. But of course they were taken away before I had the opportunity to examine them, so I have no idea how that could have been possible. Neither do I have any idea how they could have become so malformed in the first place. In the whole of my career I have never seen any foetuses that looked like them – and I have never encountered anything like that figure in a hood. How could it have torn off Mel's arms like that? And it tore off the door, too, and flung it at me. How can something made of smoke have the strength to do that?'

'Well – that is what we are doing our utmost to find out,' said Jamila. 'Meanwhile, doctor, I must ask that you do not speak to the media about this incident. That is partly because it could affect our investigation by letting the offender know how much progress we are making... or, to be honest, how *little* progress we are making. And also we do not wish to cause unnecessary public alarm, especially among expectant parents.'

'Don't worry,' Dr Pocztomski assured her. 'I haven't the slightest intention of telling anybody about this. They will think I am *zwariowałem*. In other words, that I have gone crazy.'

After they had left the pathology laboratory, they went along the corridor to the morgue. It was chilly and silent in there, and one of the fluorescent lights was flickering intermittently, like an irregular heartbeat.

A surprisingly cheerful morgue assistant with dreadlocks led them to the far end of the morgue and then rolled out the drawer on which Dr Macleod's body was lying in a white PEVA body bag. He opened it up for them with a sticky, crackling sound, and they could see that he had been flayed right down to his raw red flesh.

'Dr Kendrick is coming to examine him later,' said the morgue assistant. 'He still hasn't completed his examination of all those forensic officers who were killed in that sewer, but he said that he wants to examine this one personally. Do you know Dr Kendrick? He specialises in cases where the victims have been dismembered or mutilated. You remember that case last year when that fellow in Croydon chopped up his wife and roasted one of her legs and ate it for his Christmas dinner? It was Dr Kendrick's evidence that got him sent down.'

As they walked across to the hospital car park, Jerry said, 'I think I feel sick.'

'You and me both, Jerry,' said Jamila.

They left St George's and drove back to Peckham. For most of the way they were silent, but as they reached Peckham High Street, Jamila said, 'I've been thinking.'

'What about? What you're going to have for Christmas dinner?'

'No, Jerry, I'm a Muslim. I've been thinking about what that midwife told us that she heard. "Rise up, you shadows, and fly down, you crows." That sounds to me like the beginning of some sort of invocation.'

'Sorry, don't follow you,' said Jerry. 'What's an "invocation", exactly?'

'It's when you call on a spiritual force to help you in whatever you want to do. Like praying to God, or whatever gods you happen to believe in. Maybe it's to cure your father of cancer, or to feed you, if you're hungry, or to make you happy. Or like asking Satan or some demon to destroy your enemies, or to make you rich, or to bring you a hundred naked women for the night.'

'I'll go for that one,' said Jerry. 'You don't happen to know it, do you?'

'No... and I don't know the one about the shadows and the crows either, but when we get back to the station, I'm going to google it, and see if it's a known invocation. It might give us a clue, who knows?'

28

It was gradually beginning to grow light when Gemma and Jim Feather and a team of five radar specialists set out from the Crane's Drains building in two white vans with the crane symbol on the side.

The clouds were so low that they could hear the constant stream of planes thundering on their way to land at Heathrow airport in the west, but they couldn't see them.

Gemma had prepared a map of the five abandoned cesspits that were connected with the local sewers, based on the map used by the nineteenth-century night-soil company. Several of the houses on Mr Clarke's original map had been demolished or bombed during the war, so she had updated it to show any houses or shops or blocks of flats that had been built in their place.

They drove first to the large early-Victorian house on the corner of Talfourd Place. Gemma had already contacted the owners and asked for permission to survey the back of the property, and so the GPR team unloaded their radar equipment and carried it around to the garden.

'I hope this ain't no yeti hunt,' said Jim Feather, as he and Gemma followed them through the garden gate.

'It could be, Jim. But I don't know. I have such a strong feeling about it, that's all. I kept asking myself where would *I* hide, if I was one of those children, and I was down in the sewers?'

'If I was a kid, I'd never go down in the sewers in the first place. I grew up above ground in Lewisham and that was bad enough.'

'I tried to put myself in their place, that's all.'

'Well, respect to you for that. I can't even begin to imagine what it must be like to be living in a sewer with a bonce the size of a medicine ball or half my guts hanging out.'

It took the best part of an hour to survey the garden. The cesspit was still there, under the ground, but it had been completely filled in with topsoil, and all the GPR team could find was a hoe with a broken handle and the skeletons of three cats, which had presumably been buried by their owners when they died.

'All right, on to the next one,' said Gemma.

The next disused cesspit was located at Carlton Grove, on the corner of Peckham High Street. It had once been the site of an imposing house, which between the wars had been converted into eight flats. In the summer of 1943 it had been badly bombed and then demolished, and eventually it had been rebuilt as a four-storey block of flats with a Sainsbury's mini-market underneath it.

Luckily for Gemma and the GPR team, the street level behind the mini-market had been left open for the residents to park their cars, so they were able to roll their radar scanners over the garage floors.

Again though, they found nothing. The blurry outline of the cesspit was still visible on their radar screens, but during the construction of the flats, it had mostly been filled in with concrete and rubble from the demolished house, to act as foundations.

Jim Feather said nothing as they climbed back into their van, but Gemma could tell what he was thinking. *Waste of bloody time, this is.*

The third house was further away to the east, in Tranquil Vale, Blackheath, overlooking the grassy heath and the spire of All Saints' Church. This was an imposing five-bedroomed mansion built in 1829, with a tawny brick façade and a white-pillared porch. Although it was currently empty and up for sale, Gemma had been in touch with the estate agents, and they had given her permission to survey the rear of the property where the cesspit had been located.

'I should've brought a flask of tea, shouldn't I?' said Gemma, clapping her hands together and shuffling her feet to keep warm.

'I should've brought a full English breakfast,' said Jim. 'I'm so bloody hungry I could eat a baby through the bars of a cot.'

They watched as the GPR team systematically wheeled their instruments up and down the garden, which was laid out with octagonal rose beds and a vegetable patch and a circular patio with a sundial, although it was all beginning to look neglected and overgrown. A fine rain started falling, and still the invisible planes kept thundering overhead.

After about twenty minutes, the leader of the GPR team

called out 'Gemma!' and beckoned her. He was a short bald-headed man with enormous tortoiseshell spectacles, which gave him the appearance of a cartoon character.

Gemma and Jim crossed over to the other side of the garden.

'What is it, Norman? Don't tell me you've found something.'

Norman pointed to the video screen attached to the handles of the ground-penetrating radar scanner.

'See for yourself. The cesspit's all covered over, but it's never been filled in with soil or rubble, not like that last one at Carlton Grove. Now, see the breach in its left-hand side? That gives direct access to and from the main Blackheath sewer. I'd say that it was broken into when the sewer was first built, either by accident or on purpose.'

The other four members of Norman's team were now gathered around them, and they were all watching Gemma intently to see what her reaction was going to be. Norman turned the radar scanner around through ninety degrees, and then he said, 'There. Is this what we've been looking for?'

Gemma leaned forward, shading the screen with her hand so that she could see it more clearly. Along the right-hand side of the cesspit, at least twenty small figures were heaped up, their legs and arms intertwined with each other. The radar couldn't show them in perfect detail, but it was obvious that some of them had oversized heads and others had distorted bodies and awkwardly angled legs. On the video screen, they had the appearance of a nest of grasshoppers.

None of them was moving, so Gemma could only assume that they were sleeping. Or – if they weren't sleeping – that they were dead.

'Yes,' she said to Norman. She needed to take a moment to steady herself. 'This is exactly what we've been looking for. Well done.'

Jim Feather took a look and sucked in his breath. 'Bloody hell,' he said. 'What do we do now? We can't just leave them there, can we? But they're not really our responsibility, are they? I mean, without splitting hairs, Crane's Drains are only contracted to take care of public sewers and storm drains – not disused cesspits on private property.'

'Jim – these are the children who attacked us. These are the children who took Martin away so that he could have his legs cut off and his eyes pulled out. That's if they *are* children, which I'm beginning to doubt. They've made it impossible for us to carry out our contract and maintain the sewers, so – yes, we *are* responsible for them, in a way. Responsible for getting rid of them, anyway.'

'So do we dig down and haul them out? And then what do we do with them?'

'No, we don't dig them out,' said Gemma. 'That cesspit is at least two metres deep, and the moment they heard us digging, they'd probably try to escape through the sewers. God alone knows where they'd find to hide themselves then.

'The first thing I'm going to do is call Detective Sergeant Patel and tell her that we've found them. We're going to need police officers, aren't we, and probably first-aiders too. Then the best way to get them out of there would be to approach them through the sewer, the same way they got in there. I noticed that there's manhole access on the far side of the heath.'

'You don't think there's any danger of the same thing happening like it did at Southampton Way?' asked Jim Feather. 'Sewage blasting out, and us all getting chopped to bits?'

'I don't know, Jim. I hope not. We'll need to stay hyper-alert, that's all. If there's any sign of flooding, or wind, or the lights going funny, we'll have to get out of there fast. But this is much higher ground than Southampton Way and it's only about two hundred metres from the manhole to the cesspit. And we can't just leave those children in there. There's no way.'

'If you say so,' said Jim Feather. 'If it was up to me, I'd brick them up and fucking forget about them.'

***

Jerry was in the kitchenette of his flat in Tooting, frying himself two eggs, when his phone played 'My Old Man's A Dustman'.

'Jerry? It's Jamila. She's found them.'

'Oh, yeah? Who's found what?'

'Gemma Bright. That hunch she had about cesspits – she was right. She took out a team of ground radar specialists early this morning, and she's found where the children are hiding. They're in a disused cesspit under a house on the edge of Blackheath. She thinks there must be at least twenty of them.'

'Blackheath? That's posh. At least they're not hiding anywhere downmarket.'

'She's still out there now, with her radar team. She says the children look as if they're asleep, but she's keeping a watch on them to make sure they don't wake up and make a run for it. Her suggestion is that we go down the sewer from the nearest manhole and bring them out from the cesspit the way they got in.'

'Oh, no. Not down the sewer again. And if there's twenty of them – Jesus, we're going to need at least two dozen uniforms to back us up... plus paramedics, in case any of them are sick, or put up a fight and get injured, plus at least two buses, or vans. And what are we going to do with them, once we've got them all out? Every one of them has some kind of special need or another, and that's putting it mildly.'

'I know, Jerry. But I'll be contacting DCI Walters right away, to get it all set up. We need to do this as soon as possible.'

'I'm supposed to be picking up Alice this morning.'

'I'm sorry. You will have to put her off.'

'Great. The ex is going to love me even less than she does already. And Alice has been looking forward to it for a fortnight.'

'I'm sorry. But DCI Walters will expect us to be there, and it's imperative that we are. The MIT may be in overall charge, but this is *our* investigation, after all – yours and mine.'

'To be honest with you, sarge, I never believed that Gemma would actually find them. But there's something else we need to think about. What happens if everything goes green again, and that smoky cloaky hoody thing shows up and starts throwing keys at us and tearing us all to bits?'

'I don't know, Jerry. But we'll never understand what this is all about unless we do everything we can to confront it. Look – I'll meet you at the station at ten. DCI Walters should have been able to get most of the task force together by then.'

Jerry's eggs were becoming crisp and burned around the edges, and his kitchenette started to fill with smoke, so he quickly lifted the frying pan off the hob. 'Okay, sarge, okay. I'll see you then. By the way, did you manage to find out what that song was all about – "come up you shadows and come down you crows" or whatever it was?'

'Not yet, no. I googled it, but I couldn't find anything that matched.'

'I told you. She couldn't have heard it right – that's if she heard it at all and it wasn't just a figleaf of her imagination.'

'Never mind. I will see you later. I am truly sorry about your access visit with Alice, but I am afraid such disappointments are part of the job.'

'Tell me about it. I knew I should have been an accountant.'

'Jerry – you can't even work out the tip on a restaurant bill.'

'Well, maybe a golf pro. Or a masseur. I wouldn't have minded being a masseur.'

'Try to be early, if you can. We'll have a great deal of preparation to do.'

29

By 11:15 a team of seventeen uniformed officers had been assembled at Peckham police station, as well as six paramedics and five flushers from Crane's Drains, who had brought with them all the helmets and breathing packs and LED lights they would need when they entered the Blackheath sewer.

They gathered together in the briefing room, and when they had finished coughing and scraping their chairs, DCI Walters stood up to give them a short introduction. He spoke in a dry monotone, as if he were addressing the shareholders' meeting of a struggling restaurant chain.

'You're all familiar with the major incident here in Peckham two days ago when the main drain forcibly discharged a huge quantity of sewage. Tragically, as you well know, five of the Met's forensic officers and an employee of the drain company were fatally injured.

'What you *won't* be aware of is that over the past few days we've had several other serious incidents in the same sewer and in other sewers in the Peckham area. Even though they've all involved assault and critical injury, and they all appear to be related, we've kept them strictly confidential. This is because of their highly unusual nature.

'You've been gathered here this morning because we've located a considerable number of suspects involved in these incidents – approximately twenty in total – and we need you to go down into the sewers where they're hiding and fetch them out, by force if necessary.

'DS Patel here, along with DC Pardoe, has been running this investigation day-to-day, and I think she is the best person to explain what you can expect to encounter.'

Jamila stood up, and Jerry could tell from the expressions on some of the officers' faces that they were thinking, *Hallo, a woman, and a Pakistani woman at that*, and rolling their eyes at each other.

Their expressions soon changed though, when she started to describe everything that had happened in the Southampton Way sewer, and how Martin Elliot had been dragged away and mutilated. She left nothing out – the appearance of the children, the green lights, the keys, the moaning, and the hooded figure formed out of smoke.

She also explained how the fatal explosion of sewage appeared to be connected with the incidents at St George's laboratory and at the Warren BirthWell Centre, and the murder of Dr Macleod.

The officers sat in silence, and it was obvious that they were finding it hard to believe what Jamila was telling them.

'I can fully appreciate that you are finding this all incredible,' she said. 'However, you will be going down into a sewer yourselves today, and it is possible that you will be coming face to face with some or all of these phenomena. So you need to be forewarned.

'The children that you are tasked with bringing out of that cesspit are deformed beyond anything you have ever seen. Despite that, they have considerable strength, much stronger than ordinary children, so treat them with great caution and respect.

'Above all, I have to advise you that if you see or smell woodsmoke, especially if that smoke has a distinctive tang of lemons to it, then you should immediately drop what you are doing and evacuate the sewer as fast as you can.'

After Jamila had finished and sat down, nobody spoke for at least a quarter of a minute. Then one officer raised his hand and said, 'Come on, DS Patel – is this a wind-up? Is this some kind of psychological exercise to see how much bullshit we'll sit here and swallow? It's not April Fools' Day, so I can't think of any other explanation.'

There was nervous laughter all around the briefing room.

Jamila stood up again and said, 'I was expecting that reaction, and I can't say that I blame you. For that reason, I suggest you log in to this YouTube link. It shows excerpts from the videos that were taken down in the sewers at Southampton Way. It also shows you Martin Elliot, the manager of Crane's Drains, in his hospital bed, Dr Macleod's body in the morgue at St George's Hospital, and the state of the laboratory at St George's after the student pathologist had her arms torn off.'

There was a longer silence while everybody sat with their heads bowed, checking their phones. At last the officer looked up and said, 'Blimey,' and there was a rustle of shock from everyone else on the team.

DCI Walters said, 'Once we've extricated the children, we'll be taking them to Evelina Children's Hospital, next to St Thomas's. They're setting aside an outpatients ward for us on the sixth floor, which they've recently converted from offices. They'll have consultant paediatricians waiting for us, so that they can examine the children asap.'

'The technicians here from Crane's Drains will help you to put on your protective suits and helmets, and show you how to use the breathing apparatus,' said Jamila. 'And there's one more thing. We're calling this "Operation Suffer". As in "suffer little children to come unto me".'

'Amen to that,' said a woman paramedic at the back of the room.

They all stood up and noisily prepared themselves to leave for Blackheath. Jamila called Gemma to tell her that they were on their way.

'The children are still asleep,' Gemma told her. 'They're definitely not dead though. We've seen one or two of them stirring, as if they're having a bad dream.'

'Keep your eye on them,' said Jamila. 'We shouldn't be more than fifteen minutes at the outside.'

Jerry and Jamila went downstairs to the armoury. They would both be carrying Glock 26 subcompact pistols on Operation Suffer, although Jerry questioned if bullets would be any kind of deterrent to somebody who appeared to be made out of smoke – even if they *were* capable of hitting him so hard that they had almost knocked him unconscious.

As they waited to sign for their weapons and ammunition, Jamila's phone rang. After she had answered it, she stood with her pen poised over the firearms docket, listening intently. She said, 'Yes,' and then, 'Oh, no, that is so sad,' and then, 'Right, okay… was that all?'

'What is it?' Jerry asked her, as she tucked her phone back in her pocket.

'That was Dr Gupta from King's College Hospital. Martin Elliot died about an hour ago. Cardiac arrest.'

'Oh, shit. Poor bloke. He wouldn't have had much of a life though, would he? Blind, with no legs.'

'Dr Gupta said he was calling because the duty nurse spoke to him last night. She told him that Martin Elliot was highly agitated, and she was worried about him. It seems he was convinced that he'd forgotten to tell us something important.'

'Really? Did he tell the nurse what it was?'

'Yes. Even though he was totally blind he'd managed to write it down on a piece of paper. The nurse promised him she would make sure that we received it. Dr Gupta's kept it for us, but it was only two words. "Cave" and "friendship".'

'And Martin Elliot was stressed out because he'd forgotten to tell us that? "Cave" and "friendship"?'

'Apparently.'

'Maybe by "cave" he meant the cesspit where the children were hiding. I wouldn't like to guess about "friendship".'

'Who knows? And of course he's passed away now, so we can't ask him.'

'Didn't that unpronounceable doctor at St George's say that his grandmother could talk to the dead? Maybe we could ask her to ask him.'

'Jerry – Dr Pocztomski also told us that his grandmother was senile. And anyway, we need to get our skates on. Whatever Martin Elliot meant, we have to go over to Blackheath now and bring out those children.'

***

By the time Jerry and Jamila and their seventeen-strong squad of officers arrived at Blackheath, they found that flushers from Crane's Drains had already opened up the manhole on the corner of Duke Humphrey Road and surrounded it with blue canvas screens. A brisk breeze was blowing across the heath, which made the screens rumble like the sails of a yacht.

Every member of the squad was now kitted out in fluorescent-yellow PVC coveralls, as well as white helmets, gloves and boots, including Jerry and Jamila and the paramedics.

'Gordon Bennett,' said Jerry, as the officers gathered around them. 'We look like the canaries' annual reunion.'

Gemma and Jim Feather were standing by the manhole too, although they had left their ground radar team in the garden over the cesspit, to keep watch over the sleeping children and warn them if they showed any signs of movement.

'We've surveyed the whole length of the sewer between here and the house with a Troglotech camera,' said Gemma. 'It's three metres wide and it's reasonably clean, and at the moment, the sewage flow is only about nine centimetres deep.'

'What about the breach into the cesspit itself?' asked Jamila. 'How wide is that? None of our officers is exactly anorexic, and these suits are quite bulky. We don't want to reach it and then find that we can't get in.'

'It'll be a bit of a tight squeeze, I'll admit that,' said Jim Feather. 'I reckon it was originally built as an outlet duct, so that the cesspit could empty straight into the sewer. That was probably done in the 1860s, before the householder could install one of them new-fangled flushing toilets, and the S-bend plumbing that went with it. But by the looks of it some of the brickwork on both sides has been knocked out to widen it, and quite recently too. I'd guess that whoever did that was trying to give the children easier access.'

Jamila turned to the officers standing around her. 'Right, ladies and gentlemen. The plan is that we will enter the sewer in single file with an operative from Crane's Drains in between every fifth one of us, carrying LED lamps, and that's apart from the lamps on our helmets. Once we've reached the cesspit, we'll enter it immediately and flood it with light. That will make it easier for us to see what we are doing, but more importantly it will dazzle the children and hopefully catch them off their guard.

'Depending on how violently they struggle, the plan is to pass them back one by one along the line so that they can be lifted out of the manhole. If they are able to sit, they can then be fastened into their seats in the buses. If not, they can be strapped down to beds in the ambulances. Are there any questions?'

'Yes,' said one of the officers. 'Am I dreaming this?'

'If you're able to smell shit in your dreams, then maybe you are,' Jerry told her. 'If not, then you're awake, and this is real.'

He tightened the buckle on his helmet and added, 'Okay, everybody? Here goes nothing.'

A burly officer from Gipsy Hill police station climbed down into the manhole first. His name was Eddie Green, and he had been a runner-up in last year's Met Police Boxing Championships. Jerry and Jamila climbed down immediately after him. It was up to them to enter the cesspit before any of the other officers so that they could assess which children should be taken away first, and which children might be aggressive or even dangerous. Eddie Green would give them some protection if the children started to attack them. Apart from being a trained boxer, he was carrying a Taser attached to his belt, as well as a telescopic baton. Both Jerry and Jamila, of course, had their Glock 26s.

They sloshed their way along the brightly lit sewer, with Eddie Green in front, his head bowed so that he wouldn't hit it on the curving brick roof. Jim Feather followed close behind, carrying an LED lamp and a video camera.

Jerry sniffed. He could smell sewage, but he couldn't smell woodsmoke, or lemons. He couldn't say anything to Jamila because they were keeping strict silence until they entered the cesspit, in case they woke and alerted the children. His heart was beating hard and his Perspex face mask was steaming up, and for the first time in a long time, he realised that he was genuinely frightened, to the point where he could almost have wet himself.

This was completely different to his first experience down in the sewers – even when the wind had howled and the lights had turned green and he and Jamila had been struck by that blizzard of keys. He had felt alarmed then, and disorientated, but he had also felt a self-surviving thrill of adrenaline. Today, he felt nothing but sheer shivering dread. He couldn't stop thinking about the body parts that had come thumping down onto the pavement out of that cascade of sewage on Peckham High Street, and the way that hooded figure had attacked him.

He had the irrational sensation that the sewer was gradually closing in on him, becoming narrower and narrower, and that the air was becoming increasingly foetid and lacking in oxygen. He had to focus all of his mental strength not to turn around and blunder his way back to the manhole, and scramble out, and breathe in the fresh chilly breeze that was blowing across Blackheath.

It took them less than five minutes of wading through sewage to reach the ragged breach in the sewer wall. It was about half a metre wide and slightly less than one and a half metres high. The brick quoins on either side of it had been broken away, and some of them were still lying in lumps among the sewage.

Jim Feather was careful not to shine his LED lamp directly into the breach. He looked back to the line of police officers and flushers who were following behind him and gave them a thumbs-up signal to make sure that they were all ready. He was given a series of thumbs ups in return.

'Okay, go,' said Jamila softly, and patted PC Green on the shoulder. He ducked his helmeted head down and shouldered his way into the breach, his PVC coveralls rustling against the broken bricks.

Jamila turned to Jerry, and although she didn't say anything, he could see that she was just as frightened as he was. They had both seen Dr Macleod lying scarlet and skinned in the morgue, and there was nothing to reassure them that they weren't going to meet the same fate.

Jamila went into the breach first, with Jerry close behind her. Jim Feather followed, with the light from his LED lamp swivelling and dancing all around him.

They stepped into the cesspit and immediately filled it with light, so bright that it made them blink. Its ceiling and its walls were dry and fibrous with tree roots, and its floor had been spread with grubby brown blankets. The children were lying together in the far corner, most of them dressed in the white nightgowns that they had been wearing when Jerry and Jamila had seen them running away into Charles Coveney Road. Their arms and legs were all interlocked, as if they were clinging on to each other for security and warmth. As Eddie Green and Jamila and Jerry came in, three or four of them lifted their heads and looked up in surprise.

Three more officers and one of the flushers entered the cesspit behind them, and they all stood there confronting the children. For the first few moments, it was a silent stand-off, as the children stared at the police in bewilderment, and the police stared at the children in utter disbelief.

Every child was malformed in a different way. Some had
enormous heads, with thinning hair on them, as if they
were suffering from encephalitis. Others had tiny heads,
with near-together eyes as dark as rabbits. More than one
of them had several arms and legs, or conjoined bodies
protruding from their chests, or no limbs at all. One of
them was little more than a head, with two arms and a
neck that inflated when it breathed.

'Where's old smoky?' hissed Jerry, under his breath.

'I have no idea,' said Jamila. 'But the longer she stays
away, the better.'

With that, she approached the children and lifted both
hands to show them that she meant them no harm.

'Please – do not be scared of us,' she said. 'We have come
to take you away to somewhere safe and comfortable. We
are not going to hurt you.'

She reached down and took hold of the arm of
the nearest child, a little girl with tousled blonde hair. The
girl's eyes were both milky white, and there was nothing
but an empty cavity where her nose should have been.
When Jamila tried to lift her up, she held on tightly to the
boy lying next to her, whose body underneath his
nightgown looked plump and childish, but who had thick
hairy arms like a grown man.

'Listen, I promise you, we're going to look after you,'
Jamila told her. 'Do you understand me? Do any of
you understand me?'

The little girl held on to the plump boy even tighter
and started to cry. Then more and more of the children
started to sob. Some of their crying was high-pitched and

squeaking, others made strange breathy sounds, because they had no larynxes or sinuses, and one small boy had no lower jaw, so that they could see his windpipe bulging out of his neck when he cried.

At least seven of the police officers were crowded into the cesspit now, and they looked at each other as if they were trying to persuade themselves that none of this was real, that it was impossible for these children to be alive, let alone crying.

Jamila tugged at the little girl's arm again, and this time Eddie Green bent over and prised her hand free from the plump boy's arm. The little girl let out a whistling sound, but instead of fighting, she reached out for Jamila and held on to her, and as Jamila lifted her up, she hugged her closely.

Next, a boy with a large head climbed to his feet, with tears running down his cheeks. He held out his arms, and Eddie Green picked him up and passed him over to one of the officers waiting by the breach in the cesspit wall. One after another, the children who could manage to stand up came limping and hobbling toward them, all of them with their arms raised, all of them wordlessly pleading to be taken away.

Those who had no arms or legs or who were so misshapen that they were unable to get up off the floor continued to sob, but they sounded less panicky now, because they could see that they were not going to be forgotten.

'I'm not going to write about this in my memoirs,' said Jerry, shaking his head. 'People will say I'm taking the piss.'

All of the children were passed along the sewer by the

line of officers and then lifted out of the manhole. They all smelled of stale urine and something pungent and herbal.

Jamila sniffed and said, 'Mugwort. You can burn it as incense – it's supposed to keep evil spirits away.'

'Mugwort? I'll have to get some of that for the ex-wife,' said Jerry. His feeling of dread had completely faded now, and he was beginning to feel confident that they might be making some real progress with this investigation, for all of its insanity. If there was one thing he had learned, working with Jamila, it was that the supernatural was only terrifying if you didn't understand it. Once you did, it was nothing more than deeply unsettling.

He was hugely relieved that the children hadn't struggled or tried to attack them. He saw the girl who Gemma had sketched, with her intestines hanging below the hem of her nightgown, but she had her eyes half closed and a dreamy expression on her face, like the picture of Ophelia floating in the stream.

The remaining children were lifted up and handed along the sewer with exceptional care and tenderness, despite their deformities. There were twenty-two children altogether, and by the time they had removed the last of them from the cesspit, Jerry could see that the officers had begun to accept their extreme abnormality and treat them with the same consideration that they treated the victims of horrific accidents, like fires or car crashes.

'That's it then, sarge,' said Jerry, once the last child had been carried away and the cesspit was empty. 'The lights didn't go green, and we didn't get a howling gale, and old smoky didn't put in an appearance.'

'I still don't think we've seen the last of her... or it, or whatever it is,' said Jamila. 'You remember what she said about touching her nestlings. "*You'll suffer like your friends have suffered.*"'

'Well, yes. And I still don't believe that she's only made out of smoke. She bloody hit me hard enough, and if it *was* her that killed Dr MacLeod and pulled that poor girl's arms off...'

Jamila looked around the cesspit. 'I'll call Lambeth Road and ask them to send a forensics team to check this out... these blankets and everything. And there's faeces in the far corner. They need to examine that to see what those children have been eating and where they might have got it from. That could help us to find "old smoky", as you call her.'

They waded their way back along the sewer and climbed out on to the corner of Duke Humphreys Road, their boots dripping. All of the children who were able to sit up had now been lifted into the buses, and the remaining eight were being taken to the Evelina Children's Hospital by ambulance.

Jim Feather came up to them and said, 'Mission accomplished, folks. I don't know about you, but I could do with a very stiff drink.'

'Mission accomplished for you, perhaps,' said Jamila. 'For us, this is only the beginning.'

Behind her back, Jerry gave Jim Feather a hand-waggling gesture as if he were knocking back a glass of Scotch.

30

Jamila and Jerry followed the second ambulance to Lambeth. They had left DC Pettigrew at Blackheath to brief the forensic officers when they arrived. DC O'Brien had gone to King's College Hospital to talk to Dr Gupta and the nurse who had been present before Martin Elliot died, and to collect the piece of paper on which he had managed to scrawl 'cave' and 'friendship', whatever that meant.

Evelina Children's Hospital was a modern brick-and-glass annexe to St Thomas' Hospital, on the opposite bank of the River Thames from the Houses of Parliament. They arrived in a convoy, two squad cars, two buses and two ambulances, with Jamila and Jerry behind them.

They had driven there in silence, but as they turned into the entrance, Jerry suddenly jammed on his brakes and said, 'There! *Look!* Look, sarge! It's only him! It's only that old geezer who set us alight!'

Standing beneath a metal sculpture of fish and seaweed and seagulls, smiling mockingly at them, was the white-haired old man in the brown tweed coat. Jerry was about to climb out of the car and go after him when an ambulance blew its horn at him for blocking the gateway. He drove further into the hospital grounds and pulled up on the left-hand side, with two wheels on the pavement.

'You can't park there, mate!' the ambulance driver shouted at him, as he drove past.

'Police!' Jerry shouted back, and went running after the old man standing at the front entrance. The gate was less than fifty metres away, but when he reached it, the old man had gone. As far as Jerry could see along Lambeth Bridge Road, there was no sign of him at all – only five or six distant pedestrians, and none of them were him.

He walked back to the car and climbed in. 'Scarpered,' he said. 'Don't know how he does it. Must have rocket-propelled underpants.'

'You've been able to get a good look at him though, haven't you? You could try posting an EvoFIT of him on social media. Somebody must recognise him.'

'I was *sure* I took a photo of him outside McDonald's, but he simply didn't appear in it. And when I went outside there, he'd vanished into thin air. Poof! Gone, like he didn't exist.'

'You were right though. He has to be connected with the children somehow. That green lemony-smelling fire that burned out your car, that couldn't have been a coincidence. And now what is he doing *here*, of all places – at the very moment when we're bringing in the children from the cesspit?'

'I can't think how the hell he knows where we're going and how he manages to follow us around. But, yes, I'll have an EvoFIT done. I'll get the bastard yet.'

After Jerry had parked, they walked together into the shiny reception area, which had a curved glass ceiling that reached almost up to the top of the building. Two armed police officers were standing on either side of the lifts and asked to see their ID, even though they both knew who Jerry was. It was Jerry who had made sure that they were posted there.

'Who have they got up there then?' one of the officers asked him, pointing to the ceiling. 'Some VIP? Some royal kid?'

'You don't want to know, squire,' Jerry told him. 'I don't want you having nightmares.'

They went up in the lift to the sixth floor. Here, the children were being settled into what was temporarily being called Peaceful Ward, although they could still hear sobbing as they walked along the corridor toward it. The other wards in the hospital were named after creatures like seahorses and turtles and bears.

Inside the ward, twenty-two beds had been arranged for the children along the walls and under the windows. A paediatric consultant, two junior doctors, a ward sister and five police officers were gathered in between them. Four nurses were already going from bed to bed, wheeling screens across so that they could take off the children's filthy nightgowns and give each of them a blanket bath. A few of the children were still weeping, but most of them were silent now. Those children who were able to see were staring at the adults as if they expected something dramatic to happen at any moment, but the ward was true to its name, and it remained peaceful. Apart from the plaintive mewling of two or three of the children, the only sound was the concentrated murmuring of the medical staff and the rustle of paper as they leafed through their clipboards.

'... work out some kind of priority... those who need urgent attention and those who can wait for a while...'

Jamila and Jerry walked up to the consultants and the junior doctors and introduced themselves.

'Oh, good to meet you. I'm Andrew Tanner,' said the paediatric consultant – a short, broad-chested, fair-haired man who looked to Jerry more like a swimming coach. 'Quite a challenge we're faced with here. I can't say I've ever come across anything like it, not in twenty-three years of practice.'

'Mr Tanner's a specialist in osseointegration,' put in the ward sister.

'I see,' said Jerry, nodding his head sagely, as if he knew what that meant.

'Osseointegration is when you fuse synthetic materials with living bone to reconstruct missing limbs or other parts of the body,' said Andrew Tanner. 'It's especially useful when children are born without their arms or their legs, or any other bits of them are missing.'

He looked around the ward. 'Not to beat around the bush, I think I have my work cut out for me here. It's quite beyond me how most of these unfortunate children have managed to survive at all. That one there... I'm guessing he's a boy... he's little more than a head and a neck. How in the world am I going to be able to reconstruct him?'

Jamila said, 'I am sorry, doctor. At the moment, we cannot fully explain to you where these children came from and why we think they are still alive. This is partly because we don't know ourselves, and partly because their existence must remain confidential, at least for the time being. We don't want the press making a big thing out of it, but we're also thinking about the safety of those specialists like yourself who will be treating them.'

'Our *safety*?' said Andrew Tanner. 'Do you mean there's some kind of risk attached to treating these children? Why should there be?'

Jamila was about to answer when they were interrupted by a boy who was lying in the bed next to them. He was one of the least malformed, although his spine was bent into such an extreme U-shape that his shoulder blades stuck out like two angular wings and his chin was resting on his chest, making it difficult for him to speak clearly. He also had two smaller subsidiary hands protruding from his wrists behind his thumbs.

'When... when is our mama coming?' he asked, in a croaking voice.

Jerry found it difficult to understand what he was saying at first – not only because his lower jaw was jammed so tightly against his breastbone, but because he had such a strong accent. It sounded partly American and partly like somebody pretending to be a yokel.

'*Whenzaah mama cumunh?*'

Jamila went around the end of his bed and stood close to him, although she didn't reach out and hold his hand. His small subsidiary hands were both prehensile, and they were clutching the sheet on his bed. It almost looked as if he were hiding another doll-sized boy up inside his sleeves.

'When is your mama coming, is that what you asked?'

The boy lifted his head as much as he could. 'She promised to come and fetch us after we slept.'

'What's your name? You do have a name, don't you?'

'Not yet. Not time for names yet.'

'No? What about your mama? Does your mama have a name?'

'Liz, Liza, Adeliza. That's her name.'

'*Don't say!*' shrilled out a girl from two beds away. It was the girl with the blonde hair and the eyes like two white pebbles and no nose. 'You mustn't tell them where she is! She always says that! It's a *speak*-ret!'

'It doesn't matter – it's only her name,' the boy retorted. 'Anyway, we don't know where she is. She only said that she's sleeping.'

'Sleeping?' said Jamila, pulling over a chair so that she could sit down next to him. 'Is that why she wasn't there, when we came to get you?'

The boy nodded again and sucked in the extra saliva that had flooded his mouth.

'Did she say how long she would be sleeping for?'

'Don't say!' the girl shrilled out again. 'If they know how long, they'll know how far!'

'We only want to help you,' said Jamila. 'None of you are well at all, so you shouldn't be living down in drains. You could have your back made straight, do you know that? Then you could walk around like every other boy.'

'I'm sacred,' said the boy.

'What do you mean, you're sacred? Your life is sacred,

of course, but you don't have to have a bent back like that. And neither do you have to have those extra hands.'

'These are *my* hands. They're sacred. My back is sacred.'

'Who says that?'

'Mama says that. We are all sacred.'

'We're mama's nestlings!' the girl piped up. 'If you touch us, mama will be angry as angry!'

'You don't understand. We don't want to hurt you in any way at all. We want to make your life better.'

'*This* is better. *This.*'

'Better than living in a sewer, yes. But your life could be so much happier than this… not only for you, but for all of these other children. I am not pretending for a moment that I can offer you Heaven, but at least you won't be living in Hell.'

The boy stared at Jamila for a few moments, as if he were no longer interested in what she had to say.

'Well?' she asked him, but he didn't answer and looked away. After a while, Jamila stood up and came back to the group of doctors and police officers.

Another consultant had arrived, and he held out his hand to her. He was a tall, lean man with a flop of black hair, as if a raven had landed badly on top of his head and one of its wings was dangling over his left eye.

'Edward Latimer,' he announced himself. 'I've had a very quick look around at our unfortunate patients. My first impression is that what we seem to be seeing here are various extreme examples of VACTERL association.'

'Oh, yes,' said Jerry. 'The old VACTERL association. That.'

Dr Latimer gave Jerry a tight smile, because it was obvious that he didn't have the faintest idea what VACTERL meant. 'It's a rare combination of vertebral defects, anal atresia, cardiac defects, renal anomalies and limb abnormalities. Very rarely all of these can occur together.'

'How do you treat them if they do?' asked Jamila.

'Of course, if it's detected early, in the first or second trimester, we usually recommend a termination.'

'But supposing the child comes to term, and is born, and survives?'

'Then the poor thing will have a dreadful struggle ahead of it, I'm afraid, as *these* children must have done. We're constantly having to ask ourselves whether it's kinder to end a child's life before it's properly begun, or whether to regard its life as sacred from the very moment of conception, no matter how malformed it happens to be. The trouble with *that* is, we would then be condemning it to nothing but years of pain and suffering, and only a few short years too – so how considerate is that?'

'We fully understand that you have to make some very difficult decisions,' said Jamila. 'But we're police, not doctors, and we haven't rescued these children to judge what's sacred and what isn't. We're trying to find out how they could have been born like this, and where they've been living, and who's been taking care of them, and how. To do that, we need to make them feel that we accept them, even though they look the way they do, and then hopefully we can win their confidence. Those who are capable of talking, anyhow.'

'We'll do our very best here, detective sergeant. This is

one of the best children's hospitals in the world, if not *the* best. But what is really baffling us is how they survived long enough to be born at all.'

He paused and looked down to the far end of the ward. Screens were still being unfolded around the beds as the last of the children were being washed and changed.

'We're using the word "children", but you have only to look around. All of them are malformed in one way or another, but some of them can barely be defined as human. They're almost like that appalling joke about the child who was nothing but a head. I mean, who gave birth to them, and how were they born, and when, and where? And who could have gathered them all together like this, as they grew up? Sister Machen here tells me that they were absolutely filthy when they were brought in, covered in excrement.'

Jamila said, 'We should be able to tell you much more later, sir, when our investigation has made a little more progress. Meanwhile, we'll leave the children in your hands. Two officers will be staying here at the hospital in constant attendance, in case the children give you any trouble or you need any urgent help. There are two more officers downstairs too, in the lobby, to make sure that you aren't bothered by intruders – media, or anybody like that.'

'Yes – I saw those officers when I came in. I can't say I'm used to having an armed guard.'

Jerry was about to say, 'Let's hope you won't need it,' but he decided against it. If he were left in this ward with these twenty-two children, he would find that quite disturbing enough.

He and Jamila walked toward the doors. 'Have you had a chance to look at all of them?' Jamila asked him.

'Not all of them. But we'll be sending a photographer along, won't we?'

'Yes... and a forensic team. At least three of them have fingernails like claws, and they need to match them with the scratches on Martin Elliot's body. We need anything that can link all these incidents together and make some sense out of them.'

As they pushed their way out of the ward, the boy with the curved spine shouted out, 'I'm sacred! Mama says so! You ask her, when she wakes up! You ask Liz-Lizzie-Lizzibet! She'll tell you!'

'She'll be angry as angry!' the little blonde girl piped up.

31

After he had dropped Jamila off at Peckham, Jerry drove down to Tooting police station. While the image was still fresh in his mind, he wanted to sit down in front of a computer screen with the EvoFIT operator and give her a description of the white-haired old man in the brown tweed coat.

He managed to eat two Jaffa cakes and drink a cup of tea while he picked out faces from a database. First it was pictures of men of different ethnicities – white, black, Asian or Hispanic. Then – when he had chosen the old man's race – he selected his age group, and his hairstyle, and his demeanour, and gradually, he was able to evolve a picture that looked so much like the old man himself that it was eerie.

'That's him, you've nailed the bastard,' he told the EvoFIT operator.

'Oh. He looks *nice*. Just like my grandpa.'

'Believe me, love, you wouldn't want this old geezer for your grandpa. He'd probably cut your throat as soon as look at you.'

He left and drove back to Peckham. The sky was

strangely dark, the greenish colour of corroded copper, as if a downpour was imminent. The EvoFIT operator would post the image of the old man on Twitter and Facebook and send it around to the local papers and all the other police stations in the south-west London area, those that were still open. As Jerry drove, he glanced at the print-out of the old man's picture on the seat beside him. He couldn't help wondering if the man really existed, or if he had imagined him. It was a mystery how he had vanished each time Jerry came looking for him. But Jamila had seen him too, so he must be real.

When he arrived back at Peckham, he found that Jamila was talking to Alan Pattinson, the lock and key expert. She had been trying to eat a spiced keema pasty, which was lying on its paper wrapper in front of her with a single bite taken out of it. Alan Pattinson, however, was droning on, and every time she raised the pasty to her mouth to take another bite, he would ask her a question, and she would have to put it down again.

'So you've never heard of William Trench?' he asked her.

'No, I'm afraid not. The name means nothing.'

'Well, not to worry. There's plenty of British people who've never heard of him either.'

'I *am* British, Mr Pattinson.'

'Well, I mean people who were born and bred in Britain. They've never heard of Matthew Hopkins either. He was the Witchfinder General, born 1620, died 1647.'

'I saw a film about him once, with old what's-his-name in it,' said Jerry. 'Vincent Price.'

'That's right,' said Alan Pattinson. 'Matthew Hopkins

always claimed that he was appointed Witchfinder General by Parliament, but he never actually was. He did it for the money that local towns gave him. It's recorded that he caught twenty-three witches, four of whom died in prison and nineteen of whom were hanged, although he probably killed hundreds more.'

Jerry sat down next to Jamila. She offered him one of her keema pasties, but he shook his head. 'Thanks, sarge, but I've already had a couple of biscuits, and I'm still feeling a bit dicky after, you know...' He didn't mention the children in front of Alan Pattinson.

'So who was this William Trench?' asked Jamila.

'Ah, now *he* was a witchfinder too, in his way. He was originally appointed as the vicar of St George-in-the-East in Wapping, but when he took over the church, he discovered that almost the whole of that parish was dominated by a woman who purported to have supernatural powers. In fact, she was said to be the most powerful single witch in English history. People still went to church on a Sunday, but if they were seriously ill and were looking to be healed, or if they badly needed money, or if they wanted something nasty to happen to somebody they didn't like – they'd always go to this woman.'

'Pity she's not still with us,' said Jerry. 'I could use a bit of dosh to buy myself a new car, and my neighbours downstairs are right getting on my nerves with their bloody music. Do you know how many times they've played "Shape of You" by old ginger-knob?'

Alan Pattinson gave Jerry the quick, impatient smile of a man who wasn't used to being interrupted.

'William Trench heard from one of his parishioners that this woman was holding ceremonies to summon Satan. He went to her house on Artichoke Hill and demanded that she stop calling on the Devil, especially in his parish. When she told him to rot in Hell, he went to his friend the magistrate and had her arrested on charges of fraud and extortion.'

'How did he manage to do that?' asked Jamila.

'Well – she'd been making pin money as a faith healer and a fortune teller, but most of her profit came from being an abortionist. If a pregnant woman came to her seeking a termination, she would ask them for what seemed like a reasonable amount of money – five shillings, which is worth about thirty pounds today. But once she'd carried out the abortion, it was a different matter. She would threaten to inform the woman's husband and parents and all of her friends about it – especially if the woman was pregnant because of what you might call a bit on the side.'

'So she'd demand even more money to keep schtum?' said Jerry.

'Exactly. As much as twenty or thirty pounds in some cases. And any woman who didn't pay up was threatened that her children would go down with the measles, or her pets would all die, or her husband's business would go bankrupt. And it was widely believed that she would be able to do that.

'There was one thing more said about her. Although she was an abortionist, she believed that all human life was sacrosanct. Even if a child was miscarried or aborted, she believed that it still had an inviolable right to life. Quite obviously it's an apocryphal story, but it was said that she kept alive every one of the foetuses she aborted, no matter what was wrong with it. It was even said that sometimes she could be seen at night, walking through the streets of Wapping with the children running and limping behind her. Impossible, of course, but a good ghost story.'

Alan Pattinson held up a brown leather-bound book with a broken spine. 'It's all in here. The diaries of William Trench. I've borrowed this from Carmine's, the locksmiths. They were taken over years ago by the Handykeys group, but they still have all their old records. Carmine's were the company who made the seventy-two keys with sigils in them, and they made them to William Trench's personal order.'

'So it was this vicar, William Trench, who had them made? Does he say why?'

'Oh, yes. It was quite a tragedy. The witch-woman was tried and found guilty of extortion and sent to Tothill Fields prison, but she was there no longer than a single night before she disappeared. Vanished, even though her cell was still locked. Either she picked the lock or bribed one of the warders, that's my guess. But the following weekend, William Trench's twenty-seven-year-old wife, Miranda, was driving along Cannon Street when her carriage caught fire.'

'It caught *fire*?' asked Jerry. 'How does a horse-drawn carriage catch fire?'

'Nobody knows. It was right in the middle of the street, and even though it was open-sided, Miranda got herself tangled up in the reins somehow and couldn't get out. The horse panicked and dragged the carriage along the street, and so nobody could stop it to put out the fire and pull Miranda out. William Trench heard all the shouting and screaming and came out of the church, just in time to see his wife being incinerated in front of his eyes.

'Here,' said Alan Pattinson. He opened the book, where he had inserted an orange train ticket as a bookmark, and slid it across the table.

Jamila read from it, out loud. '*I knew instanter who was guilty of this hideous murder, for the flames which enveloped Miranda's whisky were the most lurid emerald in colour, such as I had seen in the kitchen when I paid my visit to Artichoke Hill.*'

Alan Pattinson said, 'He was convinced that the witch-woman had escaped from Tothill and killed his wife in revenge for him having her put in prison. The day after he'd conducted his wife's funeral, he gave up the vicarship of St George's and went in search of the witch-woman, to get his revenge. He says he became the new Witchfinder General, except that he was in pursuit of only one witch.'

Jamila looked at Jerry, and he knew what she was thinking. *We* were nearly cremated by green flames ourselves. Maybe this hooded figure that we're trying to nail down has the same kind of supernatural powers as the witch-woman that William Trench was after. Maybe she's a descendant of that witch-woman. Surely she couldn't be the same witch-woman – not after more than a hundred and sixty years.

'If William Trench ordered those keys, I'm assuming he found her,' said Jerry.

'He did. He *did* find her, although it took him more than three years.' Alan Pattinson took the book back and turned to another page that he had bookmarked. 'Here, look – in January of 1859 he heard from the vicar of St Paul's in Deptford, south of the river. Some woman was supposed to be getting up to all kinds of satanic shenanigans around the Royal Naval Dockyards. It's all here, in his diary, how he took the ferry across the Thames almost every day to try to track her down.

'In the end, he had the idea of persuading a young woman friend of his to pretend that she was pregnant. She went all around Deptford, asking barmaids and waitresses and nannies and serving girls if they knew of anyone who could help her to get rid of an unwanted baby. They directed her to a house on Tanner's Hill, and that's where he found her.'

'And? What did he do once he'd found her?'

'Here, read it. "*I confronted her at her front door, but I was hurl'd back on to the road as if I had been kick'd by a horse. Two of my ribs were fractur'd and I lost a front tooth.*"'

'So – even if she didn't have supernatural powers, she was incredibly strong?'

'William Trench was convinced she had supernatural powers, and that she was invested with those powers by Satan himself. He says here that after she had hit him like that, he realised he couldn't tackle her on his own. He didn't know enough about demonology. He went to the Reverend Boniface at the nearest Catholic church, Our Lady of the Assumption, because the Reverend Boniface had qualified in Rome as an exorcist, a dismisser of demons.'

Jerry sat back. Then he turned to Jamila and said, 'What do you call it when you don't believe for a moment that something's true, but you pretend to yourself that it is, like when you go to the pictures and watch a horror film, and you almost shit yourself?'

'Suspension of disbelief,' said Jamila.

'William Trench certainly believed in her powers,' said Alan Pattinson. 'He convinced the Reverend Boniface, too. "*On the night of September the eleventh, myself and the Reverend set out for Tanner's Hill with Mr Dash and five men of the church whom the Reverend had sworn to silence. We had with us the casket with the seventy-two padlocks and keys which had been made for me at Carmine's in St Martin's Lane.*

'"*When the witch-woman answered her door, Mr Dash held her at bay while the rest of us entered the house. The Reverend spoke the prayer of exorcism, which put her into a state of paralysis, whereupon we carried her out into the yard at the rear of the house. We laid her down and heaped her with lemons, since lemons are symbolic of purification. Then we covered her with yew-tree branches, dowsed her in several gallons of whale oil and set her alight, whereupon she burned with the fiercest green flames. She burned with such intense heat that we were obliged to stay well back.*

'"*She neither screamed nor protested, but continued to curse us even as the fire consumed her. On the advice of the Reverend Boniface, we lifted her charred carcass into the casket as soon as life appeared to be extinct, and firmly sealed the lid. He had warned that the smoke from her cremation would still contain her spirit and that her spirit would never be extinct. I locked all of the seventy-two padlocks and left the quarantine keys in each of them, as instructed. The five men then carried the casket away to a site they had dug not far from Deptford Park, three times as deep as the deepest grave. They buried it there, and filled the grave with concrete and aggregate, so that there would never be a chance of it being accidentally exhumed, even in the far future.*

"'The gravediggers were paid a guinea each, and for his part, Mr Dash too was well rewarded.'"

'Who's this Mr Dash?' asked Jamila. 'Is he mentioned anywhere else in the diary?'

Alan Pattinson riffled through the book and shook his head. 'Not that I can see. I can only presume that he was somebody who knew something about exorcism. Perhaps he was a friend of this Reverend Boniface. I've tried googling it, but all I've been able to find is *Mrs* Dash, which is a brand of American seasoning – you know, like chilli and garlic and onion salt.'

'Whoever he was, he "held her at bay", didn't he?' said Jerry. 'Long enough for the priest to paralyse her anyway. It would be useful to know how he did that. Maybe he was just a big tough bloke like that PC Eddie Green.'

'All the same, you've given us a tremendous amount of very helpful background, Mr Pattinson,' said Jamila. 'I'll make sure that you get well rewarded – just like Mr Dash, whoever he was.'

'Oh, please, call me Alan. It's reward enough, DS Patel, knowing that I can do my bit to help solve a crime. I would have liked to have been a detective myself, don't you know, but it's my asthma, and my eyesight's not particularly brilliant either.'

Once he had left, Jamila called PC Jane Dyer, one of the two officers she had left at the Evelina Children's Hospital.

'How is it going with the children? Everything still quiet?'

'The nurses have cleaned them all up, and they're trying to feed them now, but it isn't easy. Some of them have throats so constricted that they can't swallow. Others don't even have stomachs. Some of them are asleep and can't be woken up, and some of them are starting to get a bit bolshie. Two or three of the nurses have broken down in tears.'

'Keep us up to date, please. We can come straight across there if you need us. We're going to take a few hours' break, but we're always on call.'

Jerry looked at his watch. 'All quiet on the western front? I think I've got enough time to visit my own witch, and take Alice out for a burger.'

'I'm sorry,' said Jamila, as they went down the stairs. 'I am completely out of whale oil.'

32

The coppery green clouds had drifted away to the east by the time Jerry arrived at Moyser Road in Tooting, and now a dazzling orange sun was reflected from all the upstairs windows in the long line of Victorian terraced houses.

He rang the doorbell outside the house that used to be his, and immediately he heard barking. He didn't regret leaving Nancy, and he didn't regret leaving Tuffnut either. He had never particularly liked dogs, and he particularly detested Tuffnut, a Staffordshire bull terrier that Nancy had owned when he first met her. The dislike had been mutual, and when Tuffnut wasn't barking and snarling at him, he was staring at him with those piggy little eyes and baring his teeth as if he would love to bite a sizeable chunk out of his leg.

Nancy opened the door, holding Tuffnut by his collar, and she scowled as soon as she saw that it was him. She had cut her brunette hair into a short bob since he had last seen her, and he had to admit to himself that it suited her. She was petite and dark-eyed and still pretty, and it was a pity that almost every conversation between them had ended up as a blazing argument.

'I thought you weren't coming,' she snapped.

'I couldn't this morning, but I've got a couple of hours free now. I thought I could take Alice out for a happy meal.'

'I've planned something for her tea already, and anyway I don't like her eating junk food.'

'An occasional burger isn't going to kill her.'

'You never feed her on anything else. You don't think of the planet, do you?'

'One happy meal once a fortnight isn't going to lead to any polar bears getting drowned.'

'Oh, you're hopeless. But you can take her for a walk if you like, and you can take Tuffnut with you. He hasn't been out since this morning, and I've got some accounts to finish.'

'Tuffnut hates my guts.'

'That's the deal, Jerry. Either you take Tuffnut along with Alice, or you don't take either of them.'

'Okay, okay. I'll take him. But you'd better give me a bag for when he does what I think you want me to take him out for. I'm not going to put it in my pocket.'

Nancy called Alice to come down from her room. Usually she was ready and waiting when Jerry rang the doorbell, but she hadn't recognised his borrowed Datsun when he parked outside. She came galloping down the stairs at once. She was eight now, all arms and legs and nearly as tall as her mother, as well as being as pretty as her mother. She ran out onto the porch and gave him a hug before she went back inside for her bright red coat. Nancy came out and handed him Tuffnut's lead and three scented biodegradable dog mess bags, with built-in scoops.

'Three? What have you been feeding him on?'

'Yora. It doesn't have meat in it. Only dried grubs and beetroot and oats.'

'Sounds delicious. You don't have any to spare, do you? I've been wondering what to cook for supper tonight.'

'Why do you always have to be so sarcastic?'

'I was trained as a detective, Nance. They make you pass an exam in Advanced Sarcasm. After that you have to sit for a degree in Taking The Mick.'

Alice came out, and Nancy said, 'Have a nice time, darling. And make sure your father behaves himself.'

Alice giggled and said that she would. Then the two of them walked off along Moyser Road, hand in hand, with Tuffnut straining at his lead so hard that he was wheezing. Nancy had never trained him to walk to heel, but then she had never been able to make Jerry walk to heel either.

'I was going to take you on the London Eye today,' said Jerry. 'This case came up though, with all these children who needed to be rescued. Twenty-two of them.'

'Where did you have to rescue them from?'

'You're not going to believe it, but they were all hiding down a drain.'

'Is that a story or is it true?'

'It's true, but I wish it was a story. You should see these kids. On the other hand, you shouldn't.'

'Why not?'

'Because there are some things in life that are so terrible it's better not to see them, not unless you really have to.'

'What, are they ill?'

'Sort of. But let's talk about something else, shall we? Did you go on that outing to the Science Museum?'

'Yes. It was boring. But Miss Miller can make anything boring. She's the most boring teacher in the world. No, she's not. She's the most boring teacher in the universe.'

They walked up to Tooting Bec Common, a hundred and fifty acres of grass and trees with a lake in the middle. Tuffnut was tugging violently at his lead as they waited by the kerb, and Jerry was almost tempted to unclip his collar and let him get run over by a bus.

'Mummy's got a new boyfriend,' said Alice, as they crossed the grass toward the lake. The surface of the water was metallic grey and rippled by the breeze, with three ducks bobbing up and down on it.

'Oh, yes. What's his name?'

'Nigel. I don't like him. He's bald, and he thinks he's funny. Tuffnut doesn't like him either.'

'I don't think Tuffnut likes anybody. But, you know, all credit to him if he doesn't like Nigel.'

They were halfway around the lake when Jerry caught sight of a family walking on the opposite side. A father was pushing a pram and a mother was holding the hands of two children – one about five years old and the other about Alice's age – and a Skye terrier was trotting along with them too. It looked as if they had their grandfather with them, although Jerry couldn't see him clearly at first, because he was walking behind the father.

'What does Nigel do?' he asked Alice. But before she had the chance to answer he said, 'Never mind about that.

I think we need to take Tuffnut somewhere else for his walk.'

'Why? What's the matter?'

The grandfather's pace had slowed, so that Jerry could now see him clearly. He wasn't their grandfather at all, but the white-haired old man in the brown tweed coat. He stopped, and Jerry could see that he was staring in their direction, his hands in his pockets, although he was too far away to make out if he was smiling, the way he had smiled at the junction of Daneville Road before Jerry's car had burst into flames.

'I've just seen somebody who's not very friendly,' Jerry told Alice. 'That happens sometimes, when you're a police detective. You have to arrest somebody for doing wrong and forever after that they bear a grudge.'

'What's a "grudge"?'

'I'll explain later. Let's get away from here first.'

He turned around and started to walk back quickly to Tooting Bec Road, glancing over his shoulder now and again to see if the old man was following them. To his relief the old man stayed where he was, his hands still in his pockets, as if he had derived enough satisfaction simply from scaring them away.

Tuffnut was confused at first, because he had seen and smelled the family's dog. He had been wheezing and spitting and spoiling for a fight, but once Jerry had pulled him around he forgot about it and started tugging relentlessly forward as he always did.

'Where are we going to go now?' asked Alice, skipping to keep up with them.

'I don't know. Streatham Common. It's only ten minutes away.'

She looked back toward the lake. 'Was it that old man you didn't want us to meet?'

'That's right, love. He looks harmless, but he's a bit of a bad lot.'

They had nearly reached the road when Jerry saw a cloud of black smoke drifting toward them. It came twisting in between the trunks of the silver birches that bordered the common, as sinuous as a snake, even though the breeze was blowing in the opposite direction. He reached out for Alice's hand and said, 'Come on, let's get our skates on!'

As they neared the trees though, the smoke poured out in front of them and began to take on the shape of a tall hooded figure in a cloak – the same hooded figure that had struck Jerry when he tried to follow it up Southampton Way.

'*What's that?*' shrilled Alice. '*Daddy, I'm scared!*'

Jerry stopped, winding Tuffnut's lead tighter around his fist to hold him still. Tuffnut reared up and snuffled but couldn't seem to understand what this smoky apparition actually was. It was the *shape* of a human, but it didn't *smell* like a human. It smelled of woodsmoke, and the sharp tang of lemons.

Jerry started to edge away to the right. He was calculating that they might be able to make a run for it across the road, but as he did so, the smoky figure wavered to the right as well, as if it anticipated what he had in mind. Not only that, but the old man in the brown tweed coat appeared, about a hundred metres away, and stood there, smiling.

The smoky figure drifted closer, and Tuffnut growled.

'Easy, boy,' Jerry told him.

It was then that Alice looked up at him and said, in a hoarse, threatening voice, '*You have stolen my nestlings.*'

'Alice?' he said. 'Alice, keep your mouth tight shut – try not to let her talk.'

'*You came like thieves when I was asleep, and you stole my nestlings. They are mine. Without me, they would have had no life at all. They are mine, and I want them back.*'

Jerry was shaking, but he managed to say, 'You can't have them back. They're in no condition to be living down a sewer. And you can stop maiming and murdering innocent people just because you have some lunatic idea about keeping aborted children alive.'

'*All life is sacred. All children deserve life, even if God has forgotten them.*'

'A foetus isn't a child. A foetus with no arms or legs or body isn't a baby.'

'*All life is sacred. And those of my nestlings who need arms or legs can have arms and legs belonging to those who were lucky enough to be smiled upon by God.*'

Alice's eyes were closed now, and she was standing completely rigid, holding on to Jerry's hand so hard that her fingernails were digging into his palm. Tuffnut started to claw the grass and whine, and he kept looking from Alice to the smoky figure and back again, and it was obvious that he was growing increasingly distressed.

'*I want my nestlings back,*' said Alice. '*I want all of them*

back – back where they belong. Before you know it, they
will have grown beyond your ability to take care of them.
Only I can do that. So return them, or else I will come and
fetch them.'

'Just get the hell out of here,' Jerry retorted. 'Get the hell
out of here and get the hell out of my daughter.'

'*Your daughter can make a sacrifice too. What lovely*
long legs she has.'

'I said – get the hell out of here! Don't you dare to touch
my daughter!'

The smoky figure started to roll nearer, and Jerry pulled
Alice back. He was sure he glimpsed something shiny
and metallic glinting in the smoke – a knife or a saw. But
at that moment, Tuffnut leaped up and started furiously
barking and dancing up and down. Jerry had seen him
angry before. He had seen him wriggle his way out of
the half-open front door and chase the postman all the
way down the road, but he had never seen him go totally
berserk, not like this.

The smoky figure hesitated and appeared to shrink
back. Jerry looked around and saw that the old man in
the brown tweed coat was walking quickly away, like a
man on an urgent errand.

Tuffnut kept on barking and jumping until his legs were
tangled up in his lead. The smoky figure shrank away even
further and started to shudder. Jerry took a chance and
reached down to unclip Tuffnut's collar, and the instant
that he was free, Tuffnut shot toward the smoky figure,
his barking so furious now that it had reached the point
of hysteria.

The smoky figure curled away and disappeared between the silver birches, with Tuffnut in pursuit. After a few moments, Tuffnut stopped barking and circled around the trees, wondering how the smoky figure could have vanished. Eventually he came back, trotting up to Jerry with a mystified expression.

Alice opened her eyes and looked around her. 'Are we still on the common?'

'Yes, darling,' said Jerry, stroking her hair. 'Are you all right?'

'I feel strange,' she said. 'I feel like I've been asleep, and I've just woken up.'

'Are you okay though?'

'Yes... I feel strange, that's all. Why is Tuffnut off his lead?'

Tuffnut was sitting obediently at Jerry's feet, waiting to have his lead clipped back on. Jerry had never seen him so docile.

'He... er... he wanted to go for a bit of a run, that's all.'

'Mummy *never* allows him off the lead. She says he'd attack the first person he saw.'

'Well, today he's been a good boy, haven't you, Tuffers? In fact, he's been more than a good boy. I think he's given me one of the best clues I've had in a long time.'

They walked back toward the road. As they passed the trees, Alice stopped for a moment, and frowned, and sucked her tongue.

'I can taste lemons,' she said.

'Lemons? Really?'

'Yes. But I haven't eaten any lemons. I don't even *like* lemons.'

'I'm not too keen on them myself, love. Not these days, anyway.'

She smiled up at him, and he gave her a smile back, but he could almost have cried.

33

As soon as Jerry returned to Peckham police station, he found Jamila to tell her what had happened.

'If it hadn't been for Tuffnut, I'm sure that smoky woman would have attacked us. From what she said, I think she was all ready to cut off Alice's legs, the same as she did to Martin Elliot. It looked like she was holding something that could have been a saw, although I don't know what happened to it, whether she dropped it or what.'

'What about the old man?'

'He buggered off too, as soon as I let Tuffnut off his lead. So I reckon there's at least one thing they're definitely scared of, and that's dogs. That "Mr Dash" that William Trench mentioned in his diary – the one that kept the witch-woman at bay while the priest said a prayer to paralyse her. Perhaps he wasn't a man after all. Perhaps *he* was a dog.'

Jamila swivelled around in her chair and started to prod at her laptop.

'I'm googling for dogs called Mr Dash. You never know.'

'I'll bet you ten to one he was a dog. You should have seen how fast that witch-woman blew away out of there, as soon as Tuffnut went for her.'

After only a few seconds, Jamila said, 'Here we are. It's not *Mr* Dash but simply *Dash*. He was one of Queen Victoria's favourite dogs when she was young. He was painted by Sir Edwin Landseer and it says here that many people in Britain also named their dogs Dash in tribute to him.'

'Right then. That's something we've learned. When we go looking for this witch-woman we need to take a dog with us. Or maybe a couple of dogs. And we need to make sure that there's a dog on guard outside the children's ward, over at the hospital.'

'I'll contact the dog support unit. Unit Five at Nine Elms is probably the nearest, isn't it? We're going over to the hospital anyway, aren't we? So I can arrange for a handler to meet us there.'

'If this William Trench was able to catch her with a dog and lock her up, sarge, then there's no reason why *we* can't, even if she is nothing but smoke.'

'The only problem is, Jerry, what do we do with her, even if we *can* catch her?'

'Same as he did. Lock her up. And this time make sure that nobody lets her out.'

★

They had just climbed into their car when Jamila's phone rang. It was PC Jane Dyer, from Peaceful Ward, and she sounded panicky.

'Please get over here, DS Patel. The children are going wild. Listen... you can hear them screaming and crying and throwing things around, those that have got hands to throw things around with. We've had to evacuate the doctors and the nurses out of the ward and lock the doors.'

'All right, constable. We were on our way over to check up on the children in any case. Jerry – PC Dyer says the children are going crazy. You need to put your foot down.'

They slewed out of the police station car park on skittering tyres. The Datsun was fitted with a siren and a blue flashing light behind the radiator grille, and they sped along Peckham Road and then Camberwell New Road at sixty miles an hour, weaving in and out between buses and taxis and delivery vans. It took them less than ten minutes to reach the Albert Embankment, and although they were stuck for nearly a minute behind a council dustcart, Jerry managed to steer up onto the pavement and then back onto the road, and within another three minutes, they were pulling up outside the Evelina Children's Hospital.

They ran into the hospital, where the two armed officers were waiting for them, holding the lift doors open. They could hear the screaming as soon as they reached the sixth floor. The paediatricians and the nurses and the police constables were gathered in the corridor outside Peaceful Ward, looking stressed, while inside the children were howling and screeching and tossing chairs from one side of the room to the other.

Jamila and Jerry went up to the circular windows in the doors and looked inside. The children who had arms and legs were hobbling up and down, kicking the bedside cupboards and dragging the sheets and blankets off the beds. Those who were too malformed to climb off their beds were screaming as loud as they could and bouncing frenetically up and down.

Dr Latimer came up to them. His white lab coat was stained with parallel streaks of blood as if he had been clawed, and Jerry didn't think he had ever seen a doctor look so grim.

'They're uncontrollable,' he said. 'And they're insanely strong. Look at that poor nurse over there – they've scratched her cheek so badly she'll be lucky not to have permanent scars.'

'When did this start?' asked Jamila.

'About an hour ago. First of all they began to get restless and noisy and uncooperative. Then they started shouting and screaming and knocking over the glasses of water on their bedside tables. After that they gradually grew more and more aggressive.'

'That's so strange. When we first carried them out of the sewer, they seemed to be thankful. They weren't aggressive at all.'

Even as Jamila spoke, three or four of the children were kicking at the doors. They kicked at them again and again until the veneer around the lock split apart.

'Can't you sedate them?' asked Jerry. 'Give them a dose of the old Rohypnol or something like that?'

'I've already tried to tranquillise two of the most violent. I gave them four milligram doses of lorazepam, which usually works very quickly, but it had absolutely no effect at all. Some of them are so severely malformed that I wouldn't know where to start injecting them, or if they had a stomach to digest a tablet if they allowed me to feed it to them.'

'Do you have any idea why they're behaving like this?'

Dr Latimer shook his head. 'It's like some form of mass hysteria. I've called Dr Feldman – he's the head of our psychiatric team and he should be here at any moment. But I personally think it's connected to their physical malformation. They're feeling deeply frustrated because they're so seriously disabled, and I'm sure some of them are suffering chronic pain too.'

He paused, and beckoned them over to the opposite side of the corridor, so that none of the nurses or police officers could hear what he had to say next.

'I think they're all fully aware too, how limited their lifespan is going to be. At least five of them wanted to know how long they can expect to live. "When am I going to die?" they asked me. They said that their mother would never tell them. By their "mother", I presume they mean a woman who adopted them all.'

'Yes – well, sort of,' said Jamila.

'They have every reason to be worried though,' said Dr Latimer. 'I doubt if even the least malformed of them will survive for more than a month, at the outside. The worst I expect to go within a week or so. No human beings can exist for long if they have no stomach or intestines or their heart is so misshapen it can barely manage to pump blood around their bodies. Some of them are suffering from mesocardia too.'

'Sorry to be ignorant, but what's that?' asked Jerry.

'For the first six weeks of their development, the internal

organs of all embryos are symmetrical. After that, the heart makes its way to the left and the liver rotates into place on the right. It makes for a more efficient body if the organs are arranged as compactly as possible. But sometimes the heart remains in the centre of the body, and this is a serious condition that affects circulation. At least three of these children have this condition. They are like embryos that have grown in size but never developed in the way that they should.'

'So what's your verdict? I mean, medically speaking?'

'To be absolutely frank with you, I believe the kindest option would be to euthanise them. I have suggested it in cases of VACTERL association that are far less debilitating than these. They have no meaningful future. They face nothing but pain and frustration and an early death. If an ultrasound scan had shown me children in this condition while they were still *in utero*, I would immediately have recommended that they be aborted.'

'We believe they were,' Jamila told him.

'I'm sorry? They *were* aborted? Then how did they survive and grow to such a size? That's impossible.'

'We're not entirely sure ourselves how they survived,' said Jerry. 'But we think that this "mother" you referred to has some way of keeping a foetus alive and kicking even if it's been given the old heave-ho.'

'I've never heard of such a thing. I simply can't understand how it could be done.'

'It may be done by transplanting the aborted foetus into the womb of another woman,' said Jamila. 'We have come across several cases recently where this appears to have happened. Like hatching cuckoos in another bird's nest.'

Dr Latimer shook his head again. 'I keep up to date with every advancement in paediatrics, and I've seen no mention of any procedure like that. Not even with a healthy foetus, let alone a foetus so malformed that it can barely breathe or digest any nutrition. I mean – why would anyone do that?'

'I don't know what else to say to you at this stage, Dr Latimer. We are making some progress with this investigation, but only slowly, and there is a long way to go.'

They waited outside Peaceful Ward for another hour. Gradually the screaming and the kicking and the chair-throwing petered out, and eventually, when they looked in through the windows, they could see that all the children had fallen asleep. Some of them were lying on the floor. Others had dropped on top of heaps of blankets. The whole ward was wrecked, with broken glass and tipped-over bedside cupboards and ripped-open pillows strewn everywhere, but when they unlocked the doors and opened them, it was silent inside except for thin, constricted breathing.

Andrew Tanner came up and said, 'What's the next move then? They may be asleep now, but they're not going to stay asleep for ever, are they?'

'I'm going to try dosing them all with propofol,' said Dr Latimer. 'That's what we usually use here to induce a coma. I still have several further tests I want to carry out, and it'll be much easier to do that if they're all unconscious. Then we can sit down and discuss what the way forward is going to be – both medically and legally and, I suppose, morally too.'

'I've examined all of them now,' said Andrew Tanner. 'It's extraordinary, because three or four of them have limbs that have been transplanted from other people – some of them quite unsuitable, such as adult arms on a young child's torso. And what's even more extraordinary is that they've taken, and grown. I can't think how that's been done, or how the limbs could possibly not have been rejected.'

'What about the children as a whole though?' asked Jamila. 'Do you think it's possible to save them?'

'It depends what you mean by "saving" them. Myself, I think that it would be futile to attempt to give them arms and legs, even prosthetics. Almost all of them are beyond physical reconstruction. And that's not even counting the ones who are missing parts of their brains. All we would be doing is putting them through extreme and unnecessary suffering. From my point of view, the answer is palliative care until they naturally pass away.'

They were still talking when a uniformed police constable came along the corridor with a beige-haired Belgian Malinois. He told the dog to sit and it obeyed instantly, its tongue hanging out.

Jamila said, 'Thank you for coming so promptly. We have a very unusual situation here.'

'Maitland's the name,' said the dog handler. He had dark circles around his eyes, like his dog. 'There's two armed PCs downstairs so I'm wondering what you need me and Blizzard for.'

'Inside that ward we have a number of sick children – twenty-two in all. They are sleeping at the moment, although when they wake up they can be highly aggressive. But it's not the children who are really the problem. Dr Latimer here is going to try and sedate them so that they stay reasonably calm. The problem is that they have what you might call a guardian... or a foster parent, for want of a better description.'

'I take it this foster parent's being a bit of a nuisance, then? Male or female?'

'Female. But no ordinary woman, I warn you. She has the ability to get past security, although we are not certain how she does it. She is always dressed in a cloak and a hood, so that she looks like somebody wearing fancy dress for Hallowe'en. However, this is not fancy dress. She is extremely dangerous, and if she appears here, you need to treat her with the greatest caution.'

PC Maitland narrowed his eyes, and it was clear that he was having difficulty in believing any of this.

'A woman in a cloak and a hood, and she can get past two armed PCs without them seeing her?'

'We believe so, yes. But we also believe that there is one way of chasing her away. We're not 100 per cent certain, but we think that she has a fear of dogs.'

'She needs to be afraid of Blizzard here, I'll tell you. He's the most obedient dog I've ever had the pleasure to train, so long as you keep him active all day, and throw him his ball every five minutes. On the other hand, if you was a tea leaf making a run for it, and I told him to go for the k-i-l-l, you wouldn't stand a chance in hell. He's like *Jaws* with legs.'

Jerry lifted his hand to pat Blizzard on the head, but Blizzard looked up at him and snarled, in the same way that Tuffnut snarled at him.

'No, best not,' said PC Maitland. 'Surprising how many people make that mistake, patting a dog on the head. If you do that, dogs always think that you're going to hit them, or that you're telling them off. Blizzard here, he'd bite your fingers off, right to the knuckles, and once he'd chewed them he wouldn't spit them out either.'

'Good boy, Blizzard,' said Jerry, raising one hand in a high five. 'Respect.'

Jamila and Jerry had a last few words with the paediatricians and the nurses and the police officers who would be staying on duty here at the hospital. Dr Latimer had already started to put each of the children into a medically induced coma, and he told them that so far the propofol seemed to be taking effect, and that none of the comatose children had stirred.

'Bloody hell, I'm cream-crackered,' said Jerry, as they went down in the lift.

Jamila was looking at herself in the mirror at the back of the lift. 'I used to think that I would love to have children,' she said. 'Now, I'm not so sure.'

'What, not even *my* kids?' said Jerry, and immediately wished that he hadn't.

Jamila didn't answer that and walked out of the lift ahead of him. She didn't speak again until they were back at Peckham police station.

34

Louise was woken at 2:10 a.m. by a churning sensation inside her womb, as if the blades of a kitchen blender were slowly turning over.

She reached over to switch on her bedside lamp, and then sat up. When she pulled up her nightgown, she could actually see her stomach lumping up. She gagged, and her mouth filled with bile, although she couldn't vomit. Since Dr Gupta had shown her the scans of the two foetuses that were growing inside her, she hadn't been able to eat.

She felt desperate, but she had nobody to confide in. Her sister, Suzanne, hadn't spoken to her for more than five years. Her mother would only react with disgust that she was pregnant, even if she protested that she hadn't slept with anybody. Two or three of the elderly residents of the Whittington were kind and sympathetic, and treated her like a granddaughter, but they were suffering from varying degrees of dementia or memory loss, and they wouldn't have understood what she meant if she told them that she was expecting two distorted babies.

There had been several times in her life when she had wondered if she would be better off committing suicide.

When she was thirteen, she had been so badly bullied at school she had taken to cutting her arms with a broken test tube from the science lab. When Alan had left her, she had even gone to the hardware shop and bought a washing line to hang herself. Each time though, she had sat on her bed and decided that tomorrow might be better. Tomorrow she might have lost at least another two pounds. The day after tomorrow, when she had lost even more weight, she might meet another man. His name would be Roger, and he would have dark hair and an infectious grin.

So far, she had lost no weight and met no men called Roger, and now her womb had been invaded by these two hideous foetuses. Not only her womb, but her nervous system and her whole personality. If it would kill her to get rid of them, she might as well die anyway. She had the key to the rest home pharmacy cupboard, where there was enough Quetiapine to treat eleven residents with Alzheimer's, and that would certainly be enough to stop her heart.

Her womb contracted with another agonising pang, and she felt an abrasive sensation all the way up her back, as if her spinal cord had been rubbed with glasspaper. She bent forward, her eyes squeezed tight shut, until the spasm had passed. Then she thought, *That's it. I can't bear this. I just want it to be over. Dying can't be any worse than going to sleep. The only difference is you don't wake up. And why should I want to wake up, with these monsters inside me?*

She opened her eyes and sat up. Suddenly she felt peaceful. All her life she had done what other people had told her to do, and tried to please them even when they had mocked her and criticised her. Now these hideous scratchy foetuses were trying to take possession not only of her body but her soul as well. Enough was enough. From this moment, only one person was going to control her destiny, and that was her.

She stood up, but as she stood up, she became aware of that smoky smell again. Surely the groundsman hadn't lit another bonfire – not *now*, in the middle of the night? Her window was shut, so how had it penetrated into her bedroom?

The smell had a sharp acidic overtone too. She didn't know why, but she imagined this was what you smelled like after you had died, and you were lying in the suffocating darkness of your own coffin. A smell both pungent and sour. Although how could you smell anything, when your lungs were deflated, and you couldn't breathe, and your heart was empty, and your liquefying brain was trickling out of your ears?

'*Louise*,' she said, in a thick, clogged-up voice.

She looked around, shocked. She had said '*Louise*', but she hadn't spoken. The voice had come out of her throat, but she had felt that somebody was squeezing her larynx in their hand, and that was where her name had come from. It was a horrible, choking sensation.

'*Louise, look at me.*'

She turned, and it was then that she saw the dark smoky figure standing by the door. It wasn't completely opaque – she could make out the panels of the door through it, and the notice pinned up with her daily rosters on it. Yet she could clearly see its pointed hood, and its long dangling sleeves, and she thought she could see its eyes too, reflecting the light from her bedside lamp.

'*I sense that you wish yourself harm,*' she said.

She wanted to scream at this figure that it couldn't be real, and to go, because she must be dreaming about it. But her lips and her tongue felt numb, like they did when she went to the dentist, and her lungs refused to fill with air, and it seemed as if she could only say the words that the hooded figure wanted her to say.

'*You must take care of yourself, Louise, because you are carrying my nestlings inside you. If you harm yourself, my nestlings will come to harm, and their lives are sacred.* Your *life is sacred too. Always remember that.*'

Louise took a step toward the hooded figure. She wanted to flap her hands so that the smoke was dispersed, or at least to pull back its hood to see what it looked like. But her legs felt as numb as her lips, and when she tried to take another step, her brain couldn't work out how to make her legs work. The foetuses inside her had entangled themselves into her spinal cord, and taken over her speech and her movement and even the beating of her heart.

'*You have thought of yourself as ugly,*' she said. '*The cruel words of others have made you believe that your life has no value. But I tell you this: every single life has value. Every single life is sacred. Those children inside you were aborted and flushed away, but I was able to save them. Now you are bearing them for me, my nestlings, in a womb, which I no longer possess.*'

Louise felt another sharp pain and took a step back, and then sat down heavily on her bed. Her eyes were so blurred with tears that she could hardly see the hooded figure as it drifted closer, but she could smell it even more strongly. Woodsmoke, and lemons.

'*You will not have to carry my nestlings for long. I am invested with the power to turn their bodily clocks much faster than those of other children. You feel pain inside you mostly because they are growing so quickly, and within a week, they will be ready to emerge. You will be a mother, Louise. The proud mother of different but sacred lives.*'

Louise could do nothing but sit on her bed, rocking backward and forward because she was hurting so much.

'*You will not harm yourself,*' she said, and now her voice sounded even harsher, and more threatening. '*I forbid you to harm yourself, under any circumstances. If you try to, you will know pain that makes* this *pain feel like nothing at all. Every nerve in your body will be ripped out, one by one, and you will have to eat your own eyes.*'

With that, the hooded figure began to collapse. It swirled around and was sucked under the door, and disappeared, although it left behind that distinctive sickening smell of smoke and lemons.

Louise lay back on her bed, trembling uncontrollably, as if she had a fever. She could feel those foetuses turning around inside her and scraping at the lining of her womb, and her despair was total. How much worse could her life become, if she wasn't even allowed to die?

35

Before he drove to Peckham the next morning, Jerry stopped off at Tooting police station. He had three minor investigations to catch up on, and he wanted to check the date of his next appearance at Wimbledon Magistrates' Court, to give evidence in a case of car theft.

As he walked into the entrance hall, PC Susan Lawrence called out, 'Oh! DC Pardoe! DC Mallett's looking for you!'

'Okay, love. How was your ice-skating?'

'Not much fun. Actually, it was a disaster. I slipped over about a hundred times and now I'm all over bruises.'

'You should come out with me next time. At least you'll get fed, and you won't end up looking like you're the victim of domestic violence.'

He went upstairs and found DC Mallett sitting at his desk, reading the *Sun* online and sipping a cup of Starbucks coffee.

'How's it going, 'Edge? The lovely PC Lawrence said you wanted to see me.'

'Wotcher, Jerry. Yes. That Tweet you twatted about that old geezer you were looking for, the one you reckon set fire to your motor. Well, this woman's been in touch, and she says she knows him.'

'You're having a giraffe, aren't you?'

'No,' said DC Mallett, reaching across his desk and picking up a sheet of notepaper. 'Her name's Mary Stebbings, and she lives in St Norbert Road in Brockley. Here's her phone number. She says the old geezer's name was Malcolm Venables, and he used to live just across the road from her.'

'What do you mean, his name "was" Malcolm Venables? Has he changed it or something?'

'No, he's dead. He died about a year ago.'

'It can't be him then, can it?'

'That's what I told her, but she said she was sure it was him. One hundred and ten per cent positive.'

Jerry stood holding the sheet of notepaper and biting his lip. This was ridiculous. It was obviously a case of mistaken identity. EvoFIT was the most successful method yet invented for identifying criminals, but even so, it led to the arrest of only six offenders out of ten. Malcolm Venables must be one of the four out of ten who had been mistaken for somebody else.

'How's it all going, this sewer business?' asked DC Mallett. 'I haven't seen nothing about it in the news.'

'That's because it's all embargoed. But I tell you, 'Edge, it's a bleeding nightmare. Those deformed kids I was telling you about, we found nearly two dozen of them in an old cesspit over in Blackheath, and now they're all at Evelina's Children's Hospital. You should see the state of them. No arms and no legs, some of them. One of them, he's only got half a brain and the top of his bonce is flat as a pancake. I had to take a couple of Nytol last night, or I never could have got to sleep.'

'So what are you going to do about this Mary Stebbings? Give her a bell?'

'I don't know. I'm on my way to Peckham later, so I could go via Brockley. I don't want to dismiss this completely out of hand. Maybe this Malcolm Venables has a brother who looks just like him. Or a cousin.'

'What about all them forensic officers what got killed?'

'What's left of them is still at St George's, in the morgue. They were all chopped up into bits, but the pathologists haven't finished working out which bits belonged to which other bits. And some of the bits are missing. Fingers, feet, even a couple of heads. There's sewage workers still combing through the slush to see if they can find them.'

'It's mad, isn't it? I'm glad you're on it, and not me. I'm still chasing that Maxi drug gang over at Streatham, and that's enough to drive you mental. We had another gang-related stabbing last night, and some young bloke got his ear chopped off with a machete.'

Jerry went across to his own desk, leafed through the messages that had been left for him and checked his PC for any reports. To his relief, there was nothing urgent. His insurance company had written to say that his car was a total write-off, but that was no surprise.

He drove to Brockley and found the small terraced house on St Norbert Road where Mary Stebbings lived. When he rang the doorbell, she answered at once, almost as if she had been expecting him. She was a small, sixtyish woman with her hair pinned up in a bun like a wire-wool pan scourer, and a droopy brown cardigan. Jerry reckoned he could have used the lenses in her glasses to start a campfire, if the sun had been out.

'Mary Stebbings? Detective Constable Pardoe. Here's my ID.'

'Oh,' she said, peering at his warrant card. 'You've come about Malcolm.'

'That's right. You told my colleague that you saw his picture on Twitter.'

'I did, yes. No doubt about it. Do you want to come on inside?'

She led him through to a small stuffy living room, clearly the 'best' room, with china dogs in the fireplace and lace antimacassars on the back of the armchairs. It smelled of lavender, and damp.

'Can I get you a cup of tea?' she asked him.

'No thanks, I'm fine. I've got a lot on today. You know what they say, no peace for the wicked.'

'Malcolm wasn't wicked. Malcolm was always very helpful. He used to put my bins out for me. Always smiling too.'

'When did he die, Mary? You don't mind if I call you Mary?'

'November last year. November the nineteenth, because it was the day before my birthday. I saw him the day before, and he looked as fit as a fiddle. But he had one of those pulmonary embolisms. His daughter Penny said he went out like a light. One minute he was eating his cornflakes. The next he was dead as a doornail. Just shows you, doesn't it? Relish every moment, because you never know when it's going to be your turn next.'

'Mary – it was me who posted that picture on Twitter. It's an old man I've seen several times in the past few days, walking around the streets of Peckham and Tooting and Denmark Hill. This old man was very much alive, so I don't think there's much chance that it could have been your Malcolm.'

'I'm sure it was Malcolm. I took a long hard look at it, and I'm sure.'

'How's your eyesight?'

'Very good, as a matter of fact. I know I wear these glasses, but I had my eyes tested at Specsavers only last week, and they said my vision was clear as a bell.'

'Malcolm doesn't have a brother, does he? Or a cousin that you know of, who looks like him?'

Mary Stebbings shook her head. 'He mentioned an older sister, but she died a long time ago. Cancer, I think he said. And his wife had passed away, too.'

'In that case, the old man I saw must have been the spitting image of Malcolm, even if he wasn't Malcolm.'

'It said on the Twitter that he was wearing a brown tweed coat. Malcolm always wore a brown tweed coat. You never saw him in nothing else – not in the winter, anyway. He said it was his lucky coat because he was coming out of the Brockley Barge pub, and he stopped for a moment to button it up. They were building a whole lot of new flats right opposite, and when he crossed the road, a load of bricks dropped down and missed him by inches.'

'He always wore a brown tweed coat?'

'That's right. His lucky coat. Another time when he was wearing it, he won £75 on a scratch card. They buried him in it.'

'They *buried* him in it? Where?'

'Deptford Park cemetery. I saw him in his coffin, wearing it. I went to the funeral myself.'

Jerry felt the same icy-cold dread that had made him shiver when he was down the sewer in Blackheath. Malcolm Venables was dead. He had been dead for months. There was no possibility that Jerry could have seen him in the reception area at the King's College Hospital, or outside McDonald's in Peckham, or standing by the Evelina Children's Hospital, or on Tooting Bec Common. He was dead. Dead as a doughnut, as Jerry's late father used to say.

'Right, Mary. I won't take up any more of your time.'

'That's all right. I haven't got anything to do all day anyway, not since my Rodney got married and moved out. That's why I spend so much time on the Twitter. It's a blessing that Twitter, if you're living on your own.'

*

Jerry knew he would have to go to Deptford Park cemetery, even if there was no earthly possibility that Malcolm Venables could have been the old man in the brown tweed coat who he and Jamila had seen.

The cemetery was in a fenced-off area on the east side of Deptford Park, surrounded by plane trees. Jerry parked in the street outside and pushed open the squeaking iron gate. A plaque by the entrance told him that it had originally been used for the burial of naval officers who had died at sea and who had no surviving relatives in England to give them a funeral. He was immediately taken by the cemetery's quietness, despite the traffic in the streets all around the park and the aircraft flying low overhead. He was also struck by how neglected it was, its borders overgrown and cluttered with dead leaves and the trees around it in need of trimming.

He walked along the pathways between the graves. A light chilly wind was blowing, so that the leaves scurried around his ankles. Most of the gravestones were plain marble or granite and engraved with nothing more than the names of the men buried beneath them. A few of them were decorated with urns or railings, and four or five angels were standing with their wings folded and their heads bent in sorrow. Some of the gravestones had fallen over and some had grown such thick pelts of moss that it was impossible to read what was written on them.

Jerry found the grave of Malcolm Venables at the far end of the cemetery. It was one of a row of newer graves, although they were all overgrown with nettles. His headstone was light grey polished granite with the inscription *Malcolm Arthur Venables, Died November 19 aged 81, Mal would always walk that extra mile, To help his friends and cheer them with a smile.*

This Malcolm Venables certainly didn't sound like the old man in the brown tweed coat that Jerry had encountered. That old man had smiled, yes, but his smile had been gloating rather than friendly, and if he had walked an extra mile it had been to find Jerry and Jamila, so that the hooded figure and her children could attack them.

What was noticeable though, was that the centre of Malcolm Venables' grave was depressed to a depth of nearly a metre, unlike the other graves beside it. It looked to Jerry as if not enough soil had been shovelled into it when his coffin was buried, or else the ground beneath it had dramatically subsided after his interment and nobody had bothered to fill it in.

He was still standing in front of the grave when a short, middle-aged man in an olive waxed jacket appeared around the corner of the pathway and came strolling straight up to him as if he knew him. The man's cheeks were reddened and rough, like somebody who spends a lot of his time outdoors, and he had a cast in one eye, so it was difficult to tell if he was looking directly at Jerry or over his left shoulder.

'Paying your respects?' he said.

'I suppose you could call it that.'

'Not an old friend then?'

'No.'

The man stood with his hands behind his back, looking around. 'I must admit that we don't get an overwhelming number of people in here, paying their respects. Sometimes days will go by, and we don't even get one.'

'You work here then?'

'As part of my supervisory duties, yes. Colin Burroughs, that's me, if you ever need advice or assistance about parks or cemeteries. Outdoor Recreational Facilities

Administrator, that's my official title. What they used to call a park-keeper.'

'It's got a lot of atmosphere, hasn't it, this cemetery? A hell of a lot of history too, judging by the gravestones. I didn't even know it existed.'

'Oh, it goes right back to the days of Nelson. Lately it's all got rather run-down though, I'm sorry to say. Cuts in the council budget, that's the problem. What limited funds the council have these days, they'd rather spend on those residents who are still above ground.'

Jerry nodded toward Malcolm Venables' sunken grave. 'What happened here then? Had a bit of an earthquake, did you?'

Colin Burroughs let out a sharp bark of laughter that sounded like Tuffnut. 'No, no! That was your Thames Tideway, that was. They've been digging a new overflow tunnel, and it runs right underneath this cemetery. When it's all done, it's going to connect the Greenwich Pumping Station with the super sewer under the Thames. We've had two or three sinkholes appearing, and this is one of them. Once the tunnelling work's all completed, we'll be filling them all in, but it's not worth doing it yet.'

He pointed over to the trees that overhung the north-west side of the cemetery. Jerry could see that there was a line of orange plastic barriers underneath them, and what looked like a warning sign, although from this distance he couldn't read what it said.

'This hole's nothing though – not compared with the one we've got over there. Nearly ten metres deep, that one is. If any coffins had been buried there, they probably would have dropped down into the tunnel that they were digging. That would have given them a shock, wouldn't it?'

'But there weren't any? Coffins, I mean?'

'No. Nobody's been buried there since the cemetery first opened, and I don't think anybody ever will be. There's a story about that end of the cemetery, that it's cursed. They say that a witch's ashes were sprinkled there, after she was burned at the stake.'

'A witch? When?'

'I don't know. It would have been more than a hundred and fifty years ago because that's as far as the records for this cemetery go back. And it's only a story. But they've always called that the Witch's Quarter-Acre, and they say that if you're buried there your soul will never be able to escape from your coffin and go to Heaven.'

'I can't say I've ever heard that story before.'

'Ha! No, I'm not surprised! We don't exactly go spreading it around!'

Colin Burroughs took out a packet of cigarettes and offered one to Jerry. When Jerry shook his head, he shrugged and lit one, and stood puffing up smoke into the grey afternoon air. Jerry waited for him to tell him something more about the cemetery and its history, but he stayed silent and carried on smoking, one eye looking north and the other eye looking north-east. Perhaps he didn't know any more than he had already told him.

'Okay if I take some pictures?' Jerry asked him.

'Be my guest, squire. Be my guest.'

Jerry took out his phone and filmed a short video of

Malcolm Venables' headstone and the deep depression in his grave. Then he walked over and took more pictures of the sinkhole in the Witch's Quarter-Acre. Down at the bottom of the sinkhole, he could see tussocks of grass and lumps of soil, so it didn't appear as if it had collapsed completely into the drainage tunnel below it.

As he was walking back, Colin Burroughs beckoned him over.

'I'll tell you one thing,' he said, blowing smoke out through his nostrils. 'I don't believe that old story about the witch, not for a single moment. Just an old wives' tale. But you won't catch me coming into this cemetery at night. Nor during a thunderstorm neither.'

'Oh, no?' said Jerry, with a smile. 'What are you afraid of?'

'What are we *all* afraid of?' said Colin Burroughs, tapping his forehead with his finger. 'The spooky things that go on inside here. The human brain. More like a chamber of horrors if you ask me.'

★★★

Back at the station, Jamila listened in silence while Jerry told her about his visit to Mary Stebbings and to Deptford Park cemetery.

Then she sat back and said, 'What do *you* think? It could be a coincidence that William Trench buried his witch-woman's smoke near Deptford Park, and that there's a story about a witch's ashes being scattered there. And it could be another coincidence that this Malcolm Venables should be buried so close nearby.'

'Two coincidences I could just about believe in,' said Jerry. 'But it's the brown tweed coat that clinched it for me, because that makes it three.'

'I can understand that, Jerry, but if Malcolm Venables is dead, how could it have been him?'

'Sarge – how could a woman made of nothing but smoke almost knock me unconscious? How could children with no arms and no legs and no stomachs stay alive in a cesspit, even for five minutes? How could all those forensic officers get chopped into pieces and blown out into the street in a fountain of shit? I mean, Jesus – one old-age pensioner walking around Peckham when he's been dead since last November, that's practically normal by comparison.'

'Well, yes, you're right. But, I don't know. The more we find out, the more bizarre this whole investigation seems to become. It's like some horrible story about demons that my grandmother used to tell me.'

'It wasn't only the brown tweed coat. It was the sinkholes. William Trench wrote in his diary, didn't he, that he and his mates buried the witch-woman's coffin three times as deep as a normal grave, and piled a whole lot of concrete and stuff on top of it. They did that so it would be almost impossible to dig it up, but that means it would have been a whole lot closer to the tunnel that the Thames Tideway engineers were digging underneath. Supposing the roof of the tunnel collapsed, and the witch-woman's coffin fell down into the tunnel?'

'She would still have been locked inside it, with those seventy-two locks. How would she have got out?'

'You remember what Alan Pattinson said? Nobody

could turn those keys except for priests, or people whose hearts had stopped beating and then started up again. *Or* – the witch's children, natural or adopted. If any of those kids had already been down in the sewers, they could have opened the locks around her coffin and got her out.'

'You really think some of those children could have been living down in the sewers *before* she escaped from her coffin?'

'I'm only guessing, sarge. But we've both seen what kind of power she has. Maybe she was able to keep them alive even when she was still locked up inside it. Who knows?'

Jamila stood up and went to the window. 'We can't allow this to continue. We have to do what William Trench did, and hunt her down and lock her away for good. Or better still, destroy her completely, so that she can never come back in any shape or form. But how do we find her, and more to the point, how do we destroy her? She is nothing but smoke.'

'Didn't you say that your granny used to know all about ghosts? What were they called?'

'Churels. They can be made out of smoke too. But Churels are Pakistani spirits. And besides, my grandmother passed away a long time ago.'

'There's nobody in your family who might be able to do a spot of exorcism for us?'

'Perhaps. But I couldn't ask any of them to risk their lives, and I truly believe they *would* be risking their lives if they tried to catch her. Whatever she really is, and wherever she gets her strength from, this witch-woman is more malicious than any murderer I have ever had to go after.'

Jamila paused, and then she said, 'As it is, Jerry, I believe that both you and I are in considerable danger. It seems as if she knows how to find us, wherever we are. We could so easily have been burned to death in your car, and she might try it again at any time. For all we know, she could burn us to death in this room, while we are talking. Or tonight, while we are sleeping in our beds.'

'Oh, cheers. I'm having enough trouble getting to kip as it is. But if we're going to catch her, and put her out of action, I reckon we need to do exactly what William Trench says he did, don't you think? Number one, we need a dog, which won't be any problem. We could always use Tuffnut, my ex-wife's Staffie, if she'll let us. Number two, we need a priest who can do exorcisms. I was reading about it the other day, and apparently, the Vatican still insists that every Catholic diocese has a priest trained in driving out devils.'

'Even if we can find a priest, we will still have to convince him to help us.'

'Come on, sarge. You can persuade anybody to do anything. You only had to flutter your eyelashes at DCI Walters and he approved all that overtime.'

'*Jerry*,' said Jamila.

'All right, sorry. But I don't think we'll have too much of a problem getting hold of a priest. We won't need the yew twigs and the whale oil, because the witch has been cremated already – apart from which, I don't have a clue where we could find any whale oil. I've never seen any in

Lidl. But, number three, we'll need a coffin with seventy-two locks to shut her up in. With any luck, we'll find *that* somewhere down in the Greenwich overflow tunnel.'

'You really think so?'

'We can but try. I'll give that Gemma Bright a bell and see what she has to say about it. She's the expert when it comes to finding things down drains.'

'And what about this Malcolm Venables? This old man in his brown tweed coat?'

'It could be that *his* coffin dropped down into the tunnel as well, and that's why there's such a bloody great dent in his grave. If it didn't, we'll have to get a court order to have his coffin dug up, if only to make sure that he's still in it. And I know what you're going to ask next – what if he *isn't* still in it?'

'Then, for the first time in my life, I shall have to seek an arrest warrant for a man who is dead.'

36

DCI Walters came in, looking more like a bird of prey than usual. He had cut himself shaving and had stuck a pink plaster to the side of his chin, but it had come loose and waggled when he spoke.

'We've got ourselves a bit of a problem,' he announced.

'A bit of a problem?' said Jerry. 'That's the understatement of the century.'

'The problem I'm talking about, Pardoe, is that the media have got on to this. Somebody at St George's Hospital has tipped them off that the forensic officers who were fatally injured in the sewer in Peckham didn't die by accident. The pathologist has found that they weren't dismembered by water pressure or any kind of gas explosion. They were deliberately cut apart by what must have been some kind of a saw.'

'Even *we* haven't been told that yet,' said Jamila.

'I've already been on to the pathologist about it. He apologised for the leak and said that he'll be sending us his full report later this afternoon. He doesn't know who leaked it, but he has a fair idea, and he's going to look into it. He said that when he finds out who was responsible, heads are going to roll.'

'That's an appropriate way of putting it, under the circumstances,' said Jerry.

'That's not all,' said DCI Walters. 'Somebody at Evelina's Children's Hospital has spilled the beans about the children you rescued. The media don't have the full details, but they know that there's a number of sick children being kept in isolation and that they've all been put into an induced coma. A reporter from the *Daily Telegraph* asked me why it was necessary to have armed officers preventing people from going up to the sixth floor and why a police dog was guarding the ward.'

'What did you tell them?' asked Jamila.

'As far as the forensic officers were concerned, I said that we were still waiting for a full post-mortem report and until then I couldn't comment. As far as the children were concerned, I said that they were suffering from a serious illness that medical experts had not yet been able to identify, but we were keeping them isolated to prevent the possibility of it spreading any further.'

'And how did the press react to that?'

'They were very persistent, I'll give them that. They kept asking what kind of a serious illness, and where had it come from, was it like Ebola or something like that, but they got no more details out of me. The last thing we want is a public panic.'

'We were coming up to see you anyway, sir,' Jamila put in. 'DC Pardoe has turned up some information that may help us to make some real progress with this investigation.'

'I can't guarantee it,' said Jerry. 'But, you know – you never know.'

He told DCI Walters about the cemetery and the Witch's Quarter-Acre. DCI Walters sat and listened like a man who doesn't want to believe anything that he is being told but knows he has no alternative, because nothing else that he has yet heard makes any sense.

'We're planning to go down into the tunnel and see if we can find that coffin,' Jamila told him. 'If we can do that, we might at least have some way of holding our offender, always supposing that we can catch her.'

DCI Walters looked at her for a long time before he answered. Offender, he repeated at last. 'That's the first time I've ever heard a puff of smoke called an offender. Every day that passes, the happier I am that you're the front-line investigators in this case, and not me.'

*

Jamila called Gemma at Crane's Drains. Gemma agreed to get in touch with the engineering contractors who were digging the overflow tunnel between Greenwich and Chambers Wharf.

'I'm sure they'll let us go down and take a look,' Gemma told her. 'It's possible that the coffin could have dropped down into the excavation. They're digging the tunnel with this massive boring machine called Annie that's about as wide as two London buses. It creeps along about four metres an hour, and the engineers line the tunnel behind it with these precast concrete panels. Maybe the coffin fell through before they'd had the chance to do that. Something similar happened when they were digging the Channel Tunnel and water started to pour through the ceiling.'

'Well, we have to check anyway,' Jamila told her. 'If you can get a team together sometime later today, that would be great.'

'No problem. They're working on that tunnel twenty-four hours a day, and I know the engineer in charge, so there shouldn't be any difficulty in us getting access.'

Almost as soon as she had put down her phone, it warbled again. It was PC Dyer, calling from the children's hospital.

'PC Dyer. Is everything okay?'

'You need to get here right away, sergeant. There's something very weird happening.'

'What do you mean by "very weird"? Are the children still in a coma?'

'Yes. But it's like we're seeing things. I don't like to say ghosts.'

'When you say you're seeing things, is that all of you, or just you?'

'All of us. The doctors and the nurses too.'

'Very well. We'll be right with you.'

Jerry had been prodding at his phone and catching up with his WhatsApp messages. He looked up and said, 'Don't tell me. It's something else bloody scary.'

'PC Dyer says they're seeing ghosts.'

Jerry dropped his head forward in resignation. 'This is

never going to end, is it? We're going to be fighting this bleeding witch until we're drawing our pensions.'

He shrugged on his raincoat and the two of them clattered downstairs to the car park. As he started the Datsun's engine, Jerry said, 'Just one thing, sarge. If you see that old fellow in the brown tweed coat... or even somebody who looks like him... shout out. I don't fancy getting barbecued a second time.'

He drove at high speed to the children's hospital, with the Datsun's blue light flashing, and one or two quick bursts on the siren. When they arrived, they found that the two armed officers guarding the lifts were both looking confused and edgy.

'Don't exactly know what's going on up there, sarge, but they've warned us to watch out for any intruders.'

'Yes, you need to,' said Jamila. 'Keep your eyes open in particular for an old man in a brown coat. He looks quite harmless, but his appearance is deceptive. Quite apart from him though, do not let anybody up to any of the floors unless they are a member of staff and have ID. And I mean *nobody*. No visitors, not until we give you the all-clear.'

'Okay, got you.'

Jerry and Jamila said nothing to each other as they went up in the lift. They didn't even look at each other. On the sixth floor, as before, they found the paediatricians and the nurses and the police officers milling around in the corridor, all of them looking as rattled as the two armed officers down in reception. PC Maitland was still there, with Blizzard, and even Blizzard appeared to be nervous, clawing impatiently at the floor and repeatedly lifting up his hindquarters, even though he had been ordered to sit.

Jamila and Jerry went up to PC Dyer, who was standing by the doors of Peaceful Ward, peering in through the windows. She had that strained expression on her face that Jerry had seen before on young constables when they encountered a bizarre and frightening situation for which they hadn't been prepared at Hendon training college.

'There,' she said. 'If they're not ghosts, what are they?'

Jamila and Jerry looked into the ward. The children were still lying on their beds, each of them deeply asleep and covered in a light blue hospital blanket. Yet sitting up on every bed, there was another figure, adult-sized, but physically afflicted in exactly the same way – a grown-up version of the comatose child lying beneath it. These figures were little more than watery outlines, and Jerry could see right through them, but they were distinct enough for him to be able to make out their faces and their various malformations.

Several of them were moving, turning their heads and lifting their arms as if they were swimming, and at least three of them were opening and closing their mouths, although Jerry couldn't hear anything.

'It's *them*, isn't it?' said Jamila, her voice hushed with awe. 'It's the children, only grown up.'

Dr Latimer came up behind them. 'As soon as they appeared, I told all the nursing staff to clear the ward. I have no idea if they're dangerous or not. I've never seen anything like them. But after that last outburst of violence, I didn't want to take any chances.'

Jamila bit her lip thoughtfully, and then she said, 'Let's go in. I'd like to see how they react to us, if at all. It could be that they're nothing more than holograms. Maybe somebody has found a way of projecting images remotely. If so, it's possible that we could trace where they're being sent from.'

Dr Latimer looked dubious. 'How would anybody else know what their deformities are? We've kept a total security blackout ever since the children were first brought here.'

'Nothing in this investigation is logical, doctor,' said Jamila. 'We've stopped trying to discount any lines of inquiry simply because they don't make sense.'

Jerry pushed open the doors and they stepped inside. The first thing he noticed was how chilly it was. It was like walking into the freezer at the back of the butcher's shop where he had worked on Saturdays when he was at school. The windows were white with frost, although the sun was still shining through them, and their breath smoked.

Jamila and Jerry approached the first bed cautiously, with Dr Latimer close behind them. They could see the flattened head of the boy who was lying under the blanket, and the phantom figure that was sitting up on top of him had a flattened head too. Its eyes were opaque, and its mouth was dragged down at the sides, although it kept opening and closing its jaw as if it were chewing a lump of gristle.

Jerry went up close to the figure. It slowly turned its head and stared back at him, its jaw still opening and closing.

'Who are you?' Jerry asked it, although he knew that it was probably futile trying to talk to it if it was nothing but a hologram.

The figure kept on staring at him and chewing, and then suddenly, it flung up both of its arms and screamed at him – a scream that sounded like the blade of a knife being dragged along a railway line. Jerry stumbled back, but the figure kept on screaming, and then all of the other phantom figures in the ward began to scream too. The noise was so piercing that he couldn't hear himself think.

Both Jamila and Dr Latimer had their hands pressed to their ears, and Jamila shouted, 'Come on, let's get out of here before we go deaf!'

The three of them pushed their way back out into the corridor. As the doors swung shut behind them, the screaming sank down to a quivering whistle and then died out altogether. PC Dyer and Andrew Tanner and the ward sister came hurrying up to them, and Andrew Tanner said, 'My God, Ted! What *are* those things?'

'I couldn't even begin to tell you,' said Dr Latimer. He was visibly shaken. 'Maybe they're some kind of optical illusion, but I can't imagine what makes them scream like that.'

Jerry looked back through one of the windows. The phantom figures were still sitting on the beds, although now their heads were bowed as if they were meditating, or praying, or beginning to fall asleep.

'What do you think, sarge?'

'I think we should wait and see. Maybe they will fade away of their own accord. If they stay for much longer,

I might call for the drone unit to see if they can jam the signal. That's if they *are* being created by a signal.'

The ward sister said, 'In the meantime, I think my nurses here can all take a break. They've had quite enough stress for one morning. We have to deal with some heart-rending cases here, believe me, but we've never had to cope with anything like this.'

They were still talking when Blizzard abruptly barked, and then growled, and then scrabbled his claws on the floor. His handler said, 'Sit, Blizzard! I said, *sit!*'

Jerry turned around and couldn't stop himself giving a shiver. Standing in the corridor less than ten metres away was the white-haired old man in the brown tweed coat. The old man lifted one hand and smiled, and then he called out, 'There you are! I guessed you'd be in 'ere somewhere!' His voice was oddly muffled, like somebody with a scarf wrapped over his mouth.

'*Right*, you!' Jerry snapped at him, and started to stride toward him. 'You're nicked, you are, sunshine!'

He had taken only three or four steps when – close behind the old man – a dark cloud of smoke began to fill the corridor. Blizzard barked even more hysterically and bounced up and down, and Jerry slowed down and then stopped.

The smoke rolled around and around and rapidly took on the shape of the hooded woman, her arms outstretched so wide that they reached both sides of the corridor. The peak of her hood almost touched the ceiling.

'What in the effing eff is *that*?' said PC Maitland. He was straining so hard to keep Blizzard in check that he was leaning backward and digging in his heels. 'And where did that old bloke come from? We're not supposed to be letting anybody up here, are we?'

Before Jerry or Jamila could answer, PC Dyer spoke in the harsh, unmistakeable tones of the witch-woman. Jerry looked around at her, and he could see how shocked she was that she was speaking at all, and even more by the words that were coming out of her mouth.

'*I have come to take my nestlings home.*'

'Not a chance,' Jamila retorted, although Jerry could hear how stressed she was.

'*Do not try to defy me! I have shown you how they will grow and what they will become! Now you must leave them alone and let them lead their own sacred lives, not the lives that you think you can impose on them.*'

Jamila stepped forward, her arms by her sides, both fists clenched. 'You are not taking them. You have destroyed enough lives already. We are going to take care of them for as long as they live, which will not be long. But we are not going to let them go back to live in a sewer.'

'*The sewer is their home. It was the fat in the sewer that fed them before they set me free. You call that fat, waste. For my nestlings, it is nourishment. Now, stand aside and I will take them back where they belong.*'

'Oh, yes, and how do you propose to do that?' Jerry challenged her. 'There's twenty-two of them in there.'

'*They are mine! They are my nestlings! Without me, they never could have lived any life at all!*'

'You should let 'er 'ave 'em!' shouted the old man in the brown tweed coat, although he still sounded muffled. 'They ain't yours, them kids! You ain't got no right!'

The hooded figure kept on rolling and swirling as if she were agitated, but she didn't approach any closer. Jerry laid his hand on PC Maitland's shoulder and said, 'Go on. Give them a bit of Blizzard.'

PC Maitland bent down and unclipped Blizzard's collar, and Blizzard shot off along the corridor like a bullet fired from a gun. He went for the old man in the brown tweed coat first, leaping on top of him and knocking him sideways onto the floor. The hooded figure did nothing to defend the old man, but shrank further back, her clouds of smoke becoming more and more turbulent. Jerry could see that he had been right, and that she *was* afraid of dogs, especially ferocious dogs like Tuffnut and Blizzard.

The old man flapped one arm, trying to beat Blizzard off him, but Blizzard growled and gripped his sleeve between his teeth, shaking his head violently from side to side. The tweed was so fragile that Blizzard ripped it into shreds, and when he tossed his head back, he wrenched the old man's arm completely out of its socket.

This excited Blizzard so much that he went berserk. He snarled and tore at the old man's throat, pulling out strings of dried flesh and tendons. But there was no blood. Jerry could see that the old man was desiccated, almost mummified. Blizzard bit with a crunch right through his spinal cord, and the old man's head rolled off and tumbled across the floor, ending up with his face against a radiator.

Now Blizzard turned his attention to the hooded witch-woman, his tail erect and his hind legs trembling as if he were sexually aroused. The witch-woman was gradually retreating down the corridor, waving her smoky sleeves slowly from side to side as if that might keep Blizzard from coming any closer.

'*You will regret this*,' said PC Dyer, coming forward and standing so close to Jerry and Jamila that she was almost touching them. '*You will be punished for it, I swear in the name of original sin. You think you can take my nestlings away from me? Nobody can take my nestlings away from me. If I cannot have them, nobody can have them.* Nobody!'

Her sleeves waved more wildly, making a soft rumbling sound, as if they were being blown by a hurricane. Even Blizzard took two or three steps back. PC Dyer screamed out something that sounded like '*Amulet!*' and then there was a devastating bang from Peaceful Ward, so loud that Jerry thought his eardrums had burst. The doors were ripped off their hinges and crashed into the paediatricians and nurses and police officers gathered outside, knocking several of them up against the opposite wall and some of them onto the floor.

Out of the ward roared a huge billow of green fire, searingly hot. The flames filled the corridor, scorching everybody in it and devouring all the oxygen like some ravenous dragon. Jerry grabbed Jamila's arm and pulled her away, and between them, they stumbled toward the lifts. They were only halfway there, when the flames shrank back into the ward, although they were still burning fiercely inside.

Jerry looked further down the corridor. Blizzard

had stopped chasing the witch-woman for a moment, distracted by the flames bursting out, but now he was after her again, furiously barking. The witch-woman was backing away, still waving her sleeves. She passed the lifts and retreated as far as the stairwell, and then she collapsed and folded up and dropped down onto the floor. Her smoke poured away between the banisters and vanished. Blizzard reached the top of the stairs and stood there baffled, his ears erect and his fur bristling, unable to understand how the witch-woman could have simply slid away out of his sight.

Jerry and Jamila turned back toward the ward. The paediatricians and the nurses and the police officers were climbing back onto their feet, their faces reddened and their hair singed and their clothes still smoking. Inside the ward, every one of the twenty-two beds was on fire, consumed by raging green flames that twisted and danced and leaped up almost as high as the ceiling. The witch-woman's nestlings were being cremated alive.

The ward sister, her cap askew, had already called for the fire brigade. PC Maitland came hurrying toward them, lugging a fire extinguisher that he had found at the opposite end of the corridor. He pulled the pin and aimed it at the flames, but the heat was so intense that there was little he could do except spray dry powder into the middle of the open doorway.

Until the firefighters arrived, all they could do was stand and watch the beds blaze. There was no sign of the phantom figures, and they saw no movement from the children. There was no more screaming either. The only sounds were the crackling of fire and a strange mournful twanging as the fabric of each of the mattresses was burned away and their springs uncoiled.

Nobody spoke – not even to share their feeling that these children should never have survived anyway, and that it was a tragic blessing that their lives should have ended, although not like this.

Abruptly, and belatedly, the sprinklers in the ceiling started to rain down water all along the ward. They continued gushing until the green flames dipped and guttered and dwindled, and one after another, all the fires were put out. The twenty-two beds were left blackened and sodden and smoking, like two rows of funeral biers.

Five firefighters arrived with a noisy bustle of waterproof fire kit, although there was no more fire for them to extinguish. While they were making sure that there was no chance of any of the smouldering mattresses bursting into flame again, Jerry and Jamila walked slowly down the middle of the ward. There was little left on each of the beds except for springs and ashes and ribcages and other assorted bones. The smoke was as thick as a winter fog.

'That witch-woman,' said Jamila, shaking her head, 'she is just like those terrorists who would rather kill their own children than let the infidels have them.'

They went back out into the corridor. Jerry nodded toward the body of the old man in the brown tweed coat, his head still lying next to the radiator.

'I bet that *was* him, that Malcolm Venables. I mean, the way Blizzard could just pull him apart like that. I reckon that witch brought him back to life, like a zombie. I'll have Lambeth test him for DNA, anyhow.'

Jamila wiped her eyes. 'It is urgent that we find her now, before she can cause any more death and damage. Those poor children. They should never have been alive, but she was right in a way. Since they *were* alive, their lives were sacred.'

Jerry shrugged. 'I think we've got her on the run though. All we've got to do now is find her – and, like you say, sarge, have some way of neutralising her once we have.'

'"Neutralising", that's a very non-committal way of putting it.'

'Well, yes. But you can't arrest smoke, can you? You can't put handcuffs on it, and you can't Taser it, and you can't shoot it.'

PC Maitland came up to them, his face smudged with soot. 'Poor old Blizzard. He's still sniffing around, wondering where that smoky woman went. But I thought you'd like to know that we can probably track her down, when you're ready.'

He held up a white hospital hand towel with a black smear on it.

'Her smoke left a residue on the walls. It has quite a strong smell to it too. If ever she turns up again, it won't matter where, Blizzard and some of our other dogs will be able to track her down. I'll tell you something about Blizzard. If somebody's frying sausages five miles away, he can smell it, and it's all I can do to stop him from tearing off trying to find them.'

He passed the hand towel to Jamila, and Jamila sniffed it. Then she gave it to Jerry.

'Woodsmoke and lemons,' he said. 'That's her all right. Now we need to find her coffin, and a priest, and we'll have everything we need to get her banged up.'

37

They didn't get back to Peckham police station for another three hours. When they did though, Jerry found to his surprise that the Reverend Denis O'Sullivan was waiting for him. He was upstairs in their office, leafing through a copy of *Police* magazine.

'I was passed the message that you wanted to speak to me about exorcism,' he said, in a very precise Sligo accent. 'I happened to be here in Peckham this afternoon visiting St Thomas's, so I thought I'd call in. The young lady downstairs told me that you wouldn't be too long.'

The Reverend O'Sullivan was deacon of the Church of Our Lady of Eternal Grief in Nunhead. Jerry had tried to contact him earlier because the diocese office had informed him that he was the only practising exorcist south of the river. He was short and balding with large ears and dramatically sprouting eyebrows. He wasn't wearing a dog collar, but he was dressed all in black – black shirt, black suit and black overcoat, and there was a black bucket hat on the table next to him.

Jamila went off to the toilet to wash while Jerry said, 'Do sit down, reverend. I appreciate your calling in.

You haven't been waiting too long, have you? I was planning on paying you a visit this evening as it was.'

'No, no,' said the Reverend O'Sullivan. 'I've been here only twenty minutes, and I have all the time in the world.'

He sat down and laced his fingers together, leaning forward with a concerned expression on his face as if he expected Jerry to start confessing that he had committed adultery or stolen a six-pack of Stella from his local off-licence.

'Sorry, I pen-and-ink a bit,' said Jerry. 'DS Patel and I have just been attending a rather tragic fire.'

'A fire? Dear Heaven. Did somebody lose their life?'

'It's all part of the reason I wanted to talk to you, reverend. I don't suppose you get many people contacting you about exorcisms, but I think you'll understand when I've explained exactly why.'

'Well, you may not credit it, but I've had four or five parishioners asking about exorcisms recently. More than usual. We live in such a Godless world these days that people believe that demons are running amok. And I think that too. Once you close the door on God, you open the door for the Devil.'

Jerry quickly gave the Reverend O'Sullivan all the historical background about the witch-woman and how William Trench had burned her and sealed her smoke in a coffin. He mentioned her apparent fear of dogs. Then he went on to tell him about the malformed children, the fatberg and the deaths of all the forensic officers in the sewer, as well as the mutilation of Martin Elliot and the skinning of Dr Macleod. The Reverend O'Sullivan listened with his eyes closed, although he nodded from time to time to indicate that he was concentrating, and not bored, or half asleep.

When Jerry had finished describing this afternoon's fire at the Evelina Children's Hospital, he crossed himself and opened his eyes.

'You're not making any of this up, are you?' he asked.

'No, reverend. I know it all sounds stark staring bonkers, but every word of it's true. The only reason you haven't read about it in the papers or seen it on the news is because we've imposed a very strict media embargo. I'm also going to ask you to sign a non-disclosure agreement before you leave here.'

'I believe you,' said the Reverend O'Sullivan. 'I've read about this kind of thing in the books I studied for exorcism – aborted children being revived – although I've not heard about it being done recently. The thinking behind it was that they would resent God because they would feel that He had turned his back on them. They weren't growing in His image, as all children are supposed to, and that is why they had been terminated. But if they could be brought back to life by satanic witchcraft, they would be so grateful that they would become the Devil's willing servants.'

He paused, and then he said, 'Tell me – did this William Trench happen to mention the witch-woman's name?'

'No, not as far as I know. Alan Pattinson only had the diary on loan. If he hasn't returned it yet, I could give him a bell and ask him, but I didn't see a name mentioned in any of the bits I read. He called her the "witch-woman", that was all.'

'It would be most helpful to know who she was,

since you say that this William Trench believed her to be the most powerful witch that England has ever known. More than one witch claimed in the sixteenth and seventeenth centuries that they were the most powerful, but women who were rash enough to profess that they were witches were usually mentally unstable, since the consequence usually was that they were burned at the stake or drowned in the village pond or stoned to death.'

At that moment, Jamila came back into the office, smelling of Titan Celeste perfume. Jerry knew what it was, because he had sent it to her on her last birthday, on the recommendation of another Pakistani woman officer.

'The Reverend O'Sullivan says it would help him to find out the witch-woman's name.'

'But we don't know it, do we? Have you told him everything else? About the keys with the demon's sigils on them? About those ghosts we saw, at the hospital? About Martin Elliot being taken away and having his legs cut off?'

'Everything.'

'Did you tell him about the message that Martin Elliot wrote to us before he died?'

'Oh, no. I forgot about that. But I don't think that meant anything anyway. He wrote "cave" and then he wrote "friendship". That was all. According to the doctor, he was really worried that he hadn't told us before, but by then he wasn't exactly the full shilling, if you know what I mean. Like I told you, he'd been blinded, as well as having his legs amputated.'

The Reverend O'Sullivan was staring at Jerry as if Jerry had just blasphemed.

'He wrote "cave" and then "friendship"?'

'That's right.'

'Did you know that when people are possessed by a demon or other malevolent being, they are unable to tell anybody else the name of that demon or other malevolent being? They are simply incapable of saying it.'

'No, I didn't know that. But I suppose if I was a demon I wouldn't want anybody to know either, in case somebody like you came along and exorcised me.'

'But did you know that in the few minutes before people die, they are returned to God, no matter what they have done, and in those few minutes, they can speak the name of the demon or the other malevolent being who possesses them, and in those few minutes, that demon or other malevolent being no longer has the power to keep them silent, or to punish them?'

'I can't say I knew that either, to be honest with you.'

'What do you think this unfortunate man meant when he wrote "cave"?'

'I guessed he was telling us that the children were hiding in a cave. As it turned out, it was an abandoned cesspit.'

'"*Cave*" in Latin means "beware". And if he was warning you to beware, I'm not at all surprised. Especially if "friendship" didn't mean "friendship" in the sense of camaraderie. Friendship was the name of Adeliza Friendship, who is recorded in the Vatican library as having been the only mortal woman to have been mistress of Satan.'

Jerry and Jamila looked at each other, and then back to the Reverend O'Sullivan.

'The mistress of Satan?' said Jamila. 'Surely Satan is

imaginary. A theological concept. How can a woman be the mistress of a theological concept?'

'You're wrong,' said the Reverend O'Sullivan, shaking his head emphatically. 'It was Pope Francis who said that Satan is not a diffuse thing. "He is not like a mist," that's what Pope Francis said. "He is a person." Look it up for yourself if you don't believe me.'

'So this Adeliza Friendship was Satan's mistress. Is that why she was the most powerful witch that ever was?'

'Exactly. Satan lavished everything on her. He gave her gifts beyond all imagination. The gift of prediction. The gift of lighting fires by spontaneous combustion, which you've witnessed for yourselves. The gift of healing the sick, because she could kill viruses, even before anybody knew that viruses existed. The gift of curing the mad, because she could shrink brain tumours, even before anybody knew about brain tumours. Above all, he gave her the power to raise the dead.'

'That old man who kept following us around – he really could have been Malcolm Venables then?'

'From what you've told me, it's not only possible but highly likely. Adeliza Friendship would always have had a familiar. Not a black cat, like witches in storybooks, but a dead person she had resurrected. They would do all her dirty work for her... cleaning her house for her, running errands, spying on her enemies. They would be so grateful to her for bringing them back to life that they would do anything for her. They also knew that if they disobeyed her, they would be shut back up in their coffins before they could blink.'

'And you really believe that this smoky figure could be her? Or some kind of ghost of her?'

'You said that she was frightened by your dog. That helped to convince me. One of the better known stories about Adeliza Friendship is that she renewed the ancient pagan tradition of sacrificing dogs to cure children born with birth defects.'

'They really used to do that?'

'Oh, yes. Thousands of dogs were sacrificed in China and Greece and Hungary, right up until the twelfth century. But you can't commit mass murder against a whole species without that species seeking revenge, as the priests of China and Greece and Hungary found out, to their cost. And Adeliza Friendship too. It was said that dogs would ruthlessly attack her wherever she went.'

Jamila said, 'I'm not sure I can take this all in. She was actually Satan's mistress? But doesn't Satan have horns and a tail and live in Hell?'

'Of course not. As Pope Francis said, he's a person, a very evil person, in the sense that he has human shape. But he still has command of all the demons of Hell, and those demons can possess people so that they do Satan's work for him. That's why he wants to revive all those aborted foetuses... so that they will always be his children.'

'I still can't understand how it's done,' said Jamila. 'I can understand the science of reviving people by CPR or electric shock. But those aborted foetuses... some of them were found back in their mother's wombs, or in other women's wombs.'

'That's right. If they had been aborted before they had

developed enough to survive for any sustained period of time outside the womb, Adeliza Friendship would return them to the wombs of their original mothers or, if that was impracticable, to the womb of any other woman who could be used as a surrogate mother. Then again, if a foetus was capable of independent movement, it might seek out a surrogate mother by itself. Even from a distance, Adeliza Friendship would be able to invest it with the power to crawl, and to find what you might call a nest.'

'Yes,' said Jamila. 'We have had several cases of that. Now they begin to make some sort of sense. Maybe "sense" is not the right word, but at least we can understand what's been going on, and why.'

'There's a book in the Vatican library, *Progeniem Nidosque Diaboli Est Scriptor*,' the Reverend O'Sullivan told her. 'It literally means "The Devil's Nestlings", and it describes in full how aborted foetuses were revived and then inserted by so-called witches into the wombs of innocent women while they slept. Either that, or they crawled in by themselves. The practice of "airing" beds by throwing back the covers was not originally done to dry the sheets after a night's sleep, but to make sure that there were no aborted foetuses lurking under the blankets. That was one of the reasons duvets became so popular... it was so much easier to check for some unwelcome visitor hiding in your bed.'

While he was talking, Jamila had switched on her computer and googled Adeliza Friendship. Apart from the text describing her as 'the most notorious self-proclaimed witch of the nineteenth century', there were several engravings. One was of Adeliza Friendship herself, staring directly at the viewer. She had huge eyes and high cheekbones and a sensual mouth, and her hair was elaborately pinned up in braids. Her left hand was lifted with her fingers parted in the sign of Satan.

Another picture – a crude woodcut – showed her dressed in a voluminous skirt and dancing with the Devil. Unlike the Devil that the Reverend O'Sullivan had described, this Devil had horns and a tail and cloven hoofs, and was carrying a trident.

Jerry studied the pictures and read the text. It made no mention of William Trench and how he had burned Adeliza Friendship. It said only that she had 'disappeared' one day in September 1859, and that nobody knew what had become of her.

'She's a looker though, isn't she?' said Jerry. 'If I bumped into her in my local, I'd have a go at chatting her up, I can tell you.'

'Even if she wasn't made of smoke, Jerry, she's already spoken for,' said Jamila. Then she turned to the Reverend O'Sullivan. 'Before she set fire to those poor children, reverend, she shouted out "*Amulet!*" or something like it. Do you have any idea what that could have meant?'

The Reverend O'Sullivan thought for a moment, and then he said, 'It's possible that she was calling on the demon Adramalech. In the Bible, it is mentioned that the Sepharvites used to make sacrifices to Adramalech by burning their children alive. So even though she killed them, what she did would have met with Satan's approval.'

'You know what we're going to ask you, reverend, don't you?'

'Yes, of course. I can't say that I've ever performed an exorcism on anybody who's already been exorcised once before, and cremated, and who is nothing more substantial than smoke. She obviously has extraordinary powers, and I think I can say with some certainty that those powers come directly from Satan himself – her lover.'

He frowned at his bucket hat for a moment, as if he expected it to move, or to speak to him. 'I've exorcised what I believe to be real demons before now. A secondary school teacher in Bermondsey was possessed by the demon Crocell, who had taken over her brain by the cunning use of numbers. I was able to dismiss him by decoding his numbers, almost like cleaning malware out of a hard drive.

'I have to admit though, that I've never had to face Satan himself. It frightens me, to be truthful. Satan has a reputation for emptying the minds of anybody who tries to challenge him, so that they lose all of their memories, all of their emotions, all of their personality. They stay alive, but they might as well be dead.'

'Will you do it though?' asked Jamila.

The Reverend O'Sullivan looked at her and gave her a weary smile. 'This is obviously what my whole life has been leading up to. This is why I was born and this is why I took the cloth and then went on to study exorcism. This is my date with destiny. You ask me if I'll do it, but I have no choice.'

'Don't get too doomy about it,' said Jerry. 'We've got to find her first.'

38

They were still talking to the Reverend O'Sullivan when Jamila's phone rang, and she was told that Gemma had arrived in reception, along with Jim Feather and two flushers.

As soon as they had all come upstairs and crowded into their office, Gemma said, 'Here we are! Ready when you are.'

'If you can give us just a few minutes,' said Jamila. 'We have had a deeply disturbing day today, and we are still trying to recover from it. This, by the way, is the Reverend O'Sullivan. I suppose you could call him our spiritual adviser.'

'I think that's just what we need, a spiritual adviser,' said Gemma. 'You're not going to believe this, but I've been in touch with the contractors digging the Greenwich overflow, Argent Pelle. I know their chief engineer, Dan Beavis. He's the best in the business, Dan. He was one of the leading engineers on Crossrail. And guess what he told me? They *did* find a coffin when they were digging under Deptford Park. *Two* coffins, in fact.'

'You're joking, aren't you?' said Jerry. 'How come that wasn't reported?'

'It wasn't reported because it happened in the middle of the night, about 2:30 a.m. as a matter of fact. One coffin fell into the tunnel almost as soon as the boring machine had passed by, and the other one approximately twenty minutes later. They were stacked by the side of the tunnel so that they could be picked up and loaded onto the maintenance train the following day. But the following day, they were gone.'

'Gone? Gone where?'

'That's what Dan said they couldn't work out. The tunnellers on the night shift began to think that they might have dreamed it. They weren't drunk because they're not allowed to take alcohol down the tunnel, although they have been known to inject vodka into an apple or a banana using a hypodermic syringe.'

'This gets more loony by the minute,' said Jerry. 'Disappearing coffins and alcoholic bananas. I think I need a holiday.'

Gemma said, 'Dan told me that they didn't report the coffins, partly because there was no sign of them but mostly because it would have meant stopping work while the police were called to investigate where they might have gone, and the tunnelling contract is on such a tight schedule. Even stopping for a few hours would have cost them tens of thousands. Each tunneller gets paid nearly six hundred pounds a day, plus a bonus if they beat their target.'

'I'm in the wrong job,' said Jerry. 'Mind you, I'm claustrophobic, especially down those sewers.'

'Dan admitted that he'd put the coffins completely out

of his mind. He'd had far too many other things to worry about. When I called him though, he started thinking seriously about where they could have disappeared to. They couldn't have been lifted out of the tunnel by way of the main entrance shaft at Greenwich because somebody would have seen them. But there's an overflow duct between the tunnel and the existing Deptford main sewer, which is just about wide enough to push a coffin through. Dan said that if there had been enough people to lift them, they could have been carried out of the tunnel, pushed through the overflow and into the sewer. After that they could have been taken anywhere.'

'It's all very well saying "enough people",' Jerry put in. 'But *what* people? If it was the tunnellers, why would they even do that?'

'Think about it the other way round,' said Jamila. 'What if the people who took the coffins were down in the sewers already? Every one of those tunnellers would have been totally preoccupied with their work, wouldn't they? Because it's so hard, and so dangerous, and maybe they didn't notice them.'

'You're right,' Gemma agreed. 'When they're drilling, they need 100 per cent concentration. The chalk and the clay strata that they're boring through are very undulating and uneven, and they constantly need to make sure that the TBM doesn't veer off course, not even by a few centimetres. Besides, I can't see *them* having the time to carry off two coffins. Or like you say, Detective Pardoe – the motive.'

'You're talking about the children, aren't you?' Jerry

asked Jamila. 'You're suggesting it was the children who came and carried them away.'

'Well, who else? Who else would have wanted a coffin filled with a witch's smoke?'

'We're all ready,' said Gemma. 'I suggest we make a start at the Deptford sewer and see where we go from there. I've arranged for a team to follow us on the surface with ground-penetrating radar so that even if the coffin's submerged in sewage or buried in saponified fat, we'll be able to locate it.'

Jerry said, 'Good thinking. But there's something else we need to take with us, and that's Blizzard. If that witch-woman's anywhere down in the sewers, Blizzard should be able to find her for us. Apart from which, he's about the only thing we know for sure that she's afraid of.'

He looked across at the Reverend O'Sullivan. 'How about you, reverend? Are you coming with us?'

'Oh, my God,' said the Reverend O'Sullivan, and crossed himself.

***

They gathered on the corner of Oxestalls Road and Evelyn Street, the long straight road that runs from Deptford past the Surrey Quays. Three more flushers had already lifted the manhole cover and fenced it off with barriers, and two vans from Crane's Drains were parked in the bus lane.

It had started to rain, quite heavily. The forecast was that it would continue to rain for the rest of the day, and so the flushers were fixing up a blue PVC-coated tent.

'Don't want you getting wet, do we?' said one of the flushers, with a soggy roll-up cigarette waggling between his lips.

'We're going down a sewer, mate,' said Jerry. 'We're going to get wet anyway.'

'Ah, but you ain't been down a sewer when it's flooded in a rainstorm. That is your definitive definition of getting wet.'

While Jamila and Jerry and the Reverend O'Sullivan were pulling on their waterproof suits and gloves and fitting on their plastic face masks, one of the radar team opened up the tent flap. He was an earnest-looking young man in a fluorescent yellow jerkin, with oversized spectacles and a tiny brown moustache.

Gemma said, 'You look as if you've found something.'

'You said you were looking for two coffins, didn't you? We've located a metallic object in the sewer about eight hundred metres north of here, under Chilton Grove. It's rectangular, about two and a half metres in length and one metre wide. I'll have a print-out for you in a minute.'

'Only one?'

'We're still scanning. We've come across a doll's pram too, although how *that* got down into the sewer, God only knows.'

'I'm sure He does,' said the Reverend O'Sullivan. 'But I doubt if He will trouble to tell us.'

Almost as soon as the radar surveyor had left, the tent flap opened again, and PC Maitland appeared.

'Got here as soon as I could. Blizzard had to finish his lunch. I normally take him for a walk after he's eaten, but since we're going down a sewer…'

One of the flushers handed PC Maitland a waterproof suit and a splash-proof face mask.

'What about Blizzard?' asked Jerry, as PC Maitland zipped himself up.

'Blizzard's got his own waterproof suit, with legs. He hates wearing it, but that may be a bonus if we come across that smoke thing again, because it makes him twice as aggressive. I've brought that towel with me, the one from the hospital with the smoke-smudge on it, and I'll give him another sniff of it before we go down the sewer. I'll go and fetch him. He's in the back of the van, sulking.'

He returned after a few minutes with Blizzard on a short lead. Blizzard was wearing a black vinyl one-piece dog coat with only his head and his tail showing. His tongue was lolling to one side and his eyes were bulging, and he looked as if he fiercely resented being dressed to look foolish.

When everybody was ready, they climbed down the manhole into the sewer. In the bright swivelling beams from the LED lamps, Jerry could see that it was about the same diameter as the sewer that ran underneath Southampton Way, but the sewage was only ankle-deep because no fatberg was blocking it and it was able to flow more freely. When he inhaled for the first time though, he found that the smell was equally pungent. He looked around at Jamila and wrinkled up his nose, but she ignored him. For her, this hunt for the spirit of Adeliza Friendship was too frightening and too serious to be making jokes. She was looking for a woman possessed by the Devil from another culture and another religion than her own, and that made her feel strangely defenceless, as if none of her prayers could protect her.

PC Maitland splashed along the sewer first, with Blizzard straining at his lead, and Jerry and Jamila followed closely behind him. Behind Jamila came Gemma, since she was familiar with the layout of the sewers and would immediately recognise if something was wrong, such as the sewage starting to back up, or if there was any sign that the brick walls were in danger of caving in.

After Gemma came Jim Feather, and then the Reverend O'Sullivan, with two burly flushers bringing up the rear. One of them was Nigerian, and a Catholic, and he kept his hand resting on the Reverend O'Sullivan's right shoulder to make sure that he didn't slip and to reassure him that he was being looked after.

It took them nearly a quarter of an hour to wade their way as far as the junction with Chilton Grove. As they came nearer, Blizzard began to grow more and more excited, and to yap and splash and tug at his lead.

'He's picked up a scent,' said PC Maitland, over his shoulder.

'Really?' said Jerry. 'He's not the only one.'

It was then that Jamila said 'Yes' and 'yes' on her RT, and tapped Jerry on the back.

'The GPR team think they've found the other coffin. It's up at the end of Chilton Grove. It looks as if it's badly damaged, but they're fairly sure that it's a coffin.'

'Looks like we're in luck then, if you can call it luck. You know – finding two coffins down a sewer.'

They reached the corner of Chilton Grove, and there it was, lying at an angle against the right-hand wall.

Blizzard was dancing in the sewage with excitement, and PC Maitland had to snap at him to calm him down. Even then he stood quivering and sniffing and trampling his paws up and down.

'It's *her* coffin, isn't it?' said Jerry. He approached it cautiously and reached out his hand, but something told him not to touch it, even with his thick protective gloves.

The coffin was made of dark grey metal with greenish corrosion, probably bronze. It was completely rectangular, like a box, not coffin-shaped, and all around its lid dozens of open padlocks were dangling like earrings.

Blizzard could hardly contain himself and urinated into the sewage. At the same time, the Reverend O'Sullivan came forward, holding up a large silver crucifix. Behind his protective mask, his face was ashen.

'It's heating up,' he said. 'I've read of this before, but never witnessed it myself. It's so hot that I don't know if I can hold on to it much longer.'

Blizzard barked, and barked again, and kept trying to jump up onto the coffin, his claws scrabbling against its sides.

'She's in there,' said PC Maitland, in a haunted voice. 'She's only effing in there.'

39

'Dear God!' the Reverend O'Sullivan shouted out. The silver crucifix was melting. The arms of the cross were drooping down over his fingers and the head of Jesus had liquefied into a shining featureless blob, which clung to his glove for a moment and then dripped down into the sewage below.

All their LED lamps abruptly went out, followed by the lamps on their helmets, and they were plunged into absolute darkness.

'Don't panic!' said Jim Feather. 'Try your emergency lamps and if they don't work make an orderly exit, back the way we came!'

A few seconds of rustling and splashing followed, and then Gemma said, 'Mine's dead, Jim. Let's get out of here.'

Jerry reached into the blackness and found Jamila's arm, and then her hand. 'Come on, sarge. This is one of those times when running like fuck is the better part of valour.'

Gemma had already turned around, and he could feel that she was pushing up against Jim Feather. Before any of them could wade more than two or three metres though, there was a deafening bang and a crackle like fireworks, and the sewer ahead of them was filled to the roof with raging green flames. Jerry felt the same ferocious heat that he had felt when the children's ward had been set on fire, and he had to turn his face to one side, even though he was wearing a protective plastic mask.

'We'll have to go the other way!' shouted Gemma. 'There's another manhole further up, at Plough Way!'

Blizzard was still jumping up at the side of the coffin, but PC Maitland dragged him off and started to splash northward. Jerry turned to make sure that none of their party had been injured, and then he and Jamila followed PC Maitland. All around them, the green flames threw frantic patterns on the walls of the sewer. They looked like dancing demons, and the dazzling reflections around their boots made it appear as if the sewage itself was on fire.

They had waded fewer than fifteen metres when the sewer ahead of them exploded with another bang, and was blocked with more roaring green fire.

'Holy Saint Patrick!' said the Reverend O'Sullivan, crossing himself twice. 'She's trapped us, the witch!'

Jerry stopped and looked back. When he breathed in, he could feel that the fire was rapidly consuming all the oxygen in the sewer, and the air was becoming hotter and hotter with every second. He could also see that the fires were creeping closer and closer together, and that it would not be long before all seven of them were incinerated, like the children in Peaceful Ward.

'Jerry – what can we do?' said Jamila, gripping his hand even tighter. 'We're not going to die, are we?'

For a split second, Jerry thought that they could save

themselves by lying down under the sewage, but then they wouldn't be able to hold their breath for more than a few seconds, and there was no way of knowing if the fires wouldn't carry on burning even if they were submerged. Besides, if he was going to die, he would rather be cremated alive than drowned in human waste.

But then he thought of the way in which Adeliza Friendship had immolated those twenty-two children. She had done it immediately, *whoomph*, without giving them even the slightest chance to escape. So – even though these two walls of green fire were gradually edging nearer – why hadn't she killed them all instantly?

He looked down and saw that Blizzard was gasping for air, but was still desperately tugging at his lead to get at the coffin. *That's it*, he thought. *It's Blizzard. He's a dog, and she's afraid of dogs. Maybe she daren't touch them. Not directly, anyway. Maybe she can allow him to suffocate, but she can't kill him herself.*

He let go of Jamila's hand and went over to PC Maitland.

'Give me Blizzard.'

'What? Why? He won't go with you.'

'Tell him he has to. Come on, mate. This is our only chance. You want to be barbecued to death, or what?'

PC Maitland bent down to Blizzard and said, 'Go with DC Pardoe. Now!'

He handed Blizzard's lead to Jerry, and Jerry let Blizzard drag him toward the coffin. He had little choice – he hadn't realised how strong Blizzard was, and he was almost pulled clear off his feet.

The fires on each side of them were burning even closer

now. Gemma had dropped to her knees, and Jim Feather was standing over her, trying to shield her from the heat. The Reverend O'Sullivan was standing with his eyes closed and his head bowed and his hands together, praying. The two flushers were holding on to each other like long-lost brothers.

Jerry went up to the coffin, and Blizzard jumped up against it.

'Down!' Jerry told him, and from behind him PC Maitland shouted out, 'Down, Blizzard! Sit! Do as you're told!'

Blizzard sat down, although he was still twitchy. He kept snuffling and licking his lips and making mewling sounds in the back of his throat.

Jerry hooked his fingers into four of the rings on the side of the coffin, two in each hand. He took in a deep breath of hot air, coughed, and then prised the lid up. It was much heavier than he had thought it would be, and for a few seconds, he thought he would have to let it drop back down again. But then he gritted his teeth and gave it another heave, and it fell off the coffin and clattered down against the side of the sewer.

There was a shrieking howl, and out of the coffin boiled the smoky figure of Adeliza Friendship, her hood stretched up into a high point and her sleeves flapping wide. Jerry staggered back and nearly lost his balance. He looked up into Adeliza Friendship's hood and saw her face, her eyes incandescent white, her mouth stretched wide open, her teeth bared – Satan's mistress in a satanic fury.

'*Kill, Blizzard!*' Jerry shouted at him, almost screaming,

and let go of his lead. '*Kill!*'

Blizzard leaped up at Adeliza Friendship, but his jaws met nothing but smoke, and he dropped back down again. All the same, he leaped up a second time, snarling at her.

Adeliza Friendship whirled around and around like a dust devil. She flowed out of the coffin and up to the roof of the sewer, opening her sleeves out wide.

The Reverend O'Sullivan stood beneath her, looking up at her and making the sign of the cross.

'I command thee, demon, to be gone! I command thee to leave this world and return to the depths of Hell in which you were spawned! In the name of the Father, and of the Son, and of the Holy Ghost, I dismiss thee! I dismiss thee! I dismiss thee!'

Adeliza Friendship's smoky figure remained spreadeagled against the bricks. The green fires were still blazing on either side, and Jerry thought that she was showing her contempt for the Reverend O'Sullivan by refusing to leave. But then Blizzard leaped up again and started to bark, and she twisted around, turned to the north side of the sewer, and disappeared into the flames.

At once, the flames sank down, and then flickered, and then died out altogether. The seven of them were left staring at each other in disbelief.

Jerry looked down into the coffin. The bottom of it was covered by a fine layer of grey ash, and lying on top of the ash was a handsaw, its serrated blade still stained with amber spots of dried blood.

He beckoned to Jamila. 'There's our murder weapon, unless I'm greatly mistaken.'

'So how do we explain to the coroner that a woman made of nothing but smoke could carry a saw?'

'We lie,' said Jerry. 'It won't be the first time.'

A fresh draught blew down the tunnel, and it smelled strongly of sewage, but at least it was breathable.

'Holy shit,' said PC Maitland.

The Reverend O'Sullivan crossed himself again. 'I'm afraid to say that sums it up to a T.'

***

Eleven days later, Louise woke up and saw that the sun was shining. She sat up in bed and realised that she wasn't in her room at The Whittington Rest Home, but in a hospital ward, surrounded by screens. She felt swimmy, and bruised between her legs, as if somebody had been repeatedly kicking her.

Then she remembered. The sudden cramps. And then the contractions. Her fellow carer Linda Pearson driving her to the BirthWell centre. After that though, she couldn't remember anything.

She reached across and pressed the call button. After only a few moments, the screens parted and a smiling nurse appeared.

'You're awake! How are you feeling?'

'Terrible. Confused.'

'Well, we had to give you a general anaesthetic.'

'Have I had them?'

The nurse had an oddly doll-like face, with bright red lipstick, and kept on smiling. 'Yes, you've had them.'

'What – what are they like?'

'Like all babies. What were you expecting?'

'They were... the scans showed that they weren't normal.'

'It depends what you mean by "normal", doesn't it?'

'Where are they? I don't want to see them, but where are they? What's going to happen to them?'

'They've gone.'

'Gone? Gone where?'

The nurse sat down on the bed and took hold of Louise's hand.

'*I took them,*' she said, and her voice was suddenly hoarse, like a woman who has been smoking all her life.

'*You* took them? I don't understand.'

'*They're my nestlings. Don't worry. I'll take good care of them. They're sacred. All children are sacred. Even the children God forgot.*'